SOARING FLIGHT

Book Seven of The Extraordinaries

MELISSA MCSHANE

Night Harbor Publishing

Night Harbor Publishing

www.nightharborpublishing.com

Cover design by Amalia Chitulescu https://www.amaliach.com

For Jacob,
who said "Make her be Batman"
and for Jay,
who was so thrilled about the idea

CONTENTS

CHAPTER 1

IN WHICH CLEMENCY'S FAMILY CHALLENGES HER PATIENCE

C lemency aligned her knife and fork precisely on either side of her dinner plate, reaching for a moment's calm. She was struck by the pattern of curves impressed upon the handles, worn down from generations of Northrups handling the silverware. She had seen many different silver patterns over the years from dining with other well-to-do families, and yet she had never really noticed her own. Familiarity might not breed contempt, but it certainly encouraged inattention, at least in her case.

Her gaze wandered from the silverware to the rest of the dining room. She had nothing to complain about with regard to the beauty of her home, Emeraude House. Fine white tapers on the table and in sconces along the walls lit the dining room, their little flames combining to drive back the chill of a November evening. They illuminated the snowy linens and the many dishes of the second remove, most of which showed signs of the inroads already made upon them. Delicious aromas of beef and mutton and fish Bounded fresh from the Atlantic mingled with the scent of hot wax. The scene should have comforted her. Instead, she suppressed a sigh. And the evening had been going so well.

"Mama," she said, "you cannot expect me to approve of Lord Winder."

Mama's delicate chin quivered, and her cornflower-blue eyes widened. "Whyever not, dearest? He is titled, and wealthy—everyone says he has no less than six thousand pounds a year! And he pays me the most devoted attention, entirely proper."

"Because he is a notorious gamester," Clemency said wearily. "His estates are sadly encumbered by debt, he never pays his bills—"

"How crass, Clemency! A lady never speaks of such things!" Mama's lips, pink and perfectly Shaped, pinched tight with disapproval. "I am sure your father never told me of his financial doings, and I declare your time should not be taken up with such matters."

"Oh, but Clem is the Countess of Ashford now," Clemency's brother Roger said. "She has no choice but to entangle herself in such matters." He shot Clemency a narrow-eyed, mocking look, and added, "And it was her choice to become so, so she has only herself to blame if she is unfeminine."

Clemency ignored Roger's jab. He had never forgiven her for being the eldest, and an Extraordinary, and therefore eligible to inherit their father's title over him—though possibly it was the fact that Father had not wished him to inherit that griped at Roger. "I am the head of the family," she said, aiming her words if not her gaze at Roger, "and it is my responsibility to protect you, Mama. That means from fortune-hunters as well as anyone ineligible on other grounds."

"For *shame*, Clemency." Mama dabbed at her eyes with a snowy linen napkin. "Lord Winder cares for me, not my fortune."

"Mama, Lord Winder has set his sights on half a dozen other women this past year," Mercy said. Clemency's younger sister had been eating placidly, with no sign that the conversation mattered to her, but now she laid down knife and fork and turned her attention on Mama. "I had it from Cybele Younge that he courted her older sister Niobe until he discovered the Younge family estate is entailed upon their cousin, and the girls will have no dowry to speak of."

"Rank gossip, and nothing you should listen to, Mercy," Mama scoffed.

"I do not gossip with my Speaker's reticulum, Mama. I listen only to facts. As you well know." Mercy's soft voice hardened briefly, and Mama blushed at the chastisement. "Heed Clemency, please. She has your best interests at heart."

"Hence her tight hold on the purse strings," Roger said.

"If you have need of money, you have only to ask," Clemency told him.

Roger's face also reddened, but with anger. "I don't need to go begging to you."

"Then I fail to see why your opinion of my money management is relevant," Clemency shot back, and immediately regretted being drawn into yet another argument with Roger. To avoid entangling herself further, she said, "Mama, if you choose to permit Lord Winder to squire you about town, I will not stop you. You are a grown woman and not my child. However, if he approaches me for permission to make his addresses more intimate, I will refuse."

"Clemency!" Mama's shocked exclamation drowned out the sound of Prudence shoving back her chair. Clemency's youngest sister stood and dropped her napkin on her seat.

"Prudence, if you are finished, you should ask politely to be excused," Clemency said, wishing she did not sound so hopelessly priggish.

Prudence did not look at Clemency. "I see no reason to remain for another squabble," she said. "It's not as if it has anything to do with me." She pushed her chair back into place and strode out of the room at a pace nearer running than walking.

Clemency realized she was gripping her knife like a weapon and relaxed her hand. She glanced at Mercy, who was watching the door Prudence had left by, a grim expression on her face. "She could use some occupation," Mercy said.

"She should have her own coming-out ball," Mama said. "Clemency, there is no reason she should not. She has been presented at court, but we have done nothing to mark the event, no celebration—she has been as isolated as if she were not yet out."

"Mama, I have been home from my War Office service for barely a month," Clemency said. Again, weariness descended on her, the sensation of having had this discussion several times already. Which she had. "I agree that Prudence will benefit from a greater presence in society, but there simply has not been time for a ball."

"You should leave it to me, dearest," Mama said with a smile. Her earlier anger had vanished. "It is not as if I do not know what is appropriate."

"Let me consider a while longer, Mama, a few weeks only," Clemency replied.

Mama pouted. "Very well. But no later than after Christmas!"

Clemency did not respond. She took another bite and found her appetite had vanished. Sighing inwardly, she rose from her seat, prompting everyone but Mercy, whose lower limbs were paralyzed, and Roger to do the same. Roger smirked at Clemency, daring her to react. Smirking and remaining seated was his usual response when they dined as a family. She hated his disrespect and lack of manners, but insisting on him changing his behavior would only start another battle, and so long as he behaved properly at social functions, it was a battle she chose not to fight.

With her Moving talent, she lifted Mercy from her seat into her wheeled chair, then led the way across the hall to the drawing room, propelling Mercy's heavy chair ahead of her with her talent. Using her talent eased her heart. She could never explain how it felt to Move things, how to her the world was full of shifting currents that pressed upon her like the waves of the sea. How it was the simplest thing to take hold of those currents to shift the inanimate objects surrounding her, Moving them wherever she chose. People were harder to Move, but Clemency was among the highest-rated Extraordinary Movers in the War Office, and her skill even in that respect was exceptional.

She rolled Mercy's chair to its usual position next to the fire and took the seat opposite her. Their mother seated herself upon a divan and reclined against its arm, her gaze intent upon a hand mirror. Clemency observed that Mercy's work basket lay just outside her sister's comfortable reach, but she did not Move it to her. Mercy detested the slightest whiff of pity, and Clemency would never insult her by implying she was less capable because she was an invalid.

Mercy stretched and got her fingertips on the edge of the basket.

She pulled it closer and removed the reticule she was embroidering. "Would you light another candle?" she asked.

Clemency brought a taper closer to Mercy's side. "I can read aloud if you wish."

"No, I am too restless to listen to a story," Mercy said. "You should entertain yourself, Clemency."

Clemency watched as servants brought in the tea things and Mama set about pouring. "I am unaccustomed to idleness, after nearly four years with the War Office. Perhaps I should take up needlework."

"That strikes me as a rather passive occupation for one as active as you." Mercy lowered her needlework to her lap. "And, forgive me, but you seem different—though perhaps it is natural, after going to war, that you should have changed."

Memory struck Clemency so unexpectedly it felt like a blow to the chest: a dimly-lit room, the touch of a hand, the smell of roses blooming indoors. She blinked, and with a tremendous effort wrenched herself back to the present. "I am used to having direction, and now I am the sole guardian of my time," she said. "I will find new purpose, I am certain. But for now I wish to enjoy my time with my family."

"For whatever pleasure that brings," Mercy said wryly. "Roger is, well, Roger, Prudence is sulky, Gawain is at school. And we are none of us good at meaningless pleasantries. I wonder that you did not choose to remain in Europe."

This time, Clemency deflected her memories before they could trouble her. "With Napoleon defeated and his generals on the run, there is little purpose for me with the War Office."

"I meant for pleasure. You always liked to travel, Clemency. And Europe has so many wonderful sights, so many grand experiences." Mercy's fingers played through the balls of fine wool in her basket.

"I saw enough of France and Spain to last me many years, and now I wish only for home." Clemency accepted a cup of tea from her mother, but did not drink. She considered asking Mercy if travel was something *she* wished for, but she hated seeing Mercy's face grow still and angry when she contemplated something her crippled legs made impossible. No amount of cajoling, of assurances that Clemency was more than capable of making up for Mercy's weakness, had ever convinced her sister that her inability to walk did not make her on some level a burden.

Mercy sipped tea and set the cup aside. "Mama, are you leaving?"

Mama set her mirror aside. "I intend to visit the theatre. With Lord Winder," she said, chin held high in defiance. She had Shaped her face to give her cheeks better definition and looked far younger than her four-and-forty years.

Clemency chose not to give her the argument she clearly wished for. "I hope you have a lovely evening, then," she said politely. Mama waited a moment longer, but when she realized no further response was forthcoming, she turned on her heel and flounced out of the drawing room.

This time, Clemency did not conceal her sigh. "I should not keep her from her pleasures," she said. "I know she felt constrained by Father's lack of interest in society. But it stings, a little, to see her so completely given over to entertainment. It is as if Father never existed."

"She is also kind, and fond of showing that kindness to others," Mercy said. "If there is not much more to her than that, what does it matter? There is no point wishing her more sensible."

"I know."

Clemency sat looking into the fire, watching the flames shift and trace patterns she could almost convince herself were words. The idea that the fire might speak to her amused her, as she was no Scorcher like Roger and certainly no Extraordinary Scorcher to manipulate the fire with her hands. Besides, what message could a fire possibly have for her? Something to rein Roger in, or convince Prudence to give up her hostility?

Mercy resumed her sewing. "I notice *you* have not gone out in public more than twice in the past month," she said, so placidly it roused Clemency's suspicions.

"Do you have a criticism?" she said, smiling so Mercy would know she was not angry.

Mercy did not smile in turn. "You used to have many friends. You still have, based on the number of invitations and callers we receive.

And yet you never attend parties or dinners, and you frequently pretend to be out when someone pays us a visit."

"I have little in common with those who did not serve in the war," Clemency said.

"Many of your Extraordinary Mover friends *did* serve in the war," Mercy countered. "And your disdain for the others is unworthy of you."

"It is not disdain, only a sad realization. I realize how proud I sound, but it's nothing but the truth. I feel awkward, as if I have forgotten how to converse naturally."

"It will come back to you." Mercy's needle flew deftly through the fabric. "I envy you your ease of manner. I am not nearly so quick to make friends."

"No, but with your Speaker's reticulum, you are never out of reach of a listening ear." A pang of loneliness struck Clemency's heart, and for once she did not immediately suppress it. So much of what had happened in France, she dared not tell anyone, not even her friends in the War Office. She had spoken her darkest secret to only one woman, and that woman was far away now, nowhere that Clemency could reach.

Impatient with herself, she rose. "Forgive me, Mercy, but I am so tired. I believe I should go to bed early."

"Go, then, but—promise you will consider what I said?" Mercy laid her needlework in her lap again. "That you will stop shutting your friends out?"

"I will consider it. Thank you for caring." Clemency clasped her sister's hand briefly and then left the drawing room.

She had not changed rooms when her father died, feeling ghoulish about occupying the master's bedroom. Her own rooms suited her well. They had been modified to meet her needs when she turned eighteen, and now the windows opened wide enough to permit an Extraordinary Mover to pass through so she could Fly wherever she wished. Her mother had been shocked that Clemency's father had approved of his daughter having the ability to, as she put it, sneak away for clandestine assignations. Lord Ashford had chastised her for thinking so poorly of his own daughter's character. "Do you want her to Fly away from us entirely?" he had said, and "Keeping her a prisoner will only hurt her, and us." The memory of that conversation always moved Clemency to tears.

In her chambers, she summoned her maid, Tatton, and undressed with the woman's help. Tatton folded away Clemency's gown in silence, but when Clemency was in her nightdress with her hair braided for sleep, she said, "My lady, if I may be so bold?"

"Of course." Tatton had been in Clemency's service since before her elevation to countess, and her frequent outspokenness suited Clemency, who was herself quick to speak her mind. "Is something wrong?"

"It's my lady's footwear," Tatton said. "There is a pair of boots in the dressing room I do not believe is suited to any of the occasions my lady is likely to attend. Shall I have them removed? The gardener may make use of them, if it's your wish."

Clemency kept her expression placid, as if nothing about Tatton's words agitated her. "They are from my War Office uniform, Tatton. I keep them as a memento of that time."

"Of course, my lady. I hope I did not presume."

"You know you can be frank with me. I prefer it."

With Tatton gone, Clemency disordered the coverlet, but did not climb into bed. She stared at the mattresses in their fine linen sheets for a few moments, then walked to the window and drew back the drapes. Her room looked out over the back garden, and beyond that, the rooftops of London made a frozen grey sea as far as she could perceive. The skies were clear that night, and the waning moon, only a few days past full, sailed high in the eastern sky, touching the peaks of the stony sea with silver.

It was perfect Flying weather.

Clemency doused the lights and waited briefly for her eyes to adjust. Then she lifted the uppermost mattress and retrieved a flattened bundle of cloth. She shook it out, revealing it to be several items of clothing: dark green trousers, a coarsely woven shirt of undyed cotton, a heavy grey coat the color of a stormy sky that buttoned all the way to the neck, and a knit cap matching the coat in color. Stripping off her nightgown, she dressed quickly, tucking the shirt into the trousers' waistband and buttoning the coat over it so none of its lightness showed. The trousers came from a rifleman's uniform and fit her poorly, being rather snug over the hips, but that kept them from falling down and removed the need for a belt or braces.

She wound her braid around her head and pulled the cap over it, securing her hair in place. Settling her goggles over her eyes, she tightened the straps so they would not shift no matter how fast she Flew. She did not need to look in her mirror to know that her clothes obscured her figure enough that between those and the goggles covering her upper face, people had mistaken her for male on previous night flights.

A pair of thick socks she had stolen from the boot boy came next, heavy and scratchy but warm. She fetched the boots Tatton had fretted about and put them on, wriggling her toes in pleasure. Padded gloves tucked into the inner pocket of the coat completed her strange attire. She felt strong, competent, capable of anything.

She pushed open the window with a gloved hand and floated to where she could stand on the sill. Balancing with one hand on the frame, she looked down at the garden below. No Extraordinary Mover was afraid of heights, and Clemency enjoyed seeing the world from an unusual perspective, the dark growth apparently a wall before her, the side of the house the floor beneath her feet. Then she stepped off the sill and deliberately fell a few feet before catching hold of the currents and swooping away across the rooftops, scorning gravity's pull.

CHAPTER 2

IN WHICH CLEMENCY DISRUPTS THE PEACE AND IS IN TURN DISRUPTED

The freezing air chilled her cheeks and threaded its way through the seams of her clothes, but she was accustomed to enduring much greater cold than this. Her old War Office uniform was better for keeping out the cold than her clandestinely-acquired clothing, but it would have been useless for what she intended tonight. The trousers did not slow her the way her War Office uniform would have, either, or her Extraordinary Mover's civilian garb, with its heavy divided skirts. Clemency indulged in a moment's frustration at the limitations of her wardrobe. Surely she would win the Extraordinary Movers' Flying races more often if she were not hampered by all that fabric, flapping and catching the wind.

She soared through the night, following the gas lamps until they gave way to ordinary lanterns and then disappeared entirely. The streets made thin, pale ribbons through the city, some straight, others weaving like the cow trails they had once been. Tall houses, dark under the moonlight, loomed over the streets, their plain façades revealing nothing of what might be found within. Lights gleamed at some of the windows, not very brightly, but Clemency did not Fly to where she could peer inside. That would be inappropriate.

The idea made her laugh. This was not a part of London a well-bred lady should visit, let alone a titled Extraordinary, which of course was what made it exciting. Given her intent in Flying through London on this night, inappropriateness was hardly something she cared about.

Clemency dropped lower and slowed her speed, watching and listening as she followed one of the narrower streets. It was hard hearing anything but the loudest noises with the wind in her ears, but she had been well trained in reconnaissance by her Flight Corps superiors, and she knew how to compensate.

She also knew how to recognize her prey, after so many nights hunting the streets of London. Furtive movements, slow pacing that turned to rapid movement in the space of a heartbeat, hands held where they could conceal a weapon. And there, walking along below her with no apparent awareness that she watched, were two men, sidling from shadow to shadow after a third.

Clemency descended to a rooftop and leaned out, watching the two. They wore dark clothes, too dark to successfully hide in; one of Clemency's earliest Flight Corps lessons in the War Office was in the principles of camouflage, how pure black stood out in a way dark grey or green did not. Tracking their progress was easy. Clemency lifted off from the roof and found another, following them the way they followed their intended victim.

The victim, Clemency noticed, gave every indication of being the worse for drink. It was the only explanation for why he walked slowly and in a wobbling line. Clemency made for another rooftop. She would not act until the assailants did.

But they did not act; they continued to trail their intended victim, moving so furtively Clemency nearly lost patience with them. Surely they need not be so very cautious? Then she had to control a laugh at how in her impatience she had mentally sided with the robbers, if only in a sideways manner.

Her frustration with their slowness had nearly overcome her amusement when the two men finally sped up, running toward their victim, who still walked insensible of his danger. Clemency leaped off the roof and dropped, coming to a halt well above the trio's heads. Moving a living person was easier if one caught the person off guard, so

MELISSA MCSHANE

before the men could register her presence, she snatched both assailants by their ankles and hauled them into the sky, screaming.

That drew the victim's attention. To Clemency's surprise, instead of fleeing, he turned and gaped at the dangling figures. Clemency swung them to crash into each other, turning their screams into groans. She kept them hanging head-down in midair and descended to stand on the paving stones about twenty feet from the victim.

"You should be more careful," she said in her deepest voice. Her natural voice was already low for a woman, but she did not wish to give herself away if she could help it. "They might have killed you."

"An Extraordinary," the man said. His accent was that of the working classes, and it slurred drunkenly over the vowels. "Why'd'ye stop them?"

No one had ever challenged her on her rescues before. "I don't think even fools deserve to be beaten and robbed," she said, feeling foolish at having to put this into words. "Get along home, now, and watch yourself in future."

The man's head bobbed, and he veered away and ran, still weaving somewhat. Clemency turned her attention back to the dangling men. With a tug on the invisible currents, she sent them crashing into one another again, sending up a new chorus of groans. "And you two," she said. "What am I to do with you?"

"We didn't do nothing," one said, his voice surprisingly clear. "You can't prove nothing."

"I don't have to prove anything," Clemency said. "I just have to let you fall."

"No!" the other man shrieked. Clemency wrinkled her nose at the faint smell of ammonia wafting from him. "I won't do nothing bad no more, I swear! Just let me go!"

"Milt, you coward," the first man said. "He's an Extraordinary. They're all law-abiding rich types. He ain't going to do anything to us."

"Really?" Clemency said, and dropped them.

She caught them inches from the hard, stony street. Milt had fainted. The first man had screamed in such terror Clemency felt guilty at having caused it, but not for very long.

"I believe we understand each other better now," she said. "This

12

was not the first time you've attacked and robbed someone, is it? I would be doing the world a favor by stopping you permanently. But I have never killed anyone, and if I am to start, it will not be with petty criminals such as you."

She Moved both men, rotating their helpless bodies until they were no longer head-down, and dropped them the last few inches to land on their backs in the street. "Choose another line of work," she said harshly. "If I catch you again, I'll reconsider my position." It was a lie; she was unlikely to ever see these men again, let alone kill them. But she knew from experience that terror was a salutary lesson for those of the criminal type.

She didn't wait to see what the man made of this statement, or if Milt roused from his faint; she launched herself into the sky, Flying fast enough to ruffle her coat. She sped across the roofs, rolling onto her back briefly to look at the moon. The encounter had raised her heart rate and sent the blood pumping fast and hot through her body, and she barely felt the chill in the air. That had been bracing. These nocturnal escapades made her feel alive as she never had since leaving the War Office.

She Flew with her arms outstretched so the wind buffeted her and she felt she was fighting it, fighting and winning. This was no race, or she would orient herself to slip between air currents, her arms by her side to make herself an arrow slicing through the sky. Even without the slim-fitting trousers, she was among the fastest Extraordinary Movers in England, or had been before leaving for the War Office.

She had not raced for months. When she considered competing in the public tests of Moving skill, though she had done so many times as a young woman, she felt an odd mixture of shame and guilt and fear, none of which made any sense. She did not fear losing, for there was always another trial, another chance to win. And she did not believe her added experience from her Flight Corps training was an unfair advantage.

No, it was the attention she disliked now, the public notice that came from ranking high among England's Movers. Ever since— She veered once more away from memory, but here in the sky, with no one around to distract her, memory would not be deterred.

She made herself consider the past objectively, with a detachment that rivaled the air in its coldness. She had been captured and Coerced by Napoleon, her emotions altered so she adored him and believed his cause was just. She had turned her skills toward aiding his Grande Armée. And—she swallowed bitter bile—he had Coerced feelings of love and desire in her toward one of his generals, and she had gone to that man's bed willingly.

She still could not remember Armand de Villiers with anything but confusion and horror. Though her memories insisted she had loved him, the knowledge that that love had been forced upon her tangled with those memories until they were like a terrible nightmare that did not fade upon waking. Sometimes, she imagined she felt his hands on her, rousing her desires, and at those times she took to the skies and Flew until she was too numb to feel anything.

She hated her weakness. She was no fragile blossom, easily crushed by tragedy—had she not endured her father's death, held her family together against the many hearings and Roger's suit demanding that he be made Earl of Ashford? Was she not among the five highest ranked Extraordinary Movers in the War Office, possibly in all of England? Yet Coercion had robbed her of her confidence, and now she could not bear to see her old friends, though they could not possibly know the truth simply by looking at her. She felt her shame was written on her face regardless.

A distant cry, almost too faint to hear, drew her out of her reverie. She rolled over to survey the streets. She was near Hanover Square, where the gaslit streets pushed most crime to the outskirts. But the wealthy weren't immune to being robbed.

The cry sounded again, louder this time, and Clemency altered her flight path slightly. She saw nothing, no movement that could be a fight, but as she dropped lower, someone came stumbling out of one of the houses as if he had been pushed. Three figures followed him, rushing forward with fists raised. Those were the kind of odds Clemency detested.

She swooped low and prepared to Move one or all of the men—and their victim vanished. A scant second later, he appeared again behind the group and punched the nearest one low in the back, making him grunt in pain.

Clemency did not stop to admire the Bounder's work. Instead, she took hold of the other two and Moved them, flinging them apart so one struck the house opposite and one fell to the ground. Briefly, she hoped she had chosen the right side in this conflict, but—well, three against one could never leave any doubt as to which the right side was.

These two men were harder to control than her earlier captives, which meant they were stronger-willed and less inherently fearful; courage and emotional fortitude affected one's ability to resist Moving. With both struggling against her grip, she was forced to turn her efforts toward containing just one. Hovering above the fight, she Moved that one man, swinging him around like a stone from a sling until he slammed into the second man and both went down.

She turned her attention to the fistfight, but the Bounder seemed to need no assistance. He had the stance of an accomplished pugilist, something Clemency recognized from unauthorized visits to boxing matches, and between that and his flickering Skips out of reach, the third man could not land a hit.

"Stay down," she commanded the other two, pressing down hard on their recumbent bodies. They ignored her, wriggling and thrashing until despite her skill they were on hands and knees. Clemency shifted her attention to the one she had Moved before, holding him still. The other man bolted, and although she made a snatch for him, he soon disappeared down the street.

A cry of pain distracted her, and her captive jerked away from her hold. She let him go as well and Flew lower over the fight, where the third man had landed a lucky punch on the Bounder, knocking him back. She dragged the assailant away despite his struggles and held him pinned against the wall. Then she almost lost her grip when the Bounder popped into being right in front of the man, startling her. One punch was all it took to slam the man's head into the wall, making him sag unconscious.

Clemency continued to hold the thug upright as she alighted in the street some distance away. The Bounder turned to face her. He was shaking his hand as if it pained him. "Thank you," he said.

"I'm glad I could help," Clemency said.

The Bounder jerked in surprise. Then he vanished, and appeared in front of her with a *whoosh* of displaced air. His eyes were pale green in the lamplight, and he stared at Clemency in wonder. "Good G—I beg your pardon," he exclaimed. "You're a woman."

Clemency realized she had failed to modulate her voice. She surveyed the Bounder, who despite his heavy breathing seemed unaffected by the fight. He was not overly tall, but he was built like a fighter, with shoulders like a bull and well-muscled arms poorly concealed by his shirtsleeves. Even had he not been a Bounder, with the ability to Skip away from a blow, he might have been able to hold his own against all three assailants. "Did those men attack you in your home?" she said, choosing not to be drawn into a conversation about her sex.

"More or less," the Bounder said. "What are you doing abroad at this hour? Who are you?"

"You might thank me, you know." Clemency glanced at the unconscious thief. "It's hardly gracious of you to interrogate me when I have saved you a beating."

"I have fought off worse than this." The Bounder took another step forward. "No Extraordinary lady should be out alone at this hour. I insist you tell me your name."

"It is Northrup," Clemency improvised. If he did not recognize the Countess of Ashford, she did not intend to aid his memory. And Northrup was not so uncommon that he would identify it as the Countess of Ashford's family name. "And you are...?"

"Colin?" A light, high-pitched voice spoke from behind the Bounder. Clemency saw a young woman in a nightdress standing in the open doorway. Her short, fair hair hung loose around her face, which was in shadow.

"Lydia. Go back to bed," the Bounder said. "It's all right. They're gone."

Lydia stepped away from the door and approached them, her bare feet making no noise on the pavement. "They are not all gone," she said. "That one is waking." She pointed at Clemency's captive. He had begun to move, the tiny shifts of arms and legs that mean conscious-ness is returning.

Clemency bore down on the man, restraining him before he could come to full consciousness and fight her. "What would you like me to do with him?" she asked. "I doubt those men will return, not if they believe this place as well-guarded as it is."

The Bounder turned his head away and muttered a profanity under his breath. Clemency, who had heard much worse from soldiers in the field, did not react. "I ought to beat him senseless, scaring my sister as he did," the Bounder said, "but I believe you are correct that he is no longer a danger." He stepped forward and grabbed the thief's chin, forcing the man to look at him. "There is nothing here worth stealing," he said. "If you return, it will be the worse for you."

Clemency continued to hold him fast. "They must have believed there was *something* here worth stealing," she said. "Most thieves will not attempt a robbery when there are people present. So, what did they believe you had?"

The Bounder raised one eyebrow, giving him a sardonic air. "Miss Northrup, I don't recall giving you permission to pry into my affairs."

"You are well spoken, and genteel, and yet you know how to fight," Clemency persisted. "You are an odd mystery, Mr....?"

The Bounder did not rise to her challenge. "Many gentlemen know how to fight. That is not so odd."

"They know how to *box*," Clemency corrected him. "Very few Bounders know how to use their talent to give them a pugilistic advan-tage. You fought like someone interested in winning, not like someone displaying his skill."

The Bounder tilted his head, his eyes narrowing. "What is the point of this interrogation, Miss Northrup?"

Clemency's captive strained against her hold, bringing her to her senses. She had no reason to pester this man, and no idea why she felt compelled to discover his secrets. "I beg your pardon," she said. "That was impertinent. Shall I dispose of this criminal for you?"

"Dispose?" The Bounder's alarm was the first uncontrolled reaction she had seen from him.

Clemency looked past him at Lydia, who continued to regard them both placidly. She did not appear frightened as the Bounder had suggested; instead, she wore a look of inward-turned concentration, as if she were solving a difficult puzzle. Then her gaze lifted, and she looked, not at Clemency, but at the thief. "He should be more afraid," she said. "He doesn't believe he is in any danger. But you do not intend his death— oh, perhaps I should not have said that, because now he feels confident."

"Lydia, please, go back inside," the Bounder said. "You will become overwhelmed."

Surprised, Clemency removed her goggles to see Lydia more clearly. "She's an Extraordinary Discerner," she said in astonishment. "But she —" In time, she kept from commenting on Lydia's apparent sanity. Clemency had never met an Extraordinary Discerner, and the only one she knew of was the king, whose ability to feel the emotions of everyone around him had driven him mad.

The thief laughed. "Go on, let me go," he said. His accent was surprisingly fine, not that of the lower classes as Clemency's earlier victims had been. "You cannot stop me returning."

Clemency and the Bounder exchanged glances. The Bounder looked furious, but his hands clenched in a way that suggested he had no solution. "I should Bound him away," he said.

"To where? No, sir, I have a better idea," Clemency said. She patted the thief's cheek kindly. "I suggest you do not struggle," she told him, and Moved him straight up, fast and sure as a rifle shot.

The man's screams faded as he rose higher. "That is not enough," Clemency said, and brought him back to earth as fast as before. She repeated her Moving twice more before discovering the man was once again unconscious and setting him gently on the ground between herself and the Bounder.

The Bounder's eyes were wide, but he said nothing until she stopped. Then he spoke, enunciating clearly. "That was not the act of a lady. You astonish me, Miss Northrup."

He sounded admiring, not critical, and to her surprise her heart warmed at his appreciation for her skill. "Not being ladylike is gener-ally considered a bad thing, Mr....?"

Those odd green eyes looked her up and down. "Wescott," he said.

"And I have never believed a lady should be constrained by the opinions of others."

Clemency blushed, feeling awkward in the face of his directness. Beyond Mr. Wescott, his sister smiled happily and closed her eyes as if enjoying some rare pleasure. That brought Clemency to her senses. She knew Discerners, ordinary Discerners, were capable of ferreting out lies, and while Lydia Wescott might or might not be mad, she certainly could tell what Clemency felt—and might be able to tell that Northrup was not the full truth of Clemency's name.

"I will take this man on a ride across London," she said. "And then I will leave him somewhere not very pleasant. We will see if he takes my threats seriously then."

"I thank you, Miss Northrup." Mr. Wescott bowed, an ironic gesture Clemency recognized was aimed at himself. Again, she felt flustered, as if he had offered her a more intimate gesture instead. She secured the thief, binding him with her Moving so he would not free himself when he woke, and Flew into the sky as rapidly as she had Moved the thief before.

She headed for the Thames, which was a murky moving strip of darkness against the lighter backdrop of the city. The thief woke when she was within sight of the river's shore. "Let me go," he shouted, flexing his arms and legs against her hold.

"You do not wish for that, I assure you. Not when we are a hundred feet in the air," Clemency said. The thief froze.

"Now," Clemency added, "I imagine you still believe I can do nothing to you. I invite you to regard the river." She rotated the man so he had a good view of the Thames. "I would not drown you, of course. But on a night like this one—it is rather cold, is it not?—well, wet clothes might not kill you, but I daresay you do not like to take that risk, do you?"

The struggles began again. "Damn your eyes, you—"

Clemency released him, and let him fall for a moment before catching him. "What did you want with Mr. Wescott?"

The thief was silent.

Clemency dropped him a second time, and waited a moment longer before catching him. "Answer me."

"Rich bastard," the man growled. "That house is full of treasures. We were told the place was empty by night, but he and his sister live there. Let me go. I swear I'll never trouble him again."

Clemency considered his words. They did not sound sufficiently terrified. "If you are dead from exposure, that will certainly be true," she said, and flew low over the river's dark, constantly moving surface.

The man screamed. "No! I swear it! Please!"

That response satisfied her. She crossed the Thames and put him down on its far bank. "Find another line of work," she said, and shot away into the sky.

She flew homeward slowly, feeling the cold in every part of her. Nevertheless, she felt cheerful for the first time in months. That her good cheer did not come from her family, or from her legitimate pursuits, troubled her only a little. There was nothing illegal about her nocturnal activities, because how was justice to be served if people did not defend themselves and others? These small crimes went unnoticed by magistrates, and the Bow Street Runners had their own concerns. But if her actions were to become known, society's disapprobation would likely be harsh.

She circled the house near Hanover Square, though it was difficult to see in the darkness. An impulse struck her. She might return tomorrow, during the daytime, and see for herself whether the thief had been telling the truth about the Wescotts having great treasures. The idea excited her, and she sped up, hastening toward Emeraude House.

She unlatched the window—another feature her mother had objected to, protesting that any thief might gain access to her daughter's bedroom for nefarious purposes. "Then he deserves what he gets," the earl had said. He had said it in Clemency's hearing, making her laugh. The memory ached a little. Oh, how she missed her father! Strangely, he was the only one she felt she could have told the truth about Armand de Villiers and trusted that he would have the right reaction, which would be to have Armand shot.

She climbed inside and shut the window, latching it securely before drawing the drapes and undressing in the darkness. Hiding her clothes between the mattresses again, she climbed into bed, wishing she dared call for a warming pan. But Tatton was clever, and would know her mistress had been Flying, and while there was nothing sinister about night Flying, Clemency still did not like giving away her secrets.

It took a very long time for the bed to warm, and Clemency shivered, flexing her fingers and toes to keep them agile. She disliked winter, for all she was accustomed to the cold; the heights at which she often Flew were freezing even in summer. Perhaps she should travel, after all, go to some sunny southern country and bask in the winter warmth. But that would mean returning to society, and she could not bear that.

Instead of dwelling on the past, she remembered Mr. Wescott and his sister Lydia. So unusual, to find a gentleman who knew real fighting, for why would any gentleman need such underhanded tricks? And an Extraordinary Discerner who seemed, well, a little dazed by reality, but not mad—that was unusual as well. She found herself as curious to know them better as she was to see their house.

With those pleasant thoughts, she drifted off to sleep.

CHAPTER 3

IN WHICH CLEMENCY DISCOVERS A TREASURE TROVE OF WONDERS

O nly Mercy joined Clemency at the breakfast-table the following morning. Clemency had slept well, invigorated by her night flight and untroubled by dreams, and had wakened early by town standards. When she had been with the War Office, she was accustomed to waking even earlier, and she had not yet decided what habits she intended to keep or shed now she was once more a civilian.

The mid-morning sun illuminated the breakfast room clearly, shedding a bright light diffused by the diaphanous drapes over the windows. Clemency poured a thin stream of milk into her tea and stirred a few times before sipping. "The day is pretty enough for spring," she observed.

Mercy had her head down over her newspaper. "I suppose," she said absently. "Clemency, only listen to this. A terrible fire ravaged Wapping last night, destroying several streets' worth of buildings and warehouses."

"How dreadful! I suppose we should be grateful the fire did not encompass the city, but that is still great devastation. Were many killed?"

"This says at least ten people." Mercy lowered the paper. "I should not feel relief that it was no more. Even ten deaths is a tragedy. And I am certain the final toll will be higher."

Clemency nodded. "Does the report say anything more?"

"Most of the warehouses were the property of a Mr. Ruskin, an Extraordinary Mover—do you know him, Clemency?"

"I know of him. We may have raced once or twice. He has no strong talent, though in the face of his loss I feel guilty at indirectly slighting his ability." Clemency set her cup down. "He is quite wealthy, but I imagine this will be a terrible blow to his fortunes."

Mercy was already taking up a second newspaper. "The *Morning Herald* will have more...yes, here it is." She raised her eyebrows. "They claim the fire was the result of a bomb."

"How can they know that? Really, I sometimes believe these journalists invent things to sell more newspapers." But Clemency leaned forward anyway to read the tiny print sideways.

"Witnesses say anonymous figures were seen running from the fire, and that one of them hurled a bomb through a window. No one was captured. There is also some speculation as to the supposed bomber's motives." Mercy looked unusually pensive. "Do you suppose Mr. Ruskin has an enemy?"

"It is my experience that wealthy men always have enemies, whether they built their wealth as Mr. Ruskin did or inherited it. But it might have nothing to do with him." Clemency sat back and drank more tea. "It might be some disaffected worker who lost his job and wished to take his revenge."

"You are as inventive as any journalist," Mercy said with a smile.

"Merely considering the possibilities. Which are horrid, and therefore I will consider them no longer." Clemency spared a thought for all those families who mourned their dead today. Mr. Ruskin might suffer financially from this disaster, but at least he was alive to suffer.

Mercy folded the newspaper and set it aside. "I feel so restless. I wish it really were spring, and I might enjoy the garden. At this time of year, it is too dreary to make me feel anything but despondency."

"We might go to the park," Clemency suggested. "It is not too far a walk, and the fresh air will do us both good."

Mercy eyed her sister up and down. "You wish to go Flying, though," she said, gesturing at Clemency's attire.

Clemency plucked at the fabric of her divided skirt, which was full enough to disguise the contours of her legs and gathered into snug cuffs circling her ankles. "I can do that later."

"I will not have you delaying your own pleasures to wait on me," Mercy said. "I will read in the drawing room."

"Mercy," Clemency began.

"You devote enough of your time to this family, I refuse to add to your burden," Mercy said.

"You are not a burden, Mercy."

Mercy's lips pinched tightly together. "Excuse me, I am being addressed," she said, and closed her eyes and tilted her head back in the attitude of a Speaker.

Clemency ground her back teeth in frustration. She was certain Mercy had just lied to end the uncomfortable conversation, but she had no way of challenging her sister on her deception. She thrust her chair back from the table. "I hope you have a pleasant morning," she said, not bothering to conceal her anger.

In the foyer, she donned her full-length wool Flying coat and kid gloves, then tugged a white knit cap over her head, completely concealing her hair and covering the tips of her ears. When she had left London for her War Office service four years previously, custom for female Extraordinary Movers' headgear had been ordinary bonnets. Clemency had hated them because they interfered with her Flying, the wind catching in their folds and threatening to drag them off her head entirely. She did not know who had changed the fashion, but she was grateful to that unknown woman. Now, if only someone would permit women to wear pantaloons or even trousers while Flying...

She stepped out into the sunshine, squinting against the brightness. For all the day was clear, the sun's rays had no warmth in them. A chill wind blew, fluttering her skirts and stinging her cheeks and making her grateful for her warm coat and gloves. She drew in a deep, invigorating breath and launched herself into the sky.

She almost never had the skies to herself during the day, what with all the Bounders engaged in Skipping across the city, running errands or carrying messages. Occasionally she saw other Extraordinary Movers Flying past, but she never drew near enough to identify them. She knew many, if not most, of the Extraordinary Movers in London, having competed against them often over the years, and the idea of exchanging pleasantries in midair discomfited Clemency, as if her pleasure in Flying might be diminished by sharing it with another.

Today, it seemed the sunshine had brought the Bounders out in droves. Clemency flew higher to stay out of their paths, though she knew a collision was so unlikely as to be reasonably called impossible. It was something young Extraordinary Movers whispered about to frighten one another, tales of Bounders appearing exactly where a Mover Flew to their mutual annihilation, and stopped whispering about as they grew older and learned more of the nature and limitations of talents. A higher flight path made it possible for Clemency to watch them popping in and out, which entertained her for a few minutes until she grew cold. Then she dropped lower and headed for Hanover Square.

She drew attention as she alighted on the street where the fight had taken place last night and removed her goggles. Men and women slowed or even stopped to gawk, though none were crass enough to point. Clemency ignored them. She preferred to behave as if she was nothing unusual, which was almost true; Extraordinary Movers were not as commonplace as Extraordinary Speakers or Extraordinary Bounders in London, but there were enough of them that the sight of one should cause only moderate excitement in the street.

She slowed her steps as she approached the Wescotts' house. A small brass plaque screwed to the wall beside the door read, in curling script:

WESCOTT'S CABINET OF CURIOSITIES

Clemency touched the deeply incised letters with a gloved finger. Curiosities indeed. She understood each word, but she could not imagine what the words meant when laid out all together.

She turned her attention to the door itself, upon which was affixed a piece of card. Handwritten upon the card, in bold printed letters rather than script, read *Admission 1s. 3d. Tuesdays and Thursdays, 1 p.m. to 4 p.m., Saturdays 12 noon to 5 p.m. Private showing by appointment only.*

Clemency tucked away her goggles and extracted her pocket watch with some difficulty from within her coat. It was of finest Swiss manufacture, showing seconds as well as minutes and hours, and guaranteed accurate under the harshest conditions, such as Flying at top speed through an obstacle course with one's competitors nipping at one's heels. The time was 10:56 and thirteen seconds. Grumbling, Clemency put her watch away. She had no desire to wait in the street for one hour, three minutes, and forty-three seconds, assuming Mr. Wescott's watch was as accurate as her own, which was by no means guaranteed.

She stepped back and examined the row of houses. They were three stories tall, with sloping roofs, and gave no hint as to what lay behind them. She might Fly over and see if there were gardens behind, or accessible windows, but she disliked looking like a thief, searching for an illicit entrance. She might go elsewhere for an hour, perhaps a tea shop, but that idea left her feeling restless. Instead, she rapped sharply on the door and waited.

The stir over her arrival had faded, and the people passing now paid her no attention, at least none she was aware of. In her white cap and divided skirts, she was obviously an Extraordinary Mover, but as she currently was doing nothing overt with her talent, she was as unremarkable as she had hoped.

No one came to the door. Clemency waited for a few seconds longer, then rapped on the door again, harder this time. She considered how long she was willing to stand there, and her curiosity insisted it would be a while.

She had her hand raised to knock a third time when the door flew open with some force. "Can't you read the sign? Twelve o'clock and no earlier," Mr. Wescott said.

"I did read the sign," Clemency said. "I hoped you would admit me anyway."

Mr. Wescott blinked. Now that he was not illuminated by stark gaslight, Clemency realized his eyes were closer to blue than green, but they were still odd in how light a shade they were. He was dressed informally, in shirt and cravat but no frock coat, but he seemed unconcerned about his state of undress. He took a step closer. "You," he said. "I did not recognize you in full daylight."

"That is understandable." Clemency smiled politely. "May I enter, or would I presume too much on our very brief but intense relationship?"

Mr. Wescott's eyebrow raised in a familiar expression. "Miss Northrup, welcome." He stepped back to hold the door open for her.

Beyond, the foyer extended chimney-like high above, much taller than it was wide. To the left, two steps rose to a double door stained so dark a brown as to be nearly black. The doors were shut, and a key extended from the brass lock plate beneath two ornate brass handles shaped like pine cones. Directly ahead, stairs rose to the first floor landing.

Brass lamps hung on either side of the black doors and to both sides of the front door, providing most of the light; the chandelier hanging from the ceiling was too high for any but a Mover to reach and shed most of its light on the landing above. The narrow foyer felt nearly as cold as outdoors, though the wind did not follow them inside. Its high, white walls reminded Clemency of packed snow and ice, and she suppressed a shiver.

Apparently she did not suppress it well enough, for Mr. Wescott said, "If you'll follow me, the collection rooms are much warmer." He gestured toward the stairs, which were also narrow, with barely enough room for two to ascend side by side. The whole place looked more like servants' quarters than an elegant mansion.

Clemency followed Mr. Wescott up the stairs to a hallway painted as white as the foyer. A strip of carpet worked in an elaborate leaf and flower pattern extended the hall's length to a second set of stairs leading up. The hall was dim, illuminated mainly by lamps in wall sconces but also by the indirect light from the foyer. Three doors, two on the left and one on the right, lined the hall. All were closed.

Mr. Wescott opened the first door on the left and entered. "One moment, Miss Northrup," he said, and Clemency, who had been about to follow him, hesitated on the threshold. The room beyond was dimmer than the hallway, the drapes closed, but as she squinted, trying to see clearly, she heard the rustle of drapes drawing back, and bright sunlight streamed through a window.

Clemency stepped inside. At first, she could make nothing of what she saw. Low cabinets and tables filled the space, none of them matching any of the others. Mahogany stood side by side with oak; delicate gilded tables in the style of the previous century contrasted oddly with cabinets lacquered black and painted with elegant designs from the far East. The range of colors from ash blond wood to darkest ebony gave Clemency the impression of a patchwork blanket filling the room from edge to edge. The tables crowded the room so thoroughly one could not freely walk from one end of the room to the other.

Objects rested upon every surface, statuettes and ornate boxes covered in brass or silver filigree and other items she did not recognize. The room smelled of oil and of something like the tang of copper when one bit one's tongue.

Mr. Wescott pulled back another set of curtains, illuminating the room further. "Welcome to the Cabinet of Curiosities," he said, deliberately inflecting his voice so he sounded like an actor declaiming Shakespeare on a stage. In a more normal voice, he went on, "Feel free to look, but I must ask you not to touch. Some of these objects are rather fragile."

Clemency walked to the nearest cabinet. It contained a silver birdcage some two feet tall, wrought with such skill she did not at first notice the birds within. When she realized they were not moving, she took a closer look and discovered they were not living birds, but constructions of steel and brass. And what constructions! The wings were not solid, but made of dozens of steel feathers, each etched to mimic real feathers so cleverly that only their steel construction identified them as artificial. Their glass eyes gazed back at her with startling intelligence.

Mr. Wescott joined her. "Watch this," he said. He turned a key in the base of the cage five times, then pressed a spot next to the key, making part of the silver filigree slide sideways. Immediately, the birds' wings lifted, flexed, and settled back into place, and they moved their heads, tilting them inquisitively to look in all directions.

Clemency gasped and took a startled step backward. "They are mechanical," she exclaimed.

"Indeed they are," Mr. Wescott said. He sounded pleased with her reaction. "A perfect mimicry of life. Watch, now."

Clemency watched as one of the birds took a step along its perch and then ducked low to peck at the floor of the cage. "It is remarkable. How is it their motions are so lifelike?"

"It is a matter of timing the mechanisms." Mr. Wescott worked a couple of latches and lifted the silver cage away, revealing the birds more clearly. "Life is not so regular as clockwork, so replicating the movement of a living creature means building mechanisms that stutter and hop rather than moving smoothly."

"Did you make this, Mr. Wescott?"

Mr. Wescott smiled. "Not I. This is the work of Mr. Merlin, who built the foundation of the collection. Most of these things are his inventions, and some are marvels he purchased from other inventors. My own inventions tend toward the practical." He put the cage back over the birds as their movements slowed and came to a halt.

Clemency cast an eye over the rest of the room. "And all of these are mechanical?"

"Hence the Cabinet of Curiosities." Mr. Wescott's hand rested on the back of a steel spider the same size as his palm. His fingers were large and sturdy and did not strike Clemency as those of a craftsman.

"Will you show me one of your own creations?" she said.

Mr. Wescott's smile was wry and curved up on one side. "They are not so remarkable as all that, Miss Northrup."

"Nevertheless."

Mr. Wescott shrugged and led the way across the room to a round table upon which rested five music boxes in a circle facing outward. The boxes were of different sizes ranging from the length of Clemency's forearm to the width of her palm. Two of them were of mahogany decorated with silver or gold traceries resembling leafy vines; the other three were of steel and brass.

Mr. Wescott lifted the lid of one of the steel boxes, revealing a detailed figure of a wolfhound. All its joints were articulated, its fur traced in loving detail, and Clemency exclaimed over it.

"Ah, but that is only half the marvel," Mr. Wescott said. He turned the key at the back a few times. The wolfhound immediately sat erect, and as a tinkling melody played, it rose to its hind legs and began to dance. Delighted, Clemency leaned forward, putting her hands behind her back to control the impulse to pet the creature.

"I cannot think why you would call this a lesser creation, Mr. Wescott," she exclaimed. "It is perfectly beautiful."

"Thank you," Mr. Wescott said. "My real interest is in developing a more accurate timing mechanism for use in clocks, one that will permit a clock to sound an alarm at a chosen time. But my failures—" He gestured at the table— "still work, and I don't believe in wasting what is perfectly functional simply because it does not do what I intended."

Clemency listened to the tune and identified it as a Bach prelude. Prudence had played it often when she was a child, but Clemency had not heard her touch the pianoforte since Clemency's return from the War Office. Though this was a sprightly melody, the tune made her heart ache. She gently closed the lid of the music box, and the sound cut off. "You must put a great deal of time into your inventions, if they are all so beautiful as that," she said.

"What time I can spare," Mr. Wescott said. "I am employed with Padgett's Deliveries during the week, and I show the Cabinet as—well, you saw the card."

"Then I wonder that you have *any* time for invention."

Mr. Wescott's wry smile reappeared. "The Cabinet of Curiosities is not so well-known as it was in its heyday," he said. "We have few visitors, and I keep it open mainly out of inertia."

"That cannot be the only reason," Clemency protested.

For a moment, Mr. Wescott's smile broadened. "Has no one ever told you you are too forthright, Miss Northrup?"

"Surprisingly, no," Clemency said. Her father had encouraged her plain speaking and bluntness, teaching her only that rudeness was not the same as honesty. "How is one to learn anything if one does not ask the question?"

"Presumably, polite society believes some questions should not be asked," Mr. Wescott said.

"Well, that is foolish behavior," Clemency declared. "And I do not believe my inquiry was impertinent or rude, merely curious. It seems to me that such a marvel as your Cabinet requires more effort to maintain than mere inertia would provide."

Mr. Wescott shook his head in mock despair. "Miss Northrup," he began, then fell silent for a moment. "I feel a great fondness for the collection," he finally said. "I purchased it from my master in mechanics, Thomas Weeks, who had it from Mr. Merlin before that. At the height of its popularity, it filled a much larger space, and was popular among the upper classes. Mr. Weeks grew tired of maintaining it as the shillings stopped pouring in, and I could not bear the thought of it being sold off piecemeal. Already some of the most valuable objects had left the collection when Mr. Weeks purchased it. So I paid more than I could technically afford, and now it is a beloved millstone around my neck. Hence my employment at Padgett's."

Clemency had not expected quite so much candor, but his confidences warmed her heart. "I quite understand," she said, gazing around the room. "It is not their value, correct? It is the wonder of their existence."

"You have it exactly, Miss Northrup." Mr. Wescott's fingers drummed on the table next to the music box. "Let me show you something else."

Clemency expected him to guide her elsewhere in the room, but instead he returned to the hall and descended the stairs. She followed him, curious. He was as much a series of contradictions as his Cabinet, that miraculous collection of marvels hidden behind an ordinary house front. He was built like a ruffian, fought like a soldier, and spoke like a gentleman. He had the hands of a boxer, and yet those hands created the most delicate mechanisms she had ever seen. And he had seen her at her least ladylike and been impressed rather than appalled. Mr. Wescott, she decided, was someone she wished to know better.

CHAPTER 4

IN WHICH POLITICAL DISCOURSE, WHILE DISCOURAGED, IS ENGAGED IN ANYWAY

In the foyer, Mr. Wescott walked up the two steps and turned the key, unlocking the double doors. He put a hand on one pine-cone knob and said, "This is not so much in demand as it once was, so I keep it locked. But I believe you will appreciate it." He pushed the door open and bowed Clemency inside.

Clemency stopped just inside the threshold, her mouth falling open. The room was unexpectedly warm and was brightly lit by sunlight at its far end, where the ceiling curved to meet the back wall in a series of glass panels set in an iron framework. Planters filled with tall grasses and clipped boxwood hedges outlined paths through the room, exactly as in an outdoor garden. The air smelled damp and green and made Clemency's skin tingle.

Here and there throughout the garden stood metal sculptures, birds and small deer and people no taller than a foot high. All were as intricately made as the objects of the Cabinet. Clemency walked forward, dazed with wonder. She passed a small pond and then doubled back; it was not water, but glass, and copper and silver flowers speckled with steel bees surrounded it. Their transparent wings were tiny marvels of stained glass, iridescent with faint rainbows.

"This way," Mr. Wescott said, breaking through her reverie.

She followed him along the paths until the garden opened up into a wider, stone-paved expanse with a fountain at its center. As she approached, she realized it was not so much a fountain as a pool in a marble basin, ten feet in diameter and raised to waist height. It, too, was filled not with water, but with glass shaped and blown to appear rippling. In the center of the pool sailed an enormous silver swan, its neck arched proudly and its wings folded at its side.

"The jewel of the collection," Mr. Wescott said. He walked around to the far side of the pool and did something Clemency could not see. With a mechanical purr, the swan came to life, lowering its head. The glass water surrounded it began moving, creating the illusion that the swan was swimming upstream in a shining river. Music came from nowhere, a soft, chiming, slightly atonal tune Clemency did not recognize.

Delighted, she moved forward. From her new position, she could see silver fish bobbing within the glass water, which now was obviously a set of glass rods that moved in a complex pattern. The swan arched its neck, stretched, and appeared to snatch up one of the fish. It lifted its head, and the muscles of its throat moved exactly as if it had swallowed the fish.

She did not know how long she watched before the mechanism whirred to a stop, and the swan resumed its noble, frozen pose. "Mr. Wescott, thank you," she said. "I cannot imagine why you do not have the cream of London society beating down your door."

Mr. Wescott walked around the pool to join her. "The war has abridged many pleasures," he said, "and this has been forgotten, for the most part."

"Well, it is a shame. Though—it cannot have been entirely forgotten, if someone knew enough to try to steal from you. These creations must be incredibly valuable."

Mr. Wescott's smile disappeared. "Which is why I live above the museum. Last night's was only one of several attempts on the collection."

"How dreadful! But, then, why do you not—" Clemency blushed and fell silent. Living in an elegant neighborhood, surrounded by expensive things, did not mean wealth, and if Mr. Wescott did not have the resources to hire personal guards or retain the Bow Street Runners, she might embarrass him by the question.

But Mr. Wescott gave her another of his sardonic smiles that said he knew what she had not asked. "The attacks are not so regular that guards would be practical. I cannot afford to pay a Mover or a handful of ruffians to loiter in the street all night, every night, on the chance someone will attempt a robbery. Instead, I remain vigilant, and—I will show you another of my creations. It is not so much a marvel as a practicality, but sometimes practical is more important."

Clemency followed him out to the front door, where he pointed at the upper right corner of the frame. A thin silk rope ending in a fat tassel draped over the frame and then extended up the wall and through the ceiling. Mr. Wescott took hold of the tassel and moved it into a different position so the rope stretched across that corner of the door.

"In this position," he said, "if the door is opened, the rope pulls on a mechanism in my rooms that sets off an alarm I can hear from anywhere on the second floor. There are similar mechanisms attached to the windows of the first floor. And no one can access the back garden without alerting the neighbor's dog, who makes an almighty racket when she is disturbed."

"And you are not unskilled at defending yourself," Clemency said with a smile.

"Not so skilled that I reject the aid of passing Extraordinary Movers," Mr. Wescott said, returning her smile. Clemency found she liked his smile. It was amused, and invited her to share in its amusement.

From the landing above, a soft voice said, "Oh, it's you again. You're not at all the same today, but then that kind of anger cannot be sustained forever."

Unexpected embarrassment flashed through Clemency, as if she had suddenly been stripped naked. She looked up at Lydia Wescott, who leaned on the upper rail with her hands clasped in front of her. "I was not angry," she said. It was true; she felt no anger at the criminals she stopped, and she could not imagine why an Extraordinary Discerner would make such a mistake.

Miss Wescott kicked idly at her skirts with one foot. She wore a simple muslin gown figured with daisies, and her blonde hair was pinned neatly back from her face, though it was still obviously much too short for fashion. "I apologize," she said, though she did not look contrite, or embarrassed, or anything but placid. "Mama says I am not to disturb others by commenting on their emotional states. She says it is bad manners, like criticizing an unattractive dress or a tuneless singing voice."

"Lydia, you should return to your room," Mr. Wescott said. His entire demeanor had changed; his shoulders were tense, and he sounded as if he wished to coax a wounded animal down from a tree.

The young woman's eyes crinkled at the corners as she smiled merrily. "Colin, you needn't fret. I am perfectly well, and not at all confused. There is I, and you, and...Miss Northrup, and all of us are coherent in my heart."

That, to Clemency, sounded extremely confused. But she had not missed the pause before the young woman said her name, nor the sharp-eyed glance Miss Wescott had given her before returning her attention to her brother. "I should go," she said. "Thank you for showing me the collection. I—" She fumbled in her coat for her purse, then hesitated. Paying for the privilege of seeing the Cabinet felt awkward and wrong, a rejection of Mr. Wescott's candor and friendliness, and yet there was no reason for her to receive special treatment. And surely the Wescotts needed the money.

Mr. Wescott's gaze returned to rest on her, and he smiled again, the familiar wry smile that warmed her heart. "No charge, in thanks for your assistance," he said.

"Oh! If you are certain...that is, I would not wish to presume," Clemency said.

"Not at all, Miss Northrup." Mr. Wescott swept her a bow elaborate enough that Clemency laughed. "I hope you will return—and bring your friends," he added with a wink.

Clemency swept him an equally elaborate curtsey. "Naturally, sir."

On the street outside the Cabinet of Curiosities, she took a moment to tuck a stray lock of hair beneath her cap before taking to the skies. That had been unexpected, and not just because of the mechanical wonders. She did not know why Mr. Wescott's manners appealed to her, unless—well, he did not know who she was, and had no expectations of her based on her identity, and she found that refreshing and comforting. And he was well-mannered without being affected, amusing without being crass, and she saw that so infrequently among men of her own class, most of whom tried too hard to impress her, she found herself wishing for more of the same.

Yes, she decided, she would return, and she would tell her friends— oh. Clemency was grateful for the cold wind chilling her face. Her friends. The ones she had been avoiding. She could hardly spread the word about Wescott's Cabinet of Curiosities if she remained an isolated shut-in. Mr. Wescott's face rose up in memory, with that wry smile, and she imagined how he might look if she never returned, if she decided to avoid him too rather than explain why she could not share his genius with the world.

Impatience suddenly gripped her, and she sped up her Flight, rising higher and looping back on her trail once, twice, three times until she was dizzy. She was a fool, a self-indulgent fool. No one would ever know what had happened to her in France unless she told them, and she would never tell anyone. And in staying away from society, she let Armand win.

She hovered in midair with her eyes closed until the dizziness faded, then Flew for home. It was past time she took her own affairs in hand. She was Clemency, Countess of Ashford, Extraordinary Mover of extraordinary talent, and she refused to permit a handful of terrible memories to destroy any of that.

❧

Two evenings later, she sat by her window, turning a piece of card over and over in her hand. Her earlier daring decision was faint and weak now that the moment had come. She glanced at the lettering, barely taking in the words: invited to the Pilgrim residence for an evening of cards and conversation. By what her friend Jane did not write, the other guests would likely all be friends, Movers and Extraordinary Movers she knew well and had competed against often.

Such a gathering should be enjoyable at the least. The idea still made her cringe.

She tossed the card edge-on at the bedpost and caught it with her Moving before it could strike the wood. Then she made it sail around the room like a soaring bird before depositing it neatly on the mantel. She could not remain in this room forever, hiding from everyone she knew; at the very least, people would talk, and suppose that talk led to them discovering her secret shame? If she were to reenter society, she could control that talk to an extent.

She rose and straightened her gown. No Flying tonight, because it would disrupt Jane's party if a quarter of her guests were to leave in favor of a nocturnal race. Better not to wear her Flying gear and thus avoid temptation. So she wore a gown of cochineal-red silk figured around the neck and short sleeves with pearls, with her hair strung with more pearls, and a matching pearl necklace with a garnet pendant around her neck. The necklace had been a gift from her father on her coming-out, and she had chosen it as her armor that evening.

She examined herself in the mirror and ran her fingers along the smooth circle of pearls. She looked perfectly normal. Anything else was her imagination.

The carriage deposited her at Mr. Pilgrim's house with a minimum of fuss; she accepted the footman's assistance down, though she hardly needed it. She had not remembered that Jane's father lived only a short distance from the Cabinet of Curiosities when she had visited the Wescotts, and the realization reminded her of her resolve to mention it to her friends. She let out a deep breath and unwound her hands from the fabric of her cloak. This was nothing. An evening with friends. Some of them, in accordance with Mover tradition, were good enough friends that they used one another's given names in gatherings of similarly-acquainted Movers. It would not be so terrible.

It had been several years since she had visited Jane's father's home, but Clemency had never forgotten the faint, enticing scent of cloves that emanated from every public room. Jane had told her Mr. Pilgrim, an avid world traveler, never felt comfortable unless he was surrounded by relics of his travels. So, exotic spices scented the foyer, whose walls were covered not with paint or paper but fine silk. A series of masks, their faces strangely elongated and their mouths and eyes round holes behind the carved wood, hung on the walls where in an ordinary house landscapes would have been displayed. Nothing about it had changed since Clemency's last visit, and that fact comforted her, making some of her apprehension disappear.

She had barely entered and removed her cloak when she heard Jane exclaim, "Oh, Clemency! How good to see you! Pray, do come in—it is dreadfully cold weather, is it not?"

Clemency clasped her friend's hands and smiled, a natural, unforced expression. Jane was short and stout and never looked quite at ease in a gown the way she did in her Extraordinary Mover's garb, but her expressive eyes and animated features made her as popular with her many suitors as a more traditionally beautiful woman would be. "Thank you for the invitation. I fear I have been so busy with family matters, and with the last responsibilities of my War Office service, that I have become a sad recluse."

"Oh, bah, you needn't explain yourself to *me,* I recall very well the last months of my own service. One would think knowing the date of one's release would mean a general easing of responsibilities, but of course it only meant more work piled up until the very end." Jane hooked Clemency's arm through hers and tugged her toward the drawing room. "Francis is here—you must promise me not to challenge him tonight, he is in a rather foul mood at having come third in the last races, and losing again so soon would make him impossible."

"You have such faith in me. Suppose it is I who lose?" Clemency said with a laugh.

Jane raised both eyebrows. "You amuse me. Obviously I am the one who would win."

They laughed together, drawing the attention of the others gathered in the drawing room. Clemency caught the eye of one of the women seated near the door. She was older than Clemency by nearly a decade and dressed very somberly by comparison to the others, though not in mourning black. Next to her clothes and her black hair and her naturally red lips, her skin was pale as linen, almost bloodless. But her presence reassured Clemency, and she quickly took a seat next to her.

"Elizabeth," she said. "It is so good to see you. Is Mr. Cantrell well?"

Lady Elizabeth Cantrell smiled, the faintest twitch of her lips. "As well as can be expected. We believe the new treatment will be successful. Thank you for asking, my dear. And you—how are you? It has been so long."

For the briefest moment, Clemency considered telling her friend the truth. Elizabeth would not condemn her, she was sure. But with so many others present and listening, it was an impossible desire. "I am quite well. It has been a difficult adjustment, returning home after years of War Office service."

"You must tell us all the many stories you must have accumulated," the Honorable Francis Daubney said. He lounged with one elbow resting on the mantel, a position close enough to the fire that he must surely be scorched, but Clemency had known him for years, well enough to realize he would never admit to any discomfort. His round, cherubic face gave no hint of the black mood Jane had warned her of, but Clemency recognized in his posture his wish to forget his recent defeat.

Clemency shook her head. "I am afraid all my stories are rather tedious, as I'm sure you know—you are not so far from your own years of service to have forgotten that much of what we do in the Flight Corps is boring. Repairs, and lifting supply wagons out of the muck, and innumerable overland flights."

"Or they are forbidden for us to discuss," Francis said with a nod. "All those hours of reconnaissance. Though I imagine secrecy is no longer a concern, not with Napoleon vanquished." He extracted his enamel snuff box from within his coat and took a pinch.

"Oh, but that is something you must know more about than we, Lady Ashford," said a young woman, another Extraordinary Mover. Clemency remembered racing against her, but could not recall her name. "Is it true that another Extraordinary Coercer fought Napoleon and destroyed his talent?"

Fear and shame struck Clemency at this casual reference to the man who had humiliated her. This young woman did not know Clemency had met Napoleon personally, and her comment referred only to Clemency's presence in the field during the Battle of Waterloo. But Clemency could not think how to respond in a way that did not mean being drawn into a conversation that could end in only one place. "Well, I—" she began, fumbling for words.

"I heard it was a head injury," Francis said, closing his snuff box and holding it loosely between thumb and forefinger. "Those have been known to incapacitate someone's talent."

"So completely, though? And he has not recovered even though by now he must have healed any such injury," the young woman said. "Lady Ashford, tell us what you know."

Clemency gained control of herself. "I know only what everyone does, that Napoleon is no longer an Extraordinary Coercer," she said. "And why would another Extraordinary Coercer have attacked Napoleon? One would imagine they had more in common than not."

"Unless they were in competition with one another," the young woman said. "But in that case, why would not that second Extraordinary Coercer have taken up Napoleon's mantle?"

"Which is why I believe the explanation involving a head injury. It is the simplest and most reasonable," Francis said. "However much more interesting the idea of another Extraordinary Coercer is."

"If that were true, though, we would owe that man a great debt," Clemency said. "Still, I agree with you. And I suppose in the end it hardly matters how Napoleon was defeated so much as that he was." This time, anger swept through her at the memory of what Napoleon had done to her, and she closed her fists to keep it at bay.

"His defeat has certainly brought the soldiers home in droves," Elizabeth said in her quiet voice that nevertheless silenced others. "Many of whom know no trade, and are dependent on charity. And that does not include those who are too wounded to work. I feel such pity for them."

"What do you speak of?" Jane said, approaching their little group. "You know I dislike talk of politics."

"No, it is only Elizabeth displaying her boundless capacity for compassion," Clemency said with a smile. "We speak of those who return from war with no means of support."

"Oh, in that case, it is these returning Extraordinaries who concern me," Jane said. "It is selfishness, I know, but I fear being displaced at my employment by some male Extraordinary Mover who believes his sex makes him my superior."

"Oh, Miss Pilgrim, surely not!" the same unknown young woman exclaimed. "Not when you are ranked so high among the Extraordinaries."

"The war afforded women greater freedoms, at least the talented ones," Jane said, "so is it any wonder that we do not wish to be curtailed again now that the war is over? And yet there are those who demand that very thing."

"Mrs. Bonner," Francis said with a look of distaste. "She is loud in her protestations that Extraordinary women are unfeminine if they do anything but what society has always prescribed." He rolled his shoulders as if the mention of Mrs. Bonner gave him an itch between the shoulder blades.

"She is but one voice, however loud," Clemency declared, "and no one of sense pays her any heed."

"I still believe she is dangerous," Francis said. "Because she is herself an Extraordinary Mover, her words are every bit as disruptive as these complaints that Extraordinaries care more for their privileges than for the service they can give society."

"Now *that* is political talk," Jane said.

"Disturbing talk, though," Elizabeth said. "I dislike the rising feeling that the mob might dictate the behavior of others."

"I've heard nothing of this," Clemency said, feeling a twinge of guilt at having permitted herself to be so isolated. "How, a mob?"

"There are many who demand Extraordinaries use their talents according to government mandate, irrespective of the Extraordinaries' opinions on the matter," Elizabeth said. "Registration, required hours of service, just as if they were beasts of burden rather than, in most cases, titled and powerful."

"As if we do not already turn our talents toward helping others," Francis said. "I have spent the last two weeks assisting in building that new theatre in Covent Garden for no remuneration. I could as easily have turned down that request on the grounds that it is beneath someone who is the son of an earl. If we are privileged, it is because we have earned that privilege."

"Not everyone has," said the same unknown woman. "Most titled Extraordinaries inherited their titles from ancestors ennobled by King Charles, not on their own merit. And some of us *do* care more for privilege than for earned respect."

Clemency's opinion of the young woman rose. Challenging a roomful of Extraordinary Movers on their possibly undeserved status could not be easy, even for one who was herself an Extraordinary. "But should all of us therefore be treated disrespectfully, simply because some are selfish?" she asked.

"I will not submit to someone else's control, however noble their motives," Jane said. Her eyes widened, and she put a hand to her lips to hold back a laugh. "And now you have drawn me in against my will. Let us bring out the cards, and talk of lighter matters."

Francis drew near Clemency. "Care for a pinch?" he asked, extending the snuff box.

Clemency choked on a laugh. "You are wicked to remind me of my foolishness in the past," she said. "I cannot believe I ever permitted you to dare me to take snuff. So unladylike."

"Movers are not Movers unless they are engaged in a challenge," Francis said with a smile. "And, speaking of which, I know Jane made you promise not to challenge me at Moving," he said in a lower voice. "Shall we make it a duel at cards instead?"

"I accept," Clemency said. She and Francis had never been anything but the kind of rivals who delight in each other's successes almost as well as in their own, but his smile comforted her. Her earlier fears had faded to nothing. "And I have so much to tell you. Have you heard of Wescott's Cabinet of Curiosities?"

CHAPTER 5

IN WHICH AN IMPOSSIBLE THEFT OCCURS

Storms kept Clemency indoors the next two days, cold rain that seeped inside at every window and door and made her regret her impulsive declaration that she did not wish to travel. So much of Europe was warmer at this time of year than England, and she recalled mild winters in Spain and a few glorious weeks on the Italian coast and muttered curses under her breath no lady should voice. Everything irritated her, particularly her family, whose minor quirks of behavior became major vexations when they were all trapped in the house together.

But Thursday dawned clear and unexpectedly warm, and relief at being released from captivity sent Clemency into the skies before breakfast, racing no one except herself. That she did not beat her best time on a straight flight from Emeraude House to Carlton House and back did not disturb her, so pleased was she at Flying again.

After breakfast, she cajoled Mercy into a walk through the nearby park. Mercy's irritability had been as great as Clemency's despite her frequent Spoken conversations with her reticulum, and she had not yet fully recovered. Clemency ignored her sullen silence and talked cheerfully of anything she could conceive of.

"We should go to Wescott's Cabinet of Curiosities this afternoon," she said. "It truly is remarkable, and I believe you will enjoy it."

"I see no way for us to manage it," Mercy said. "It is not as if my chair will fit on the carriage, and I cannot walk between the cabinets as you describe them."

"Mercy, you know I do not mind carrying you."

"And *you* know I despise being seen as an invalid." Mercy's hands, folded in her lap, gripped one another tightly. "It is bad enough that everyone who passes us now feels entitled to stare."

"They are staring at a chair propelling itself, dearest," Clemency said. Her maximum Moving capacity was almost nine thousand pounds, and Mercy's chair weighed nothing by comparison, but in relative terms it was quite heavy, with its padded iron frame and enormous wheels that creaked as they rolled. Mercy could not manage it by herself, and Clemency did not believe she could manage it with her natural strength, either. But it was sturdy, and capable of easily traversing rough ground, and gave Mercy a measure of freedom Clemency appreciated.

"They are still staring," Mercy griped.

Clemency stopped, and the chair stopped with her. "That is quite enough," she said. "It is a beautiful day, we are both in good health, and you cannot enjoy being in such a foul mood. Should we race? The path ahead is clear."

Mercy gripped the arm rests of her chair reflexively. "You would not dare make a spectacle of us."

"I would so dare, if it made you laugh."

Mercy looked up at her sister. Clemency wrinkled her nose and stuck out her tongue. Mercy's eyes widened in astonishment. Then she laughed. "Very well, I am out of sorts, but do not you dare race with me. You know I fear falling out of my chair."

"I know." Clemency resumed her leisurely gait. "Does anything trouble you?"

"My reticulum has been abuzz with terrible news this morning," Mercy said. "I intended to wait to tell you until I had more facts, because it affects you indirectly. But the information burdens my heart."

"Mercy, you should not keep secrets. I would rather know only a little than see you unhappy. What is this terrible news?"

Mercy sighed. "An explosion in Covent Garden."

"Explosion?" For a moment, Clemency was transported to the battlefield, with the sound of cannons echoing in her ears. "An explosion, here in London? Where in Covent Garden?"

"You know of the construction going on there? A new theatre being built?"

"I have heard, yes. I have friends working there."

"Which is why I chose to remain silent. Part of the building collapsed, and five people are dead and a dozen seriously injured. My reticulum did not know names."

Clemency realized she had come to a halt. Her chest ached with a terrible premonition. "Francis was there," she breathed. "It cannot be —not Francis."

"Mr. Daubney was there?" Mercy exclaimed, and put a hand over her mouth as if keeping back words might protect Francis. "I did not realize—oh, Clemency, that is terrible!"

"Surely someone will be able to tell you," Clemency said. "Ask again."

Mercy lowered her hand and wound it in the fabric of her skirt. "As I said, they did not know names, and I hoped to discover those facts before telling you what can only cause you pain. But that is not the terrible thing."

"What could be more terrible than the death of friends?"

"It is that there is strong evidence the explosion was caused by a bomb." Mercy's face was paler than usual. "No one has claimed responsibility, but witnesses saw two men running from the devastation, and my reticulum says there was nothing in the building site that could have exploded accidentally."

"Why would anyone wish to bomb a theatre?" Clemency paced a few steps away, then back. Her imagination persisted in throwing up images of dead soldiers with Francis' face. "There must be some mistake."

"That is the extent of my knowledge, Clemency." Tears filled Mercy's eyes without spilling over. "How I wish I knew more!"

Only the fact that Mercy would be helpless if she left kept Clemency from Flying to Covent Garden to discover the truth for herself. "We must return home. I need to know—Mercy, forgive me for cutting our walk short."

"I understand," Mercy said.

They were most of the way back to the house when Mercy gasped and tilted her head back in the attitude of a Speaker. Clemency's heart lurched in fear. This might be any communication, but the hope that there was more news of Covent Garden stopped her in her tracks. Francis could not be dead. It was impossible.

Mercy's eyes were closed against the sun striking her face, and a muscle leaped in her jaw as she clenched it tightly. Then she relaxed, and smiled. "Mr. Daubney is well," she said without opening her eyes. "I do not recognize any of the names of the dead."

"I should mourn their deaths regardless," Clemency said, breathing out heavily in relief, "but I cannot help but be grateful it is not a more personal kind of mourning."

Mercy lowered her head and opened her eyes. "I am told there are Movers clearing the debris, and the injured have been taken to hospital. But if you still wish to go there—"

"I would only be in the way," Clemency said. "I will send word to Francis, though. He will know more. Perhaps I will invite him for supper."

"That would be lovely," Mercy said. "He is a charming guest."

"And we are still free to visit Mr. Wescott," Clemency said, eyeing Mercy.

Mercy scowled, but half-heartedly. "If it will give you pleasure, I will not object," she said.

"Such self-sacrifice," Clemency teased.

At two o'clock that afternoon, she Moved Mercy from her chair through the front door and into the carriage, which was equipped with a special seat that kept Mercy from sliding off and falling to the floor. Mercy gripped the seat's handles lightly, with the ease of long experience. "I still say this is a terrible idea," she said.

"You will appreciate the sights, I assure you." Clemency took her seat beside Mercy and arranged her skirts. She had chosen not to wear her Extraordinary Mover clothing because it was unlikely she would need to leave Mercy behind for an unexpected Flight, and because she liked the idea of being anonymous, as far as that was possible. Seated side by side, she and Mercy looked like ordinary women, not at all talented. It was an amusing notion, and Clemency entertained herself by watching those they passed and observing how little attention she and Mercy garnered.

Hanover Square was busier today than it had been on Monday, no doubt because of the clement weather, and the streets were crowded enough that their carriage could not approach the Wescotts' house closely. Clemency ordered the driver to stop as near as he might and climbed down without assistance. Then she Moved Mercy past the open carriage door and brought her to float next to her, her legs dangling so her feet were some two inches above the street. Mercy's face was set and pale, though Clemency knew she was in no pain; her legs were truly paralyzed and free of most sensations. It was being conspicuous that angered and saddened her.

Clemency hooked her arm through Mercy's and walked to the Wescotts' door. As she Moved her sister, she made her bob slightly, imitating the up and down movement of ordinary walking. Almost no casual observer ever realized Mercy could not walk. Clemency's heart ached for her, though, for her impairment that curtailed her freedom and for her proud spirit that hated to be dependent on anyone, even a beloved sister.

She opened the door without knocking—it was well within the hours of admission, and this was a public place during that time, Clemency reasoned—and guided Mercy within. The white, uninviting foyer was empty, but Clemency heard the distant murmur of voices coming from the floor above.

Mercy was looking at the narrow stairs. "There is no graceful way for me to ascend," she said, but with a resigned smile that heartened Clemency.

"Then we will Fly together," Clemency said. She tightened her grip on Mercy's arm and drifted upward along the stairs, bringing Mercy with her. Even this small exercise of her talent warmed her heart. She Moved between invisible currents, tugging on some and being tugged on by others, a sensation that thrilled through her. Surely no other talent could surpass the beauty of Moving.

At the top of the stairs, she halted before the open door to the Cabinet of Curiosities. "Are you quite comfortable?"

Mercy rolled her shoulders out. "This position will weary me after a time, but I have enough support as yet."

Clemency nodded. Her talent encompassed Mercy's hips and lower extremities, holding them gently but firmly rigid, but she knew from years of doing so that even with such firm support, Mercy's own weight bore down on her hips over time, causing her discomfort or even pain. "We can—"

A door farther down the corridor opened, and Mr. Wescott appeared, speaking intently to an elderly woman dressed even more warmly than the winter air would merit. The two approached Clemency and Mercy, and Mr. Wescott looked up briefly before taking a longer look. He smiled, that wry expression that said he was laughing at a shared joke, though Clemency had said nothing.

"Lady Spalding, thank you for your conversation," he said to his companion. "I did not realize just how storied a history the collection has."

"Oh, I recall Mr. Merlin's antics well," the old woman said. She smiled a merry, conspiratorial smile, and tapped the side of her nose. "I was present the night he broke Mrs. Cornelys' mirror. Oh, how we all laughed! Not Mrs. Cornelys, of course. It was a very valuable mirror. I did not see the skates on display, Mr. Wescott. Surely they would make an interesting relic, perhaps with a card describing the story?"

"That is an excellent idea, Lady Spalding. It is true, not all of the collection is on display, but I will search the skates out immediately." Mr. Wescott passed Clemency with a look that clearly said "wait there" and descended the stairs with Lady Spalding.

"That is Mr. Wescott?" Mercy said in a whisper. "He looks like a prizefighter, but he sounds like a gentleman."

"A remarkable contrast, is it not?" Clemency whispered back.

Mr. Wescott showed Lady Spalding the door and walked back up the stairs. "How good to see you again, Miss Northrup. Have I you to thank for my increased custom?"

Mercy's arm jerked in surprise. Clemency's heart thumped once, hard, and then sped up as if trying to propel her out of the house and into the sky. She had completely forgotten she had given Mr. Wescott her family name and not her title. Possibilities sleeted madly through her mind. If any of her friends had come here, and said Lady Ashford had suggested it—but Mr. Wescott had called her Miss Northrup, so he did not know—unless he knew, and was pretending otherwise for some reason—

She heard her own voice saying, "I may have mentioned the Cabinet of Curiosities to a few people, but I am certain it entertains on its own merits. This is Mr. Wescott, Mercy—my sister, Miss Mercy Northrup, Mr. Wescott."

She squeezed Mercy's arm and prayed her clever sister would understand. Mercy coughed. "Mr. Wescott," she said. "Such a pleasure to meet you. My sister has spoken so highly of your museum, I was eager to see it for myself."

"I am pleased to show you around, ladies," Mr. Wescott said with a bow.

Clemency pulled Mercy along beside her as Mr. Wescott escorted them through the aisles, pointing out interesting objects or turning keys to bring mechanical marvels to life. She watched the man rather than the clockwork creations. His large hands fascinated her with their deftness, so unusual for their size, especially when she recalled how skilled he was at fighting. Darting in and out, landing a blow and then Skipping away in seconds: so unexpected. She remembered how admiring he had been of her Moving skill and suppressed a smile. No one believed a lady would Fly secretly through the city by night, punishing criminals. They were both of them unexpected.

When they came to a narrower aisle, Clemency guided Mercy ahead of her, waiting for a stout, mustachioed man escorting a slender woman to pass. The man bumped against Mercy, who let out a small cry. "I beg your pardon," the stout man said, rubbing his large stomach, and continued on his way. Clemency glared at his retreating back.

"I did not realize you are both Extraordinary Movers," Mr. Wescott said.

49

"We are not," Clemency said absently, her eyes still on the stout man. Then she came to herself. "Why would you believe that?"

Mr. Wescott made a gesture with one hand, waving it up and down like a cork bobbing on water. "You are Flying," he said to Mercy. "You drifted when he pushed you."

Mercy's face reddened. "My sister Moves me," she said in a low voice. "I cannot walk."

Mr. Wescott's eyebrows flew nearly to his hairline. "I had no idea," he said. "How remarkable. You are completely without use of your lower body?"

"We prefer not to discuss it," Clemency said coldly. She had seen Mercy's face go from red to pale and did not need a Discerner's talent to sense her humiliation.

"I beg your pardon," Mr. Wescott said. "I should not have made such a personal inquiry. Please forgive my rudeness." He did not look embarrassed, or ashamed, merely concerned, and Clemency was struck once more by the difference between his physique and his demeanor.

"Thank you," Mercy said. "I prefer not to be an object of pity."

"I assure you, that was the farthest thing from my mind." Mr. Wescott smiled again. "Will you permit me to show you the frogs? They are said to croak in the key of F, but I am not musical and have no idea if this is true."

"Not musical, and yet you build those wonderful music boxes?" Clemency exclaimed.

"Music boxes?" Mercy said.

"I have my sister's help in tuning those," Mr. Wescott said. "Miss Wescott's ear is expert. She has mastered the pianoforte and the harp as well as the flute."

"And where is Miss Wescott?" Mercy asked.

"Oh, she is resting," Mr. Wescott said. "Here, I will show you the music boxes."

His steps slowed as he approached the table. "Odd," he said.

Clemency looked past him. There were only four boxes on the table. The fifth, which Clemency recalled was made of mahogany and was the largest of the set, was missing. "Is something wrong?"

"They were all here this morning," Mr. Wescott said. "Pray, excuse me." He vanished with a *pop* that drew the attention of a trio of women standing in the next aisle over.

"I don't understand," Mercy said.

"One of the boxes is missing," Clemency said. "There were five here when I visited last week." She tipped open the lid of the steel box containing the wolfhound, then, with only the smallest hesitation, turned the key a few times. Mercy leaned forward, resting her hand on the table for balance.

"It's beautiful," she said. "So precise, and so delicate. I don't suppose Mr. Wescott takes commissions?"

"Would you like one?"

"I was thinking of Prudence. She loves this tune, and I believe she could use cheering up."

Clemency, who was used to feeling nothing but impatience with her youngest sister's sulks, said, "Cheering up?"

"You have been gone so long—oh, I do not mean that as a criticism! It is just that perhaps you do not know how greatly she suffered from our father's death. They were very close, you know—the two of them the only non-talented ones among the Northrups." Mercy's eyes narrowed. "You did not tell Mr. Wescott your identity."

"We met in such a way that I did not wish him to know me as the Countess of Ashford," Clemency said. "And it is not as if Northrup is not our name."

"Yes, but it is misleading at the very least." Mercy continued to regard Clemency with an intensity that made her wish to be elsewhere. "Is there some reason you cannot now tell him the truth?"

"Have you never wished to be other than you are?" Clemency said in a low, harsh voice. "To be free of your identity and everything that goes with it? I wished for that, Mercy, for just once to be simply Miss Northrup, not Lady Clemency or Lady Ashford and not the Countess. Surely that is not so terrible."

Mercy blinked. "Is it not? Dearest, what bears down on you so much you reject our family?"

"Not our family—oh, I cannot explain!" She would not share with her sister her greatest shame, or the memories that took her late at night and propelled her into the freezing sky. "Please, Mercy. Do not tell him. Let me have this for a little longer."

"I—" Mercy closed her mouth as Mr. Wescott entered the room the conventional way, via the door. To Clemency's surprise, Lydia Wescott followed close behind him. She was dressed plainly in pink muslin and looked like a normal young woman except for her eyes, which were unfocused, and the drifting way she walked as if she were a tethered boat swinging with the current.

"It's probably too late, but I will not give up hope yet," Mr. Wescott said. "My sister, Miss Wescott, Miss Northrup, Miss Mercy Northrup. Lydia, what can you Discern?"

Miss Wescott stared past Clemency and Mercy at the music boxes as if she could see the missing one sitting with the rest. Then she turned and wandered away, walking near those who still wandered the Cabinet. Mr. Wescott watched her go. His hands were clenched into the powerful fists Clemency remembered seeing put to such good use in the fight.

"Miss Wescott is an Extraordinary Discerner," she told Mercy. "Mr. Wescott, has the music box been stolen?"

"By someone who came here in the guise of a paying visitor," Mr. Wescott said. "This is the second time this week someone has stolen from the collection during visiting hours. I have been a fool."

"A *second* theft?" Clemency exclaimed. "How dreadful! What was stolen before?"

"One of the birds—you recall, the ones with metal feathers?" Mr. Wescott's voice was low and rough with anger, and Clemency was grateful he did not direct his anger at her. He sounded like a dangerous enemy, and she almost pitied the thief. "But that is nothing by comparison to the music box. I must hope whoever took it has not got far."

"Because if the thief is still here, Miss Wescott will Discern his guilt," Mercy said. "But—" She fell silent.

"I know," Mr. Wescott said. "Why would that person have lingered to potentially be found out? More to the point, how did that person conceal the box? It is quite large. And no one has Bounded out of here all day, so they did not simply snatch the box and Bound elsewhere. But I must try."

"How astonishing that a thief might be so bold," Clemency said. "So many of these objects are small enough to conceal on one's person, and yet he took that music box." She cast her mind back to their approach to the Cabinet of Curiosities, searching the crowd outside in memory for anyone carrying a box or bundle, but she had been paying close attention to Mercy, and the crowd had made little impression on her. Nor had anyone left as they entered.

Mr. Wescott was watching Miss Wescott make her way through the room. She still drifted, as aimless as a leaf floating downstream, but she looked closely at everyone she passed. Finally, she walked out the door, causing Mr. Wescott to mutter something under his breath and hurry after her on foot. Clemency, feeling awkward about continuing to look at the exhibits as if nothing had happened, once more turned her gaze on the music boxes. "I wonder," she said. "Why this?"

"They must be extremely valuable," Mercy said. "I have seen ones not as fine as these offered for sale at twenty pounds or more. And you said there have been attempts at theft before."

"Yes, but Mr. Wescott is correct that this object would be difficult to remove from the premises without someone noticing." Clemency remembered the stout man who had bumped into Mercy. He had certainly been in a hurry—and yet she had not seen anything about his person that could have been a music box of the correct size. Sighing, she said, "It is a terrible shame. He does so much to protect this place."

"Does he?" Mercy's voice lowered, and there was an arch tone to it that startled Clemency. "And you know of this, how?"

Clemency refused to be drawn. "We have spoken more than once, that is all."

"Is it?" Again Mercy's voice was heavy with meaning.

"I fail to see what about my words requires you to question them." Clemency lifted the lid of another music box, revealing a pair of dancers, male and female.

"Only that I have never known you to be interested in any man to the extent of knowing his activities." Mercy rested her hands on the edge of the table as if supporting herself. "And you did not tell him the truth of your identity. Clemency, if you—"

53

"You are growing tired," Clemency said, pointing at Mercy's hands, which trembled. "Perhaps we should leave."

"Do not try to change the subject," Mercy said. "If you have an interest in Mr. Wescott, that is not terrible."

"Of course I do not," Clemency protested. "He is simply in an interesting line of work. Dearest, I will take us home." She Moved Mercy away from the table and through the aisles as rapidly as she dared.

"I—" Mercy shut her mouth in a thin, hard line. Clemency felt instantly guilty at using her talent to take advantage of her sister's infirmity. She slowed her pace, though she did not stop. Interested in Mr. Wescott indeed. They had barely spoken two words to one another, and he did not know her true identity—though he *was* the only person who knew the secret of her nocturnal flights, and that was a different sort of true identity... She shook her head violently.

"Is something wrong?" Mercy asked.

"No, it is nothing," Clemency lied.

CHAPTER 6

IN WHICH MR. WESCOTT'S GENEROUS GESTURE CAUSES CLEMENCY CONFLICTING EMOTIONS

They had reached the foot of the stairs when Clemency heard someone calling her name from above—the false name she had given Mr. Wescott. She turned to see the man himself descending the stairs. "Are you leaving? I had hoped to ask your opinion on another marvel."

"I take it there is no sign of the stolen box?" Clemency asked.

"None." Mr. Wescott stopped on the bottommost step and gripped the newel as if he might wrench it free. "Miss Wescott says no one here feels any guilt over a theft, and the music box might have gone missing any time in the past hour and a half."

"Is there nothing you can do?"

Mr. Wescott shrugged. "I have set my sister to watching the door in case someone else intends theft, and I will have to commission a Seer to Dream the stolen objects' location if I wish to find them. But that will take time, and who knows what might happen to the box before that?"

"What do you mean?" Mercy said. "Surely it will end up in someone's private collection?"

"Or it might be disassembled for its clockwork." Mr. Wescott looked even grimmer. "I have made many innovations in the past few years, and someone might have wished to copy my work for his own profit. But I do not mean to trouble you ladies with my problem." He smiled, though Clemency thought it looked forced, and turned to Mercy. "I need some assistance that I believe you, Miss Northrup, can provide."

"I?" Mercy asked, startled.

"Please, permit me to show you, and you will understand." Mr. Wescott strode to the locked double doors and turned the key, then dropped the key into his coat pocket. He pushed the door open. "This way."

Clemency guided Mercy through the door and along the paths, moving slowly so Mercy could appreciate the wonderful creations of the garden. Mr. Wescott passed the silver swan without setting it in motion, so Clemency only paused there a moment, explaining to Mercy what the mechanical bird did.

"This is astonishing," Mercy breathed as they passed a row of miniature human figures holding musical instruments, a flute and a violin and a drum. "I see now why you were so eager to bring me here. How perfectly delightful!"

"I believe I could spend an hour here and not see everything it has to offer," Clemency said. "But we have fallen behind."

She sped their pace toward the wall of windows and the large open space beneath them. The garden ended some twenty feet from the wall, and the area beyond was floored with much-scuffed wood that looked as if hundreds of hand-sized carriage wheels had raced across it. More planters lined the wall beneath the windows, each overflowing with boxwood shrubs. Unlike the others, these had not been trimmed in months, possibly years, and the resinous smell of the shrubs was strong enough to be nearly overpowering.

Mr. Wescott had opened a door to the left of the windows and disappeared inside. Curious, Clemency followed him. The door did not open on a second large room; it appeared to be the entrance to a closet, filled with shelves that were themselves filled with mechanical objects similar to those in the Cabinet above. These, however, were not arranged in a way to give visitors a good view of them. Clemency's impression was of clutter and disuse.

"Oh, yes," Mr. Wescott said. "Here, hold these." Without turning around, he extended a hand behind himself to Clemency and thrust a pair of metal objects into her hands. Clemency controlled an expression of distaste, for the metal things were dusty and rust-spotted. They were a pair of metal frames about the length of her forearm into each of which were set a row of four small wheels, all in a line. She turned one of the wheels with her forefinger, and it rotated with a little difficulty, letting out a faint squeal of metal grinding against metal. She had no idea what they were for.

"Here we are," Mr. Wescott said. He backed out of the closet, bringing with him an armchair set on enormous wheels. It was similar in design to Mercy's chair, but slimmer and, based on how easily Mr. Wescott moved it, lighter.

"I assume you have seen these before," he said.

"I have one," Mercy said. "Its frame is iron, and it is designed to maneuver over rough terrain because I am fond of wild places such as those near our home in Norfolk."

"Mr. Merlin designed the original of this invalid chair," Mr. Wescott said. He pushed on the chair's back, making it roll gently forward. "I have added some modifications of my own that I would like to bring to market. Specifically, lightening the chair itself and making the wheels more maneuverable so it is manageable by women. I fear Mr. Merlin, and his successors, considered only the convenience of men when they built these. Miss Northrup, would you do me the honor of giving me your opinion? I hope I do not presume too much on our very short acquaintance."

"You wish me to use this chair?" Mercy said.

"It would benefit me greatly if you could tell me where I need to improve." Mr. Wescott sounded perfectly matter of fact, not at all as if he felt he was insulting Mercy by alluding so directly to her infirmity.

"I—" Mercy looked at Clemency. "Well, I suppose."

Clemency immediately lowered Mercy into the chair. Mercy rested her hands on the circular rails mounted on the wheels. "What are these for?" she asked.

"You use them to move the wheels. They are to prevent one

dirtying one's hands by touching the wheels directly." Mr. Wescott pushed on one of the rails, demonstrating.

Mercy gripped the rails harder and pushed, propelling herself forward a few inches. "It is not at all heavy," she exclaimed. She rolled herself away, slowly, then gaining momentum until she was moving at a slightly faster than walking gait. At the edge of the garden, she glanced at Mr. Wescott for permission, and at his encouraging nod, she wheeled herself into the nearest path.

Clemency watched Mercy pass through the garden, stopping now and then with no apparent effort to look more closely at some wonder. "She could not do that with her own chair," she murmured.

"Those heavy ones are indeed better for traversing rough ground," Mr. Wescott said, "but at the cost of one's freedom. I assume you must Move her chair now?"

Clemency nodded. "But this—" She nodded at Mercy. "This is miraculous."

"As I said, I am in her debt if she can prove my modifications beneficial. At the risk of sounding ill-bred, I would prefer to support myself and Miss Wescott by my inventions rather than by Bounding."

Clemency glanced at her companion. He was watching Mercy, not her, but his brow was furrowed as if he was thinking of something else. "The Cabinet is expensive to maintain?"

Mr. Wescott looked her way. "My Bounding employment pays the bills, but it requires me to spend time away from Lydia, and she..." His voice trailed off, and he looked away again. "She is occasionally confused and disoriented, thanks to her talent. Today there are not many visitors here, and she has not been overwhelmed, but when the museum is busy, she suffers. I would prefer to be near at all times."

"She does not appear mad."

"She is not mad," Mr. Wescott said in an intense, low voice like the growl of an angry animal. "She perceives the world around her, and she knows the difference between what is real and what is not. But an Extraordinary Discerner feels the emotions of those around her as if they are her own, and learning to distinguish between them is difficult. Miss Wescott is still learning."

"I understand," Clemency said. "I apologize if I gave offense."

Mr. Wescott shook his head. "No, it is just that I fear—but I should not burden you with my own troubles."

Clemency watched Mercy lean over to examine the steel bees with their iridescent wings. Her face shone with happiness. "You have given my sister her freedom," she said. "I believe you may burden me with anything you like."

Mr. Wescott laughed. "That is quite the offer. Suppose what I want is to see you again?"

Warmth flooded through Clemency, heating her cheeks and making her heart beat faster. "I do not call that a burden," she said, finding herself unable to look at him.

"Such a relief," Mr. Wescott said, sounding amused. "I am to deliver a lecture at the Society for the Promotion of the Sciences on Wednesday next; will you attend?"

Clemency made herself look at him, hoping she appeared nonchalant. "What is the subject?"

"I'm afraid it is quite dull. 'On the Motion of Mechanical Creatures, With Special Attention to Beasts of the Natural World.' Your presence would prevent me falling asleep with boredom as I speak."

The drollness of his expression made Clemency laugh. "You offer a very powerful incentive, sir," she said, bobbing a curtsey. "I will attend."

Mr. Wescott's smile broadened. "For once, I look forward to one of these lectures with great anticipation."

Clemency blushed again. To distract herself, she once more turned her attention on her sister. Mercy had nearly reached the outer door, and as Clemency watched, she turned the chair in a tight circle and returned the way she had come. The delight and wonder in her face made Clemency's heart beat faster for a completely different reason. Impulsively, she said, "We must have one of your chairs. Please, how much will it cost to commission one?"

"Not as much as you imagine. The true cost is in how long it will take me to build another." Mr. Wescott turned to face Clemency. "I would like you to take this one—not to purchase, but to use while I build a second."

"Oh!" Guilt and embarrassment flooded through Clemency. "Oh, we could not possibly—"

"Again, I remind you that you will be doing me a favor in testing the prototype thoroughly," Mr. Wescott said. "And of course you are free to tell everyone who admires it where they might acquire one of their own."

His expression was once more that knowing, wry smile, and Clemency felt flustered enough she could not meet his eyes. "Such mercenary motives," she managed, smiling so he would know it was not an insult.

"Miss Wescott and I must eat, Miss Northrup," Mr. Wescott said. His gaze fell on the metal things she held, and he abruptly took them from her. His fingers grazed hers, those heavy, thick fingers that looked nothing like a craftsman's. They were warm and slightly rough against her skin, and again heat flooded through her. She must look ridiculous, with her cheeks bright red and her hands suddenly feeling twice their normal size.

"What are they?" she asked, trying to distract herself.

"They are wheeled skates," Mr. Wescott said. "They fasten to one's shoes and permit one to skate on wood or stone rather than ice. Mr. Merlin invented these, but I'm afraid he did not invent a way for the user to stop. I understand that lack led to great amusement among those watching the skater." He lifted one of the skates to eye level and murmured, "Though I can see a possibility..."

"You must live in a marvelous world, to have so many ideas," Clemency said.

"Such a polite way of saying my ideas possess my every waking hour," Mr. Wescott said. "Miss Northrup, I find you remarkable."

Clemency was saved having to answer this by Mercy's return. She was breathing more heavily than usual, but her cheeks and eyes were bright, and Clemency had not seen her smile so brilliantly since before their father's death. "Clemency, it is amazing," she said. "Mr. Wescott, you are a marvel. What can I tell you that will be of use?"

"You will have many days to experiment," Mr. Wescott said, "if you will do me the honor of using the chair for a week or two."

"Truly?" With that exclamation, Mercy looked much younger than her twenty years. "Oh, Mr. Wescott, if you're sure it won't be an imposition?"

"Your sister and I have established that some impositions are no burden," Mr. Wescott said, smiling. "Miss Northrup, I shall have the new chair ready by a week from next Monday, if that suits."

"Of course, Mr. Wescott." Daringly, Clemency extended her hand to clasp his, ostensibly to seal the agreement, but in truth she simply wanted to feel his hand in hers again. The tiny part of her that spoke with her mother's voice chided her for her wantonness, but it was shouted down by her father's memory, saying *There's nothing wrong with desiring things, and if the thing you desire is worthy, why not do whatever it takes to grab hold of it?*

Mr. Wescott took her hand with no hesitation, his firm grasp making her heart beat faster. Likely she was being foolish, but she had not felt this way in a very long time—

—and with that, memory struck her a blow that shook her to her core, the memory of Armand's hand touching hers, drawing her close so her body was pressed against his. Her hand closed convulsively over Mr. Wescott's. She opened eyes she had not realized were closed and found him regarding her with a puzzled expression. She smiled, hoping it looked natural and not like a parody of a smile, and released his hand, saying, "I look forward to Wednesday next, sir, and thank you again for your generosity."

"It is all my own pleasure, I assure you," Mr. Wescott said, but he still looked puzzled, as if he knew she was not being fully forthcoming.

Mercy wheeled herself to the door, where Clemency carefully Moved her down the two steps to the foyer. Then she Moved her sister, lifting her out of the invalid chair, and carried Mercy and the chair to their carriage. Mr. Wescott held the door open for her, then stood in the doorway as she settled her burdens for travel. Clemency concealed her disquiet in the bustle of getting Mercy into her seat, carefully not meeting Mr. Wescott's eyes.

"If you are well, dearest, I will Fly home with the chair," she said.

"But you are not wearing your Flying clothes," Mercy protested.

"It is not so long a journey, and I will Fly high enough no one will see me as anything but a bird," Clemency assured her.

To Mr. Wescott, she said, "I wish you luck in retrieving the music box."

Mr. Wescott's smile faded, and he nodded, but said nothing more. Clemency took hold of the chair and sped away into the sky.

This was not her first time Flying while not wearing her Extraordinary Mover's garb or her Flight Corps uniform, but every time, the chill that touched her legs sent an unexpected shiver through her. She Moved the folds of her gown to wrap more securely around her legs and Flew faster. It was unlikely she would arrive after Mercy and the carriage however slowly she Flew, but the chill was more than she liked to endure for long.

She berated herself silently for letting memory affect her. What must Mr. Wescott believe her momentary stiffness meant? She herself did not know what it meant. It was not as if she loved Armand, but her memories were so tangled between remembered desire and present abhorrence that she sometimes had to insist to herself that all those loving feelings had been Coerced.

This attraction—yes, attraction, she was not ashamed to own it— she felt to Mr. Wescott bore no resemblance to what Napoleon had Coerced in her toward Armand. She remembered how her body had reacted to Armand's touch and felt ill at how Napoleon had made her complicit in Armand's seduction. She swallowed bile and sped faster, though the drag of the wind on the chair prevented her reaching her top speed. She would not permit that past Coercion to interfere with her true emotions now.

She descended rapidly and alit on the stoop, bringing the chair to rest on the street. The carriage had not yet arrived, so she opened the door and Moved the chair into the foyer. Though narrower than Mercy's own chair, it was still wide enough for comfort, Clemency guessed from how eagerly Mercy had taken to it. Then she waited on the stoop, not caring that it made her look foolish; she did not intend to take to the skies again in her drafty gown, and she did not wish for Mercy to have to wait in the carriage for Clemency to be fetched.

Her time in the air had chilled her despite her wool spencer, and she rubbed her arms rapidly to warm them. She could not attend Mr. Wescott's lecture alone, not if she wished to remain Miss Northrup and not Lady Ashford. Mercy disliked being conspicuous in public, and even the new invalid chair might be awkward in a lecture hall. Perhaps Francis might accompany her. He would feel entitled to tease her about her bluestocking tendencies, but she did not mind that.

The carriage rattled around the corner and came to a stop at the front door. Clemency opened the carriage door, too impatient and too cold to wait on the footman. "Inside," she said, "and I must write to Francis. Do you suppose tonight is too soon to invite him for supper?"

CHAPTER 7

IN WHICH A PLEASANT PARTY
IS INTERRUPTED, AND
CLEMENCY MAKES A WAGER

C lemency patted her lips with her napkin and spread it across her lap again. She surveyed the table, and the guests seated around it, with contentment. Francis had not been immediately available to dine with her, and she had invited him for the following Monday. But when she had mentioned the engagement to Jane, Jane had been so enthusiastic Clemency could not help but invite her, as well.

With Jane attending, it was only natural Clemency should invite the Honorable Tobias Wortham and Jonathan Howell, Lord Paxton, both Movers of renown, both among those Clemency referred to as "Jane's swains." And then Jane had mentioned that Elizabeth had seemed dejected when last she saw her, prompting Clemency to offer her an invitation as well. By Monday evening, the proposed quiet family dinner had grown into quite the event.

Now Clemency watched Mercy, seated at the end of the table opposite her, and felt even greater contentment. By tradition, it should have been her mother's place, but the invalid chair did not fit anywhere else along the dining room table, and Clemency had decided, after several days of watching Mercy wheel herself around the house, that she would not deprive her sister of her mobility simply for propriety's sake.

She was too far away to hear the details of Mercy's conversation with Francis, who sat at Mercy's left, but her face was alight with enthusiasm, and Francis' lips occasionally quirked in the smile that meant he had said something clever. In anyone else, it might have been an annoying habit, saying things one knew to be witty and preening oneself on one's wit, but Francis was genuinely amusing, and Clemency appreciated his turning that skill toward entertaining Mercy.

The Dowager Countess, seated on Mercy's right, did not look at all charmed by Francis' wit, nor by the conversational sallies of Tobias on her other side. Clemency had hoped Tobias, who was the soul of patience and a very good listener, would draw her out of the sulk she had been in ever since Clemency refused to invite Lord Winder to the party. It occasionally struck Clemency as absurd that she had to coddle her mother the way she might a stubborn child. Surely the coddling ought to go the other way around?

And the Dowager Countess was not the only stubborn child at the table. Prudence sat midway along the table, picking at her food and not meeting anyone's eye. Clemency regretted giving in to Mercy's persuasion and permitting Prudence to join the party. "She is lonely, and I believe she feels unwanted and overlooked," Mercy had said. Clemency had ignored the unspoken criticism and made her invitation to Prudence as genuine as possible. But looking at her sister now, she guessed whatever impulse had prompted Prudence to accept had not filled her with unalloyed enthusiasm.

With the same inward sigh that always accompanied her thoughts of her family, she turned her attention to more immediate matters. "You are bold, Jonathan, to claim I am afraid to race you," she said to Lord Paxton, seated at her left. "I have beaten you two out of the last five times we have competed."

"Those are bold words as well," Jonathan said with a smile. "You have been away these four years. Much can change in that time."

"She chooses not to race against me, either," Jane said. "That, to me, is the mark of someone unprepared to lose."

"You both know War Office service means training daily,"

Clemency said, pretending to lecture them. "Racing must needs be set aside."

"Oh, bah, we always raced anyway," Jane said. "Come now, Clemency, you cannot put us off forever."

Clemency could not understand why the idea of a simple race—of Flying in competition with other Extraordinary Movers, which she had done often since her talent manifested—should leave her feeling so uncomfortable. "Very well," she said. "We shall set a date." She refused to let fear rule her, and this uncomfortable feeling was far too close to fear.

"The public trials are coming up soon," Jonathan said. "Why make it a private race when one can have one's time registered officially?"

The uncomfortable feeling surged, and Clemency crushed it ruthlessly. "If you are not afraid of being outraced in front of the world," she said, smiling archly.

"Then it is settled," Jane said.

Clemency rose from her seat, prompting the others to rise as well. Irritation at Roger's absence flashed through her, twinned with relief at the same. She did not miss his sullen, spiteful presence, nor his veiled —sometimes not so veiled—barbs directed her way, but with him gone, there were no male members of the family to play host to the men. So she said, "I realize it is not custom, but I invite you all to join me in the drawing room—if you men do not mind forgoing your usual pleasures?"

She did not wait for agreement; what could they say if they disagreed with Lady Ashford? Instead, she accepted Jonathan's arm and led the way from the dining room and across the hall to the drawing room, whose doors were flung wide and welcoming. The fire burned high enough that the room was already warm, and Clemency seated herself with pleasure some distance from it, politely leaving room for other of her guests to take advantage of the warmer seats.

She watched Francis accompany Mercy to her usual spot near the fire, left open to accommodate her chair. He was a good friend, to be so attentive to her sister. As he handed Mercy her workbasket, he said something that made Mercy laugh, and Clemency's heart lightened even more. If only Prudence—but if Mercy was right, it was Clemency who was partly to blame there. Clemency cast about the room and saw

Prudence seated near their mother, both still looking sulky. Ah, well, at least Prudence had not hared off to her bedroom.

"I have missed this," Francis said as he took a seat beside Clemency.

"This, what? The clamor of too many Movers in one space?" Clemency said with a smile.

"Good friends, good food, good fun," Francis said. "I take it you have decided to leave your self-imposed isolation? I heartily approve."

"I simply fell out of the habit of entertaining," Clemency lied. "Will you join us at the public trials at the end of the month? My reputation is apparently on the line."

"With pleasure," Francis exclaimed. "We will see if the War Office has blunted your edge. And when I have outraced you, well, you must pay a forfeit."

"Must I?" Clemency tilted her head inquiringly. "And what should this famous forfeit be?"

"An introduction," Francis said. "To a lady of my choosing."

"Really? Francis, have you your eye on someone? Does your mother know?"

Francis shrugged. "Mama is in perennial despair at my refusal to court any of the eligible and wealthy and occasionally titled young ladies she parades before me. Do not read too much into my request."

"Oh, but now I am so curious I cannot help but pry."

"You need only lose, and your curiosity will be satisfied." Francis smiled a rather secretive smile.

"Very well," Clemency said. "However, when I win, you will...oh, dear, I cannot conjure an appropriate forfeit of my own. It is not as if you can introduce me to any of the gentlemen of your acquaintance." She laughed. "I know! Your forfeit will be to tell me the name of this young lady you wish to meet. Then we are both the winner."

"You must be curious indeed to sacrifice your forfeit. Now I fear you will be disappointed." Francis' smile deepened into a wry, self-deprecating expression that reminded Clemency of Mr. Wescott.

"I will not, as you have yet to disappoint me," Clemency said. "Though on that note, I have a request." She leaned closer so she might speak without shouting over the growing noise of many conversations.

"A request? Are you certain you have not come up with a forfeit?" Francis removed his snuff box from inside his coat and took a pinch.

"No, this is by way of being a favor." Clemency's cheeks felt hot, and she fixed her gaze on the snuff box so she did not have to meet Francis' eyes. "I wish to attend a lecture in two days, and I require an escort. I wondered if you might join me."

"Lady Ashford requires an escort?" Francis sounded more puzzled than surprised. "Since when have you needed anyone to give you countenance in public?"

Clemency felt her head might burst into flame from embarrassed self-consciousness. "In truth, I do not, except that I choose to attend not as Lady Ashford. I wish to be anonymous."

"Anonymous?" Francis' tone became increasingly perplexed. "Clemency, what are you failing to tell me? You are redder than an apple, and your hands are fidgeting the way they do when you are not being completely forthright."

Clemency glanced at Francis, who looked curious but not condemning, and made a decision. "The lecturer is someone I find interesting," she said. "He is a Mr. Wescott, and he—"

"Of Wescott's Cabinet of Curiosities?" Francis interrupted. "And you were so enthusiastic about it. I begin to see."

Clemency blushed harder, but managed to say, "He has asked me to attend the lecture, but he knows me only as Miss Northrup, and of course Miss Northrup cannot go to a lecture unaccompanied. Will you come?"

Francis regarded her in silence for so long Clemency finally had to look at him. The smile had vanished, leaving him looking more sober than she had ever seen him. "Why do you not tell him your name?" he asked.

"Oh, because I met him under conditions that prevented me telling him the truth, and now it will be awkward if I reveal myself like the villain of a melodrama." Clemency did not add her suspicion that Miss Wescott knew she had given a false name, or at least a not entirely truthful one.

Francis shook his head slowly. "Clemency, if you admire this man—if you have more than a passing interest—it will do neither of you any good for that interest to develop while there are secrets between you. You are Countess of Ashford, titled in your own right, and that gives you social consequence Mr. Wescott may feel intimidated by."

"I will tell him the truth," Clemency said. "But not now. Soon, I promise."

"It is not I to whom you should make that promise," Francis said. He smiled, and clapped her on the shoulder in a friendly way, and his soberness vanished. "Very well. When shall I call for you? I hope for your sake this is an interesting lecture, as I am certain you do not wish to attend with a companion who thinks nothing of sleeping through the boring bits."

"Never fear," Clemency said, "I am prepared to pinch you if you do."

"Francis!" Jane called out from across the room. "Oh, forgive me for interrupting, Clemency."

"It is no interruption, and you know your father would be extremely disappointed in your unladylike behavior at shouting across a drawing room," Clemency said, taking refuge from her embarrassment in a faux reprimand.

Jane rose and crossed the room, walking in exaggeratedly tiny, mincing steps that were apparently her interpretation of ladylike behavior. "I wish to know more of the disaster at Covent Garden," she said. "In fact, I believe we all do."

"That is a rather serious subject for after-supper conversation." Francis rose to meet her.

"Oh, bah, it is what we have all wondered for days," Jane said.

Clemency caught Elizabeth's eye. Her friend had been seated next to Jane, and now she shrugged slightly, inviting Clemency to speak. "It is true I have been worried at the reports of a bomb causing the disaster," Clemency said.

The room quieted. Francis once more removed his snuff box from within his frock coat, but he did not open it, merely tapped its lid with his index finger. "I was far enough away that I only heard the explosion, and then the noise of the building collapsing. But those Movers who helped us clear the debris, the ones who had been on the ground, said the smell was unmistakable."

"Then it was a bomb," Elizabeth said. She closed her hand on her skirt and twisted the fabric in a tight knot.

"Someone in power believes so," Francis said, "because men came later to ask many, many questions about the event. They were the sort of questions that indicate someone is suspicious of events."

"You mean they accused you all of complicity?" Clemency exclaimed.

"Not in so many words," Francis said. His restless tapping of the snuff box became more pronounced. "But it was clear they believed that any bomb that exploded where and when and how this one did could easily have been placed by someone working on the theatre's construction."

"And then there are those who blame the Extraordinaries at the site for not acting quickly enough, and allowing the disaster to be greater than it should have been," Jane said. "Have none of you heard those rumors?" she added as a clamor rose up.

"Now *that* I do not believe," Clemency said. "Five people died, all of them Movers or Extraordinary Movers; how can anyone suggest they were negligent?"

"I have heard those rumors as well," Francis said. His hand closed entirely over the snuff box, and he gripped it as if he might crush it to powder. "That we were careless, or that we took unnecessary risks, which led to our being incapable of stopping the building's collapse."

Clemency rose and put a hand on his arm. "No one who knows you will believe it."

Francis shook his head. "This is the first time Extraordinary Movers have been blamed for an accident involving their talents, or the misuse of their talents. I am angry at being traduced so, but in the abstract, it disturbs me that someone has made such a claim."

"Do you believe they are deliberate lies, then?" Tobias asked. He took a position next to Jane as was his habit, but he did not look at her, only at Francis. "Spoken with malicious intent?"

"I do," Francis said. "But the allegations of careless misconduct have all been anonymous, whispers in the night, so to speak. There is no way to counter rumor."

"That makes no sense," Jane declared. "Why lie about something the Extraordinaries involved will deny? Surely there are witnesses to corroborate their statements."

"As if the word of an Extraordinary were not his bond," Jonathan said, taking his usual position at Jane's other side. "You say there was no carelessness, and that is the end of it."

"Not for those who believe Extraordinaries should have less influence in our society than they do," Elizabeth said, drawing everyone's attention. "Francis, you say this is the first time Extraordinary Movers have been blamed for the misuse of their talent, but that is not entirely true, is it?"

Francis shrugged. "Very well, it is more accurate to say that this is the first time such an accusation has been taken seriously. Not every Extraordinary Mover is conscious of his responsibility to society, and we have all heard tales of Movers and Extraordinary Movers using their talents to gain an advantage over others, or even to commit crimes."

"But those are nothing but tales," Jonathan said. "The law privileges Extraordinaries, true, but it does not overlook crimes. The Catterwell prison exists solely for the purpose of confining criminals with talent; what would be the point of it if those with talent could break the law with impunity, and thus not need to be imprisoned?"

"Such naivete, Jonathan," Jane said, but with a fond smile to take away the sting of her words. "Wealthy people commit crimes, if not the same kind of crimes the poor do, and many of them never suffer the slightest repercussions. I believe, if Extraordinaries do not appear to commit crimes, it is because they are good at hiding their criminal activities."

"Bold words," Clemency said, amused at Jane's forthright speech. "But I see Elizabeth's point. Extraordinaries enjoy many privileges, and to the jealous, it might not be such a stretch to imagine they enjoy many immunities as well."

"Jealous?"

Clemency startled. Prudence had shot to her feet as if that one word had propelled her. "You believe it is jealousy that makes us question whether you deserve what you are given?" she continued. "Perhaps it is simply common sense to question whether an accident of birth makes you our superior."

Clemency swallowed her first, hasty response. "I don't believe anyone here considers him- or herself superior to others simply by virtue of having talent, Prudence," she said instead. "And you know Father never permitted others to treat him poorly simply because he lacked talent."

Prudence's face was mottled with rage. "Don't speak of him to me," she shouted. "You have no right—" She closed her mouth tightly and rushed from the room.

Clemency stared at the place where her sister had been. "I beg your pardon, everyone," she said. "Lady Prudence has been unwell."

"She loved her father dearly," Elizabeth said. "It is a hard thing to lose someone one loves."

Tobias cleared his throat. "I wonder how many others are reasoning along those lines?" he said in his soft, diffident voice. "That those of us with talent believe we are better or more deserving human beings?"

"I have met those who hold that opinion," Clemency said, grateful to Tobias for redirecting the awkward conversation, "but no one of sense agrees with them. In fact, I have heard them actively derided as fools."

"That is the case in the War Office," Francis said, "where rank is more important than talent. Lord Wellington, for example, is a Mover of no very great talent, far outstripped by his subordinates, and yet only a fool would consider him a lesser person. But outside the Army, that opinion is far more widespread than it should be."

"I worry more that in the Covent Garden matter, Extraordinaries are being criticized for failing to act when that is not the case," Jane said. "That may start people wondering whether Extraordinary Movers can be trusted. So many of us are engaged in building and demolition, and those can be dangerous activities even without involving Movers. Suppose some other disaster occurs, and Movers are blamed for it simply because they *might* have acted inappropriately?"

"Surely not," Clemency said, but she did not feel confident in her assertion. "There must still be proof of a crime, mustn't there? Allegations are not enough."

"According to the men who spoke to us, no one involved in the disaster will be charged with a crime, not even with willful negligence, but that will not stop the talk of collusion," Francis said. He turned his gaze on Mercy, who sat with her hands clasped tightly in her lap. "And this talk is disturbing some of us. I propose a game of whist, if Lady Mercy will consent to be my partner?"

Mercy's face lightened. "You know I cannot bear to lose at whist, Mr. Daubney. I hope you are prepared to fight for our victory."

"Always, Lady Mercy." To Clemency, Francis said, "Permit me to set out the tables?"

"Of course." Clemency rose and Moved the tea tray to the console table nearest the door. She was not overly fond of cards, but she enjoyed watching others play. Now, however, the unease roused by their conversation would not leave her. She politely declined an invitation to one of the tables and took a seat nearer the fire. Jane had called Jonathan naïve, but Clemency felt the term applied to her as well; she had never considered that anyone might misuse their talent, certainly not for criminal gain, but of course there was nothing stopping a Mover or a Bounder from stealing, or a Seer from Dreaming something to give herself advantage over another, or a Scorcher from committing arson.

What truly disturbed her was her contemplation of her own nocturnal activities. In a sense, she used her Moving in opposition to others, and she was not certain whether doing so to prevent crime rather than engage in it was enough of a distinction. That was doubly true when she remembered that society would not look kindly on her for Flying through the city at night, searching for criminals she could turn her talent on. If stopping crime was not something she dared share with the world, how legitimate was it, really? Clemency had the feeling this was not a question she could easily answer.

CHAPTER 8

IN WHICH A LECTURE ENDS IN AN UNREASONABLE DEMAND

The hackney Francis had hailed rattled through the streets with unusual alacrity, as if the driver had somewhere else he wished to be. Since it was also poorly sprung, the rattling jounced Clemency until she wished she had suggested Flying instead, given how beautiful and bright a day it was. It was vanity that had led to the hackney; Clemency had decided to wear a gown of fine dark blue wool that flattered her more than did her Flying garb, and had Tatton arrange her hair in a way that her knit cap would immediately disorder. She refused to listen to the little voice that taunted her for her foolishness in wishing Mr. Wescott to admire her appearance.

Beside her, Francis watched the streets pass by, apparently absorbed in his own reflections. But then he said, "I have been contemplating all the possible circumstances that might have led to your not telling Mr. Wescott your true identity. What secrets are you keeping, Clemency?"

"It is not so mysterious as that," Clemency said, inwardly scrambling for a plausible lie. "We struck up a conversation without an introduction, and when it came time to correct that misstep, I had already given him the impression that I am no one. I found that unexpectedly satisfying." The explanation sounded threadbare—when would someone ever not be introduced to the Countess of Ashford?—and she hoped she had taken the right assertive tone.

"I see," Francis said. "I did not realize you chafed at your rank, not after how you fought to gain it."

"That is essentially what Mercy said. But—oh, I cannot explain. People believe they know who Lady Ashford is, her habits and her opinions, and they expect things of me based on those beliefs. I occasionally weary of those expectations, that is all."

"I suppose I understand that," Francis said. "During my service there were many who expected great military things from me, simply because my uncle is Major Daubney who is high in Lord Wellington's confidences. Still—"

Clemency waved her hand in a dismissive gesture. "I have said I will tell Mr. Wescott the truth soon. Do not fear, I have no intention of pursuing the connection, growing ever more intimate, with the burden of that secret resting on me."

"And you believe that is where this connection will go? Clemency, you astonish me."

Clemency blushed. "I do not know anything. Perhaps I am wrong, and Mr. Wescott will simply be a friend. But suppose I am right?"

Francis gripped her hand briefly. "You know I wish you nothing but the best." He removed his hand and added, with an impish smile, "Except when it is a matter of competition. You have yet to outrace me."

"Brag if you like, but my maximum Moving weight has always surpassed yours," Clemency replied, laughing.

They continued their banter for the few minutes it took for the hackney to arrive at their destination. Francis handed Clemency out of the carriage, and she shook her skirts out and examined the building. The forbidding grey stone façade looked more appropriate to one of the more dreadful government buildings than to anything that housed a society dedicated to furthering knowledge. Its windows were unusually small and narrow, in contrast to its wide, pillared porch and double doors of some dark wood.

A largish brass plaque fastened beside the door bore the inscription *Society for the Promotion of the Sciences* and, in smaller letters beneath,

Timendi causa est nescire. Clemency stood for a moment, puzzling this out. Her father had not been fond of Latin or classical Greek, saying often he preferred communicating with the living than with the dead, but Clemency had enough grounding in the classics to recognize these words, though she could not recall who had originally said them. "Ignorance causes fear, I believe is the meaning," she told Francis.

"I never gave Latin space in my mind for longer than necessary to satisfy my tutor," Francis said. He pushed the door open and held it for Clemency to enter. "Though that is an excellent motto for such a society."

The foyer was no more appealing than the exterior of the building; it was cramped and narrow, with closed doors to right and left and a staircase not wide enough for Clemency and Francis to ascend side by side filling the rest of the space. A gentleman had nearly reached the top of the stairs, but he did not look down at their entrance, merely turned and disappeared down a hall leading deeper into the building.

Clemency and Francis exchanged glances. "I expected someone to tell us where to go," Clemency said in a low voice. "Shall we venture upstairs?"

Francis tried the handle of the nearer door and found the door locked. "I suppose we must."

The upper hall, with its dark paneling, felt like a tunnel reaching deep beneath a mountain, dimly lit by lanterns shaped like upside-down tulips. The lantern glass appeared dirty, but was on closer inspection merely cloudy with inclusions Clemency concluded were too uniform not to be intentional. The dimness made her feel she was seeing the world through black gauze. Possibly the Society members were the kind of science-oriented men who took no interest in such mundanities as a welcoming environment. Mr. Wescott had not struck her as one such, but she had only met him three times, and she could not have learned everything about him in so few encounters.

The gentleman who had entered before them was visible at the end of the hall. He opened a door, letting bright sunlight into the hall before closing the door behind him. Clemency quickened her pace, though there was no reason to believe reaching that room quickly would benefit her. The hall unnerved her, as low and narrow as it was.

Extraordinary Movers were creatures of the sky and wide-open spaces, not burrowers.

She opened the door into the lighted room with some force, causing Francis to sneeze as was his habit when entering a brightly-sunlit space. She walked forward, gazing in awe at her surroundings. Unlike the hall, the room had ceilings easily twenty feet in height, studded with skylights polished so clear she could almost imagine them open holes to the sky rather than glass. Narrow windows like the ones she had seen on the building's façade lined the wall opposite the door, but these let through plenty of light and gave Clemency the impression of cozy reading nooks or embrasures holding telescopes for viewing the stars.

Chairs that did not all match one another had been lined up in rows facing the right-hand wall, where stood a lectern and a series of high-backed desks made of some glossy reddish wood. The desks, rather than their tall backs being set flush against the wall, stood in pairs extending perpendicular to the wall, like medieval confessionals. Clemency could easily imagine tonsured monks in black robes poring over illuminated manuscripts at such desks.

Clemency's eye was drawn to the table next to the lectern. Its ornate carvings made it look even more out of place than the mismatched chairs. Mr. Wescott stood in front of it with his back to her, busying himself with setting out a number of mechanical contraptions whose purpose Clemency could not determine. She told her heart to calm itself and made her way to a seat near the center, not so close to the front as to seem overly eager, but affording her a good view of the lectern.

"I see this will be a demonstration as well as a lecture," Francis said as he seated himself beside her. "Are these some of Mr. Wescott's curiosities?"

Clemency's cheeks heated with the private embarrassment of having temporarily forgotten her companion. "You have not seen the Cabinet?"

"I am not much for museums, Clemency," Francis said. He took a delicate pinch of snuff and tucked the snuff box away in his coat.

"Though you are so interested in this one, perhaps I should make an exception."

"It is remarkable. I never realized the possibilities of clockwork beyond what makes my pocket watch run." Clemency adjusted her bonnet to give her restless hands something to do. Francis was correct; she fidgeted when she was nervous.

At that moment, Mr. Wescott straightened and turned around. His gaze immediately fell on Clemency, and he smiled, that wry, amused expression that invited her to join in his amusement. Clemency could not help but smile in return. Mr. Wescott eyed the chairs between himself and her, raising an eyebrow in clear indication that her position made it impossible for him to approach. Then he glanced at Francis, and his smile faded. He nodded politely at Clemency and turned away.

A cold fist gripped Clemency's heart. Surely he did not believe Francis was anything but a companion—oh, but why should he not? On the other hand, she and Mr. Wescott had built such an accord between them, he could not possibly believe she would taunt him so? The urge to leap from her seat and confront him filled her. She folded her hands in her lap to control the impulse. They would speak later, and she would convince him—she was not certain of what she must convince him, but anything to stop him looking at her with indifference.

The room was filling up now, and Clemency found herself flanked on her other side by a large, sweaty man who breathed heavily, as if he had found the stairs too much of a challenge. Clemency smiled politely at him and received a somewhat strained smile in return. The air had grown warm with the advent of dozens of bodies, and Clemency wished she had removed her cape before sitting. Now, crowded in as she was, that was impossible.

A tall, slender man stepped up to the lectern and cleared his throat. "Thank you all for coming. We are pleased to hear today from one of our most prominent members, Mr. Wescott, whose popularity has preceded him based on today's attendance. Mr. Wescott will speak to us on the topic 'On the Motion of Mechanical Creatures, With Special Attention to Beasts of the Natural World.' Mr. Wescott."

Clemency applauded politely with the others as Mr. Wescott took his place at the lectern. "Thank you," he said. "I appreciate your interest in a subject that has long fascinated me. Of course, when one is fascinated by a topic, one runs the risk of boring others by prattling on about it. I hope I will avoid this pitfall today." He smiled that familiar smile again, and added, "If I fail, I assure you those seats are quite comfortable for napping." Subdued laughter filled the room.

"I will not begin with an exhaustive history of clockwork," Mr. Wescott continued, "but a few points are necessary to provide a foundation for my subject, primarily that the regular motion demanded for the successful operation of clocks and watches is not always desirable in other mechanisms. The living world is erratic, and mimicking its motions requires a similar irregularity. Timing is everything, ladies and gentlemen, and today I will demonstrate how timing permits the aping of the natural world."

Clemency leaned forward slightly, captivated by the motion of his hands as he gestured in time with his words. As the lecture continued, her appreciation for his intelligence grew; he spoke clearly and concisely, never descending into abstruse and tedious theory, explaining obscure terms without distracting from his presentation. She could not imagine anything less boring than this subject.

Her interest increased when he began demonstrating his work. She recognized most of the mechanical marvels, having seen them in operation at the Cabinet, and hearing the audience gasp or murmur in surprise gave her a feeling of satisfaction, as if she had a proprietary interest in their success. As the music box wolfhound danced, she looked instead at its creator and was startled to find him watching her. His expression was thoughtful, somber, and she found herself unable to look away.

Then he closed the music box and set it on the table, turning away from her. She felt as if she had been released from a Mover's grip, her breathing rapid, her heart pounding. Once more she clasped her hands in her lap, stilling them.

Finally, Mr. Wescott concluded his remarks and invited questions from the audience. Clemency again fixed her gaze on the table with all its many marvels, paying only half her attention to the questions and

Mr. Wescott's responses. She found herself remembering the stolen music box and wondering what would be the purpose of such a theft. Perhaps it was simple greed, but having now heard Mr. Wescott discourse on the uses of mechanics, she now wondered if he had not been correct before in suggesting someone might wish to steal the mechanism to reproduce it.

"Thank you very much," Mr. Wescott said, and the applause that followed brought Clemency back to herself. She applauded as well, but remained seated while the large, sweaty man rose with the others. Mr. Wescott was thronged with people interested in a personal word; she would wait for the tide to ebb, and then speak to him.

"You were right, Clemency," Francis said. "That was fascinating. I had no idea how much was possible with mechanical contraptions. It quite makes me see my watch in a new light."

"And that is not all he creates," Clemency said. "You saw Mercy's new chair—that is of his design, based on an earlier creation."

"Lady Mercy was more animated than I have ever seen her last Monday evening." Francis removed his snuff box from his coat, but did not open it. "She was positively radiant."

"I owe Mr. Wescott a great debt for that."

Francis looked at Clemency closely. "But that is not the root of your attachment. I have never seen you so interested in anyone as you are in Mr. Wescott."

"I fear he believes you and I are..." Clemency's voice trailed off. She watched Mr. Wescott demonstrate one of the mechanical creations to an elderly woman, and her heart ached. "I am a fool, Francis."

"No more a fool than anyone who feels a budding attachment. And you know your friends wish only for your happiness." Francis turned the snuff box over in his hand idly, as if he was not fully conscious of doing so.

Clemency sighed. "Let us speak to him, and then we should go. I don't know what I expected."

She rose and followed Francis along the row of chairs. The crowd surrounding Mr. Wescott had thinned somewhat, but there were still enough people Clemency did not like to push past them. She waited, feeling increasingly awkward. Perhaps she should simply leave.

She surveyed the room to distract herself. Portraits hung on the wall nearest the windows, dour and forbidding with dark backgrounds matching dark clothes so the subjects' faces appeared to float in the centers of the frames. Beside the door, a bust on a plinth cast its blank gaze over the room. Clemency felt she should recognize its subject, but the memory escaped her.

As she looked away from the bust, the door opened, admitting five men in unremarkable suits. Though they were of different heights and complexions, they gave Clemency the impression of uniformity, as if they were produced from a mold. Possibly that was because of the way they moved, their strides identical, their heads turning constantly as they surveyed the room. One's gaze crossed Clemency's and moved on, showing no interest in her, not even the idle interest of a man who finds a woman attractive. Clemency had never been regarded with such dispassionate indifference, and it chilled her.

The men spread out through the room like a seed pod bursting, examining their surroundings closely. One man approached Mr. Wescott, somehow parting the crowd without doing anything so crass as shoving people aside. Mr. Wescott turned away from the woman he was speaking to and said, "Yes?"

"Mr. Wescott?" The man's voice was as bland as his appearance.

"I am he," Mr. Wescott said. He did not sound annoyed, but Clemency saw him close one hand into a loose fist as if holding on to his patience.

"Mr. Wescott, you will come with us," the man said. He gestured in the direction of the door, where the other four men had gathered.

"I will?" Mr. Wescott arched an eyebrow. "Who are you?"

"That is unimportant." The man continued to hold his hand out toward the door, as if he intended to ask Mr. Wescott to dance. "You are required to come with us to answer some questions regarding the Covent Garden bombing."

CHAPTER 9

IN WHICH CLEMENCY DIVULGES HER IDENTITY AND REAPS THE FRUITS OF DECEPTION

Mr. Wescott's eyes narrowed. "I know nothing about that incident, and if you intend to claim I was complicit, I assure you I was nowhere near at the time of the bombing. And I certainly refuse to go anywhere with strangers who fail to reveal their identities."

Clemency worked her way around the crowd, which had stilled as the conversation proceeded, until she could see the unknown man's face. His expression frightened her. It was the expression of someone who cared nothing for other people except for what they could do for him.

"We are tasked with investigating the bombing," the man said, "and I must inform you that failure to comply will be seen as an admission of guilt."

"That's irrational," Mr. Wescott said, for the first time sounding impatient. "There are any number of reasons I might not comply with your absurd demands, starting with my repeated assertion that I had nothing to do with it and can prove I was elsewhere."

"We have evidence that you were involved," the man said. "You are invited to speak to our superior on the matter. If you are innocent, you have nothing to fear."

Mr. Wescott laughed. "And now you are simply being ridiculous," he said. "I decline your so-called invitation, and suggest you leave now."

The other four men moved forward. The speaker put a hand on Mr. Wescott's arm. "You will come with us."

Mr. Wescott vanished and reappeared five feet to the left with a faint rush of displaced air. "You cannot confine a Bounder, gentlemen, if that is what you are."

"Your refusal only confirms your guilt," the man said.

"That is not how the law works," Clemency declared.

There was a rustle of fabric as everyone remaining in the room turned to look at her. The man said, "Do not interfere, miss, or it will go hard with you."

For the briefest moment, Clemency hesitated, looking past the man at Mr. Wescott. Then she lifted her chin and stared the stranger down. "I am the Countess of Ashford, and you will not take that tone with me, sir."

The man's eyes widened, and for the first time he looked uncertain. "Your ladyship," he said, "this is not your concern."

"I believe it is," Clemency said, walking forward until she was directly in front of him. "Whatever suspicions you have, you do not have the right to bully anyone into admitting guilt when he does not know the charges against him. You do not have the right to compel a private citizen to go with you to some undisclosed location, to be interrogated by unknown persons. And you do not have the right to claim a person's refusal to go along with your bullying makes him guilty."

"We have authority from our superior—"

"Who is, again, known to none of us. For all we know, you intend to make Mr. Wescott a scapegoat for the bombing because you lack the ability to discover the true culprit. Assuming you are, in fact, authorized to do so." Clemency took a step closer. She remembered standing before the House of Lords, arguing her right to inherit, and closed her hands to keep them from shaking as they had then. "I do not believe you are as convinced as you claim of Mr. Wescott's guilt, or you would not have taken the approach you did. If you have genuine questions, ask them. If not, I invite you to withdraw."

The man's eyes moved rapidly as he looked from Clemency to Mr. Wescott and back again, passing over the silent, watching crowd. "It would be better for Mr. Wescott to come voluntarily," he said, his voice not as steady as before. "To answer questions and assist in our investigation."

"Changed your mind, have you?" Mr. Wescott said. "One minute ago you had convicted me without trial. I feel no responsibility to help those who have already decided on my complicity."

The man licked his lips. "I misspoke," he said. "Will you accompany us?"

Mr. Wescott glanced at Clemency swiftly before turning his gaze on the man. "I think not," he said. "If you have questions—real questions—you may find me at the Cabinet of Curiosities. If not, I suggest you not approach me again." He crossed his arms over his chest, drawing attention to the size and breadth of his shoulders.

The man also glanced at Clemency, who glared at him. Then he turned and left the room, trailed by his companions.

The moment the door clicked shut, the room erupted into shouts and demands for explanations. Finally Mr. Wescott clambered onto the table, nudging aside the wolfhound music box, and shouted, "Please, let us have quiet!" When the noise died away, he added, "I have no idea why anyone would believe I had something to do with that dreadful bombing, so I cannot answer your questions."

"But who would have the power to attempt to haul you away?" the fat, sweaty gentleman who had sat next to Clemency asked.

"That, I also cannot explain," Mr. Wescott said. Then he smiled that wry, amused smile, and said, "This has certainly been the most exciting lecture I have ever given. I hope you do not expect my next lecture to end in a public hanging!"

Laughter that sounded rather relieved broke out, and the crowd began to disperse. Clemency waited as Mr. Wescott stepped down from the table and set about putting the mechanical marvels into boxes for transport.

"So much for anonymity," Francis murmured in her ear. "What will you tell him?"

"I don't know," Clemency said. "But I could not remain silent."

"No, you could not. Those men were armed." Francis rested his hand on her shoulder. "Shall I remain?"

"Please. I would like you to meet Mr. Wescott." She did not add that she intended to make it clear that Francis was only a friend. That made her seem so pitiful.

Though she stood only a few feet from the table, Mr. Wescott's attention never strayed from his packing. Clemency watched his hands move deftly over the clockwork marvels until she felt uncomfortable, as if she were doing something far more intimate than waiting on his attention.

The room was empty now save for the man who had introduced Mr. Wescott, who was at the door speaking to an attractive young woman. Clemency stepped forward and cleared her throat. "Mr. Wescott."

"I suppose neither of us were bored, were we?" Mr. Wescott said, not looking up. "Thank you for attending."

"Mr. Wescott, I apologize for my deception," Clemency said, feeling desperate to regain his regard. "I should not—"

"I knew who you were when you first appeared on my doorstep," Mr. Wescott said.

Startled, Clemency took a step back. "But you said nothing."

Finally, he looked at her, and her heart sank, for his expression was nothing like the amused, confiding look that had captivated her before; he looked almost as indifferent as the stranger had. "I would be no true gentleman if I challenged a lady on her right to privacy. You wished to be Miss Northrup, and I was certain you had your reasons. Though I hoped you would confide in me eventually." He stepped away from the table. "May I be introduced to your companion?"

"Oh!" Clemency shook herself out of her astonished stupor. "Mr. Wescott, this is my friend, Mr. Daubney. Mr. Daubney is a fellow Extraordinary Mover, and he and I have known each other for many years. He expressed an interest in your mechanical marvels."

Francis flicked a glance at Clemency, but otherwise did not react to her blatant lie. "Truly a marvel, Mr. Wescott. Lady Ashford has spoken of nothing else for a fortnight. You have made quite an impression on her."

Mr. Wescott smiled. "High praise indeed." He rested one large hand on the nearest box, which fastened at the top with a hasp and was equipped with straps that dangled loose over the edge of the table. "I feel I should thank you for intervening, Lady Ashford. I did not intend to go with those men, but escaping would have meant leaving my mechanicals behind, and I had a feeling the men would take advantage of my absence to confiscate them."

"You truly have no idea why they believe you complicit in the bombing?" Clemency asked.

"None." Mr. Wescott's fingers rapped restlessly on the box lid. "And I cannot imagine I have made the kind of enemies who would accuse me of a crime. There must be a mistake, but what mistake, who knows?"

"You are not afraid they will try again, this time at your home?" Clemency wound her hand into her skirt so the fine wool fabric calmed her.

"It is true, if they did not care about taking me from a room full of witnesses, they may be more inclined to do so where no one can see," Mr. Wescott said. "But in truth, my feeling is that their aggressive approach concealed their true intent, which was to throw me off balance so I would give away more than I intended."

"But you know nothing of the matter," Clemency said. "How could you give anything away?"

"Indeed," Mr. Wescott said. "I doubt they chose me at random, so there must be some truth to their allegations—or at least it must be true that *someone* has accused me of complicity. Therefore, they will still want to question me. I hope this encounter will encourage them to be less aggressive in their questioning a second time."

Clemency nodded. She cast about desperately for something else to say, and landed on, "I hope your sister is well." Immediately she felt stupid. Such an inanity!

But Mr. Wescott did not react as if he considered her words inane. "Thank you for asking, Lady Ashford. She is very well." He cleared his throat. "You must have guessed she is responsible for revealing your identity. She knew you were not who you claimed to be, and it took only a little investigating on my part to discover your true name. But she did not intend to intrude on your privacy."

"I knew it was a possibility, but—truly I am not offended, I understand Extraordinary Discerners can sometimes not help what their talent Discerns." Clemency's face felt hot, though she did not know why she should be embarrassed. She was not the one who had intruded...though she was the one who had lied, and perhaps that was the cause of her embarrassment. Or perhaps it was her knowledge that Francis was listening closely to this conversation. She did not like the idea of him learning of her nocturnal activities.

"You are very gracious." Mr. Wescott cleared his throat again. "I should return; I dislike leaving Miss Wescott alone for long periods."

"Is Miss Wescott an Extraordinary Discerner?" Francis said. "How remarkable. There are so few of them in England."

"She grows more in control of her talent every day," Mr. Wescott said, once more crossing his arms over his chest. "But I have the care of her, and I take that responsibility seriously."

"Of course," Francis said, not rising to Mr. Wescott's implied challenge. "It is what we do for those we love, is it not?"

Mr. Wescott relaxed. "It is," he said. "Which reminds me—how does my chair serve your sister, Lady Ashford?"

"Very well, Mr. Wescott, and I cannot thank you enough." He was so much more formal now, so distant, that it made Clemency's heart ache. Their friendly camaraderie, their informal discourse, all gone. She made an effort to conceal her dissatisfaction. "You have given her such freedom."

"It was my pleasure." Mr. Wescott bowed. Then he picked up the nearest box and slung its straps over his shoulder like a satchel. "Forgive me, but I must leave you. Thank you again, Lady Ashford, and I will deliver the new chair Monday next, if that is acceptable."

"Of course," Clemency said.

Mr. Wescott settled the second box's straps around his shoulders so it lay against his chest. He nodded politely to both Clemency and Francis, and then was gone with a faint *pop*.

Clemency drew in a deep breath and let it out slowly. "I suppose we should go."

"Clemency," Francis said. She looked up at him; his expression was sober, his brows drawn down to nearly meet above his nose. "Clemency, you knew this might happen."

"What might happen?" Clemency said, forcing an air of unconcern. "Come, Francis, the carriage is waiting."

"You are the Countess of Ashford," Francis said, undeterred by her breezy attitude, "and not every man wishes to be overshadowed by a titled, powerful woman. At least he was not resentful that you lied to him."

"It is nothing," Clemency said. "We barely know each other, and he has pressing responsibilities—"

Francis took her arm and swung her around, making her face him. "You need not lie to me," he said. "It breaks my heart to see you in pain. I could have him beaten, if that would soothe your spirits."

Clemency choked on a laugh. "He is an accomplished fighter, and a Bounder, and he uses both skills expertly. Anyone you hired to beat him would have quite the job ahead of him."

"My curiosity as to how you met continues to grow." Francis converted his grip on her arm to an offer of his escort. "Let us return to your house for refreshments, and later I will take you to the theatre, and we shall amuse ourselves with no thought of Mr. Wescott."

Clemency took Francis' arm. "You are the best of friends, Francis. And perhaps someday I will tell you how Mr. Wescott and I met."

"If it is not a thrilling tale of adventure, I shall feel sadly misused," Francis said, striking a pose of noble suffering that made Clemency laugh again.

Between tea and the theatre and a late supper, Clemency managed to forget Mr. Wescott for several hours. Francis was charming and pleasant, and she could understand why his mother wished so devoutly for him to be wed, because he would make any woman a wonderful husband. But Francis had never shown any interest in marriage, though he flirted in a desultory way with any attractive young lady whose path crossed his, so Clemency could not wish him luck in finding a wife when she was uncertain as to whether it would make him happy.

When she finally returned home, the house was quiet and dimly lit. Clemency handed her cape to Slater, the butler, and was about to ascend the stairs when her eye fell on a card resting on the silver salver meant for accepting such offerings. Curious, she picked it up. *Mr. Colin Wescott, Wescott's Cabinet of Curiosities*, the fine black printing read. Clemency's heart gave an unexpected lurch.

"When did this arrive?" she demanded of Slater, who paused in the doorway leading below stairs.

"Sometime after eight o'clock this evening, my lady," Slater said. His voice had the precision he adopted when someone failed to observe the social niceties. "It was after you had left for the theatre, and naturally I would have brought the card to you in the morning, at a decent hour."

"Thank you, Slater," Clemency said absently. She turned the card over. A penciled message in bold, squarish letters matching those on the door of the Cabinet of Curiosities read *Am I too bold to ask you to join me at my home tomorrow morning at 10? Am in need of your opinion.*

Her heart, which had nearly regained its composure, sped up until it fluttered against her ribcage. Her opinion? She could not imagine what Mr. Wescott could possibly need her opinion of. The sensible part of her chastised Mr. Wescott for having the effrontery to write with such informality to someone his social superior, but the rest of her shouted it down. He could not write such a message if he felt distant or indifferent to her. She clutched the card to her chest and indulged in a silly, helpless smile. Then she Flew up the stairs and over the balcony rail and down the second-floor hall to her room. Sleep suddenly seemed unlikely.

CHAPTER 10

IN WHICH A FRIENDLY VISIT
ENDS IN CONFUSION

Se Flew to the Cabinet of Curiosities the following morning, leaving early so she might indulge in a swooping, roundabout path. She looped lazily through the sky, then dove, chasing pigeons across the rooftops and laughing as they scattered in a rush of wings. Flying that low, she was aware of pedestrians with their heads tilted back, watching her pass. She waved at a child clinging to its nurse's hand and laughed again with delight as the child nearly fell over trying to keep its eyes on her.

She soared higher then, into the freezing heights where the pigeons dared not go, and made herself an arrow shooting across the sky. Her divided skirts flapped wildly in the wind, dragging at her, and she reflected, not for the first time, how much of a disadvantage female Extraordinary Movers were at when it came to racing. Surely a woman did not sacrifice modesty simply by dressing in men's clothing? And yet there were too many who agreed with Mrs. Bonner that femininity took precedence over practicality.

When her face was numb and her hands tingled inside their padded gloves, she dropped lower and headed for Hanover Square. She alit a little too rapidly and fell to one knee to keep her balance, drawing attention from passersby. She stood and straightened her cap, pretending that landing had been intentional, and knocked briskly on the Wescotts' door.

She had been waiting long enough to check the time by her pocket watch when the door swung open, revealing an unfamiliar man. "Lady Ashford," he said. "Welcome. May I take your coat?"

Mystified, Clemency entered and removed her Flying coat, a full-length wool coat heavily padded for warmth at altitude. The man accepted it from her and bowed. "If you will permit me, I will show you to the drawing room."

Clemency followed him up the stairs to the first floor and down the hall to the door on the right. The man opened the door and bowed again. "Lady Ashford, Miss Wescott," he said.

Miss Wescott rose from a chair near the fire, which burned low enough Clemency would have found the room chilly had she not just descended from the upper atmosphere. "Good morning," Miss Wescott said, curtseying just deeply enough to make Clemency feel awkward.

"Good morning," Clemency replied. The door shut behind her, and the two of them stood facing each other. Miss Wescott's head was tilted slightly to the right, like an inquisitive bird, and her fair hair hung loose around her face so she looked very young. She appeared to be waiting for something. Clemency cast about for something to say and came up blank.

"Hammond is not nearly so formal as he seems, but he sees our consequence as fitting his own." Miss Wescott clasped her hands in front of her. "I forgot," she said. "Won't you sit? I'm afraid I get lost sometimes, and then we stand for an hour saying nothing, which is terribly boring if you're aware of it."

"I suppose it would be," Clemency managed. Miss Wescott's matter-of-fact tone contrasted sharply with her words, which made just enough sense not to be confusing. And yet Clemency had never heard anyone speak the way Miss Wescott had. She no longer knew whether Miss Wescott was sane or not.

She took a seat opposite the young woman and settled her divided skirts. Miss Wescott also sat, watching Clemency with that odd, inquisitive expression. "You're confused," Miss Wescott said abruptly.

"I see the world so differently, and I don't always know how to express what I see in a way that does not sound mad. But you are also not angry that I discovered your secret. I apologize for my intrusion on your privacy."

"Thank you. I understand," Clemency said. "I did not intend to deceive, but my identity—I should not be known as Lady Ashford when I go out at night like that."

"It frees you, I know," Miss Wescott said. "And you—but I have said I should not comment on others' emotional states. Do you like Colin?"

"I beg your pardon?" Clemency did not at first remember that Colin was Mr. Wescott's given name. Then she ruthlessly suppressed a blush. "Do I—"

"Oh, I see," Miss Wescott said with a smile. "He would be angry with me if he knew how informally I speak with you, Lady Ashford. But for an Extraordinary Discerner—perhaps you do not know this, but we are always so intimately aware of those around us, we have difficulty maintaining formality. It is as if the entire world is our family, do you see?"

Clemency did not see, but she nodded.

The door opened again. "Lady Ashford," Mr. Wescott said. "I apologize for the delay. Thank you for coming. I realize my request is irregular."

"You made me curious," Clemency said. Mr. Wescott was dressed properly in frock coat and waistcoat and cravat, but on him the attire looked as odd as formal gowns did on Jane, as if it was not his natural appearance. She extended a hand to him in greeting and pretended his touch did not send a shiver of excitement through her.

"I would not have made such a request were you not already in some sense involved," Mr. Wescott said, taking a seat next to his sister. "You recall what I said yesterday about those men still wishing to question me? It turns out I was correct."

Clemency drew in a startled breath. "They came here? Surely they did not try to assault you?"

"No," Mr. Wescott said, smiling, "it was not an assault. I had a visitor late yesterday afternoon. One man, though he was remarkable in size. He gave his name as Mr. Rutledge and requested the pleasure of a conversation with me regarding the Covent Garden bombing."

"That is much more civilized, but I still fail to see why anyone would connect you with it," Clemency said.

Mr. Wescott raised one eyebrow and pursed his lips, giving himself an amused if somewhat sardonic air. "Mr. Rutledge was not only more polite, he was considerably more forthcoming. It seems the Covent Garden bomb was atypical of such devices. Most bombs, he told me, are made to be ignited and thrown immediately before detonation. This one was attached to a clockwork mechanism that permitted the bomber to choose a later time for the bomb to explode."

"A clockwork mechanism," Clemency said. "But surely you are not the only man in London who builds mechanicals?"

"I am, however, the only man in London to whom the device could be traced." Mr. Wescott's amused expression vanished, and he suddenly looked so angry Clemency was taken aback. "Mr. Merlin's stolen mechanical bird was found amidst the wreckage."

"They dared!" Clemency exclaimed. "To turn such beauty toward destruction—how horrid!"

"I can see now how the mechanism might be altered to regulate something other than the timing of a mechanical creature." Mr. Wescott's hands closed into fists, resting on his knees. "I did not create it, so I do not feel personally affronted at its abuse. But I was its care-taker, and it infuriates me to be used like that."

"Of course it does! I am infuriated on your behalf." Clemency shook her head. "But I am not sure why you asked me here. I know less about bombs than you do."

"But you do know more about the law," Mr. Wescott said, "at least, that is my understanding from how you spoke so eloquently in my defense yesterday. Mr. Rutledge, while less hostile than those men, nevertheless sounded unconvinced that I was not involved. I would like to know what you can tell me about what he can do to me. I would prefer not to see the inside of the Catterwell."

"I am no expert," Clemency protested.

"I would rather have your advice than that of an expert with no interest in my situation," Mr. Wescott said.

"You know enough," Miss Wescott said abruptly. "And it matters to you what happens to Colin."

This time, Clemency could not control a blush at Miss Wescott's frankness. "My knowledge is more specific with regard to inheritance law," she said, "but I know something of criminal justice. When the Rights of Man were enumerated in 1787 after the rebellion in the American colonies was put down, the document included protections against the unjust treatment of those accused of a crime. For example, you cannot be compelled to testify against yourself in criminal proceedings, and you have a right to know what charges you are accused of."

"And does Mr. Rutledge have the power to arrest me?"

Clemency shrugged. "I don't know. I suppose it is possible, if he has the authority, but in that case he would be required to make an official statement and proffer his credentials of authority. Did he show you any such?"

Mr. Wescott shook his head. "He did not even look as I expect an officer of the law to look. But he stated that he was not from Bow Street, and when I asked if he had been sent by the magistrates, he said his was a higher authority."

"That is chilling. Any authorities higher than the magistrates are the sort who try capital crimes. Though I suppose setting off bombs is that, regardless of whether they cause death." Clemency clasped her hands in her lap to still their restless motion. "If Mr. Rutledge was unconvinced of your innocence, it is likely because whoever Mr. Rutledge's superiors are, they have no other suspects, which means they will watch you closely to give themselves the illusion that they are acting."

"That's remarkably cynical of you, Lady Ashford." Mr. Wescott's admiring smile reminded Clemency of the night they had met, when she had turned her talent on the would-be thief. She should feel more embarrassed at her unladylike comment, but if it was a true observation, why should it embarrass her?

"I fear the law no longer overawes me," she said, "as I have seen it employed against me as well as in my favor. Though some of that may be my knowledge that my title and status afford me protections under the law that many people do not have."

"You intrigue me," Mr. Wescott said, leaning back in his seat as if settling in for a story. "May I ask you to elaborate?"

"It is no great secret." Clemency's memories of facing down the House of Lords surfaced, but in this quiet room, with Mr. and Miss Wescott's attention on her, they were not such terrible memories as once they were. "I am the eldest of my family, and my father wished me to inherit his title. He contended, before his death, that if a female Extraordinary enjoys many protections under the law, such as property rights and the ability to enter into contracts in her own name, she should be permitted to inherit a title in her own right."

"That is very sensible, and therefore I am certain you had to argue the point with someone," Miss Wescott said.

"Indeed. My brother Roger—he is next in our family after me—contended that he should be the heir on the grounds that he is male." Clemency sighed. "It was his only argument, and yet there were many who agreed with him, likely because they feared for their own inheritances. For if an Extraordinary woman can inherit, that is only a short step to a woman of any talent inheriting over her male relations, and from there...you see how that might worry some."

"It would worry anyone who knows his innate abilities are inadequate, and who must therefore depend on tradition to gain benefits," Mr. Wescott said.

"At any rate, Roger and I argued the case all the way to the House of Lords, who ultimately sided with me. Those with talent, Extraordinary or otherwise, saw the benefit of cementing the policy that talent is to be rewarded. It was not a unanimous decision, so I never take my title for granted."

"And your brother?" Miss Wescott asked.

Clemency refrained from rolling her eyes. "Roger resents me, but there is nothing he can do. I wish he would give over his anger, because he has wealth settled upon him by our great-aunt, and prestige, but he feels scorned because he is merely a Scorcher, not a talent of great remark. To him, the earldom would rectify all the slights he imagines he has endured over the years. But I would not deny my father's last wish simply to make Roger happy."

"Of course not," Mr. Wescott said. "And now you are Lady Ashford, righter of wrongs, defender of the innocent, descending under cover of night to prevent crimes..."

His droll expression made Clemency laugh even as her cheeks heated. "No one knows of my nighttime doings," she said. "They are not the sort of thing a countess should do, however much a boon they are to society."

"You needn't fear, we shan't tell," Miss Wescott said. She looked unusually grave, as if something more than Clemency's secret concerned her. Clemency considered asking what troubled her, but as she hesitated over whether this was too personal an intrusion, Miss Wescott went on, "It is actually quite thrilling to imagine you Flying over the city at night, Lady Ashford. Do you suppose others do the same?"

"I have never encountered anyone else, Extraordinary Mover or otherwise, in my flights. But now that I consider it, I cannot imagine I am the only one who has thought to use her talent in protecting others," Clemency said. Again, she recalled what Jane and Francis had said about people with talent misusing it, committing crimes, and felt vaguely uncomfortable, as if by her secrecy she had put herself among their number.

"It cannot be many, if that is true," Mr. Wescott said, "or it would be public knowledge as those saved by such protectors made their stories known." He laughed. "I admit, I find the idea of a cadre of Extraordinaries secretly preventing robberies and arson and murders very amusing. They might meet in an abandoned castle or derelict warehouse to plan their strikes against criminals, and conceal their identities so their fellows do not know the truth—why, anyone you meet might be a fellow opponent of crime, Lady Ashford!"

Clemency laughed with him. "They should carry something to indicate their identity to other protectors. Perhaps a pin—I understand Napoleon's sympathizers in France did the same, so why not turn that idea to a good cause?"

"An excellent plan." Mr. Wescott shook his head, his eyes still bright with laughter. "Ah, Lady Ashford, I cannot recall the last time I laughed so much."

"I, as well," Clemency said, and she was startled to discover it was true. The realization shook her. Surely she had laughed since France— but she could not remember feeling so light of heart in months. The knowledge made her uncomfortable, as if in sharing this laughter, she and Mr. Wescott were engaged in something more intimate.

She turned to look at Miss Wescott, hoping to dispel the awkward feeling, and caught the young woman regarding her with a smile Clemency could only describe as blissful. She remembered seeing Miss Wescott smile like that before, the night Clemency had met her, but she could not remember what she had said then to make Miss Wescott react that way. Clemency herself felt, not blissful, but deeply content; if Miss Wescott's demeanor reflected the emotions she Discerned, she should not look as if she were experiencing pure happiness. Unless it was not her emotions Miss Wescott was feeling.

Clemency covertly glanced at Mr. Wescott. He was watching, not Miss Wescott, but her, his lips curved in a smile so warm it made Clemency's heart beat faster with memory. Armand, looking at her with that smile and those knowing eyes that had seen every inch of her, his lips brushing hers—

Nerves propelled her to her feet. "I beg your pardon, but I should go—I have a prior engagement—please forgive me—"

"Of course," Mr. Wescott said, rising as well. Faint lines of puzzlement creased his forehead, but he walked to the door and opened it for her. "I appreciate your generosity in overlooking my imposition."

"It was not an imposition, and I am happy to oblige. I hope you are not troubled by those men again. Such a horrid thing—if needed, I can testify that the bird was stolen—" Clemency knew she was babbling, but she could not stop herself.

Mr. Wescott smiled, a normal, friendly expression. "I believe that will be unnecessary, but I thank you, and I will call on you if I am wrong."

"Miss Wescott, thank you for your hospitality," Clemency said.

Miss Wescott had not risen when they did, and now she looked at

Clemency with wide eyes. "It is the present, not the past," she said in a faint voice, "but Time does not know it."

Clemency blinked in confusion. Then she turned and hurried down the hall and the stairs to the foyer, where she snatched up her coat without donning it, and was out the door before Mr. Wescott could open it for her.

She launched herself into the sky and sped upward, higher and higher until her chest ached with cold and the freezing air dried her eyes painfully. Then she hovered high above London and drew in great shuddering breaths that chilled her further. This was ridiculous. She was free of Coercion, free of Armand, and permitting her memories to control her was unacceptable. Now Mr. Wescott must believe she was unstable, or fickle, or had no interest in him, and none of that was true, but how was anyone to tell the difference if she ran away whenever her memories troubled her?

She considered returning to Hanover Square to explain herself, and fear and shame flooded over her. No one need ever know what had happened; few even in the War Office knew she had been Coerced, and none of them knew about Armand. For a moment, she had the wild impulse to Fly to France and seek out Jennet Falconer and confide her turmoil to her. But Jennet, who alone knew the truth, was an ordinary woman who did not deserve to be burdened with Clemency's night terrors that apparently had become day terrors as well.

A shudder wracked her body, and for a second, perhaps two, she considered Flying higher. Then she came to herself. She was not going to abuse her body simply because she had some unpleasant memories. Blinking to moisten her eyes, she Flew homeward. Mr. Wescott would arrive on Monday with the new chair; she would make certain he knew of her regard then. Perhaps she should invite him and Miss Wescott to supper, in thanks. The idea of spending time with him warmed her chilly body. She would not be bested by anything so ridiculous as terrible memories.

CHAPTER 11

IN WHICH CLEMENCY'S FOUL MOOD IS NOT EASED BY FLYING OR FOOD

Her unhappy mood did not subside on her return to Emeraude House. She felt restless, uninterested in settling down to any sedate activity like reading, but too deeply chilled to find more Flying appealing. She eventually settled in the drawing room, contemplated ringing for tea, and decided even the scant company of the servants was too much to bear.

After a few minutes' silent grousing, she began Moving the many knickknacks her mother had collected over the years, juggling miniature figures and candlesticks in elaborate, complex patterns. It was something she had competed in often at the public trials, and a skill at which she excelled. She gradually added more and more objects until she had two score porcelain miniatures flying through the air, dipping and swirling and dodging each other like so much chaff in a whirlwind. Rather than soothe her, the rapid motion irritated her further. If this was all her talent was good for, what was the point of having it?

Anger pulsed through her, and she flung two of the statuettes at the fireplace, smashing them against the bricks and sending shards flying. Breathing heavily, she leaned forward, watching the flames blacken the smooth porcelain surfaces. The sight calmed her somewhat, as did her growing awareness that she was not behaving rationally. She could not recall the last time she had lost control of her temper.

She realized she was holding the rest of the objects stationary, frozen where their trajectories had landed them, and gently Moved them back to their original places on hearth and tables. Then she stood and wearily trod to the fireplace. She swept up the shards and splinters with her Moving and plucked the larger pieces out of the fire, depositing them all in a neat pile on the hearth. Then she rang for a servant. The man did not look at all surprised at Clemency's request to dispose of the broken figurines. She hoped that was not because her household was so eccentric such things were a matter of course.

She resumed her seat and squeezed her eyes tight shut for a few seconds. If only it were dark, she might Fly through the city, looking for crime to stop. She recalled what Mr. Wescott had said about an imagined group of Extraordinaries bent on eradicating crime from London's streets and smiled despite herself. She personally did not feel the need for companionship on her nocturnal excursions; in fact, she loved the solitude and the feeling that she was doing something no one else dared do. But the idea compelled her nonetheless.

She spent the rest of the day in motion, examining each of the rooms in her house for untidiness, walking to the park and circling it on foot many times, and finally calling for her carriage and driving herself through the city. She had not driven since her return from the War Office, because why take such a slow, roundabout mode of transportation when one could Fly instead? But on this day, staying at ground level suited her. She was not so alien as all that if she could drive through the streets without drawing attention.

She dared not venture into the seedier parts of London, not because she feared for her safety, but because she felt superstitiously that if she traveled openly into places she would later Fly secretly, the inhabitants who saw her now would somehow recognize her then. Instead, she stayed on the most public and popular thoroughfares, admiring store fronts and exchanging nods with other drivers. The ordinary, even banal activity soothed her, and she returned to the house before suppertime feeling less oppressed in spirit.

Unusually, the whole family gathered that evening for supper;

Roger frequently dined at his club, and Prudence more often than not ate off a tray in her room. Clemency tried to be generous of spirit with Roger and Prudence, but she could not help seeing their behavior as an insult. The fact that she felt easier when they were not present to start a fight or sit in sullen silence complicated her emotions. They were her siblings, and she felt she should at least not see them as a burden.

She summoned up a pleasant smile and addressed Prudence. "Mama insists you are ready for a ball to celebrate your come-out, and I agree with her. Is that something you would like?"

Prudence poked at a pile of soft, cooked potato, Bounded at great expense from South America. "I did not believe you cared about what I would like," she said, not meeting Clemency's eyes.

"Prudence! For shame!" their mother exclaimed. "Clemency cares very much for all of our well-being."

Clemency took a bite of her own potato and chewed slowly, summoning inner calm. She liked the exotic delicacy enough to make an effort to bring it to her table, but at the moment it tasted like ash. "I regret that you feel that way," she told Prudence, "and I apologize if I gave you the impression that your needs are not important. Perhaps you could choose a date?"

Prudence shrugged. "So long as you are asking me, I would like it to be as soon as may be managed." She did not sound enthusiastic, but at least she was speaking to Clemency, and Clemency would take her victories where she could get them when it came to her family.

Mama let out a sound midway between a tiny shriek and a gasp. "Oh, and you may leave the planning to me! This is the perfect time of year for a ball, and it will be so beautiful—and you will need a new gown, a new wardrobe, even!"

Prudence's lips curled in a sneer. "I see no reason to celebrate so lavishly. It is not as if I have talent, something to set me apart."

"Prudence, having talent is not so important," Clemency said. "Most of the population of England has no talent."

Prudence flung her fork down to chime loudly against her plate. "And yet those with talent consider themselves superior," she exclaimed. "Do not tell me you and Roger and Mercy and even Mama do not benefit under the law and in society because of your talents!"

"And why should we not?" Roger said. "Those of us with talent have superior abilities, so why not reward us as a result?" He patted his lips with his napkin and then attacked his beef with enthusiasm, as if there was nothing more to say.

"That is not—" Clemency began.

"You do nothing to benefit society with your Scorcher talent," Prudence shot back. "Lighting a fire in the hearth, or lighting a pipe—those might be done by anyone. And yet you are celebrated for that accident of birth."

"Prudence, you know talent is not all there is to life," Mercy said. "Father had no talent, and he was respected and admired by everyone who knew him."

Clemency winced inwardly. Mercy was right, but mentioning Father was more likely to cause an explosion than to calm Prudence.

As she expected, Prudence's face paled, and she shoved back from the table. "None of you knew Father as I did," she whispered. "None of you deserve to speak his name."

"Prudence, you are not the only one who grieved at his death," Clemency said. It was a mistake, but she could not bear receiving her sister's bile one moment longer without striking back. "He loved each of us regardless of what talent we did or did not have. You should not blame us for his loss."

Prudence turned on Clemency, a furious scowl distorting her face. "Don't pretend you care about me," she snarled. "You believe you can return home like a conquering hero and tell us all what to do?"

"Since when have I told you what to do?" Clemency raised her voice to match Prudence's. "I have given you everything you wish for, met your every need, and all I ever receive in return is vitriol and anger. Why, pray, should I respect you when you behave like this?"

"Yes, you are generosity itself," Roger said. "Lady Bountiful of the manor."

His sarcasm made Clemency's already keyed-up nerves twang further. Gritting her teeth, she said, "You would prefer I keep you all on a tight leash, make you come begging to me for favors and money? Who pays for your club, Roger?"

Roger's face darkened. "That's right, hold it over my head that I am dependent on you until I reach the age of twenty-five. I could have received my inheritance at my majority if not for Great-Aunt Edith's insistence that I wait. Everyone in my life believes me incompetent— you, Great-Aunt Edith and her solicitors, Father. Prudence is correct; you came home from the war and set about managing our lives, will-you, nil-you."

"I did no such thing!" Clemency regretted her outburst immediately. She drew in a breath and said, more calmly, "I regret that my War Office service took me away during a time when I was needed here to settle Father's affairs. But that was hardly my choice. And I am doing my best now."

"Clemency, *please*," Mama begged. "This is hardly behavior befitting a lady."

"Clem hardly cares about that," Roger drawled. "When difficulties rear their heads, she takes to the skies. Not exactly ladylike behavior, is it?"

Clemency ignored Roger. "Prudence, I do care about you," she said, hoping it was not too much of a lie. "I want you to be happy. I know I can't bring Father back, but can we not find some common ground?"

Prudence rose from her seat. Her lips were white and pinched with anger. "We have nothing in common but birth," she said. "You cannot change that." She shoved her chair against the table and broke into a run, slamming the door open and disappearing down the hall.

Clemency closed her eyes and mentally rehearsed the worst profanities she could remember hearing from soldiers in the field. When she opened her eyes, her gaze fell first on Mercy, who gripped her fork and knife as if she intended to use them in her defense. "She is in such pain," Mercy said.

"At what point does her pain become self-indulgence?" Clemency said. "She is not the only one who lost a beloved father. I cannot believe her anger and misery will bring her satisfaction. The rest of us have learned to accept our loss."

"Don't imagine you know how we feel," Roger said.

"Roger, you—" Clemency again bit back a few choice words. "I did not mean I know how you feel," she said when she regained control. "But it seems as if Prudence wishes to be miserable and rejects anything that might cheer her. I have no idea how to approach her."

"Permit me to speak with her, Clemency," Mama said. "She has agreed to a ball for her coming-out. I truly believe if she joins society, she will see how much pleasure it will give her, and that may lighten her spirits."

"I hope you are right, Mama," Clemency said. She did not believe anything would lighten Prudence's spirits so long as she clung to her misery, but she also did not wish to have Prudence stalking through the house, angry and bitter and resenting everyone, for the rest of all their lives. And perhaps Mama *was* right, and being recognized as an adult by society would give Prudence something to think about that was not her dead father.

The meal proceeded in blessed silence, but when Clemency rose at its conclusion, Roger surprised her by rising as well. "I'm off to the club," he said, then, with a mocking smile, added, "if that is acceptable to you, Lady Bountiful."

"Oh, by—" Clemency was sure at some point, her bridle on her tongue would slip, and she would shock her family with her language. She calmed herself and said instead, "If I were to oversee your every movement and every activity, Roger, you would know what true oppression looks like."

Roger's smile vanished. "So I am to be grateful you are only parsimonious, and not overbearing?"

"Stop," Mercy said. "This argument will make neither of you happy. Roger, why must you needle Clemency? She does not treat you like a poor supplicant."

"And neither does she treat me like a brother," Roger said, and turned on his heel and stalked away.

Clemency let out a long breath. "I would take that complaint more seriously," she said, "if I did not know his definition of treating him like a brother means giving him the title."

"Oh, that is not true," Mama said. "You were named countess, and Roger accepts that."

Clemency and Mercy exchanged glances. "He has stopped arguing the point," Clemency said. "I doubt that means he has accepted it."

She read to Mercy in the drawing room for an hour, hoping the peaceful activity would soothe her. Instead, the slowness of the story, in which people talked and talked endlessly without ever taking action, roused her impatience to new heights. She did her best to conceal her irritation, not wishing Mercy to be the recipient of her foul mood, but at the end of the hour, Mercy laid her needlework in her lap and said, "If you are resentful of reading to me, I would prefer you leave off and permit me to sew in peace."

Instant remorse filled Clemency. "It is not you," she said, "and I hope you will forgive me. I am simply out of sorts."

"That is natural, given the meal we had," Mercy said. She leaned forward in her chair, her eyes intent on Clemency. "You are not a villain, you know, whatever Roger and Prudence might say in their jealousy."

"You believe it is jealousy?"

"What else can you call it, when you have freedom and power they lack? Prudence suffers from the burden of being seventeen and female in a society where women's roles are constrained, and Roger—well. There is nothing you can do for Roger save abdicate, and I hope you will not do that."

"Father wished for me to inherit, so I cannot betray his memory. And it is not as if I believe Roger's needs are more important than mine." Clemency set the book aside and sighed. "I will retire now. Are you tired? I can Move you to your room."

"I am not yet sleepy. Albert can carry me." Mercy put a hand over Clemency's. "Sleep, and tomorrow will look brighter."

"I hope so," Clemency said with a smile.

She climbed the stairs rather than Flying to the second floor, feeling a need to connect with the earth, or at any rate the staircase. It occurred to her that Mercy had not sounded at all resentful when she spoke of the footman carrying her. That eased Clemency's heart somewhat. She owed Mr. Wescott a great debt.

The memory of how she had left him made her cheeks burn. He must think her fickle, or unstable, and she wished so much for his good opinion. It disturbed her slightly that she cared so much for the regard of someone still virtually a stranger. But he intrigued her, and she wished to know more about him, and that could not happen if he believed she disliked him, or however he interpreted her odd behavior.

Now that she was free of social and familial obligations, her eager-ness to be Flying over the city burned like a tiny fire in her chest. She submitted to Tatton's assistance impatiently enough that the woman said, "My lady, is something wrong?"

"No, it is just that I have been restless all day," Clemency lied. "All I need is a good night's sleep, and I am certain I will feel more myself in the morning."

She successfully kept from tapping her toe against the dressing table leg while Tatton braided her hair. Instead, she watched herself in the mirror, examining her face for signs of her hidden struggle. How easy it was to conceal one's turmoil from the casual observer! Tatton certainly did not perceive her mistress's disquiet, and Tatton was extremely shrewd. Clemency looked perfectly calm. Hers was not at all the face of someone intent on illicit doings.

She lay in bed and waited for Tatton to finish tidying the dressing room, so eager to be up and doing she quivered. The instant Tatton closed the door behind herself, Clemency sprang from the bed and rooted between the mattresses for her clothing. Dressed, shod, and gloved, she opened the window and stepped through it, pausing only to latch it closed behind her before shooting into the sky like a rocket.

For a few minutes, she Flew with no intent in mind, simply enjoying the cold air on her face. Already she felt calmer; taking action, any action, relieved the urgency that tightened her chest and tensed her muscles. The dark moon had set hours before, and although the skies were clear, the blackness was deep enough Clemency felt shrouded in velvet. Below, the lights of the city twinkled like chips of diamond shaken free of the night's velvet folds, barely illuminating the streets. Either this was a night when the criminals would be out in force, or it was too dark even for them.

Remembering her previous nocturnal flight, she headed for the Thames and followed its dark path for a few miles, then turned north and began her hunt in earnest near Whitechapel. She swept silently over the few men and women still on the streets. The darkness forced her to Fly lower than she preferred, but she was still high enough that no one looked up to perceive her. She might as well be invisible. Why there was no talent for invisibility, she could not imagine, but such a talent would benefit anyone who wished their doings to remain secret. Of course, probably most people would use the talent for crime, so it was just as well it did not exist.

She Flew in a tight pattern she had been taught in the Flight Corps, assessing the streets, and became increasingly irritated at seeing no one intent on breaking into a house or stalking a victim for robbery. Surely Londoners had not suddenly given up on crime?

Frustrated, she headed west. Perhaps she should hunt south of the Thames, in those narrow warrens that looked so unlike the streets near London's center it was hard to believe they were both part of the same city. Clemency disliked Flying there not because it was difficult to apprehend miscreants—if anything, crime was prevalent enough she might spend every night catching criminals and never run out of prey —but because the rampant poverty and illness made her heart ache. She could stop a few criminals from preying on the weak and innocent, but that left hundreds or even thousands unpunished. She could do nothing to save those who barely had enough to eat, let alone those who had nothing at all.

She made out the dome of St. Paul's in the distance and decided to swoop around it before moving south. The beautiful landmark gleamed pale even in the low light, appearing more solid, more real than anything in its surroundings. On a whim, Clemency Flew lower and alighted on the top of the dome, just where it curved beneath the cupola and the cross. Perhaps her behavior was sacrilegious, but she could not help herself.

She turned, looking out across the city. From this vantage point, the city was once more a frozen sea of rooftops and chimneys, the smells of waste and the closer odor of the Thames merely hinted at in the frigid air so Clemency could imagine herself on an island surrounded by a grey, motionless ocean.

Tilting her head, she looked up at the cross surmounting the cupola. It was so small compared to the building as a whole, and yet it symbolized so much to so many. Clemency had never been much for religion, though she paid her devotions every Sunday and at Christmas and Easter, so she felt unmoved by its presence. God had not prevented Napoleon from Coercing her and making her Armand's doxy, and while she suspected it was unfair to criticize God for failing to intervene, she could not help her resentment.

She pushed off the dome and drifted lower, examining the rest of the cathedral, though it was dull compared to many she had seen in Europe. She preferred the Gothic influences to Christopher Wren's contemporary marvel. It was beautiful, true, but much of it looked more like a government building than anything devoted to religion.

Furtive movement caught her eye, and she halted midair, peering into the dimness. Three—no, four figures crept along the base of the cathedral at its rear, moving slowly with many pauses. The figure at the head of the line occasionally gestured, beckoning his comrades forward or indicating they should stay back. From her vantage point, Clemency saw two other men approaching along the street, neither of them appearing very alert. But the thieves, or so she imagined them to be, were cautious not to be noticed by those passersby nevertheless.

Clemency floated backward until her feet rested on the edge of the dome, slowly so as not to draw attention, though the thieves did not remember to look up. She watched them creep along the foundation until they reached a spot that to Clemency did not stand out from the rest of the cathedral. It was far from the doors and well away from where most people passed. The four men gathered in a tight knot, crouching behind some bushes. Clemency decided this was her moment.

She dropped to hover about twenty feet above their heads and snatched them up, or tried to; they looked up just as she descended, and two of the men resisted her Moving. The other two, however, let out hoarse cries of shock and flailed their arms until Clemency used her talent to bind their limbs tight to their bodies.

"You should be ashamed, stealing from a house of God," she cried in her deepest voice. "I will not permit it."

The two men on the ground looked up, their eyes and mouths wide with astonishment. Then the man on the right, the one who had been at the head of the line, scowled furiously and gestured. In the next second, yellow fire filled the air, engulfing Clemency entirely.

CHAPTER 12

IN WHICH THERE IS FIRST FIRE AND THEN WATER

Instantly, Clemency's War Office-trained reflexes took charge of her body. She Flew backward, out of the Scorcher's fire, then dropped to the ground, rolling as she landed. She rolled again, extinguishing the few small fires that had ignited on her clothing, and slapped at the back of her head in case that had caught fire as well.

Then, crouching, she surveyed her surroundings. The two men she held captive with her Moving still hung struggling in the air some thirty feet off the ground, but their fear and stupidity made them powerless to override her with their own will. The Scorcher's fire sailed in her direction, but slowly, as if it was looking for a target. Since Clemency could not see the Scorcher from her location, likely the Scorcher could not see her, but if the man was capable of maintaining an unfueled fire for more than a few seconds, he was quite powerful and therefore quite dangerous. It was time to change tactics.

Clemency shot rapidly skyward. The fire immediately rushed toward her. This, too, was something she had been taught to counter, though the War Office had naturally believed she would turn this training toward fighting Napoleon's Scorchers. She was faster than the fire, but she waited for it to almost catch her before changing course midair and speeding back the way the fire had come.

She cast about as she flew, looking for the two remaining thieves. Heat warming her back told her the Scorcher's fire continued to chase her. If the Scorcher was clever, he would not bother with that fire; he would ignite a second fire around her, and a third. She hoped the Scorcher was not clever.

She spotted the two thieves when she was barely fifty feet away and closing fast. Aiming at the place where they stood, she sped up until the wind screamed in her ears. Just before she would have overrun the men, she pulled up sharply, making an abrupt upward turn, and Flew skyward again.

Shouts, and a couple of vile curses, told her the trick had worked. She rolled and hovered, looking back at the two men. The Scorcher had not dismissed the fire quickly enough, and the men danced and slapped at the fires burning here and there on their dark clothes just as she had done seconds before.

More screams, these distant, reminded her of the other thieves. She had carried them with her as she Flew, instinctively Moving them so they stayed within her reach. Now she slung them away rapidly, faster and faster until they slammed into the wall of the cathedral. She let them go, and they fell to the ground and did not rise. A tiny doubt niggled at her that perhaps she had hurt them badly, but she ignored it. They were criminals; they deserved their fate.

Instead, she turned her attention to the other thieves. The Scorcher had risen to his feet and was pointing at Clemency. Clemency dropped to avoid the burst of flame that erupted just where she had been, then Flew in a zigzag pattern back to where the Scorcher stood, avoiding more fires lighting the night.

She tried once more to Move the remaining thieves, but succeeded only in knocking the one not a Scorcher to the ground. The Scorcher sent more fire blazing in Clemency's direction. Clemency Flew away, heading directly up now. She would test the limits of this Scorcher's distance, how far away from himself he could ignite a fire.

She passed the top of the dome, then passed the cross, and rose another ten feet or so before she exceeded the Scorcher's distance. Why the Scorcher did not ignite fire near himself and then fling it at Clemency, she did not know, but that suggested the Scorcher's range for such a tactic was limited. Clemency was safe from his fire up here, but she was also at the limit of how far away she could take hold of a thing or person to Move it. They were at an impasse.

She searched the area, looking for something she could use as a missile or bludgeon. No convenient fallen trees lay nearby, the lamp posts were firmly rooted and would be awkward weapons in any case, and the cathedral grounds were irritatingly free of large stones. She might Fly elsewhere for a weapon, but she did not like to leave her prey unwatched, in case they decided to flee. She briefly considered the dome's cross before rejecting its possibilities with a shudder of horror at her impiety. She might be irreligious, but she was not profane.

She decided to drop lower and risk the fire. Cautiously, she descended, all the time dividing her attention between the thieves and her surroundings. To her surprise, no fires erupted in the air. The remaining thieves were crouched beside the cathedral, intent on something between them. One of them glanced up, and his gaze fixed on Clemency. He grabbed his partner's shoulder—the Scorcher, Clemency saw as she neared.

She made one last attempt at seizing them, and her Moving took hold of one, lifting him a few feet. His partner, the Scorcher, grabbed hold of his legs and hauled him back to earth even as fire once more blossomed around Clemency, hotter than before. Clemency released her prey and threw herself backward, landing this time in the street. Pain shot through her shoulder momentarily, but she ignored it in favor of extinguishing the flames. Then she launched herself into the sky once more.

Flying in a random path to make herself less of a target for the Scorcher, she returned to where she had last seen the thieves. They were gone.

Cursing, she rose higher, scanning the nearby streets for her prey. No one strolled near the rear of the cathedral, and to its front she saw only the sedate movement of pedestrians whose consciences did not trouble them. No one ran; no one looked up and shouted in fear; no one even exclaimed over the bursts of fire that had brightened the night. She had lost the thieves.

She returned to the cathedral, angry with herself for permitting them to escape, though she did not know what she would have done with them if she had captured them. Come to think on it, she had two captives already. She Flew to follow the wall, searching for where she had dropped the men.

Something small and dark and out of place wedged against the wall caught her attention. At first, she believed it was a stone like the one she had imagined finding to use as a weapon. Upon looking more closely, she discovered it was more regular in shape than a stone, being more oblong than round. Curious, Clemency descended and alit near the thing. It was wrapped in folded canvas and smelled sharply of black powder, a smell any veteran of the war was unlikely to forget.

Clemency knelt beside it, using her Moving to unfold the canvas. Beneath its folds lay an elegant mahogany box decorated with silver filigree. In the next second, she recognized Mr. Wescott's stolen music box. She was about to lift it with Moving when she heard, very faintly, the ticking of a clockwork mechanism unaccompanied by music.

Once more, reflex took over, and Clemency was aloft almost before her ears registered what they had heard. A bomb. Those thieves meant to blow up St. Paul's, or most of it. She hovered above the bomb, her mind running frantically through options and landing on the only possible one mere seconds later. She lifted the bomb as carefully as she could, holding the box steady with her Moving, and Flew south, gradually gaining altitude.

The little part of her that had worried about the fate of the thieves now battered at her with how stupid this was. She did not know how powerful an explosive it was, nor whether shaking the box might set the bomb off prematurely. The bomb trailed her by more than sixty feet, which was the extent of her Moving range; suppose that was not enough distance, and the bomb detonated and killed her?

She shouted down that small, cowardly part of herself. She could not leave the bomb where it might hurt or kill people. She did not know how to defuse it. That left only one alternative: sink it in the Thames, and hope she got there in time.

She felt she had never Flown so slowly. Her fear that the bomb might explode in midair made her heart race and her palms sweat inside her gloves. She was barely aware of the chill in the air, though her face below the goggles was numb and she had lost her cap at some point, probably one of the times she had rolled to extinguish the flames. The dark streets crept by beneath her. St. Paul's was not far from the Thames, and surely she should have seen the river by now!

Then the streets ended, and the vast dark moving expanse of water appeared. Relief flooded through Clemency, and she flew lower, above the water's surface. No one would be abroad on the river at this hour, but she could not help imagining accidentally dropping the box onto a passing boat.

Satisfied that the river was clear, she rose higher, much higher, Moving the bomb slowly into position beneath her. The river water should drown the horrid thing. Gradually, the box swung around until it was about forty feet above the surface of the water. Breathing slowly, Clemency edged higher without moving the box until she was at the limits of what she could control. Then she released the bomb.

For a second, as it dropped, she believed she had succeeded. Then a tremendous explosion shattered the air, and light illuminated the Thames before momentarily blinding Clemency. An enormous fist punched her, flinging her backwards so that in her stunned state she fell out of the sky like a stone. Then she hit something like a slab of concrete, and her vision, which had begun to clear, turned black.

She was only unconscious for a moment, because her next awareness was of freezing water soaking her clothes and filling her mouth and nostrils. She gasped, choked, and fought her way to the surface of the Thames, then Flew with a great rush of water out of the river to hover some few feet above it. Coughing to clear her lungs, she snatched her goggles off, blinked foul water and the afterimages of the explosion out of her eyes, and shook herself, sending sprays of water flying. Then she breathed in deeply, welcoming the shock of frigid air on her body that told her she was alive.

The shock was only pleasant for a few seconds. Then she realized if she did not get dry and warm, she would likely die. Her sodden coat, once so welcome in its weight and thickness, now dragged at her as if it were woven of iron and not wool. With shaking fingers, she unbuttoned the coat and shrugged out of it, then let it fall with a faint splash into the Thames.

Her ears rang dully with the sound of the explosion, but as the ringing faded, she began to hear the sounds of people approaching, running footsteps and shouts. Being caught now after everything she had done to protect herself was unthinkable. She shot away into the sky, rising higher until she could no longer hear anything but the whistle of the wind. Then she headed for home.

The wind numbed her soaking wet body until she was barely conscious of herself as more than a collection of impulses and desires for warmth. By the time she reached her window, her hands were too numb to operate the latch. She stripped off her gloves and dropped them, too weary and frozen to use her Moving to keep them with her. Her whole body ached with a bone-chilling cold. Finally, she wrapped one frozen hand around her other wrist as if it were a stick and used that hand to prod open the latch. With one last effort of will, she Moved the window open and then fell through it.

She lay on the floor beneath the window without moving, her mind blank, her fingers and toes pulsing painfully. Then she dragged herself across the floor to the fireplace and managed to knock the poker over. When she tried to lift it with Moving, it quivered briefly, but did not budge. She managed to wrap one hand around its handle, and again with the help of her other hand poked the fire back into life.

Then she dropped the poker, its tip still in the coals, and waited for the fire to heat her enough so she could stand. It took a few addled moments for her to realize she might die before that happened. She rolled onto her back and searched the darkened room for the bell pull. The rope hung like a headless snake near the bed. She stared at it, searching for the snake's head and finding only a knot at the lower end. The knot meant something, she was certain. She extended her Moving and wrapped the currents around the knot, then pulled. The rope did not move.

Clemency nearly wept with frustration. She wanted nothing more than to lie in her bed and sleep until she was warm again. But she was going to freeze to death beside the fire instead. That image woke her up. She had endured worse than this, and she was damned if she was going to give up now.

She focused on the knot, on her memories of how it felt to wrap her fingers around it and tug. It was a silk rope, and the threads were smooth beneath her fingers and bumpy where they wove around and under and through one another to make the knot. She drew in a deep breath and *pulled* with her Moving. The rope jerked, down and then up again.

Clemency lay back and watched the ceiling. The many foot-wide squares of carved wood covering it moved with the firelight, shifting as the flames danced below them. This was an old house, remodeled many times, and yet this antique ceiling had survived all those changes. This seemed symbolic of something, but either she was too addled to puzzle the meaning out, or her confusion made the symbolism feel important when it actually was not.

The door opened. "Yes, my—*my lady!*"

Clemency groaned as Tatton crouched beside her, putting an arm beneath Clemency's shoulders and helping her to sit upright. "I need to dry off," she muttered through clenched teeth. If she relaxed her jaw, it shivered so much her teeth rattled.

"You're wet through, my lady. What happened?"

"No questions, Tatton. Help me. Please."

Tatton stopped speaking and set to work unbuttoning the shirt that felt to Clemency as if it had soaked up half the Thames and then frozen solid. Her limbs felt slightly less numb than before, and she was able to work her arms free of the shirt. Tatton pulled off her boots while Clemency unfastened the trousers in only a few tries. Finally Clemency sat naked before the fire and let Tatton rub her dry with a warm cloth that burned against her icy skin, then accepted another fire-heated blanket to wrap around herself.

She watched Tatton gather the ruined clothes and carry them away somewhere, probably not to clean them. It was not as if Clemency could explain why they should be saved. She would simply have to acquire others. The shakes began to subside, and Clemency rested her head on her knees and let her mind drift. She had saved St. Paul's. That ought to be cause for celebration. Instead, she simply felt tired. Perhaps things would look different in the morning.

Tatton returned with a bundle of cloth that turned out to be one of Clemency's nightdresses. Clemency found she was able to stand and dress without assistance. Then Tatton freed her hair from its braid and made Clemency sit by the fire once more so she could brush it and dry it. The feel of the brush against her scalp reminded Clemency of her childhood, when her nurse would brush out her hair with a hundred strokes, claiming that would enhance its growth and beauty. She had not remembered that in years.

"My lady," Tatton said, "I apologize for prying, but...what happened?"

"I can't tell you," Clemency said. "Forgive me. It is not something I can tell anyone."

"Of course, my lady." Tatton sounded disappointed but not disapproving, and Clemency felt a twinge of guilt, given that she often shared her secrets with her maid—just not this one. And not Armand.

But that was not entirely true, was it, because there *was* someone who knew her secret. Someone she ought to tell the story to, because it was his clockwork mechanism, or at any rate his mechanism altered by the bombers, that had nearly killed her that night. Clemency's spirits lifted at the idea of speaking with Mr. Wescott again. How much of that was the simple knowledge that she did not have to keep the secret alone, and how much her desire to spend time with the man, she chose not to pursue.

She sat by the fire until her hair was dry and braided again, and then climbed into her bed, which was heated by not one, but two warming pans, and finally felt warm enough to sleep. Her last memory, just as she drifted off, was of the Scorcher's thin face, turned up toward hers as Clemency Flew past with the Scorcher's fire pursuing her. The Scorcher was a woman, she realized, but that was not an important enough realization to keep her from falling asleep.

CHAPTER 13

IN WHICH CLEMENCY HAS A DILEMMA

Clemency woke to a moment of blissful stillness, a dream of running through a field of buttercups fresh in her mind. She stretched, and the moment vanished as her muscles contracted in pain. Everything ached as if she had been beaten, with the pains greatest in her right shoulder and hip. She had landed on that side while escaping the Scorcher's fire, she remembered—and with that, the events of the previous night returned in a rush.

She lay still so the aches would hurt less and stared at the underside of her bed's canopy. What would the world make of what had happened? The sound of a bomb detonating was unmistakable, but for one to explode in midair over the Thames—that would take a Mover. And she had left the unconscious would-be bombers at the cathedral. True, they had probably recovered and fled, but if they had not, they would be able to tell the world about the mysterious Extraordinary Mover who had assaulted them. Clemency refused to dwell on the possibility that they had not recovered.

She closed her eyes and made herself breathe, in and out in a regular rhythm, until she was calm. Even if the story of an Extraordinary Mover preventing the bombing of St. Paul's became public, there was no way anyone might trace that story to her. Tatton was intelligent, and might put the clues together, but she was also loyal and would bring her suspicions to Clemency rather than spreading them abroad. Clemency was safe.

She had no appetite, but her body demanded food, so she rang for chocolate and toasted bread and ate in bed, a luxury she rarely indulged in. Food revived her, made the aches less, and eventually she was able to rise and dress with only a few twinges when she moved her shoulder incautiously. Tatton made no reference to the previous night, but Clemency caught the edges of the looks she gave her mistress when she believed Clemency was not watching, and Clemency's worries resurfaced. Perhaps she should bring Tatton in on the secret. It was something to consider, at any rate.

The morning newspapers were neatly folded in a stack at the end of the dining table, indicating either that Mercy had not yet come downstairs or that she had suddenly become tidy. Mercy was as fond of news as a Seer, and Clemency subscribed to many publications for her sake. Now she took up *The Times* and unfolded it. She found the story about the bomb halfway down the front page.

The journalist had had the report second hand, and many of the details were wrong, such as the size of the explosion—if the news article was correct about that, the blast would have killed her—but it was otherwise frighteningly accurate in its conclusions, down to the assertion that an Extraordinary Mover was seen fleeing the site. There was no mention of St. Paul's being the original target, and no mention of any criminals being apprehended. An unexpected, confusing emotion filled Clemency, a mixture of relief and affronted pride. Her identity was still secret, but she had saved who knew how many people by her actions, and no one knew to give her credit!

She riffled through the other papers, which all reported more or less the same facts. It was not until she reached the *Morning Herald* that she read an accusation that stopped her cold. "The authorities are searching for the Extraordinary Mover who was responsible for the failed bombing," the article read. "That his bomb detonated prematurely does not absolve him from culpability in this bombing and perhaps in others."

Spots danced before Clemency's eyes, and she finally remembered to breathe. Outrageous. That she could be blamed for the bombing she had prevented...! Her anger overrode the quieter voice that said she might be in danger from the law. They believed the Extraordinary Mover was a man; no one would link Lady Ashford to this incident. And fear was irrelevant in the face of such shocking injustice.

She could not wish the bomb to have detonated as the criminals intended, for that might have caused great loss of life in addition to damaging an important London landmark. But things would be much simpler if the authorities, whoever they were, knew where they should be looking for the bombers. If the same people were responsible for every bomb in the past few weeks, this one was part of a pattern, and Clemency's intervention had muddied the waters, so to speak. Again she reminded herself that none of this was her fault.

For a moment, she struggled with herself. She wished to remain anonymous; she wished the bombers to be apprehended. Those wishes were incompatible. Briefly, she considered keeping the secret, and decided she was not craven. She would have to reveal the truth to someone with the power to do something with that knowledge.

Absently folding the papers, she considered her options. She should tell Mr. Wescott what had happened. He had already been questioned by someone connected to the investigation; he would know whom she should speak to and what that person ought to know.

She was most of the way to her bedroom when she remembered it was Friday, and Mr. Wescott would be at his place of employment. Scowling, she alit on the second floor landing and trudged to her room. She would have to send a message, and wait on his return. Until then, she would Fly and let the activity stretch her sore muscles out.

Tatton again said nothing as Clemency changed into her Flying gear and tucked her hair under her white cap. Impulsively, Clemency said, "Thank you for your discretion. I am certain you are bursting with curiosity."

Tatton smiled and shrugged in the odd way she did, hunching one shoulder higher than the other. "My lady's business is her own," she said, "though if I may speak boldly, I am aware that you often go Flying at night, and I have mentioned this to no one."

"It is not that I don't trust you," Clemency said. "This is a matter I cannot speak of to anyone—but if that changes, well, you know I depend on you, Tatton."

Tatton curtseyed. "I do, my lady."

Clemency retreated to her private drawing room, where she penned a quick message to Mr. Wescott. As she was signing it, Slater appeared in the doorway with a small silver plate upon which lay a card. Clemency deposited her note on the salver and picked up the card. "Oh, Jane," she exclaimed. "Slater, do have her shown in."

Jane, when she arrived, was wearing her Flying gear, which was identical to Clemency's except for being a somber maroon instead of navy blue. "Good morning, Clemency," she said cheerfully. "Are you going somewhere?"

"Just for a flight around town," Clemency said. She found she did not wish to tell her friend about her message to Mr. Wescott. Quite aside from her involvement with the bombing, she felt tender of her growing attachment to the man. Jane would not mock her for being attracted to someone not of their social class—though Mr. Wescott was a gentleman, so what did it matter if he was neither wealthy nor titled?—but she would feel entitled to tease Clemency, and however friendly the teasing, Clemency did not wish to endure it.

"Oh, then you must come with me, I am paying calls this morning and they will be more entertaining if you are present." Jane threw herself into a chair and fanned her face ostentatiously, though she did not appear over-warm. "No one will wish to talk of anything but this mysterious Extraordinary Mover, and it will be delicious gossip."

"But I know nothing of the matter," Clemency lied.

"Oh, bah, how is that relevant? It is *gossip*, Clemency. We will speculate wildly and laugh a great deal. And on that subject—" Jane sat up in her chair and leaned forward, clasping her hands on her knees. "I am hosting a party on Tuesday next, and you must come, because it is due to you that I discovered the Cabinet of Curiosities."

Clemency raised her eyebrows. "That is a mysterious and confused sentence I beg you to untangle."

"It is nothing so confusing. The ground floor of the building is almost entirely taken up by an astonishing mechanical garden that Mr. Wescott does not display to the public. But he is willing to hire it out for gatherings, and I have engaged it for Tuesday. It is remarkable, Clemency! Mr. Wescott showed it to me and I was simply astonished. Do say you'll come."

Clemency suppressed a flash of irrational jealousy that Mr. Wescott had done something so potentially intimate as showing the garden to Jane. "Of course I will. Do you invite only our Mover friends?"

"Oh, no, I intend this to be *the* social event of the season. Everyone who is anyone will be invited." Jane rose and put a confiding hand on Clemency's arm. "And Mr. Wescott will benefit from the publicity. He is quite fascinating, don't you agree?"

The jealousy returned, hot and burning. "I agree," Clemency said, exerting herself to be pleasant, though she could not help but consider Jane's many swains and resent Jane wishing to attract yet another. "I enjoy speaking to him."

"Of course you do." Jane smiled and patted Clemency's arm. "Let us go, and we will have a race to Elizabeth's house. She serves the best refreshments. I swear I shall someday lure her cook away from her. Father cares nothing for food if it is not the cuisine of some foreign country to the far East, and how am I to find such a paragon?"

❦

CLEMENCY RETURNED TO EMERAUDE HOUSE AFTER THREE O'CLOCK, exhausted in spirit and aching in body. She had not realized how difficult it would be to refrain from telling her friends the truth of the failed bombing. She also could not bring herself to lie, to reveal details and pretend she had heard them elsewhere. So in the end, she remained mostly silent, except when it came to speculation on the identity of the Extraordinary Mover.

"I cannot believe he was involved in the bombing," she had said to Lady Deirdre when that woman had voiced the *Morning Herald's* opinion. "It is much more likely that he interrupted the real bombers and removed the bomb before it could destroy their target."

"That is highly coincidental," Lady Deirdre had said in her high-pitched, somewhat nasal voice. Clemency had never found her voice annoying until that moment. "You expect us to believe that an

Extraordinary Mover *happened* to be Flying past at just the right moment to observe someone setting a bomb?"

"Which of us do you suppose would be capable of bombing London?" Jane had said. "It is not just a matter of coincidence or accident. It is a matter of motive. We all know one another, perhaps not equally well, but enough that I cannot believe one of us might do such a horrid thing."

"People are not always what they seem," Lady Deirdre had said, lowering her voice so it sounded more like the coo of a pigeon than the twitter of a wren. "Imagine the dark secrets one of us might be hiding!"

"I refuse to believe it," Clemency had said. "Lady Deirdre, did you see in the newspaper that the authorities are investigating? Which authorities do you suppose those are? Not the Bow Street Runners?"

"Oh, certainly not," Lady Deirdre had said, "because who would pay them? Now, I have heard tell of a clandestine government organization that investigates crimes. Remember that rash of counterfeiting a few years ago? They operate in secret, and I have heard that many gentlemen and even a few ladies are in its employ."

Knowing Lady Deirdre could talk about unlikely conspiracies such as that one for hours, Clemency had been satisfied at successfully deflecting her. Now, however, she remembered Lady Deirdre's words and wondered if there was some truth to them. If one could imagine a group of Extraordinaries secretly defending the city against criminals, was it any more preposterous to posit a group within the government doing the same thing?

She left Jane at the front door and waved to her as her friend Flew heavenward, then Moved the door handle rather than touching it, more to remind herself that she could than because she needed to. She had not yet lost the memory of being unable to Move the poker and the bell pull last night. The last time her Moving talent had been suppressed, she had been seriously injured with a head wound that had nearly killed her. That the injury had broken Napoleon's Coercion of her made her remember it, not exactly fondly, but with a resigned satisfaction. Enduring her talent's suppression was the second worst thing she could imagine.

A note lay on her bedside table when she entered her room. She snatched it up and opened it. *You intrigue me,* Mr. Wescott had written. *I will be at home after four o'clock and look forward to discussing the matter.* He had not signed it, but his distinctive handwriting—not even handwriting, but printing—was as good as a stamped insignia.

Clemency read the short message twice more, her eye lingering on the bold lettering. She was well and truly smitten, was she not? She dropped the note on the table and crossed to the window to look out across the city. Should she Fly, or ride? Flying would make her appear windblown, but it was faster and more satisfying. And it was not as if Mr. Wescott did not know she was not exactly ladylike in her behavior at times. On the other hand, she had a new gown of printed cotton that flattered her complexion, and a wool spencer that complemented the gown perfectly...and now she was behaving like a simpering maiden fresh from the schoolroom. Flying it would be.

CHAPTER 14

IN WHICH CLEMENCY TAKES
HER FATHER'S GOOD ADVICE

She alit in front of the Wescotts' house at precisely seven minutes and twelve seconds after four o'clock and knocked on the door as sedately as any upstanding lady with legitimate business might. It opened only a few seconds later, and Hammond the butler bowed her inside. "Lady Ashford," he said. "Welcome. Mr. and Miss Wescott are expecting you."

Clemency had not anticipated Miss Wescott's presence, and the news dampened her spirits. If Mr. Wescott intended to protect her reputation by providing them both with a duenna, he was more careful of social mores than she had believed. She was not sure how she felt about that. She put on a cheerful smile and followed Hammond up the stairs to the sitting room.

Miss Wescott sat near the fire and did not turn at Clemency's entrance. Mr. Wescott was seated at a table upon which were spread the components of some mechanical device. He rose when Clemency entered, smiling his familiar smile that warmed Clemency's heart. She chastised herself for being so smitten, but her father's voice again echoed in her head: *Never let fear stand in the way of getting what you want, and fear of what others will say is the worst fear of all.*

"Lady Ashford," Mr. Wescott said. "It is your turn to rouse my curiosity. You have information about last night's failed bombing? Forgive me, but after reading what the newspapers reported, I suspect I know how you came about this information. But I will pretend to ignorance if it means listening to you speak."

Clemency blushed and cast a glance at Miss Wescott, who continued to watch the fire as if she had no interest in their conversation. Well, it was not as if she did not already know of Clemency's secret adventures. "If your guess is that I was the Extraordinary Mover reported seen at the site of the explosion, you are correct. I happened upon the would-be bombers when they attempted to destroy St. Paul's Cathedral. They had adapted your stolen music box to make their bomb, and I discovered it in time to remove it to where it could harm no one."

Mr. Wescott's eyes widened. "I cannot decide which of those statements to respond to first. You are unhurt?"

Clemency's shoulder still troubled her, but she said, "I took no injury to speak of."

Miss Wescott finally turned away from the fire. Her eyes were as unfocused as they had been the day of the music box theft. "That is fortunate," she said. "For you, if not for them."

Clemency did not know what to make of this statement, so she ignored it. "The bomb would not have destroyed the cathedral entirely, or at least I do not believe so, but it would have caused great damage. So it *was* quite fortunate that I was in the area."

"Given the size of London, it is also surprising that you Flew there last night and not elsewhere," Mr. Wescott said. He shook his head slightly as if breaking free of a trance. "I beg your pardon, Lady Ashford. Will you sit?"

Clemency took a seat near Miss Wescott and waited for Mr. Wescott to sit opposite her. "Mr. Wescott," she said, "I have a dilemma. My actions may have saved lives, but based on what I read in the newspapers, they have confused the issue of who the bombers are and what they intend. No one but I—and now you and Miss Wescott —know they intended harm to St. Paul's. But if there is an investigation underway, whoever your Mr. Rutledge is needs as much correct information as possible. And I seem to have robbed him of some of it."

"Yet telling anyone the truth means revealing your involvement," Mr. Wescott said, "and likely your habit of nocturnal activities as well."

"You have it exactly, Mr. Wescott." Clemency ran a hand over the smooth satiny fabric covering the sofa arm. "I would like your advice, if I may. My instinct is that my privacy is less important than the lives of those who might be hurt or killed if the bombings continue. But if those investigating are not competent, I would be sacrificing that privacy for nothing. What should I do?"

Mr. Wescott ran his hand over his chin in thought. "That is quite the dilemma," he said. "I cannot tell you what to do—that is not a responsibility either of us wants me to have. But I can tell you that Mr. Rutledge struck me as an intelligent, astute man who is strongly committed to stopping the bombings. That means, however, that he is also ruthless. My assessment is that if you were to tell him of your involvement, he would not assume you were at fault the way the *Morning Herald* did, but he also would not care about protecting your reputation."

"But is my reputation more important than saving lives?"

"You have already made a decision," Miss Wescott said. "You came here looking for reassurance. Colin and I will stand by you, you know."

Clemency blinked in surprise. "I did not," she began, cleared her throat, and said, "Is it so obvious?"

"To me," Miss Wescott said. "But I should not tell you what you feel. Mama always called me haughty and presumptuous and a naughty girl." The vacant look disappeared, and for a moment Miss Wescott looked much younger than the twenty years Clemency guessed her age to be. "That is what they all said."

Mr. Wescott rose from his seat to kneel at his sister's side. "Lydia, that is in the past. The past, remember? Mama was wrong."

Miss Wescott turned her stricken look on him. "It hurts us both," she said. "Me, and then you, and then me again. You are not a Discerner, I know, but there is so little difference."

"I know." Mr. Wescott took her hand and squeezed it. "You should lie down. You are close to being overwhelmed by your talent. Please, Lydia, go and rest."

Miss Wescott nodded. When she again looked at Clemency, her

eyes were focused and not at all distant. "Forgive me," she said. "Some-times I forget. But I know you understand how memory can hurt. Forgetting would be the wrong kind of release." She stood and walked to the door. "And remembering means nothing ever dies."

When the door shut behind her, Mr. Wescott continued to stare at it as if he could see through its wood and the walls to the Cabinet beyond. "Forgive my sister," he said. "She endured much before she learned to control her talent, and the memory is sometimes painful and takes her by surprise."

"I understand completely," Clemency said. Immediately she regretted the force with which she spoke. Who knew what Mr. Wescott might make of it? But he seemed not to notice anything was amiss. "I honor her struggle. It must be so difficult to distinguish between one's own emotions and those of everyone else."

Mr. Wescott sat beside Clemency with his hands clenched on his knees. "Our mother feared her, and treated her badly," he said, his voice harsh. "When she could no longer bear Lydia's presence, she confined her to an asylum in the country—nothing terrible, at least not physically, she was not abused or mistreated, but she was surrounded by others whose emotions were fractured and violent. You can imagine the results."

Horrified, Clemency could only nod.

"It took me three years to gain the money and influence to have her released," Mr. Wescott continued. "Mother fought the decision, but after Father's death I was the head of the family, and I swore she would never see Lydia again." He laughed, a short, bitter sound. "She probably believed I meant it to benefit her."

"Of course not," Clemency said. "It was all for Miss Wescott's sake."

Mr. Wescott nodded. He smiled, a self-deprecating expression. "Forgive me for burdening you with our family woes. I do not like anyone imagining Lydia is weak or unstable, simply because she has some painful memories."

His words stabbed at Clemency's heart. "Of course not," she repeated. "She is to be honored for enduring, and for remaining sane." She did not know if she could say the same for herself.

Mr. Wescott cleared his throat. "Mr. Rutledge left me a means to contact him," he said. "I can send a message that I have new information, and arrange for him to meet you here, if you would like. That will protect your anonymity to a degree, though of course Mr. Rutledge will wish to know your identity."

"That will be superior to him knocking on my front door," Clemency said. Mr. Wescott's nearness made her heart race; though he was not touching her, he was close enough she imagined she could feel the warmth of his body scorching her skin. His hands now curled loosely on his knees, those large, powerful hands that had gripped hers so firmly and yet so gently. She tore her gaze from his hands to discover his attention fully on her face, his gaze a steady regard that sent a shiver through her.

His smile deepened into amusement. "Surely you are not cold," he said.

Clemency had not realized her shiver was so noticeable, and she blushed—she must look awful, face bright red in contrast with her white cap, tendrils of hair flying in every direction as they did when she Flew any moderate distance. At least her Flying garb was dark enough not to show the inevitable smudges that developed when one Flew across London repeatedly. She only looked overwrought and not slovenly.

"No," she said. "I am not cold."

Mr. Wescott's smile faded, and his brow furrowed slightly, as if Clemency were a puzzle he could not solve. "And yet you shiver," he said. "Perhaps that means someone is thinking of you."

His eyes captured her attention, those sea-blue eyes with a hint of green, startling against sun-darkened skin that was the mark of a publicly employed Bounder. "That might be awful," she found herself saying. "Suppose it is someone horrid?"

The corner of his mouth turned up, just enough to be a smile. "And suppose it is not? Suppose it is someone who wishes the best for you, and whose regard is worth having?"

Her heart beat hard and fast as if it meant to propel her out of her seat and into the sky. "How will I know?" she whispered.

Mr. Wescott shrugged, and one eyebrow arched nearly to his hairline. "It may have to remain a mystery."

He was closer now, close enough that she could smell the clean scent of soap and the fainter tang of mineral oil on his hands. Her father's voice echoed in her ears again: *Why not do whatever it takes to grab hold of what you want?* Before fear and propriety asserted themselves, she leaned forward and kissed him.

His lips were warm and soft and curved to meet hers, kissing her in return as sweetly as she could ever have hoped. She put her arm around his strong shoulders and thrilled to feel his arm around her waist, drawing her close. He rested one large hand against her cheek, cradling it gently, his fingers lightly stroking the side of her face. The warmth of his skin against hers sent a flash of desire through her. For a moment, she remembered Armand, but Colin Wescott's body felt nothing like her seducer's, he smelled clean and sharp and not of the cloying scent of roses, and the memory vanished, swallowed up by the passion of the moment.

How long they sat there kissing, Clemency never knew, but at some point, they drew apart, slowly, as if they both knew when the moment should end. Mr. Wescott removed his hand from Clemency's face, resting it once more on his knee, and Clemency impulsively covered it with hers and was warmed by the delighted smile the gesture elicited.

"Well," she said, and found herself speechless.

Mr. Wescott put his other hand atop their joined ones. "That was unexpected."

"Unexpected? I feel as if we have been moving toward that ever since the night we met," Clemency said.

His smile broadened. "Very well. Unanticipated, at least in the sense that I did not lure you here in the hope that you would kiss me."

Clemency smiled impishly. "That is much more reasonable. I should apologize for being presumptuous, except you seemed to enjoy it."

"Oh, I did, I assure you." Mr. Wescott removed his hands from hers and ran them through his hair, disordering it. "But you—no."

"What is it?"

He shook his head. "Nothing but my own misunderstanding. You seemed interested in me, and then you would flee, and I could not tell where the truth lay."

Clemency drew in a breath, remembering the times her memories of Armand had intruded upon her. "Someday I will explain," she said, "but I believe I should go now." It was her choice, but the decision still sent a pang of loss through her.

Mr. Wescott looked as if he wished to protest, but he merely smiled and stood, taking her hand and bringing her with him. "You are correct," he said, "for the sake of propriety if nothing else. I will send word when I have heard from Mr. Rutledge."

"If he does not respond soon, I believe I will see you next on Monday, when you deliver my sister's chair. And—oh! Again on the following Tuesday, at Miss Pilgrim's gala here." Clemency squeezed his hand lightly and released him. "She is so eager, and I am pleased to see your inventions receive the recognition they deserve." She chose not to mention how jealous she had been of Mr. Wescott's supposed closeness to Jane. That would only make her seem unstable.

"They are not all my inventions, but I take your meaning," Mr. Wescott said. His smile when he looked at her was so warm, so tender, it caused another shiver, which made them both laugh.

Mr. Wescott escorted her to the front door, and Clemency looked back at him as she soared into the sky. He shielded his eyes with one hand so he could watch her, and she waved and saw him wave back. Delight elicited a giddy, heartfelt laugh that spilled uncontrollably out of her. Perhaps kissing a man to whom she was not married or even engaged was not what her father had intended when he encouraged her to reach for what she desired, but she remembered the face of the man who had assured her mother that Clemency deserved her freedom and felt he would not have censured her.

Mr. Wescott was right; that had been unexpected, and yet felt the more glorious for it. And she had banished her demons. She had never felt so certain that the future held something wonderful.

CHAPTER 15

IN WHICH CLEMENCY'S PAST BECOMES THE PRESENT

The following Monday, she stood beside Mr. Wescott and watched Mercy wheel her new chair around the foyer, turning and backing with ease. Mr. Wescott rested his hand on the back of the old chair, drumming his fingers against the brocade upholstery. "I believe this is my finest work yet," he said to Clemency, "if I may say so without seeming immodest. At the least, it is the one that most clearly benefits its intended user."

"I cannot speak to other invalid chairs, but this one is perfectly beautiful," Clemency declared. The chair itself was of ruddy polished wood, with heavily padded seat and back covered in rose damask. Two fat bolsters sat atop the arms, providing more padding for Mercy's forearms. Though the wheels were of iron, they were much slimmer than those of Mercy's original chair, and the rails for propelling the chair were smoothly polished to provide a comfortable grip.

Mercy rolled to a stop before them, gripping the rails to keep the chair in place. Her color was high and her eyes were bright. "Stopping is difficult, if I have achieved any great speed," she said, "but as I find I enjoy a fast ride under my own power, I do not consider this a flaw."

"If I may demonstrate," Mr. Wescott said, stepping forward, "I have made one further adjustment." He indicated a heavy latch near each wheel. "If you engage this latch, it will lock the wheels in place, removing the need for you to hold the chair steady yourself when you wish to remain still."

Mercy worked the latches, back and forth, and finally left them in place and rested her hands in her lap. The chair did not roll even the tiniest distance. "Mr. Wescott, you are a marvel," she exclaimed. "I cannot thank you enough."

"I should not claim all the credit, given that Mr. Merlin was the originator, but if my alterations suit you, then you are quite welcome." Mr. Wescott smiled and rolled the other chair back and forth a few inches. "And I can easily build those modifications into future chairs."

"So many people will benefit," Clemency said.

Mercy turned her gaze on the stairs. "If only there was a way to shift the chair between floors without depending on Moving," she mused. Then, with a look of horror, she stammered, "I do not mean to be ungrateful—this is more than enough, and I should not dismiss what I have in favor of air-dreaming—"

"We understand, dearest," Clemency said in some amusement. "And it is natural that, having experienced a measure of freedom, you should long for more of it."

"I wonder..." Mr. Wescott walked slowly toward the grand staircase, which rose straight as an arrow to the first floor balcony that over-looked the foyer. "A clockwork engine attached to a belt, or a series of links in a chain...though perhaps a chair with a passenger would be too heavy for the mechanism...but if the chair were to attach to the chain, and be wound upward—"

"Mr. Wescott," Clemency said with a laugh, "do not tell us you have conceived of a solution?"

Mr. Wescott turned, his smile once more self-deprecating. "The beginnings of a notion, which may or may not be a solution. I did mention that my ideas plague my every waking moment, did I not?"

"That must be so exciting, seeing the world as you do," Clemency said.

"That is a very generous way of putting it." Mr. Wescott returned to her side. "I beg your pardon, but I have a dinner engagement I should prepare for. Lady Mercy, if any problems develop, or if you find your needs not fully met, please contact me, and I will make any alterations you require."

"Thank you so much, Mr. Wescott," Mercy said, extending her hand.

"Yes, thank you, Mr. Wescott," Clemency said, concealing her disappointment at his abrupt departure. "I will have payment sent to your residence immediately."

"Then I thank *you*, Lady Ashford," Mr. Wescott said, bowing over her hand. He held it for longer than was strictly acceptable, though he made no other intimate gesture. Blushing, Clemency smiled at him, wishing she dared kiss him again. Since Friday, she had been unable to think of anything but their embrace and how much she longed to repeat it. But that was impossible, at least in the public setting of her foyer. So she squeezed his hand, lightly, and was rewarded with that same smile that warmed her to her core.

"I will see you tomorrow night, then," she said. "It is sure to be an exciting evening."

"I understand everyone who is anyone will be there." Mr. Wescott shook his head in mock despair. "Miss Pilgrim asked that I demonstrate the wheeled skates, but I declined on the grounds that I prefer not to kill myself in front of a hundred witnesses to my folly."

Clemency laughed. "I prefer you remain whole and uninjured, so I approve of your decision."

Mr. Wescott nodded. "Until tomorrow, Lady Ashford." With a smile, he bowed once more, and then vanished.

Clemency stood facing the door after he was gone, remembering his smile. She was startled out of her reverie by Mercy's chuckle. "Clemency," she said, "you are smitten."

Clemency turned around fast. "I am not. I have no idea why you would say that." Her face was hot, and she was sure she was bright red, giving herself the lie.

"*I* do not know why you are embarrassed," Mercy said. "He is intelligent, and charming, and he clearly has an interest in you."

"We are of such different social standing, though. He may be a gentleman, but he is not noble, and that is so difficult when it is the man who is of a lower rank than the woman."

Mercy waved a dismissive hand. "You are Lady Ashford. Who will argue with you over where you choose to bestow your heart?"

Clemency glanced over her shoulder at the door again as if Mr. Wescott were still present. "I—no one, I suppose. Oh, I am so flustered. I cannot remember ever feeling this way before." She ruthlessly suppressed memories of Armand.

"Well, he obviously shares that feeling, Clemency, which to me suggests that you should pursue the connection." Mercy wheeled herself in the direction of the stairs. "Would you Move me to the balcony? I wish to finish the reticule I am netting before supper."

"You are remarkably insightful about the ways of men and women," Clemency teased. She lifted the chair with her Moving and raised it to the upper floor, slowly so Mercy would not fall. "It is unfortunate you have made no attachments of your own."

Mercy ducked her head. "Yes, unfortunate," she said.

Clemency stopped Moving the chair in surprise. "Mercy!" she exclaimed. "There is someone!"

"Please, put me down," Mercy said. "You know how I dislike heights."

"Oh, I beg your pardon, I was—" Clemency lifted the chair over the rail and set it down gently, then Flew to follow it. "Mercy, you must tell me."

"There is no one," Mercy said, but again she would not meet Clemency's eyes. "Besides, it is not as if any man will want a crippled wife. Better for me that I make no attachments."

"Mercy—" Clemency shut her mouth on words that would only hurt her sister. She could not assure Mercy that her assertion was untrue when she knew otherwise. Mercy's lovely face had never been enough to stop men and women looking at her not in admiration, but in pity. "You should not fall into despair. You are only twenty, dearest, and there is time—"

"I would prefer not to discuss it," Mercy said, and wheeled herself away. Clemency followed her, slowly so as not to overtake her. At least Mercy had not lied about being Spoken to to distract her sister.

134

CLEMENCY STOOD BEFORE HER MIRROR THE FOLLOWING NIGHT AND admired the way her gown fell from her shoulders, Grecian style, all the way to her ankles. She looked particularly good in blue, especially the shade of blue that matched a cloudless summer sky. Silver clasps secured its silken folds to drape over her shoulders, and she wore silver shoes to match. A necklace of diamonds set in silver links and a silver band to secure her hair completed her ensemble. It was not a warm gown, but she did not intend to do any Flying tonight.

She stopped in the drawing room before leaving. Mercy sat beside the fire, for once not sewing. Mercy lowered her book and said, "Oh, you look lovely!"

"Thank you," Clemency said. "You are certain you won't join me? Jane was most insistent that you were invited."

"No, I am well enough as I am. If even half of the people Miss Pilgrim invited attend, it will be a sad crush, and I will be unable to move." Mercy's smile became impish. "You should not worry about me, not when you could be dwelling upon how *someone* will admire your appearance tonight."

This time, Clemency kept from blushing. "You are terrible."

"No, I am honest. And he will admire you greatly, I am sure. Now, go. Enjoy yourself. And bring me many exciting stories!"

In the carriage, Clemency wrapped her heavy cloak around herself and pressed her feet against the hot brick provided by Slater. The night was not actually as cold as it had been the night she Flew, drenched and shivering, from her encounter with the bombers, but the difference was not great when one was sitting rather than moving one's limbs. Fortunately, her cloak was warm, and she felt nearly comfortable.

The foyer of the Cabinet of Curiosities was, by contrast, very warm, not at all chilly as she was now accustomed to expect from the tall, white-walled room. She smiled at Hammond as he accepted her cloak, then turned to greet Jane, who stood at the bottom of the two steps leading up to the garden. The noise of many people all talking at once filled the air.

"You must be gratified that so many people accepted your invitation," she said, pitching her voice to be heard over the clamor. "I imagine most of London is here tonight."

"Oh, bah, this is nothing," Jane said as she embraced Clemency. "Just wait an hour, when everyone has arrived. Then the true event will begin! Go, explore. There are as many marvels as there are guests to converse with!"

Clemency nodded and left Jane to greet another guest. She stood in the open doorway and gazed across the garden of marvels for a moment. The paths were thronged with guests chattering to one another and exclaiming over the clockwork mechanisms. Clemency reflected that Mercy had been correct about the unlikelihood of her chair being able to fit anywhere in this crowd.

She heard someone coming up behind her and stepped away from the door. She still had not seen the person she most cared about speaking to tonight—but with that, her eye fell on the silver swan, and she beheld Mr. Wescott standing next to it, speaking to a crowd of onlookers. As she watched, he worked the mechanism, and the swan's head moved and the "water" flowed. The hushed gasp from the crowd was audible even at Clemency's distance.

She watched the swan until it finished its routine and the crowd dispersed, then made her way through the throngs of guests until she reached Mr. Wescott's side. He saw her coming, and smiled, but did not stop speaking to the lady and gentleman before him. "...the construction is remarkable," he was saying when Clemency neared. "I will spare you the details, as they are quite dull, but you can see for yourselves the end result."

"If I could not see that it is made of silver, I would believe it a real bird," the lady said.

Clemency thought this was rather fatuous, as the bird, lifelike as it was, still did not behave exactly like a real swan. She recognized this thought as a spiteful one that derived from her impatience to have Mr. Wescott's attention entirely for herself and did not comment.

"I would be interested in purchasing it," the gentleman said. "For the right sum, of course."

"I am afraid it is not for sale at any price," Mr. Wescott said, sounding suitably remorseful and yet firm. "I believe, as did my predecessors, that this mechanical should be displayed to the world rather than shut away in a private collection. But your interest is flattering. Pray excuse me, I should speak with Lady Ashford."

The lady and gentlemen looked startled to see Clemency there, so quietly had she been standing. She smiled pleasantly and waited for them to hurry away. "I did not realize anyone might wish to purchase these creations," she said to Mr. Wescott, "but of course it makes perfect sense. I suppose I believe, as you do, that they should remain where all can see them, and it did not occur to me that others might not share that opinion."

"I have received no fewer than four offers tonight for the swan alone," Mr. Wescott said. "And more for the other objects. I could likely make my fortune if I wished to sell off the collection."

"But surely you will not!"

His amused smile warmed her heart. "If I wished to do so," he said, "I would have done it years ago, and saved myself the heartache of maintaining it."

Clemency turned to face the swan. "But it is a labor of love for you."

"Indeed." Mr. Wescott sounded deeply satisfied. "Though I wish I were an artist rather than an inventor, for I should very much like to capture the scene before me in paint or pastels."

Clemency, surprised, turned back to look at him. "What scene?"

Mr. Wescott's smile vanished, and he looked so serious it made Clemency's heart race. "You, gowned like Aphrodite, with silver in your hair to match the swan."

She had blushed more since meeting this remarkable man than in the whole rest of her life to date. "You flatter me, sir," she said, unable to meet his eyes.

"It is only what anyone who sees you will say." Mr. Wescott offered her his arm. "May I show you something else? It is my latest creation."

She accepted his arm gladly. "It must be something beautiful, if you have placed it in this garden with all the other marvels."

"I hope you will find it so."

Mr. Wescott guided her to a place somewhat less crowded than the rest of the garden, primarily, Clemency believed, because there were no mechanicals at that spot. He stopped near one of the planters bearing a boxwood hedge. The top of the hedge was just below shoulder height to Clemency, and unlike the other hedges, it had not been trimmed flat, but instead waved its thin branches in a random way. Mr. Wescott bent and reached into the base of the hedge, where he did something Clemency could not see. "Watch," he said, pointing at the top of the hedge.

At first, nothing happened. Clemency could not even hear the whirr of the mechanics over the drone of the crowd, which had grown louder as the minutes passed. Then a brass figure no more than a foot long leaped from the hedge, eliciting a gasp from Clemency. The figure was shaped like a woman garbed as an Extraordinary Mover, complete with a tiny white cap and billowing divided skirts. She rose into the air, curled in on herself, and dove, somersaulting in midair and then straightening out to Fly in a smooth curve across the tops of the boxwood branches.

Clemency, marveling, took a step forward and leaned closer. Now she perceived that the figure was attached to a brass rod that carried her through her Flying path. How the figure bent and twisted and moved its head, she had no idea, but it looked just as lifelike as the swan. "Extraordinary," she breathed. "Mr. Wescott, it is amazing."

"I had the best inspiration," Mr. Wescott said.

Clemency turned to face him. He once more wore the look of tenderness she remembered, and it took all her self-control not to put her arms around him and kiss him, in full view of everyone in the garden. A wicked impulse suggested that none of those people were watching, and she might do as she pleased, but she resisted the urge.

"It is perfectly beautiful," she declared.

"I hoped you would like it," Mr. Wescott said. He looked past her, and a frown replaced his intimate smile. He swore under his breath, said, "Excuse me," and vanished with a faint *pop*.

Clemency turned in a complete circle, looking for him in case he had merely Skipped elsewhere in the garden, and eventually saw him standing beside the swan. His hands gripped the shoulders of a man who was laughing loudly enough Clemency could hear it over the riot. Mr. Wescott's words were not audible, but he looked angry.

"Mr. Ffoulkes should not have touched that thing," Francis said in Clemency's ear. She jumped and rounded on her friend, slapping his shoulder lightly.

"Do not sneak up on me; you know I hate it," she said.

"Hence my interest in doing it just often enough that I am amused and you are not truly angry," Francis said. "Did Lady Mercy not join you? I understood Jane invited her, and I wished to see this marvel of a new chair I have heard tell of."

"She would never be able to maneuver through this crowd," Clemency said absently, her attention already back on Mr. Wescott and his captive. Mr. Wescott had steered Mr. Ffoulkes away from the swan and now shook him slightly, then released him with enough force to make the man take an involuntary step backward. Mr. Ffoulkes ostentatiously dusted off his shoulders and settled his coat more securely. He was taller than Mr. Wescott, but seeing the two of them together, Clemency could not help but remember watching two dogs facing off, one of them an elegant long-haired creature, the other a compact, snarling mutt, and how that contest had ended with the elegant dog routed decisively by an animal who knew very well how to fight.

"Come, leave Mr. Wescott to fight that battle," Francis said as if he could hear her thoughts, "and I will show you the rest of this place. It is remarkable, really. To think it has been in London all this time and I never knew it."

"Mr. Wescott said it used to be quite famous, years ago."

"Ah, yes, I forgot for a moment that you have more of an interest in the Cabinet of Curiosities than simple fascination with mechanics." Francis squeezed her hand where it rested on his sleeve. "You and Mr. Wescott...?"

"You should learn to complete your sentences, Francis," Clemency chided him.

"That was by way of an invitation for you to share your feelings, my dear. I believed you did not feel you should pursue the connection, not after your encounter at the lecture, and yet you speak of him in the familiar way of one who feels an attachment."

"And if I do? Is that so horrid?" Clemency spoke more sharply than she intended, and regretted it immediately. "I beg your pardon, Francis. I feel so muddled when I consider Mr. Wescott. I find him interesting, and I believe he feels the same about me, but I am Lady Ashford now, and I do not know how I am to pursue this…whatever is between us."

Francis stopped and turned Clemency to face him. "You should follow your heart," he said, "and never fear what others will say. You are the keeper of your honor, and I have never known anyone more honorable than you."

"Thank you, Francis." Clemency looked past him toward the door, where a rush of guests had appeared—no, they were headed out, not in. "What is that?"

Francis, who was taller than she, followed the line of her gaze. "I believe…ah, yes. Jane did say she had invited everyone, and I suppose General de Villiers is part of 'everyone.'"

For a moment, the room swayed, and the sounds of speech echoed in Clemency's ears like words heard underwater. "General de Villiers?" she heard herself say, still in that hollow, echoing way.

"Yes, he has been quite the fixture about town this last week," Francis said. He did not appear to notice the room swaying. "A very romantic figure, having been Coerced from his loyalty to France's king to follow Napoleon and then defeating an entire brigade of revolutionaries after breaking his Coercion. I doubt the man will need to pay for his dinner for a fortnight or more."

Clemency removed her hand from Francis' arm. "I see," she said. She felt numb all over, rooted to the ground like that brass figure affixed to her rod and unable to move. The crowd at the door continued to shift, each person trying to be the one to reach it first. It looked like a teeming mass of shifting oils rather than a collection of individuals, and she could not make out any one person, but he was there, she was certain of it. The famous General de Villiers.

Armand.

CHAPTER 16

IN WHICH CLEMENCY MAKES HER ESCAPE, BUT DOES NOT FLEE FAR ENOUGH

F rancis took a few steps away from her. "We will never make it through the crowd, and I wish to meet this paragon," he said without looking back. "Perhaps if we wait, movement will be easier."

"I wish to look at something else first," Clemency said. Her voice had stopped echoing, and now merely sounded faint, though she could not tell if that was real or her imagination. "I will join you later."

Francis did not react as if he had heard her. Perhaps her voice really was as inaudible as she believed. She took a step backward, bumped into a hedge in a stone trough, and tripped over her feet as she turned. Grabbing the hedge to keep her balance, she used it to haul herself upright. She found she was breathing as heavily as if she had run a mile, her heart pounding, her skin clammy with sweat. Francis still did not notice her distress; he was watching the door, craning his neck for a glimpse of Armand. Clemency fled.

She knew immediately her cause was hopeless. The room had only one exit, and that was the one place she absolutely could not go. None of the many glass windows were made to open. She might Fly, but that would only make her conspicuous against the high ceiling. Possibilities whirled through her head, being discarded and then returning for consideration as if the situation might have changed.

As she cast about wildly for a solution, her feet carried her of their own volition away from the door, toward the wall of windows. The many lights illuminating the garden reflected off the glass, turning the wide panes into imperfect mirrors. By their reflection, she did not look at all like a woman fleeing in terror.

She reached the windows and stopped in front of the wild hedges. They had been trimmed, she noticed with the part of her that clung to her sanity. Behind her, the throng of people continued to move, pushing inexorably toward the doors. In the golden reflections, they looked even more like a mindless mass, a pool of water filmed with oil that swirled and ebbed with the motion of the wind blowing across its surface. She felt dizzy, and sick, and for a moment she considered breaking a window so she could escape—but that would only draw him to her faster.

She turned, putting her back to the hedges, and her gaze fell on a door she had missed before. Now she remembered; it was the closet where Mr. Wescott stored unused mechanicals, or so she supposed. Her hand was on the latch before she was aware of moving. In seconds, she was inside with the door safely closed behind her.

The little room was far larger than a closet, but the many laden shelves filling it made it feel cramped. Clemency walked down the aisle formed by the rows of shelves until she reached the back of the room. Then she leaned against the wall with her arm beneath her face and shook and shook without trying to control herself. Armand. Armand in London. Armand here at Jane's gala. She knew it was no nightmare, for she never felt anything in dreams, and the rough, unfinished wall rasped at her skin, and the air smelled of oil and grease and dust. He was here. And she was trapped.

She drew in a shuddering breath and stood upright, wrapping her arms around herself to stop the shivering. Dirt clung to her forearm where it had pressed against the wall, and some rubbed off on her beautiful gown, but that did feel like a dream, as if gowns and jewels and silver shoes were all part of some other world where people laughed and joked and cheered Armand for his victories because they knew nothing of who he truly was.

The door creaked open, and Clemency shrieked and then closed her hand over her mouth. She could not face him. Not in front of all these people.

"Lady Ashford?"

Clemency swallowed. "Mr. Wescott," she said, and could not find words to continue.

"I would prefer no one enter this room," Mr. Wescott said, "because—" He walked toward her and came to a stop several feet away. "Is something wrong?"

Her eyes felt hot and wet, and she raised her fingers to her cheeks and discovered she was weeping. "I need to leave," she said. "There is no way out."

Mr. Wescott's eyes narrowed. Then he took a few more rapid steps and slung his arm around Clemency's waist, lifting her off the ground. Before she could protest his rough handling—

—weightless floating, like Flying without air—

—they were in a small Bounding chamber that smelled of lamp oil and astringent cleanser. A tiny lantern burned on one wall, its frosted glass making the flame within seem motionless. Mr. Wescott put Clemency down without comment and opened the door opposite the Bounding symbol, which was a series of concentric circles painted in blue and green and orange. "Please," he said, gesturing for her to precede him. Clemency did.

The Bounding chamber opened on the Wescotts' sitting room, in which one lamp burned low and the fire was banked. Clemency took two steps and then halted, blinking in the dimness. Mr. Wescott brushed past her with a murmured "Excuse me," and trimmed both lamps until they burned brightly. "Will you sit?" he asked. "Permit me to build up the fire. You are shaking."

Clemency had believed her shivering had stopped. Now she realized she was genuinely cold. She sat as near to the fire as she could manage without getting in Mr. Wescott's way and clasped her hands in her lap, breathing slowly in the hope this would stop the shaking. She watched Mr. Wescott's hands as he poked the embers into life, for once not dwelling on how attractive they were. They were strong, and capable, and she wished with all her heart her problem was something those hands could solve.

Mr. Wescott sat back on his heels when he was finished. "Are you warm enough?" he asked without looking her way. "Should I call for something hot to drink, or do you require something stronger?"

"I am well," Clemency said. It was not entirely a lie; she felt less shaky now, and most of what was wrong with her, Mr. Wescott could not help. "Thank you."

Mr. Wescott stood and took a seat opposite her. "Something is wrong. You looked—pardon me, but you looked like someone who has seen a glimpse of Hell. Did someone offer you insult?"

Clemency shook her head. "I cannot explain. Please, do not ask. But I must leave now." She stood and walked to the door, but stopped with her hand on the latch. She could not leave by the front door, because she could not guarantee Armand was not near, nor that she would not receive a well-meaning invitation from an acquaintance to meet the famous General de Villiers.

She crossed instead to the windows and examined them. Each had a well-oiled latch, and when she tugged on one, it opened easily. She leaned out. It was cold, but that did not matter. She had to escape.

A hand closed over her wrist. "That is insanity," Mr. Wescott said. "You will freeze before you reach your home. Pray, come with me, and I will call for your carriage."

"No," Clemency cried, wrenching away from him. "I must not—no, *please* do not ask! I would rather freeze to death than remain here another minute."

Mr. Wescott's expression hardened, and Clemency realized too late how he must have taken her words. "Very well," he said. "If your home has a Bounding chamber, I can convey you there. If you are willing to endure my touch."

It felt like a blow to the face. Clemency could bear no more. "That is not what I—" she blurted out. "It is not that. It is not you. There is someone I cannot meet, and the only way to avoid him is Flying. If we had a Bounding chamber—but we do not, I realize it is a sad oversight, forgive me—"

Mr. Wescott put a hand on her arm again, this time gently, not as a restraint or warning. "I will not ask," he said. "But you cannot Fly in that gown, as beautiful as it is. Did you have a wrap, or a cloak?"

Clemency nodded and wiped her eyes. She was crying again and had not noticed. If knowing of Armand's presence was enough to disorder her wits so, she could not imagine what she might do if she met him in person. Fly screaming and laughing hysterically into the night, no doubt.

"Then wait here, and I will return," Mr. Wescott said.

Clemency again sat on the sofa near the fire and stared into its flames, trying to find the good in her situation. Disordered wits aside, learning of Armand's presence in London this way was for the best. She would eventually have to meet him, and she would be prepared when that happened. She would be calm, and she would know what to say, and he would not disturb her world.

Except that was a lie.

Armand's existence was a threat. He had not yet announced what they had been to each other, or she would have heard about it, from Francis or Jane if from no one else. She did not know what that meant. Either he meant never to reveal the truth, or he was waiting for the opportune moment, but in either case she needed to be prepared for the world to learn she had been Coerced into loving him. And that was no very terrible thing, was it? Napoleon had Coerced many into terrible deeds, and this one was only different because it had happened to her, a peer of the realm and an Extraordinary. Most people, the ones she cared about, would understand, and to those of low minds she would be a nine days' wonder, and then her story would be forgotten in the wake of some other scandal.

She closed her eyes and let the fire's heat burn away the last of her tears. She had had a lifetime's worth of scandal when she and Roger were battling for the title. She knew what it was like to be the center of gossip. She hated it, but she could endure. She would have to endure.

The door opened, and Mr. Wescott entered, carrying her cloak. "I still believe this is a mistake," he said, handing it to her.

"Is there anywhere else you can Bound me?" Clemency asked, hope rising within her.

"I fear all the places I know are public businesses, and closed for the night. And I do not know what I had in mind, suggesting I could Bound to your home. Even if you had a Bounding chamber, I cannot Bound to a place I have never seen." Mr. Wescott helped her arrange her cloak around her body. "I was carried away in my desire to assist you, I suppose."

"I am so grateful," Clemency said. "I cannot imagine anyone I would rather have come to my aid than you."

"And yet," Mr. Wescott said, "you cannot tell me who troubles you." His voice was gentle, inviting confidences. He reached up as if to touch her shoulder, hesitated, and straightened a fold of her cloak instead.

Tears rose up in Clemency's eyes again, and she blinked them away. Almost she told him everything. "I," she began, and memories of kissing Armand, of his naked body in her arms, filled her with such shame and humiliation they stopped her tongue. "Forgive me," she whispered. "I truly cannot. But it means more than I can say to have your regard."

Mr. Wescott nodded. "I hope for your sake you are as fast as legend has it," he said, stepping to the window and holding it open.

"Legend? I am legend now?" Clemency asked. The knot of pain in her chest loosened slightly.

"England's fastest, or one of them," Mr. Wescott said with a smile. "I wished to know more about you, and Miss Pilgrim was remarkably forthcoming. I could not tell if you were friends, or rivals."

"Both," Clemency said. "Thank you again, Mr. Wescott."

She climbed through the window and dropped a few feet before catching herself and soaring away. She did not look back to see if he was still watching.

Immediately she knew she had made a mistake. This was far worse than having cold air freezing one's legs and other body parts; the gown's thin fabric fluttered in the wind, chilling her further. Clemency was forced to wrap her cloak tightly around her legs and arms, but its edges caught the wind and slowed her progress, and although she made herself as much like an arrow as she could manage under those conditions and without her goggles, she knew she was not making good time.

By the time she reached her own safe window, she was half frozen and seeing things she was almost certain were not there, air sprites and living rainbows and clouds that bulged as if trying to give birth to monsters. She tumbled in and lay on the floor for a few seconds, breathing in warm air, before Moving the window shut. That was two times in less than a week she had nearly killed herself by Flying improperly clad. She laughed, and it came out sounding like a frog's croak. Perhaps she should petition for female Extraordinary Movers' garb to be a full-body wool suit under wool shirt and trousers. At least then she would not freeze.

She eventually managed to stand and ring for Tatton, removing her cloak and dropping it on the floor near the fire. When Tatton appeared, Clemency had poked the fire into life and was staring into it, this time remembering how helpful Mr. Wescott had been and regretting not telling him the truth. She did not believe he was the sort of man to reject a woman simply because she had been intimate with someone to whom she was not married, but if he was, well, better she know that now than when their...could she call it courtship? When whatever this was between them had progressed further.

Tatton did not act as if she found anything out of place in her mistress's demeanor. As far as she was concerned, Clemency had returned home the usual way and nothing at all strange had happened at Jane's gala. She asked a few questions about the mechanical garden that Clemency answered briefly but politely, and eventually she left, turning down the lamp as she went.

Clemency climbed into bed and curled in on herself. Her earlier terror had vanished—more accurately, it had faded to almost nothing, for Clemency had discovered years before that no fear could be maintained indefinitely without exhausting the body. She closed her eyes and remembered, not Armand, but Mr. Wescott. She had no doubt he had meant what he said about protecting her. The idea sent a shiver through her, not of fear but of happiness. He cared for her, he had built that incredible Flying woman, he found her beautiful—whatever threat Armand posed was as nothing beside that. She had been foolish to permit worry to overcome her. Smiling, she let her wonderful memories carry her off into sleep.

She woke late the next day, for once without feeling guilty about it. Most fashionable people slept until noon at any rate, and she could be fashionable if she chose. She rose and dressed, with Tatton's help, in a comfortable gown; she did not actually need Tatton's assistance, as she had retained her convenables from her War Office days, and those undergarments were not only easy for one person to put on, they were more comfortable than stays. But she enjoyed Tatton's company and did not like to make the woman feel unneeded.

After a meal, she settled in her father's study to go over business with her steward. This was the responsibility she had most dreaded when she first knew her father was dying and intended her to be his heir. She had feared the management of the estate would be too much for her. It had been a pleasant surprise to discover she understood what Baxter laid in front of her, and Baxter, for his part, treated her like a countess and not like a child. It was not exactly pleasant business, but it was not a chore, either.

She finished her estate business by three o'clock and left the study feeling more cheerful than before. Three o'clock was too early for tea, and too late to go Flying; perhaps she could read to Mercy. She had not yet seen her sister that day, and she wished to tell her—not about Armand, of course, but about the many mechanicals, particularly the Extraordinary Mover.

As she neared the drawing room, she heard voices, male and female, and saw the door was slightly ajar. She could not imagine what man might pay them a visit, unless it was Francis, and in that case someone would have notified her. She had forgotten he would have realized she was no longer at the gala, and with some chagrin she hastened her steps. She hated lying to him, but she could not tell him the truth, so she would have to determine a story that would satisfy him without being an outright lie.

She pushed the door open, and stopped, once more rooted to the spot. Mama looked up and said, "Oh, Clemency, dear, only look who accepted my invitation! He tells me you were acquainted in France— my dear, why did you not say?"

Mama's companion rose from the sofa beside her. "I am certain Lady Ashford has many memories of France," General Armand de Villiers said. "I hope I am not one she has forgotten."

CHAPTER 17

IN WHICH AN UNKNOWN THREAT LOOMS

Numb lips prevented Clemency from speaking. That Armand would dare come here— She looked past him at Mama, whose delighted expression told her how Armand had managed his infiltration of her home. Mama was exactly the kind of woman who would be most charmed by Armand's demeanor and his tragic, heroic story.

He looked exactly as she remembered, his black hair neatly combed in the latest fashion, his shoulders made broader by his well-cut coat, his warm brown eyes crinkling at the corners as he smiled. And his smile—it still dimpled on one side, and for a moment she remembered how she had loved his dimple and felt like vomiting. His regard of her was as warm as his eyes, warm and admiring as if they were any man and woman who might find one another attractive. Armand's scent, the cloying, thick smell of roses, filled the air, and a tight knot of tension twisted her stomach again.

She took a seat more rapidly than was graceful as her legs suddenly refused to support her. "General de Villiers," she said. "I did not realize you were acquainted with the Dowager Countess."

"We were introduced at the theater by my good friend Lord Winder," Armand said, resuming his seat. The knot tightened. His voice was the same, too, barely accented and deep and resonant, the kind of voice that made any woman's heart melt. "I cannot credit that she is your mother, Lady Ashford. She is far too young to have a daughter your age."

"Oh, General, that is too much!" Mama giggled and playfully slapped his wrist. "You are a charmer, that is true. You ought to turn your charm on my daughter!"

Clemency's hand clenched on the arm of the divan. "I am certain General de Villiers knows what behavior is appropriate," she said. "I understand you arrived in London last week, General. How long do you intend to stay?"

"For shame, Clemency! One would almost think you wished the dear general gone from our fair city!" Mama exclaimed.

"I am certain Lady Ashford meant nothing of the sort," Armand said with another dimpled smile. "I intend an indefinite stay, Lady Ashford. London has so many pleasures to offer."

The smile deepened, and the look in his eyes told Clemency clearly what pleasures he had in mind. The slightest hint of confusion crept into her thoughts. Armand had to know she was no longer Coerced and did not care for him, and he must also realize how she would feel about having been his Coerced lover. Yet he was behaving as if their love had been real, and as if Clemency desired his attentions as much as he wished to bestow them.

"It seems all of London agrees with you," she said. "I have heard you are quite popular."

"Ah, I am a novelty," Armand said, casting his eyes down modestly. "It is that I was Coerced, you see, and broke my Coercion. Almost no one has done that."

His words felt like a blow, an implication that *she* was not strong-willed enough to overcome what Napoleon had done to her. "How astonishing," she managed. "How is it done, pray?"

Armand shrugged. "I cannot explain the details. They are complex. But in essence, I became aware of what I truly desired, and saw the difference between that and the desires Napoleon imposed upon me. Then it was merely a matter of reaching for the truth."

"I declare that is so very confusing," Mama trilled. "I am certain I could not manage it."

"Thank heaven it is nothing you will ever need fear," Armand said. "Napoleon Coerced many women to—but that is indelicate, and I shall not mention it." He flicked a glance at Clemency, and this time his smile was wicked enough to make her blood run cold. Her confusion over his behavior vanished. Oh, he knew well how she felt about him, and he intended to make use of it. She could not imagine what he might do, but she was suddenly convinced he did not mean her well.

"But enough of such talk," Armand said. "I fear I must leave you for another engagement, but may I request the pleasure of your company as I go, Lady Ashford? We have much to reminisce about—memories of France, of course."

Clemency almost turned him down. Spending any time in his company was abhorrent to her. But she realized, if he intended her harm, she ought to know what he had in mind. So she made herself smile and offered him her hand. "Permit me to accompany you to the door, General."

Armand kept a slow pace as they left the drawing room. He tucked Clemency's hand around his arm and said, "So. You left last night before we could meet. I was terribly disappointed."

"I had another engagement," Clemency said. "And it is not as if we have anything to say to one another."

"No?" Armand's eyebrows raised in pretended surprise. "Well, you may be correct. Words never played much part in what we did together, did they?" He rested his hand over hers and squeezed it lightly.

Clemency jerked her hand away. "Stop," she said, the word rasping in her throat. "Stop it. I was made to love you, and you know it. I would never have done those things were I not Coerced."

"Coercion cannot prompt that kind of passion," Armand said. "I never would have guessed an Englishwoman of rank might behave with such abandon, but I welcomed it."

Clemency slapped him. The sharp sound rang out in the silent hall. "I was Coerced," she repeated. "You may tell yourself whatever lies you wish, but the fact remains that Napoleon gave me to you like a prize, and he made me go willingly. Now that I am free of Coercion, I remember those days with revulsion."

Armand did not react to the blow. Instead, he smiled, as pleasantly as if she had kissed him instead. "You are mine," he said. "I am the first man to bed you, and I intend to be the only man who ever will. I can wait for you to realize the truth."

Enraged, Clemency tried to Move him, to fling him against the wall and then over the balcony to hang upside down until he screamed. Armand jerked, flailed his arms, and took a step backward, swiftly regaining his balance. His smile broadened. "Your talent is useless against my fortitude," he said. "I resisted Coercion; why would you believe even the strongest Mover could affect me?"

"Get out of my house," Clemency said, breathing heavily in her fury. "Get out, and do not return."

A door farther down the hall opened, drawing both their attention. Roger emerged and strode in their direction. His steps slowed as he neared them. "Who's this, Clem?" he asked. "One of your suitors?"

Clemency drew in a breath, trying to calm herself. Armand was looking at her, his expression mocking, and Clemency saw the dilemma she faced: introduce Armand, and behave as if he was not her worst enemy, or refuse to introduce him and make Roger believe something underhanded was afoot. She let out the breath. "Roger, this is General de Villiers of the French army. General, my brother, the Honorable Mr. Northrup."

Roger's face twisted in a snarl that lasted barely a second, and Clemency remembered too late how much he hated being referred to merely as Honorable. As swiftly, his expression returned to a calm indifference. "Pleased to make your acquaintance," he said to Armand, and without waiting for Armand to respond, said, "I'm off to the club, not that you care."

"I hope you have a pleasant evening," Clemency said.

Roger saluted her with a casual, impudent wave and sauntered away toward the stairs.

When he was gone, Armand said, "Your brother does not respect you, I warrant."

"My family is none of your business," Clemency said. "Leave now, before I have you thrown out."

"You would not cause such a scandal," Armand said.

"Would I not?" Clemency said.

Smiling, Armand bowed, a perfectly correct gesture that felt as if he mocked her. Then he sauntered away, his gait and demeanor exactly matching Roger's, down the hall to the stairs.

Clemency watched until he disappeared and waited for the sound of the front door closing. Then she walked with a heavy tread to her study, feeling as if she were encased in lead, dragging her down and preventing her from Flying. She sat behind the desk and buried her face in her hands. He meant to make her his doxy again—well, that was impossible. She was still the Countess of Ashford, and he was a talentless nobody. Let him do his worst. She would endure.

She wished she were not so gifted at lying to herself.

⁂

TWO DAYS PASSED IN WHICH CLEMENCY HID IN EMERAUDE HOUSE and pretended Armand was in France. She heard nothing of his activities, though she guessed Mama saw him when she was in Lord Winder's company. None of her friends called on her, and she did not go Flying, though the public trials were rapidly approaching and she should practice. No one noticed that anything was amiss except Mercy, and Mercy, rather than teasing her secrets out of her, only looked at her on occasion with a curious expression and left Clemency to her solitude. Clemency was too grateful not to be pestered to see anything peculiar in her sister's behavior.

Late on the second day, a note arrived. Clemency's heart leaped to see the familiar blocky printing. But Mr. Wescott had nothing personal to convey: *Mr. Rutledge would like to meet with you tomorrow morning at my home*, the note read. *I apologize for the short notice, though Mr. Rutledge does not. My guess is that he is a busy man who enjoys putting others at a disadvantage so he may unbalance them. I will remain if you wish.*

Clemency considered the message. She did wish Mr. Wescott to be present during her meeting with Mr. Rutledge, and not only because she regretted leaving him so abruptly on Tuesday night; he would be an ally against someone Clemency felt increasingly disinclined to trust. She wrote a swift reply and dispatched a footman to Hanover Square. She would have to tell Mr. Rutledge the truth about her night flights, and the idea felt a little like being a child confessing the theft of a pie from the kitchen. *That* was an attitude she needed to shed. If she behaved like a child, he would treat her like one.

She rose early the next morning after a restless night and met Mercy in the dining room. "But you have eaten already?" she exclaimed, seeing the empty plate in front of her sister. "You are an early riser, true, but this is exceptional even for you."

"I slept poorly, and decided I did not wish to lie abed remembering awful dreams," Mercy said. "And then there is such news—oh, read it yourself, I cannot bear to speak of it."

Puzzled, Clemency took up the newspaper that lay open next to Mercy's seat. In the top center of the front page, exactly where it could not go unnoticed, were the words BOMB STRIKES VAUXHALL GARDENS and, beneath that line, *2 killed in blast*. She blinked, and set the newspaper down. "They must have attacked when few were present," she said, feeling instantly the inanity of the statement.

"Early this morning, after the entertainment was well over—but *why* would anyone do such a thing?" Mercy exclaimed. "And no one has yet to claim responsibility. It is horrid enough to imagine some group wishing to force the government to act in their favor, but how much more horrid to picture a lone person or group of people who kill for no reason at all?"

"Someone will stop them. I have to believe that," Clemency said. She reflected silently that if Mr. Rutledge had the power he claimed, she might be the one to help stop the bombers.

She Flew to Hanover Square and waited on the doorstep, jigging in her nervousness. If it was not nerves over meeting Mr. Rutledge, it was nerves over seeing Mr. Wescott again. She had spent a restless night unable to make a decision as to whether to tell him about Armand. In one moment, she imagined him supporting her, telling her she should not feel ashamed; in the next moment, he spurned her in horror and disgust. She leaped from one possibility to the other, believing she had settled on one decision only for the other decision to appear suddenly reasonable and right. By morning, she had not come to a conclusion. She told herself she would see how the day unfolded just as Hammond opened the door and bowed her in.

Miss Wescott was alone in the drawing room, reading. When Clemency hesitated on the threshold, she put her book down and said, "Please, join me. Colin is a late riser."

Embarrassed at her presumption, Clemency stammered, "I did not mean—Mr. Wescott only said 'morning,' and I believed—I beg your pardon for intruding."

"It is no intrusion. I enjoy speaking with you," Miss Wescott said. Today her gaze was direct and acute, not unfocused, and she displayed none of the distress Clemency had seen in her on her last visit. Clemency recalled what else had happened on that last visit, and her cheeks warmed. Miss Wescott smiled, an impish expression that again made her look younger than her age. "I am so glad. I will not tell secrets, of course, but I feel your happiness, and it is a marvelous thing."

"Can anyone keep a secret from you?" Clemency asked, laughing to cover her embarrassment.

Miss Wescott tilted her head, and her eyes narrowed in thought. "If they feel something, and I have no context for it—no speech, either their own or another's—then it is more difficult to know what they conceal. But I always know when someone lies, and if I am clever, I can discover what that lie conceals. I did not know you were Lady Ashford, for example, only that Miss Northrup was not your true name. Not the name you know yourself to be, not anymore."

"And you feel my emotions as if they are your own."

Miss Wescott did not answer at first. She bit her lower lip as if uncertain. "Sometimes that is true. I feel everything—I can't not feel the emotions of others—but now I can tell the difference between myself and everyone else. It is a matter of coherence...oh, but I cannot explain. You do not see what I see."

"I cannot explain to you what it is like to Fly, either," Clemency said, "and I imagine it is for the same reason."

"You have it exactly." Miss Wescott leaned back in her seat. "But you do like Colin, yes?"

Clemency blushed. "I do." Speaking her feelings to this young woman seemed the most natural thing in the world.

"There, that is not so terrible a thing, is it?" Miss Wescott's smile returned. "I will not tell him. I am very good at keeping secrets, which is odd considering that I am also good at ferreting secrets out, don't you agree?"

"Perhaps that is a good quality for someone who knows others' secrets," Clemency said.

"I agree. I will remember that. And I will not tell anyone of your anger." Miss Wescott raised her head as the door opened. "Colin, you should have told Lady Ashford a time. She might have waited an hour or more, and that is simply tedious."

"Not if I have you to talk to," Clemency said. The more she knew of the odd young woman, the more inclined she was to pursue the connection, and not only because Miss Wescott believed Clemency was angry when she was not. Not at all. "Mr. Wescott, I apologize for intruding so early."

"Not at all," Mr. Wescott said. He was again impeccably dressed, and again his clothes looked not quite right on his powerful frame. "I'm afraid Mr. Rutledge did not specify a time, either. More of his desire to keep you unsettled, and therefore in an uncomfortable position."

"Either he is quite powerful within the government, or he is a bully," Clemency said. "I consider myself forewarned."

Mr. Wescott smiled. "I would like to tell you that you have nothing to fear, but I don't know what to expect from the man. If he does attempt to bully you, I suggest you end the meeting and leave. You are the one with the power because you are the one with the knowledge."

Miss Wescott stood, bringing her book with her. "I will leave you now, as I have nothing to do with this meeting."

Clemency's heart leaped at the idea of being alone with Mr. Wescott, and then it began beating hard and fast with the knowledge that she had yet to make a decision. But then another idea occurred to her. "Wait," she told Miss Wescott. "You should stay."

"Why is that?" Mr. Wescott asked.

"She knows when someone lies," Clemency said. "Miss Wescott, would it be too much of an imposition to ask you to listen to my conversation with Mr. Rutledge? It might keep him honest."

"If he knows an Extraordinary Discerner is present, do you mean?" Miss Wescott looked briefly thoughtful. "I believe I can manage that. Give me a moment, I wish to change my gown."

When she was gone, Mr. Wescott said, "That would not have occurred to me."

"I hope I did not overstep," Clemency said.

Shaking his head, Mr. Wescott said, "No, not at all. I fear I may treat Lydia with too much care sometimes. I remember all she has endured, and it makes me cautious of her, and possibly that means my protectiveness is overprotectiveness. I forget that what she has endured has made her strong as well as weak."

Clemency did not know how to answer that. Her motives, now that she considered them, were likely selfish; she was afraid of Mr. Rutledge, and she wished for a defense against him, even if that defense was in the person of an occasionally infirm young woman. "She will do me a great favor by her mere presence."

"Indeed." Mr. Wescott seated himself opposite Clemency, disappointing her. She was aware of the empty seats on either side of her and wished he had chosen one of those instead. He leaned forward, resting his elbows on his knees in an informal way, and said, "You seem recovered from your distress. I hope this means your situation has improved."

"It—yes, and no." Clemency opened her mouth to tell him about Armand, about having been Coerced, and considered how quickly Miss Wescott might change her clothes. This was not a thing she wished to share with anyone except Mr. Wescott, and even speaking the truth to him filled her with dread. "I wish I could explain myself, but it is not something pleasant, and I dislike dwelling on it. Please forgive me."

"You owe me no explanations," Mr. Wescott said. Clemency imagined the faintest hint of disappointment in his voice, and she opened her mouth to protest further. But Mr. Wescott overrode her. "Tell me, or not, as you choose, but understand that I will support you, whatever your secret turns out to be."

Now Clemency was grateful he was not sitting beside her, because the depth of emotion in his expression and his words made her long to kiss him again, and that was a bad idea when his sister might return at any moment. "Someday I will tell you," she said, promising herself to make it true.

The door opened, and both Clemency and Mr. Wescott sat upright. But it was Hammond, not Miss Wescott. "Mr. Rutledge," the butler said, and made way for their guest to enter.

CHAPTER 18

IN WHICH CLEMENCY RECEIVES AN ULTIMATUM

C lemency had expected someone tall, based on Mr. Wescott's comments on Mr. Rutledge's size. Now she saw her imaginings were completely inadequate. Mr. Rutledge was indeed tall, much taller than six feet, Clemency guessed, but he was also heavily built, not quite fat, but bulky in the way some men develop as they reach middle age. He was dressed impeccably, but plainly, in coat and pantaloons that she might have called unfashionable had they not been so nondescript; unfashionable would have drawn the eye, and she judged Mr. Rutledge would despite his size draw little notice for his appearance.

"Mr. Rutledge, please have a seat," Mr. Wescott said. He did not offer to introduce the man to Clemency, and Clemency guessed Mr. Wescott had not yet divulged her identity to Mr. Rutledge. That he had been so protective of her reputation warmed her heart.

Mr. Rutledge's first words, however, dispelled that warmth. "Lady Ashford," he said, his dark brown eyes regarding her as if he could see through to her heart. "I did not imagine you might be the Extraordinary Mover involved."

"You recognize me," Clemency said.

Mr. Rutledge nodded. "My wife, before we married, followed the progress of your fight for your title with some avidity. She firmly believes in the rights of women and spoke eloquently on your behalf—she is an Extraordinary Seer and has much influence with the peers and gentry of England. Then, when Napoleon reappeared earlier this year, she was called on by the War Office to assist in his defeat, and I understand many of her Dreams related to your service."

Clemency's mouth fell open. "You are married to—I apologize, I recognized the name, but I did not realize there was a connection. Mrs. Rutledge was of great help to all of us." That this imposing man, who gave Clemency the impression of being an emotionless force of nature, should do anything so prosaic as marry struck Clemency as absurd. But she had met Mrs. Rutledge once or twice, and remembered her as a passionately driven woman who pursued her goals with single-minded fervor, and she supposed if Mr. Rutledge were to marry anyone, it made sense that it would be that woman.

"She will be pleased to know you remember her," Mr. Rutledge said. He leaned forward slightly. "Mr. Wescott informs me that you have knowledge concerning the bomb that detonated over the Thames last week. Do you intend to confess your culpability in the matter?"

Mr. Wescott twitched, but said nothing. Clemency, whose fears had told her to expect such an accusation, did not react. "If you intend to make me the villain before you have even heard my story," she said, "I do not believe we have anything to say to one another."

To her surprise, Mr. Rutledge smiled—a thin twist of the lips merely, but it warmed his eyes and made him seem finally human. "My apologies," he said. "Weak souls are of no use to me when lives are at stake. I did not believe you were the sort to wilt under attack, but I wished to see for myself what kind of woman you are."

Clemency regarded him steadily, though her heart had begun to beat more rapidly. "And now that I have passed your test, perhaps you are interested in my story—unless you wish to continue your game?"

The smile broadened into a real expression of amusement. "And that has put me in my place, right enough," Mr. Rutledge said. "Very well, Lady Ashford. Tell me what happened the night of the sixteenth."

Clemency straightened her spine. She glanced once at Mr. Wescott, who after that one restless movement had stilled. He gave her no indication of what he believed she should say, but his presence steadied her. "Some of my story that bears on what concerns you is not the business of anyone but myself," she said. "I will tell you because the details will explain how I came to be within reach of the bombers, but I expect you not to share these facts with anyone else."

"You are not in a position to make demands, Lady Ashford." Mr. Rutledge settled more deeply in his chair, which creaked under his weight. "I will use what you tell me to stop these men, and I do not need your permission to do so."

Clemency folded her hands in her lap and stared at him, saying nothing. For several seconds, they sat in silence. Clemency's heart continued to thump painfully in her chest, but she felt no fear; instead, she felt the giddy excitement she always felt before a race, when her whole body sped up in preparation.

The door opened, and Mr. Rutledge turned to face Miss Wescott in the first uncontrolled movement Clemency had seen him make. "This is private, miss," he said.

"Mr. Rutledge, this is my sister, Miss Wescott," Mr. Wescott said. "She is an Extraordinary Discerner and has agreed to sit in on this conversation at Lady Ashford's request."

"So much for privacy," Mr. Rutledge said. "You have no trust in me, Lady Ashford?"

"Should I have? The first thing you did upon arrival was accuse me of detonating a bomb within the city," Clemency shot back. "I believe Miss Wescott will keep you honest, and I *do* trust her."

Mr. Rutledge's eyes narrowed. He again shifted his weight, making the chair creak more loudly. "I intend to deal honestly with you," he said, "and I do not need to be compelled to it by a Discerner. You realize I could take her presence as an admission of guilt on your part? If you are innocent, you have nothing to fear."

"Mr. Rutledge, I am the veteran of a very nasty legal battle. Do not tell me that innocence is a protection." Clemency leaned forward. "You are a mystery, sir, and you have never to my knowledge disclosed what gives you the authority to ask me questions on any subject, let alone this bombing. If I am willing not to pry into your affairs, I hardly think you have the right to question the precautions I take to protect my legal rights."

For several seconds, Mr. Rutledge continued to regard Clemency in silence. Finally, he rubbed his chin with one massive hand and said, "Very well. Understand that if you prove guilty, your title will not protect you."

"I understand." Clemency drew in a deep breath. "I have since my return to London from the War Office made a habit of Flying through the city by night, using my talent to stop criminals from assaulting and robbing citizens. That is not a thing I would like made public, Mr. Rutledge."

"Of course." Mr. Rutledge waved a hand as if to request her to continue.

Clemency quickly told the story of the night in question, though she did not reveal that she had been knocked briefly unconscious when the bomb exploded. Mr. Rutledge shot a glance at Mr. Wescott when Clemency revealed that the bomb was attached to his music box, but did not interrupt her. The story was not long, to her surprise. When she finished, Mr. Rutledge said, "You say that the Scorcher was female?"

Confused, Clemency nodded. "I don't see how that is relevant."

"Leave that to me, Lady Ashford." Mr. Rutledge rubbed his chin again. "Did any of the others have talent?"

"None that they displayed in front of me, Mr. Rutledge."

"I see. Then they were unlikely to have been Bounders or Movers, or they would have used those talents against you, and I do not believe, if more of them were Scorchers, that only one would have attacked you with fire." His eyes focused on something past her left shoulder, but Clemency guessed he was merely deep in thought, and she did not turn to see what fascinated him.

"There has been no report of talent being used in any of the other bombings," Mr. Wescott said.

Mr. Rutledge's gaze fixed on him. "I am not at liberty to discuss my investigation," he said. "But...no. And yet a Scorcher attacked you, Lady Ashford."

Clemency said nothing. She had no idea what any of it meant, except... "It seems each target is increasingly important or public," she said. "Is that typical?"

"Again, I cannot say," Mr. Rutledge said. "But I am grateful you came forward, Lady Ashford. Until speaking with you, I believed the bombings happened at random—you heard about Vauxhall Gardens early this morning?"

Clemency nodded.

"The bomb you deflected did not fit the pattern—not that I am admitting there is a pattern." One eyelid drooped in a wink. Clemency suppressed a smile. "Now that I know it was intended for St. Paul's, much becomes clear. Your information is most helpful."

He looked at Miss Wescott, whose eyes were slightly unfocused. "Am I an honest man, then?"

"As honest as you permit yourself to be," Miss Wescott said promptly. "I understand about keeping secrets. I am very good at that myself."

"I will remember," Mr. Rutledge said, in what felt to Clemency like a sinister way to speak such an innocuous phrase. He stood, prompting Mr. Wescott to stand as well. "Lady Ashford, I must insist you give up chasing criminals by night. It is dangerous work."

"Because I am female?" Clemency said, irritated.

"Because you have responsibilities that would be abdicated were you to be injured or killed in your nighttime activities," Mr. Rutledge said. "Leave such behavior to others."

"What others?" Clemency demanded. "It is not as if there is an organization dedicated to preventing crime. Criminals are punished if they are caught, true, but that is small comfort to those who are hurt or robbed or murdered so punishment is warranted. And you cannot force me not to act."

"I can reveal your identity if you do not stop," Mr. Rutledge said.

Clemency gasped. She leapt to her feet. "I told you the truth so your investigation would not be hindered. How dare you turn my generosity back on me?"

"I agreed I would not tell anyone involved in my investigation how you came by your information," Mr. Rutledge said. "I did not say I might not reveal it for some other purpose. I would be acting in your best interests."

Her hands shook with fury, and she balled them into fists to still them. "To the devil with my best interests," she said. "You are not my parent and you are not my superior."

"I am someone who is concerned about the lawlessness endemic to London. Your continued actions will interfere with my plans. If I discover you remain active hunting criminals, I *will* tell the world." Mr. Rutledge's dark eyes were as cold as Clemency had ever seen on anything human.

Clemency stared him down, clenching her jaw to hold back stronger words. Mr. Rutledge nodded politely to her. "Your information is very welcome," he said. "Good day, Lady Ashford. Mr. Wescott, Miss Wescott." His gaze lingered on Miss Wescott for a few seconds, and then he turned and left, shutting the door behind him.

Clemency tried to calm her breathing, but her whole body shook beyond what she was capable of controlling. She made herself sit and clasp her hands tightly in her lap. Give up her nocturnal hunting, just because some stranger insisted on it? A talentless stranger who could not possibly disrupt crime the way an Extraordinary Mover could?

"It would do no good to hit him," Miss Wescott said.

"I would not have hit him," Clemency and Mr. Wescott said simultaneously. They looked at one another, startled, and then both laughed, Mr. Wescott in amusement, Clemency in embarrassment.

"He told the truth. He means to protect you," Miss Wescott said. Her voice sounded strained, and Clemency realized how her anger must be affecting the young woman. She focused on breathing, a calming exercise she had learned in her War Office days, letting her fury rush out of her with every breath. Eventually, her hands stopped shaking, and she could look at Miss Wescott without embarrassment.

But Miss Wescott did not appear disturbed. Her gaze was acute, not unfocused, and she was watching her brother rather than Clemency. "He knows more than he said, obviously," she told Mr. Wescott, "but it is true that the bombings are escalating. He fears for the day when the bombers start targeting people rather than buildings."

"But they would not need my timing mechanism to attack people," Mr. Wescott said.

"They would if they wished to control where and when they attack," Clemency said. "Throwing a bomb into a carriage risks the bomber being apprehended. Setting a bomb at, for example, Whitehall would permit the bomber to kill the First Lord of the Admiralty, again for example, while not being anywhere near at the time."

Mr. Wescott scowled. "I would like to get my hands on these murderers who have made me indirectly complicit in their crimes."

"I wish I had been the one questioned," Miss Wescott said, sounding plaintive. "I might have made him reveal the pattern, and then we would know where the next target is, and Lady Ashford might stop them."

"I?" Clemency exclaimed. "But Mr. Rutledge said—"

"It matters more to you to see justice done than it does to him," Miss Wescott said. "It is what the anger fuels, the desire to stop others being hurt. Mr. Rutledge does not understand that. He believes you are a bored countess who seeks out danger because it is a thrill. That is why he wishes to control you. But you are more than that."

"I am not angry anymore, Miss Wescott," Clemency said. "I simply wish to do some good with my talent."

Miss Wescott closed her mouth in a firm line, the very picture of someone deliberately not commenting. Before Clemency could challenge her on her assertion, Mr. Wescott said, "Lady Ashford, Mr. Rutledge is wrong about your motivations, but he is not wrong that your activities are dangerous. I will not tell you what to do, but perhaps you could consider carefully how you use your talent?"

Clemency controlled the impulse to shout at him; he had not insulted her by suggesting she was weak, and he had not told her to stop hunting criminals. "I am always careful," she said, not dwelling on the shock of falling into the Thames and that terrible frozen flight home. "And I will not be ordered about by someone to whom I owe no allegiance. I will simply have to be more cautious so I am not discovered."

"I suppose that is the best I can hope for," Mr. Wescott said, so ruefully it startled a laugh out of Clemency.

"That is two mechanicals that have been used in the creation of bombs," she said. "And yet you did not say there had been another theft."

"There has not been," Mr. Wescott said. "I presume the villains have studied my work well enough to replicate it, given the attack on Vauxhall Gardens." His jaw clenched, making him look as villainous as any bomber intent on destruction. "I cannot believe anyone would wish to turn an innocent creation into something deadly."

"People are selfish and cruel," Miss Wescott said. Her lips looked pinched, as if she were in pain. "They steal and hurt and kill because they see only themselves and not others."

"Oh, but not everyone is evil," Clemency protested.

Miss Wescott turned her haunted gaze on Clemency. "Some choose to be other than what they are, and they choose it over and over again until they are the sum of those choices. But even they feel greed and powerful self-interest. They simply decide to act otherwise."

Clemency did not know how to respond. For the first time, she considered what it must be like to be an Extraordinary Discerner not in terms of how others' emotions would overwhelm one, but from the perspective of never being fooled by the white lies society depended on. That Miss Wescott was not jaded beyond belief struck Clemency as a miracle—or perhaps she was jaded, and hid it well.

Miss Wescott closed her eyes. "Colin," she said, "either you must calm yourself or I will have to leave."

Mr. Wescott's expression immediately became remorseful. "I beg your pardon. I suppose you are correct in your assessment; I was being self-indulgent in my anger. Forgive me."

"I know it is difficult to remember. I never blame you. I never blame anyone." She opened her eyes, and this time, she smiled. "There are those capable of imposing their emotions on a Discerner, intending to overwhelm her, but to me that is no different from anything else I feel. So I consider myself lucky in that respect."

"That sounds cruel," Clemency said. "Like kicking a man's broken leg."

"I have better defenses against such things than an ordinary Discerner. But I did say that people are like that." Miss Wescott rose.

"I feel a great desire to play the harp now. It is how I distinguish between emotions, by playing what I feel."

"Mr. Wescott says you are an accomplished musician," Clemency said. "Perhaps you will play for me someday—unless it is too personal."

Miss Wescott's smile was unforced, with no hint of her previous melancholy. "Not at all. I dream of being able to evoke the emotions I feel in others. It would be a beautiful thing to be a Coercer if one elicited happiness or joy, don't you agree?"

The memory of passionately embracing Armand, of how happy she had been, struck Clemency like a brick to the face. Miss Wescott gasped and put a hand to her heart, a gesture that might have seemed affected had she not gripped her gown as if trying to stanch a mortal wound. "Why does that—" she began, and then she ran from the room, slamming the door behind her.

Clemency and Mr. Wescott exchanged startled glances. "I—please excuse my sister," Mr. Wescott said. "I do not know what prompted that."

"I cannot say," Clemency said, though she was all too certain she knew why Miss Wescott had fled.

"It was something you felt," Mr. Wescott said. He shook his head. "Do not elaborate. Your privacy is your own."

"Thank you." Her earlier impulse to explain about Armand had withered and died. There was nothing she could say that would explain the terrible tangle her memories made of her emotions. How she could remember loving Armand as if that was a natural emotion and at the same time feel revulsion over those same memories, she could not understand, and if she could not, what hope had anyone else?

"I meant to ask," she said, wishing to change the conversation, "if you and Miss Wescott would consent to dine with me and my family on Monday night? And perhaps Miss Wescott will agree to play for us. We have no harp, but we have a very fine pianoforte."

"We would be delighted," Mr. Wescott said. He sounded as relieved to steer the conversation elsewhere as Clemency was. "We can congratulate you on your victory."

"My victory?" For a moment, Clemency was puzzled. Then she remembered. "Oh! The public trials. I had nearly forgotten they are on

Monday as well." She laughed. "Perhaps I should be more diligent in my preparations. I am sure to do poorly if I cannot concentrate."

"Then we will talk of how you will improve next time," Mr. Wescott said with a wink, and Clemency laughed again.

She bade him goodbye on the doorstep and again waved as she ascended, watching him until he was a tiny figure below. Her anger over Mr. Rutledge's demand and his dismissive treatment of her had faded. She owed him no obedience, and she refused to permit him to threaten her. She would simply have to be more circumspect in her activities.

But that was something for a distant future. She had more immediate worries, namely the need to perform well at the trials. With a quick roll in midair, she straightened her body and drew in her arms to make herself an arrow. Mr. Wescott's comment about her being a legend both thrilled and unnerved her. Legends had more to live up to than ordinary folk.

Well, she would simply have to prove herself—to herself, if to no one else. She shot away through the sky toward home.

CHAPTER 19

IN WHICH THE PUBLIC TRIALS END IN AN UNEXPECTED SURPRISE

Clemency was fond of Hyde Park, of its many trails for riding or strolling with a companion, of its trees and grassy swards. At this time of year, the trees were almost entirely bare of leaves, and the park took on a different kind of beauty, stark and angular and smelling of wood smoke. From above, the paths traced out straight lines that intersected with one another in geometric splendor, with the curve at the western end of Rotten Row so slight only someone Flying above would perceive it. Usually, when Clemency Flew past, the throngs of people moving along those paths seemed like ants intent on bringing food or news back to their queen.

On the last Monday of every month, however, Hyde Park was cleared for the Moving public trials, and Flying overhead was prohibited if one was not competing. Clemency and Mercy traveled via carriage to the park, with Mercy's new chair strapped to the back where a footman would otherwise ride. The carriage stopped in Belgravia, near the eastern end of Rotten Row, and Clemency removed the chair and settled Mercy in it.

"Such a beautiful day," Mercy said. "It is not even terribly cold."

Clemency tilted her head back to look at the sky. It was the clear, cloudless blue of fine glass, with the slightest of breezes barely stirring the air, nothing that would hinder a race. "I hope you will not be bored, dearest," she told Mercy. "I am only competing in two events, and there is always some delay between competitors' runs as they clear the courses."

"I enjoy watching the juggling, though I admit what I enjoy is the moment when the Movers lose control of their objects and they all rain down around them." Mercy giggled. "The men in particular always look so chagrined. Why is it that male Movers feel more shame at losing than females?"

"That is not entirely true, because all Movers are extremely competitive and enjoy testing their skills. I believe the men feel more entitled to make a great show of their failings. Possibly it eases the pain of losing." Clemency steered Mercy's chair wide of a pair of men dressed in Extraordinary Mover's garb, close-fitting short coats and pantaloons and soft-soled shoes. The men floated as Clemency did, a few inches off the ground; the shoes were designed for speed and agility in Flying, not for durability, and the hard earth of the paths would quickly destroy them.

Clemency eyed their pantaloons with some irritation. Her divided skirt probably contained four times the fabric their garb did, and it would drag on her. And yet she would likely still outrace those two, so she did not feel complaining would do any good.

They began to pass the distance trials, with crowds of Movers milling about behind a long line of competitors. Though there were easily a hundred people there, with a few hundred more watching, no one spoke, and the only noises were faint grunts of effort and the occasional *thunk* of a wooden ball hitting the ground.

Clemency watched, but did not stop. She had competed in the distance trials, in which a competitor Moved a single colored wooden ball as far from herself as possible without losing control of it, many times as a young woman, but her range had not changed in the last four years and it had never been more than passable. There was no point in competing when one had no chance of winning and nothing to prove to anyone.

Mercy gripped the armrests. "There is Mr. Daubney."

Clemency stopped and searched the crowd. Francis was some

twenty yards distant, standing with the other Movers in the line. Clemency followed the line of his gaze to where a yellow wooden ball Moved slowly away from Francis in a smooth line. "His control is excellent," she said, suppressing a pang of jealousy. This was not a trial in which they were rivals, and she should be pleased for his success.

"I did not realize how great a range he has," Mercy said. Francis' ball was well ahead of his next closest rival's and showed no wobble or slowing. "Surely he must win!"

"I do hope so," Clemency said.

They watched for a few more minutes until the yellow ball finally dropped. A young man darted across the field to where it lay and hammered a wooden stake to mark its place. A strip of fabric with Francis' surname on it fluttered in the light breeze. Francis strode away without speaking to the Movers on either side of him, though as they remained very still in concentration, he likely did not wish to disrupt them.

Clemency Moved Mercy's chair off the path and rolled it toward Francis. Immediately she saw what must be the one flaw in Mr. Wescott's creation; the slim wheels balked at the rougher ground of the lawn, and Mercy let out a small cry as the chair bumped and jostled her. "I apologize—here, I will make a change," Clemency said, and Moved the chair an inch off the ground to float beside her. "If you latch the wheels in place, the balance will be perfect."

Mercy did so. She gripped the arm rests loosely to steady herself, though Clemency's control was perfect. Clemency was accustomed to Mercy's disquiet when the chair lifted off the ground, and took no offense.

"Mr. Daubney sees us," Mercy said. "We must congratulate him."

"He has not won yet," Clemency said, but she scanned the field and observed that Francis' marker was a good ten yards ahead of his nearest competitor. Even so, it was bad luck among Movers to assume victory before the final trial was over.

"I see you chose not to challenge me," Francis called out when he neared. "Ready to pay your forfeit?"

"I intend to beat you on the Tower run," Clemency said with a smile. "We will not talk of forfeits until then."

"Ah, such confidence." Francis bowed to Mercy. "Lady Mercy. Dare I hope you will cheer me on?"

"You present me with a dilemma, Mr. Daubney," Mercy said. "Sisterly devotion must needs win out. But I hope you run a close second."

Francis laughed and clutched his chest. "You wound me, Lady Mercy. At the very least, tell me you are impressed by my performance in the distance trials?"

"Oh, very impressed, sir," Mercy said. "But surely you need not concern yourself with also impressing would-be employers?"

"It is true the public trials act as a reference for Movers wishing to be paid to employ their talents. For me, it is more a matter of gaining consequence among my fellows. And of course it demonstrates my willingness to be approached for charity work, such as at Covent Garden." Francis' smile disappeared. "The site has been cleared, and they have begun construction again. Such a waste of resources, not to mention the lives lost."

"Forgive me for being so selfish as to be grateful yours was not one of them," Clemency said.

Again Francis smiled, an impish expression that made him look like a cherub with mischief in mind. "Your care for me is appreciated," he said, "though if you have more of an interest in me than as a friend, you are doomed to disappointment, for my heart is given elsewhere."

"Your famous forfeit," Clemency said with a laugh. "Soon enough I shall know your secret, one way or another."

"Indeed." Francis bowed grandly, making Clemency laugh again. "Are you to compete in the juggling? I would love to watch you perform."

"Yes, you and Mercy may cheer me on without hesitation." Clemency turned the chair and carried Mercy back to the path. "I have told Mercy she should wager on my success, but she is averse to risk."

"Only where you are concerned," Mercy said. She sounded oddly subdued, not at all as cheerful as she had been a moment before. Clemency examined her closely, but her expression was placid, not fearful or pained.

"Well, then, I will have to win, and then tease you with the sum you would have made on my winning!" she said, and to her relief, Mercy smiled. She so hated being treated like an invalid it was sometimes difficult for Clemency to know when she was in distress.

Beyond the field, where the trees began, more people clustered, these ones talking and laughing loudly. It was an eerie contrast to the near silence of the distance trials. "Francis, will you take charge of Mercy's chair? I must report in." Clemency waited only long enough to see Francis' nod, and then she hurried through the crowd, searching for an official witness.

The man she eventually found recognized her and greeted her with a smile. "Why, Lady Ashford! It has been years. Come to teach these whippersnappers a thing or two about Moving?"

"Mr. Hardison, I'm so pleased you remember me. I hope to do my best, of course." Clemency hoped she did not sound falsely modest. Now that she was at the moment of truth, she worried that perhaps she would look a fool by attempting more than she was capable of. But her father had always told her *Better to reach beyond your grasp and find your grasp is greater than you know than to give up too soon,* and she had never regretted taking that advice.

"You will be third up at number seventeen," Mr. Hardison said. "Good luck, my lady."

Clemency drifted to the tree marked with a card labeled 17, where a young man no more than sixteen or seventeen Moved some twenty objects in concentric circles in front of himself, rings and balls and horseshoes. She counted; twenty-two, actually. He was not very skilled, keeping the objects directly in his view and causing them to revolve slowly, but twenty-two was a respectable number for someone who could not have manifested his Moving talent more than five years ago. His skill would be a fine draw for potential employers in a year or two.

She glanced around, but did not see Mercy and Francis. They would be nearby, and she did not need a distraction. She surveyed the ground surrounding tree seventeen. Dozens of objects lay there, a few simple ones like the balls and rings the young man Moved, but many others of irregular shape, some fragile like china figurines, others large and heavy. Clemency regarded a three-inch cube of iron. Weight was nothing to her, but its mass would make it maneuver awkwardly. Which, of course, would look all the better to the judges.

She watched the young man finish his routine, then waited impatiently through the next two competitors' performances. One of the women was awkward and dropped her first object before she had Moved more than six items. The other woman was more competent, and managed thirty-one objects, many of them complex, but she was not daring in the paths she chose to Move them. Clemency tamped down on her pride. Time enough for that when she had actually competed.

The loud commentary hushed when she stepped up to the tree, and Clemency heard her title being whispered between the observers. That made her feel confident rather than nervous. She nodded at the witnesses, then scanned the ground around her and selected ten random objects to Move into the air simultaneously. A low gasp ran through the watching crowd. Clemency guessed no one had tried anything like that so far, but it was a knack she had developed during the war, and while the trick looked complex, it was actually very simple. The truly complicated maneuvers came later.

She set the objects to revolving in slow circles and gradually picked up more of the things lying around her, two at a time, until she was controlling fifty items. The crowd's excitement grew with every new addition to her constellation of Moving parts until they were counting each pair. The cry of *"Fifty!"* drowned out all the other noise, but Clemency was too intent on her Moving to notice more than that.

She judged she could handle more, but the juggling trial was not only about numbers, it was about skill. With a little effort, she divided the objects into groups by color, spinning them into four loose globes of different sizes. She Moved those for some fifteen seconds, then realigned the objects by material and again made four globes. It was an interesting challenge, but not the thing that would win her the trials that day.

Slowly, she turned until she faced the tree. She disassembled her globes and made the objects circle in front of her in a thin ring at eye level, parallel to the ground. She drew in a breath and let it out slowly. Then she spread out the ring so it circled the tree.

It looked simple. But no Mover could Move anything she could not see, and the tree's trunk was broad, producing an area behind it where Clemency could not see to Move her objects. In order to keep the ring moving, she had to throw each object hard as it vanished so it crossed back into her line of vision and then catch it before it fell. It was the most difficult maneuver Clemency knew, and the most rewarding.

Based on the gasps from the crowd, most of those watching knew how difficult the maneuver was. She heard a few cheers that were hushed by others, and one voice clearly saying, "She'll drop a few, I warrant." Those words filled her with greater determination to prove that speaker wrong.

She kept the ring moving for a full minute, then gradually caught and held still each object after it passed behind the tree until she was Moving a giant cluster of miscellaneous objects. Turning again, she carefully spread the objects back over the ground and released them. There was a moment of hushed silence—and then the cheering began.

Flushed with excitement and pride, Clemency made her way around the crowd to where Francis and Mercy waited. "What do you say?" she asked.

"That's a new trick," Francis said, clapping her on the shoulder. "Astonishing. No one will be able to top that."

"I saw her practicing, but she made me promise not to hint at what she intended," Mercy said, her eyes bright with excitement. "*I* believe everyone else should give up and go home after that."

"It is not so amazing as all that," Clemency said, blushing harder. "Besides, now that I have done it, others will know it is possible, and perhaps one of them will best me."

"Not without a great deal of practice," Francis said. "And now that we have both successfully demonstrated our greatest skills, what do you say to a race?"

At the far end of Hyde Park, within sight of Kensington Palace, stood a collection of fat pillars atop which rested circular wooden platforms, all of them painted an eye-watering white that today gleamed in the undimmed sun. Clemency always imagined them as enormous flat toadstools and herself as a tiny sprite dancing and Flying beneath them. There were no ladders or ropes or stairs; anyone wishing to stand atop the platforms either had to Fly or be Moved. Clemency saw

Mercy settled within the area roped off for bystanders and Flew with Francis to the top of the southmost pillar.

The platforms were nearly fifty feet across and sturdier than anything Clemency could imagine. A number of Extraordinary Movers dressed for racing floated lightly above the platform, none of them more than a few inches off the surface. To one side stood two Extraordinary Movers all in black; they were the monitors who announced the start of the race and took the official times. They were flanked by a man and a woman also dressed in black. Clemency recognized the woman from previous races. She and her companion were not Movers, but Speakers, and they would communicate with the Speakers at the turning point of the race to ensure each participant made the full circuit.

Clemency's attention shifted to the female Extraordinary Mover in black. She was a handsome woman of middle years with chestnut hair not fully covered by her white cap. Unlike the other monitor, she was watching the crowd of soon-to-be racers, with her attention particularly fixing on the women. Clemency recognized her, as well, and her pleasure at performing well faded. Mrs. Bonner.

Clemency quickly looked away so she would not meet Mrs. Bonner's eyes. "Why is *she* the race monitor?" she muttered to Francis.

Francis shrugged. "I believe she is concerned about the purity of the race being contaminated by female Extraordinary Movers behaving in an unladylike fashion. She has certainly become more vocal recently about how ladies should act when they have an example to set for the rising generation."

"Hang the rising generation," Clemency muttered, making Francis choke on a laugh.

"That is precisely the kind of language Mrs. Bonner deplores. Not ladylike at all," he said. "But you should not worry. I am certain Mrs. Bonner does not know how prone you are to corrupting others."

"Who is corrupting others?" Jane Flew down to join them. "Make room for Jonathan, though you should not speak to him, he has been monstrous cruel to me and I declare I wish nothing to do with him." Her smile belied her words, and she cast a fond glance on Jonathan as he followed her to alight nearby.

"My heart is broken," Jonathan said. "Shall we have a friendly wager to cheer me up? The one of us with the slowest time shall host the other three to supper."

"Oh, bah, that is nothing," Jane scoffed. "Ten pounds says I beat the lot of you. Go on, all of you, are you babies or are you Movers?"

"All right," Francis said. "Ten pounds from each of us to the winner, and the loser hosts supper."

"It must be later this week, for you know how Jane's cook dislikes unexpected guests," Clemency said, making the others laugh so loudly they drew the attention of nearby racers.

Francis glanced past Clemency. "Hush, the dragon approaches," he whispered.

Clemency composed herself, but it was too late. "Lady Ashford," Mrs. Bonner said. Her voice was more elderly than the rest of her, a raspy creak that put Clemency in mind of an unoiled hinge. "Your mirth is inappropriate."

Clemency widened her eyes in false perplexity. "Inappropriate, how, Mrs. Bonner? We are in good spirits and prepared for a good race. I see nothing wrong with that."

"Your levity is unbecoming a lady. You are a peer of the realm—it is your duty to set an example." Mrs. Bonner's frown could have stopped a wild boar in its tracks. "I believe you owe it to England."

Clemency was seized with a sudden urge to laugh at Mrs. Bonner's choice of words. As if Clemency's behavior could move a nation! "It is kind of you to share your opinion, Mrs. Bonner," she said when she could speak without a tremble of amusement, "and I believe we are in agreement that female Extraordinary Movers should set an example. We simply disagree as to what that example should be. But I am, as you say, a peer of the realm, and while I respect you as one of England's most prominent talents, I am the keeper of my honor, not you."

The frown deepened until Mrs. Bonner's jaw seemed about to detach from the rest of her face. She opened her mouth to speak, and Francis said, "Oh, Mrs. Bonner, I believe you are being summoned. It must be nearly time to begin, don't you agree?"

Mrs. Bonner narrowed her eyes at Francis, clearly suspecting him of trickery. Francis turned his most innocent cherubic smile on the lady. After another few seconds, Mrs. Bonner turned and Flew away across the platform.

"That woman," Jane said, and appeared to run out of words.

"She is harmless," Clemency said.

"I disagree," Francis said, somber now. "She has a great deal of influence as a highly rated Extraordinary Mover, and there are many who agree with her somewhat antiquated views on the womanly virtues. And since she is herself a woman, her views have added power."

A shrill whistle rang out across the platform. "Form up for the Tower run!" shouted one of the Speakers.

"She can do nothing to me at the moment, and I choose to focus my efforts on winning," Clemency said, settling her goggles over her eyes.

She and the others drifted away from the platform to where four other Extraordinary Movers made four corners of an invisible vertical square like a doorway in the air. Clemency picked a spot close to the top of the square as the other racers spread out around her, no one venturing through the "door." She preferred Flying high from the start instead of wasting time pushing up from below. Swiftly, she oriented her body so she was an arrow pointed in the direction of the distant, unseen Tower of London. Her heart beat fast with excitement. No feeling in the world could beat the anticipation of a race.

Seconds later, the whistle sounded again, two shrill blasts, and Clemency shot away from the starting field, accelerating until she was near her top speed. The wind lashed her body, her skirts flapped wildly like the wings of a dozen ravens, and she could barely breathe. She had never felt so alive.

She never bothered looking for her competitors when she raced, because that slowed one down more than the wind. As far as Clemency was concerned, she raced only herself. But she could not help noticing someone to one side keeping pace with her—Francis—and another Extraordinary Mover Flying not far ahead of her and at her same altitude. Jonathan, she saw, and silently cursed. He and she had been Flying rivals for years, and not nice ones as she was with Francis; if

Jonathan won, he would needle her with his victory for weeks. He could not be permitted to outfly her.

She sped up, pushing herself past her limit until she wished she could scream from the effort. Gradually, Jonathan grew in her sights. He never looked back, and he would have no idea she was so close until she was past him.

The tiny shape of the Tower of London appeared in the distance, growing rapidly larger. It was the halfway point, and marked the most difficult point in the race course. Not only must a racer make a sharp turn as quickly as possible, reversing to return to the finish, she had to make that turn at exactly the right moment. Too soon, and she would be disqualified; too late, and she lost valuable time. Clemency had meant to practice that turn before the trials, but she had never made time for it. Now she told herself not to worry. She would make it, or not, and it was all down to skill and luck at this point.

The Tower filled the sky. Jonathan was no more than three feet ahead of her. Clemency counted off the remaining distance to the turning point, *four, three, two...*

Jonathan made the turn, and Clemency immediately realized her mistake when he almost Flew into her. She dropped and instinctively turned, hoping she had not moved too quickly. Her skirts flapped hard as she dove and rolled, dragging at her body. By the time she finished the turn and straightened herself, Jonathan had gained three body lengths on her.

Clemency silently cursed. She would never catch him now, and he would be acclaimed the winner, damn him. Gritting her teeth, she sped up again. There was no point whingeing about what she could or could not do. There was only the race, and she still had her own time to beat. And maybe she would be lucky, and Jonathan would make a mistake, though she did not actually wish to win under those conditions.

If anyone else was near, they were not within eyesight. Francis had vanished. Clemency felt as if she and Jonathan were the only Extraordinary Movers in the sky. Jonathan seemed to have caught an air current, for she had not made up any ground; if anything, he was edging farther ahead. Clemency pushed herself harder. She would not give up even though it was impossible.

Ahead, the white platforms came into view. Jonathan streaked toward the finish point. No, she would never catch him. She would have to resign herself to teasing for the foreseeable future.

Brilliant light exploded in Clemency's face, followed by the loudest noise she had ever heard. An invisible fist punched her, knocking her backward to tumble out of the sky. Stunned, she fell for a few seconds and then caught herself. The air was full of white wings fluttering in all directions, a numberless flight of doves Clemency watched in amazement. It took her a moment to realize they were not birds, they were endless sheets of white paper scattering to fall across the ground.

She shook her head to clear it. A bomb, and a much bigger one than the one she had detonated over the Thames. Dizzily, she Flew back toward the platforms. It took her a second or two to realize that the blackened stumps she saw were all that remained of them. A few of the pillars were on fire, and the rest lay in shattered, splintered pieces surrounding them. Not a single platform remained.

The pillars were not all that lay destroyed on the ground. Clemency Flew down and alit clumsily on the grass near the first body she saw. It was Jonathan. He lay sprawled with his arms and legs awkwardly akimbo. Blood pooled beneath his shattered head.

Clemency knelt beside him and took his hand in hers. Her goggles were askew on her face, and her eyes ached, but no tears flowed. "Jonathan," she said, unable to hear her own voice through the ringing in her ears. He had been winning. He should not be dead. She remembered that moment of jealousy at the Tower, and then she could not stop weeping.

CHAPTER 20

IN WHICH A TERRIBLE LOSS PRECEDES A TERRIBLE ULTIMATUM

Someone alit nearby and stumbled toward her. It was Francis, his mouth moving in speech. Clemency shook her head. "I cannot hear you," she said, though in truth the ringing was subsiding.

Francis spoke again, and this time his words came to her as if from a great distance. Between that, and the movement of his lips, she understood him to be asking whether she was injured.

She shook her head. "Jonathan is dead," she said. She felt numb to her core. "It would have been—I lost time in the turn, Francis, it would have been I caught in the blast—"

Francis dropped to his knees and grabbed her shoulders roughly, shaking her and dislodging her goggles further. "You cannot dwell on that," he said, his distant voice harsh. "Call it luck that you were not faster today. We have lost so many, we should be grateful you were not among them."

"So many?" Clemency tugged the goggles to hang around her neck. The sound of screaming finally penetrated the fog wrapped around her. "The platforms. Francis, the platforms—they must have been lining up for the next race—"

She looked past Francis' shoulder. The fields surrounding the destroyed platforms were filled with screaming, fleeing people. The ropes defining the spectators' area were gone, torn away by the riot. It took Clemency a moment to realize what that meant.

"Mercy," she gasped.

She tore herself away from Francis and took a few stumbling steps before Flying low and fast across the ground toward the devastation. That close to the grass, she should have felt she was speeding along, but time seemed to stretch until seconds turned to minutes in her heart. It took only two of those eternal seconds before she saw the chair, fallen on its side and surrounded by grass torn and muddy from hundreds of fleeing feet. Her heart constricted with terror.

She landed awkwardly near the chair and the limp figure lying beside it, crying her sister's name in despair. Mercy lay so still, one arm flung over her head, that Clemency screamed her name again and reached for her, not knowing what she meant to do.

Before she could touch her, Mercy stirred. She lifted her head, looked Clemency in the eye, and said, "You're alive." She burst into tears. "I believed you dead—I saw you blown out of the sky, and then the crowd knocked my chair over and I couldn't see anything. I believed you were dead."

Clemency gathered her sister into her arms and clung to her, weeping tears of relief. "Are you hurt at all?"

"No, I huddled behind the chair like a barrier, and no one trampled me." Mercy swiped her sleeve across her eyes. "It is something else to thank Mr. Wescott for, that the chair is so sturdy. It was a great protection."

Clemency looked up at Francis, who stood over them, his expression grim. "I must take Mercy home, but I will return. They will need help clearing the—the destruction." She could not bring herself to say *bodies.*

"Permit me," Francis said. "Your Moving weight capacity exceeds mine, and I believe they will need someone to Move the platforms, in case there are any survivors." The bleakness in his expression told Clemency what he thought of the likelihood of there being survivors.

"Thank you, Francis. Mercy, do you mind if Mr. Daubney takes you home?"

"Not at all," Mercy said, managing a smile.

Francis had already righted the chair, and Clemency Moved Mercy into it. "I will return," Francis said, "though I hope the devastation is less than I believe, and my skills will not be needed." He Moved Mercy's chair to hover just above the grass. Mercy gripped the armrests and once more smiled reassuringly at Clemency, and she and Francis drifted away toward the nearest path.

Clemency stood and surveyed the fields. Everywhere she saw the torn grass and patches of muddy earth that marked the flight of those close enough to witness the explosion. The ravaged fields were mostly empty; the terrified crowds were gone, though a few people remained, most of them tending to the bodies that lay lifeless near the devastation. As she watched, a man's body lifted gracefully from the earth, and the woman standing beside the body folded the man's arms across his chest before maneuvering him with her Moving toward where others had gathered, all with similar burdens.

Clemency had seen more than a few battlefields, but those had always been from a distance, high in the sky. The reality of death struck her like a blow, turning her to stone. Despite what Francis had said, she could not help remembering the sight of the platforms exploding and feeling herself falling out of the sky. She would have died had she been closer.

She shook herself out of her stunned reverie and Flew above the impromptu morgue toward what remained of the platforms. Most of them still burned, sending thick clouds of black smoke into the air. Clemency had never seen the like before. It made her complaints about blocked chimneys filling the drawing room with ash and soot seem frivolous.

She tried to approach, to discover if she could see anyone she might save, but the smoke filled her lungs and sent her choking and coughing away from the fires. When she could breathe again, she tried Flying around the wreckage at a greater distance and discovered she could see the edge of a fallen platform extending beyond the smoke.

She took hold of the platform and easily Moved it, lifting it up and away from the smoke. It was only part of a platform, and to her relief there were no bodies on it. But it was still burning, and the fire grew hotter when she lifted the platform out of the choking clouds of smoke. After a moment's consideration, she Flew with it the short distance to Round Pond and lowered it gently into the water to douse the flames. Swans fluttered and flapped wildly at this intrusion into their territory and then settled down. Likely they were not intelligent enough to remember a threat once it had disappeared.

She saw another Extraordinary Mover carrying a smoking platform in her direction. The Mover was female, and although she was at a distance, Clemency believed it was Jane. She did not Fly to join her friend; exchanging pleasant greetings was out of the question, and she knew Jane preferred to do her grieving in solitude. Jane hated condolences, as Clemency recalled from when Jane's mother had died and Jane had gone into a fit of incandescent rage over a friend's innocently offered sympathy. In a week or so, Jane would be ready to talk about Jonathan, and until then, Clemency would leave her to her grief.

Dragging the remains of her platform out of the water, she returned with it to the site of the destruction. She did not know why it mattered to her that the platforms stay together, unless it was an instinct that she should not disturb the site where so many had died more than necessary. They were dead; it should not matter to them. But it mattered to her.

By the time she returned, the fires had been extinguished and the other platforms removed. One or two charred slabs of wood, all that remained of the platforms, lay to the side of the pillars, which meant she was not the only sentimental one. She descended, dropping her platform atop the others, and walked to the pillar bases, heedless of the damage to her shoes.

The fairy toadstools were broken off where the platforms had fallen, and now their jagged remains jutted skyward, blackened and shattered. Men and women moved through the wreckage, lifting charred and twisted bodies to float away from where they had fallen to their deaths. Clemency guessed some of them had actually been killed by the explosion rather than the fall, and she swallowed bile and hoped she would not vomit.

She stepped on something that rustled and crinkled that did not feel like winter-dry grass. She lifted her foot and saw one of the papers that she had mistaken for birds' wings. Curious, she picked it up and turned it over. Slightly smeared printing covered the page, declaring in bold letters at the top, A WARNING TO THE OPPRESSORS!

Clemency read on, her eyes narrowing. *I have now demonstrated five times my ability to strike and remain unseen. No one can stop me, least of all that disease that eats at the heart of England's government, those Extraordinaries who receive titles and preference beyond what they deserve. Unless they are removed from all positions of power, I will continue to attack. This was a warning. My next attack will be far more deadly.*

At the bottom, in large type to match the heading, were the words *Mr. Jinks.*

Clemency crushed the paper in her hands. Obviously Mr. Jinks was a false name; she already knew the bombings were the work of a group of people. But that was irrelevant. Whoever "Mr. Jinks" was, he —they—had struck a devastating blow. She did not know how many had died today, but if the bombers considered this a warning, she could not imagine what destruction might result from their next attack.

She continued toward the devastation, though she wished she could leave, Fly home and forget the memory of the explosion's light and the bodies falling to their deaths. But abandoning her friends would make her a stranger to herself. So she walked on and eventually drew near enough to see a familiar figure directing the efforts of the Movers. For a second or two, Clemency again considered walking away. Responsibility or not, she did not feel equal to encountering Mrs. Bonner again. Then she told herself she had a duty, and Mrs. Bonner could not dissuade her from it.

"Mrs. Bonner," she said when she was near enough.

Mrs. Bonner turned. Her white cap was missing, her hair was disordered, and soot streaked her face, but she held herself as regally as ever. "Lady Ashford," she said. "We believed you caught in the explosion."

"I almost was," Clemency said. "What can I do to help?"

Mrs. Bonner looked her up and down, silently. "There were many injured when the spectators fled. You might assist the Extraordinary Shapers in Moving the injured to where they can be treated."

"I will," Clemency said. "You were not on the platforms?"

A tight, angry frown twisted Mrs. Bonner's face. "Do you accuse me of negligence?"

Startled, Clemency stammered, "Of course not. I meant to express my relief that you survived. I had believed you still watching the end of the race."

"I was called away, and was returning to my post when the incident occurred." Mrs. Bonner still looked angry. "Go now, and make yourself useful."

Clemency bit back a furious retort and leapt skyward.

She found the Extraordinary Shapers, three of them, near where the spectators had stood, in an open grassy area bounded on the west by trees that reminded Clemency unpleasantly of the makeshift morgue. A few of the people in that area lay still, but more of them were sitting up, which dispelled the illusion. Two of the Shapers were women, one a man, but all of them wore the black caps or hats declaring their profession. Clemency alit near the man and said, "How can I help?"

"Lady Ashford," the man said. "I am Dr. Warburton. If you will, you might search for those too injured to walk here. Take care to immobilize anyone you Move, for some injuries are exacerbated by rough handling."

"I understand, doctor. I am familiar with the need for caution." Clemency Flew away with a quick nod to the other Extraordinary Shapers.

She began searching in a spiral pattern, Flying ever wider. From above, the devastation looked less terrible, the ground still gray-green with only a few brown scars where the turf had been torn up by fleeing spectators. There did not appear to be anyone left near the platforms, living or dead, but Clemency remembered searching battlefields for those too wounded to help themselves, and she determined to be thorough.

She found a man leaning up against a tree trunk with his eyes closed and one leg stretched out straight before him, and for a few seconds upon descending, she wondered if he was dead. Then she saw his chest moving, slowly but regularly, and with a sigh of relief she alit beside him and said, "Are you badly injured? How can I help?"

The man opened his eyes. "I believe my leg is broken." He shifted, winced, and said, "No, I am certain of it."

"Relax, and permit me to Move you," Clemency said. "I will immobilize your leg and you should feel very little pain."

She took hold of the man and gently Moved him off the ground, holding him in his seated position. He grimaced, and she secured the outstretched leg better and said, "Tell me if this hurts you, but I have found faster is better when one cannot avoid causing pain."

The man only nodded. Clemency took to the skies.

She heard nothing from her passenger, and a few glances told her he was still conscious, so she reassured herself that this, at least, had gone well. She Flew at a decent speed back to the Extraordinary Shapers, and as she descended, she made a quick count and decided there were fewer injured there than before. That, too, heartened her.

Having deposited her passenger, she Flew back to her search. She found only three more wounded, and she carefully brought each one back to lie on the ground where they could be treated. The Extraordinary Shapers did not acknowledge her returns, and she did not disturb them.

On her final journey, after satisfying herself that this was the last of the injured, she found Francis waiting near the improvised hospital. She set down her burden and drifted over to join him. "Mercy is well?" she asked.

"Safe and well at Emeraude House," Francis said. "You look exhausted. Sit with me and rest."

Clemency did not feel like arguing, and she was exhausted.

She and Francis sat beneath a tree that still bore a card with the number 11 printed on it. Clemency tipped her head back so the tree's rough bark caught at her hair. No doubt she looked a mess, sweaty and covered in soot with her hair disordered, but she was too tired to care. "This is not how I pictured this day ending," she said. "Mr. Wescott and his sister were to dine with us."

Francis took out his silver pocket watch. "It is barely past one o'clock," he said. "Your supper plans need not be interrupted."

"Supper seems so anticlimactic after all this. I consider it fortunate that Prudence's ball is still two days away." Clemency sighed. "And the bombers will never stop until they achieve their goal."

"What goal is that?"

"Did you not see?" Clemency handed him the wad of paper she had never thrown away. "These were all over the field. I believe they were intended to scatter when the bomb detonated."

Francis smoothed the paper over his knee and read it silently. "Those bastards," he said. "I will not beg your pardon for my language, because I do not believe they deserve any lesser epithet."

"I agree." Clemency closed her eyes. "And since what they want is impossible, the bombings will continue until the people behind them are caught."

"You believe it impossible? Clemency, there are already those in power who agree with this sentiment." Francis rolled up the paper and tapped it against his knee. "They will welcome an excuse to promote their interests and rid themselves of their Extraordinary opponents. When the public hears of this demand, who knows how many will agitate for the government to give in?"

"Surely feeling is not high against Extraordinaries?" But as she spoke, Clemency remembered Prudence's anger at her talented family, and wondered if Prudence was more representative of the population than she guessed.

Francis shrugged. "I have no idea. But it is a possibility we should be prepared for."

Clemency sighed again. "I wish everything were as it was this morning, when all I had to worry about was outracing you so I could demand the name of your inamorata."

"I would like to say you would never have done that, as you never have before, but I had a collision just after the turn. You were six yards ahead of me when the explosion—" Francis shut his mouth sharply. Clemency's heart gave one aching stab of misery.

To counter it, she said, "Well, I won, so you must pay your forfeit."

"We never finished the race. There was no victor."

"Come now, Francis. I need cheering up. You must tell me who you wished me to introduce you to." Clemency elbowed her friend gently in the side. "It will give us both pleasure."

Francis did not at first respond. Clemency elbowed him again, harder. "Francis?"

"I do not know that it will give you pleasure," Francis finally said.

"Of course it will," Clemency said.

Francis heaved a deep sigh. "It is not so much that I wished an introduction as that I need your intervention on my behalf."

Clemency's eyes widened. "It is someone you know? Someone we both know? Oh, Francis, it is not Jane, is it? Because she is already awash in swains."

"It is not Jane."

"Well, I refuse to list off the many women we are both acquainted with. Tell me before I burst with curiosity."

Francis tilted his head back as Clemency had done and closed his eyes. "Promise me you will not berate me."

Clemency frowned. "Why would I berate you?"

"Because," Francis said, "it is Lady Mercy I have fallen in love with."

Clemency's heart gave another jolt, this one of surprise. "*Mercy?*"

"Is it so impossible to believe?" Francis sighed again. "She was never anything to me but your sister when we were young, and then I left for the War Office, and then *you* left for the War Office, and I did not see her for seven years. Then you returned, bringing me back into her orbit, and she was a woman grown, and I saw her in a new light. I love her, Clemency, and I ask your permission to marry her."

Dozens of memories crowded Clemency's head, all the times Francis and Mercy had been in company, how he had made her laugh, how he had sought her out as his partner in games. She remembered now the look on his face when they had found Mercy lying helpless on the ground, and how she had in her terror for her sister not recognized the terror he felt as well.

"Mercy," she repeated. "Francis, I do not—that is, if she does not return your regard—"

Francis smiled, his familiar impish expression. "You needn't fear on my account," he said. "I told her of my love when I conveyed her home, and she confessed she had loved me since she was a girl and had despaired of me ever looking fondly in her direction. I apologize for not waiting for your official permission."

Clemency laughed. The sound carried far in the still air, and for a second or two she felt embarrassed at laughing when so many were dead or injured. But Francis' words had dispelled some of the sorrow she felt. "Francis, you have my blessing," she said, "though if I know my sister, she would have insisted on you carrying her off to Gretna Green had I refused your suit."

"She did say something of the sort," Francis admitted. "I would prefer to do this in an open manner. Are you happy for us?"

"Decidedly so." Clemency rose and brushed off her posterior. "Let us return to my house, and I will send word to Mr. Wescott that he and Miss Wescott are still invited to supper. You may join us so long as you promise not to be dull the way most people in love are."

"I promise to be at my most charming," Francis said.

"Then I—"

Clemency was interrupted by a voice from behind them. "Lady Ashford."

She turned. It was Mr. Rutledge.

"Lady Ashford," he said, "I would like a word with you."

Clemency did not know how someone of his size could possibly sneak up on anyone, let alone someone trained in surveillance by the War Office, but either her distraction or his skill had kept her from perceiving him. "A word about what?" she said, her surprise sharpening her tongue.

"Clemency, who is this?" Francis asked. He took a step forward, putting himself closer to Mr. Rutledge than Clemency, though he did not stand in front of her.

"This is Mr. Rutledge. He—" Clemency did not know what to say to explain the man who stood before them in his not quite unfashionable coat. Perhaps the investigation into the bombings was not a secret, but her nocturnal activities certainly were, and she did not trust Mr. Rutledge to keep her secret if she did not keep his.

"I have an interest in discovering who stands behind these incidents," Mr. Rutledge said, as smoothly as if bombings and investigations were perfectly normal. "Lady Ashford was close to the explosion, and I wish to discuss her observations."

Clemency's throat, which had constricted as Mr. Rutledge began speaking, relaxed. "Of course, Mr. Rutledge."

Francis still looked dubious. Before he could ask the reasonable question of how she knew Mr. Rutledge in the first place, Clemency said, "Will you return to Emeraude House and tell Mercy I will return shortly? And then we will plan for supper."

"If you wish," Francis said, and leapt skyward.

Mr. Rutledge watched him go. "He does not know what you have done at night," he said.

"No one does—well, no one but you and the Wescotts. I told you I prefer anonymity." Clemency watched Mr. Rutledge instead of Francis. The man looked perfectly relaxed, as if he had not a care in the world. His demeanor would have angered Clemency—how could anyone not feel horrified over what had happened only an hour before?—had she not guessed that whatever face Mr. Rutledge showed the world, it did not represent his true feelings.

"Walk with me," Mr. Rutledge said. Clemency, feeling dampness seeping through the seams of her almost certainly ruined shoes, chose to drift instead.

"Did you see the handbills?" Mr. Rutledge said after they had gone some two dozen steps in silence.

Clemency nodded. "I saw them scatter, and then I read one. Is it true?"

"You do not believe this 'Mr. Jinks' claim of responsibility for the other bombs?"

"I believe it is somewhat late for someone to claim responsibility. Why now, and not with the other bombs?"

Mr. Rutledge shook his head. "This is not the first message," he said. "There was another left at Covent Garden and one at Vauxhall. In both cases, my people found the messages and suppressed them. My guess is that this dramatic display of a thousand handbills was meant to prevent us suppressing this message as well."

"So they have demanded the demotion of Extraordinaries before," Clemency said.

"They have. I chose not to make that knowledge public while I searched for those guilty."

Clemency stopped. "But suppose that has made them more likely to place bombs? Suppose they are so desperate to reveal their demands to the world that more people were killed who should not have been?"

"Do you accuse me of responsibility for their actions?" Mr. Rutledge said, turning on her. "Had their demands been made public, there would have been civil unrest and very probably riots as the populace insisted the government do five mutually exclusive things to counter the bombings."

"You do not know that."

"I assure you I do." Mr. Rutledge glared at Clemency. "Tell me what you saw."

"What I—you mean, when the bomb exploded." Clemency blinked. "The explosion centered on the platform where we—the racers—waited for the race to begin, and where we would have gathered for the announcement of our official times. If it had detonated even half a minute later, it would have killed all of us, and not just those preparing for the next race."

"I hoped you would say that," Mr. Rutledge said. "It confirms what my investigation has learned, that in every case but the one you disrupted, the bomb detonated at the wrong time. Prematurely, here and in Covent Garden, and too late in Vauxhall. We are dealing with amateurs, which both reassures and terrifies me."

Clemency chose not to comment on how unexpectedly forthcoming Mr. Rutledge had become. "You mean because amateurs are not predictable."

"Precisely." Mr. Rutledge's gaze became distant. "Every mistimed bomb brings me closer to catching these criminals, but as they are amateurs, they cannot be counted on to stay with their pattern."

"You have Seers searching for them, yes?"

"Of course. But, again, their unpredictability works against Dream, and we have no foci to compel Vision." Mr. Rutledge turned his gaze on Clemency. "Thank you, Lady Ashford. I hope you took my earlier warning to heart."

Clemency ground her teeth. "I remember every word you said," she temporized.

"That is not the same as saying you will obey my instructions." Mr. Rutledge's eyes were once more cold and unfeeling. "I am quite serious, Lady Ashford, when I say your actions interfere with my business. Do not ignore me."

"I will not," Clemency said.

Mr. Rutledge nodded, a gesture not quite a bow, and strode away. Clemency watched him go. She recalled what Miss Wescott had said about how Mr. Rutledge believed she was bored and a thrill-seeker, and anger pulsed through her. Mr. Rutledge had no claim on her loyalties, and she saw no reason to obey him. She leapt into the sky and Flew toward home.

CHAPTER 21

IN WHICH MISS WESCOTT
PERFORMS A MIRACLE

C lemency's defiant anger faded as the day wore on until, as she dressed for supper, she considered whether Mr. Rutledge did not have some small point. He was arrogant and demanding, true, but if he had as much responsibility as she suspected he did, he might be justified in not wishing her to interfere. On the other hand, she had never encountered anyone else, talented or not, on her nocturnal adventures, so she did not see how Mr. Rutledge could contend that her actions were interference when there was no one with whom to interfere.

She clasped her pearl necklace around her neck and watched Tatton's reflection as she arranged Clemency's hair. "Thank you," she said impulsively.

"Thank me? For what, my lady?" Tatton pinned another stray lock.

"I have done a good many mysterious things these past weeks since my return, and you have not complained or pestered me for my secrets. Thank you for your discretion." Clemency threaded a pair of pearl drops through her earlobes and flicked one to make it tremble.

"It is only what I promised your father I would do when I entered your service," Tatton said.

Clemency resisted the urge to turn and face Tatton, as that would disorder all her maid's fine work. "My father?"

Tatton placed a final pin and laid the others on the dressing table. "Have I never told you? Your father, God rest his soul, spoke to me shortly after I was engaged. He told me you would bear many burdens someday, and that you would need someone you could rely on to be discreet and honest. I told him I would be that."

"I never knew." Clemency gently touched her hair. It was a darker blonde than it had been in her youth, and she suspected it would turn mousy in years to come, but the change had been so slow she had never looked at her reflection and seen a stranger. Not until this moment. The woman in the mirror was she, but her eyes and the way her mouth turned down at the corners were unfamiliar. Tatton had said nothing, so the change was all in Clemency's head, but it was unsettling nonetheless, as if she were seeing a future self who might bear the burdens her father had spoken of.

"Then I thank you again," she told Tatton, who smiled and walked away to tidy the dressing room.

Clemency was halfway down the stairs to the drawing room adjacent to the dining room when she heard voices, male and female, and with a shock remembered that Mr. and Miss Wescott would be joining her that evening. She had given so much consideration to Mr. Rutledge's words it had displaced her usual flutter of excitement when she imagined spending time with Mr. Wescott. Her heart sped up, and she paused on the stairs to command it to be still. It ignored her.

Finally, she gave up and proceeded to the landing and from there to the drawing room. It was a smaller room than the one her family gathered in after meals, and was only used as a cloakroom or to welcome guests for supper so they need not stand in the foyer until the bell rang. She drew in a breath, released it, and entered.

She was the last to arrive, it seemed. Francis and Mercy sat close together opposite the door, speaking in low voices. The Dowager Countess and Prudence sat on a divan nearby; by the stubborn look on Prudence's face, she did not like what her mother was saying, but Mama's face was alight with rapture.

And there was Miss Wescott, seated across from Mercy, with Mr.

Wescott standing next to her speaking to Roger. A flash of irritation shot through Clemency that she immediately suppressed. Roger was charming and interesting to everyone but his older sister, and she ought to be grateful that he was present to entertain her guests. Deep in her heart, though, she wished he had not come.

Mr. Wescott glanced her way when she entered, and his eyes lit with appreciation. "Lady Ashford," he said, turning to face her. "Thank you for the invitation. My sister and I are pleased to join you."

"The pleasure is mine," Clemency said with a smile. She stepped toward him with her hand extended and managed not to shiver with excitement as he clasped it briefly. "I see Roger has introduced himself, at least; have you met the others?"

"I have done my duty as your brother, Clem," Roger said with a pleasant smile that for once did not conceal a smirk or a scowl. "We are all good friends now. You did not say Wescott designed the grand clock at Hepburn's."

"Because I was unaware of that fact," Clemency said, smiling back at him, though she detested his casual *Clem* as if she were a favored pet. "My brother's club is famous for that clock. You are too modest, Mr. Wescott."

"Then, at the risk of becoming too *immodest*, I will say that I can hardly be expected to share the details of every one of my inventions when there are so many." Mr. Wescott shrugged as if creating mechanicals was nothing to speak of, but his eyes were alight with humor, and Clemency laughed at his droll expression.

"Roger, you have not visited the Cabinet of Curiosities, have you?" she asked. "It is quite remarkable."

"I shall have to remedy that lack," Roger said. "Come, now, shall we go in to supper? Or—I should not usurp your place, should I, Clem?"

The old familiar sneer was in his voice, and Clemency's heart sank. If Roger was to needle her during supper, she could hardly challenge him, not with the Wescotts watching. So she pretended not to hear the edge in his words, and said merely, "It is hardly usurpation to make a suggestion, don't you agree? Let us go in."

She settled herself at her usual place at the head of the table and ignored Roger's scowl at what she knew was, to him, a reminder that he had lost his chance at that place. It cheered her that Mr. Wescott seated himself to her left, enough that she could say very civilly to Roger on her right, "I'm so glad you joined us tonight."

"Indeed," Roger said as the soup course commenced. "I didn't believe you ever noticed my absence."

Clemency carefully did not look at Mr. Wescott to see what he made of that jab. "I always do," she said, though she refrained from adding *because the meal is more pleasant without your presence.*

"It is kind of you to include us in your family gathering," Mr. Wescott said. "You are fortunate to have a large family—there are five of you, is that correct?"

Clemency had never been so grateful for an innocuous interjection. "Yes, but Gawain is at school, and he will not return until next summer."

"He is glad of it, too. I have never seen anyone so desirous of leaving his family behind." Roger laughed, a harsh sound too loud for the room. "We are not a typical loving family all the time, Wescott. Not at all."

"I imagine most large families have times of disquiet," Mercy said from the foot of the table. "We are fortunate in our times of amity."

"However few there are," Roger said with a smile and a wink. Clemency guessed he meant it as a joke, but she saw no humor in it.

"I meant to ask, Lady Ashford, how the disaster at Hyde Park fell out," Mr. Wescott said with no sign that he had heard Roger despite Roger being seated across from him. "Miss Wescott and I were both very concerned when we heard the news. You were not injured, I take it?"

"No, and I consider myself very lucky, because had I been faster, I would have been caught in the blast and killed." She remembered Jonathan's shattered head and closed her eyes briefly to dispel the vision. "Mr. Daubney and I assisted in the recovery, putting out fires and bringing the injured for treatment."

"Lady Ashford is being modest," Francis said. "She was tireless in her efforts. But she will tell you it is only what anyone would have done."

"Because it *is* only what anyone would have done," Clemency said, wishing his words had not made her blush. "I do not consider myself above helping when help is needed."

"You—" Prudence began, but subsided at a glare from Mercy.

"I understood that was at the heart of the bomber's motivations," Mr. Wescott said. He looked up as the servants removed the soup bowls and brought in the dishes of the first remove. "Forgive me, I should not raise such a terrible subject at the dinner table, and one at which I am a guest."

"No, Wescott, we do not shy from speaking of serious matters, not in this family," Roger said. He served himself a prime cut of pork roast and did not offer the dish to Clemency. "And by now the news is all over London. Expel Extraordinaries from the government, or the city suffers this Mr. Jinks' reign of terror."

Clemency exchanged a glance with Mercy, who looked as if she wished she were close enough to slap sense into Roger. "It cannot be as simple as that," Clemency said. "That is, I realize those are Mr. Jinks' demands, but removing all Extraordinaries from positions of power would cripple the government." She reached for the pork only to have Mr. Wescott offer to serve her from a different dish. "And how is anyone to expel them from the House of Lords? Some of those Extraordinaries' titles are quite ancient."

"Not ours," Roger said. "Ennobled by Charles II, back in the day. The Northrups are practically upstarts by comparison to some."

"But Lady Ashford's point is valid," Mr. Wescott said. "Mr. Jinks may hate Extraordinaries, but his hatred cannot be the basis for our government."

"I think he's not wrong," Prudence declared. "Extraordinaries have more power than they should. It's not right that they get honors and benefits just because of an accident of birth."

"Prudence!" Mama gasped. "It is your sister you speak of!"

"Mama, Prudence speaks what many people have said," Clemency said. "I do not believe it is wrong to consider what they have experienced that has shaped their opinions."

Prudence stared at Clemency. She held her fork unremembered over her plate, ignoring the food on it. "You don't believe that."

"I don't agree with Mr. Jinks, no." Clemency returned her sister's stare. "But if a portion of the populace feels they are treated unfairly, I believe their grievances should be heard."

"How very generous of you, Clem," Roger said, saluting her with his glass before taking a drink.

"Generous because Lady Ashford knows how that hearing would play out," Francis said. "Extraordinaries provide valuable services to this country, and they deserve recognition for those services."

"All the Extraordinary Movers I know are generous with their talent," Clemency said, nodding at Francis. "Not all of them are titled, either, so it is unfair to claim that being an Extraordinary gains you the highest prestige. And that is true for all the talents."

"Which is the same as saying you believe those of us without talent should remain silent in the face of injustice," Prudence said.

"I beg your pardon, Lady Prudence, but I seem to have started an argument," Mr. Wescott said. He leaned forward to address her more directly. "My father had no talent, and I believe he was jealous of his children for having what he lacked. It is never easy, is it?"

Prudence glared at him, but said nothing.

"You needn't fear, you know," Miss Wescott said, her high voice cutting through the silence like birdsong. "You are yourself, and you need not borrow consequence from anyone. Do you play the pianoforte? Lady Ashford said you did."

Prudence blinked. "I do," she said, and looked startled, as if she had spoken without meaning to.

"We will have to play together—you must know some duets, yes?" Miss Wescott smiled. She seemed completely unaffected by the mood at the table, which surprised Clemency, as she would have imagined Roger's anger at the very least to hurt her.

"I would love that," Mercy said, "don't you agree, Francis?"

Francis, who had been angrily intent on Roger, startled at being addressed. "Of course," he said. His demeanor softened as he looked at his beloved. "Lady Prudence is quite talented."

"I have not played in a very long time, not since—a very long time," Prudence said.

"It hurts you, I know," Miss Wescott said. "Forgive me, I should not comment on your emotional state. I forget sometimes that what I see is not apparent to everyone."

Prudence's brow wrinkled. "I understood Extraordinary Discerners went mad."

Mama gasped. Clemency said, "Prudence, that is not appropriate—"

"I was mad, for a time," Miss Wescott said, as calmly as if she were asking for a particular dish. "But it is that we lose ourselves in everyone else, and when we find ourselves, the madness is gone. And I do not believe you hate your family as you believe you do. You are simply lost."

Prudence's mouth fell slack in astonishment. Then she pushed back her chair and stood. "Excuse me," she said, and was gone before Clemency could respond.

Silence fell, without even the chink of utensils against porcelain. Clemency cleared her throat. "Please do not mind Lady Prudence. She suffered greatly from our father's death." She was beginning to feel as if all their suppers ended the same way, with Roger sneering openly at her and Prudence leaving in a huff. Though Prudence had remembered politeness this time.

"Yes, and—but I should not say," Miss Wescott said. "We all have our secrets. But I do not believe it is a secret that you, Lady Mercy, and Mr. Daubney are quite fond of one another."

The smiles that followed this statement made Clemency feel as if a palpable cloud had lifted. "They are," she said, "at least I hope they are, if they are to marry."

Mama gasped again. "Clemency! How is it that I was not told? Oh, dearest Mercy, I am so pleased, though of course you should not consider marriage until Clemency is wed." She gripped Mercy's hand tightly. "We shall have to see about a wardrobe for you, so much is possible when one is a married woman!"

Francis grinned at Clemency, for all the world like a cheeky school-boy. "Mercy told you, did she? Well, you *did* give me your permission."

"And he took immediate advantage of it," Mercy said with a fond smile for her betrothed.

"I am so happy for both of you," Clemency said. She was acutely aware of Mr. Wescott beside her, watching the happy couple. If only Mama had not said that about Clemency needing to marry first! There was no reason for Clemency to feel awkward, but she had kissed Mr. Wescott, and they had spoken intimately, and—well, she did not believe that meant marriage was the next step, but she was not at all averse to pursuing the connection, and who knew where that might lead?

"I beg your pardon, Mama?" she asked, realizing she had been addressed.

"I said you are far too isolated. You will never marry if you do not take part in society. So many eligible men—the Duke of Craythorne, perhaps, or that wonderful General de Villiers. He is *so* charming, and you are already acquainted with him—"

"I am sure I will eventually meet someone," Clemency said through suddenly numb lips. She dared not look at Miss Wescott, to see what she made of the terrible jumble of anger and fear and desire her emotions had become. She had forgotten about Armand in the shock of the day, and now she could not help wondering what would happen the next time they met—for meet they certainly must, if Mama had anything to do with it.

She managed to survive the second remove without letting her distress show, though she imagined Mr. Wescott realized something was amiss. She knew her conversation was intelligible, but it could not have been more than superficial, and he was intelligent enough to recognize the difference. That was another thing she owed Armand for, ruining her pleasure at dining with a man who interested her.

She led the ladies to the main drawing room and left Roger, Francis, and Mr. Wescott to their port. It was a mark of how disturbed she was that she did not even feel wistful at being separated from Mr. Wescott for even a short period of time. With luck, her mood might lighten before the men appeared.

Mercy rolled herself to her usual seat by the fire. "Sit, dearest, and talk to me. I declare no one is as happy as I am today!"

Clemency took her usual seat. "I cannot believe the two of you kept such secrets from me. I never guessed Francis cared for you as anything but a friend, and you—feeling such an attachment for years and never speaking a word! I question my perspicacity."

"Your love is sweeter for having been so uncertain," Miss Wescott said, taking the other end of Clemency's sofa. "Pardon me, I did not think to ask if this was a private conversation."

"I wish the world to know," Mercy said with a laugh. "Miss Wescott, do you feel my happiness?"

"Of course. And it is beautiful." Miss Wescott closed her eyes and smiled as blissfully as Mercy. "Some secrets are easier to keep than others, Lady Ashford. And you were not here, not all of those years, so it is not as if you could be expected to know."

Clemency did not know whether that was meant as comfort or criticism. She decided to take it as a comfort. "It has all worked out splendidly, so I do not mind having been fooled," she said. "But, Miss Wescott, will you play for us? Or do you wish for the men to arrive so your audience will be greater?"

Miss Wescott was looking toward the doorway. "Oh, I do not believe it matters, not when the performance is not the point."

She rose, leaving Clemency mystified at her words, and walked to the pianoforte. Clemency had taken a look at it that afternoon and been surprised to find it in tune and free of dust. For an instrument that had not been played in years, it was in excellent condition.

Miss Wescott sat gracefully at the pianoforte like a butterfly coming to rest on a leaf. "What shall I play?" she said, quietly enough Clemency guessed she was speaking only to herself. "What indeed." She lifted her hands and held them above the keyboard as if waiting for them to be inspired. Then, lowering her hands to the keys, she began playing a piece Clemency recognized as a Mozart sonata.

Clemency's sour mood evaporated as Miss Wescott played on. She had a more delicate touch than Prudence, but Clemency did not believe that was a flaw in either of their abilities. Clemency knew only enough of music to recognize that Prudence was unusually skilled, but she could tell Miss Wescott was equally talented.

When the sonata came to an end, Clemency said, "That was beautiful."

"It was the first piece I learned to completion," Miss Wescott said.

"I like Mozart, though I imagine he would not have been a comfortable companion for a Discerner. All excitement and passion."

"Do you know any popular songs?" Mama asked. "I do love it when Prudence sings. She knows so many sweet melodies."

"I do not often accompany a singer." Miss Wescott stood and rummaged in the nearby cabinet. "But I am competent enough at sight reading that I believe this one will be no trouble."

She went into a new melody, something light and clearly intended as accompaniment for a voice, but she did not sing. Clemency knew the words, but she was as musical as a frog, and joining in would ruin the performance.

"I like that song," Roger said as he and the other men entered. "You have quite the touch, Miss Wescott."

Miss Wescott smiled, but did not divert her attention from the pages of music. Again, Clemency marveled at her lightness of touch.

Francis strolled toward the fire with a smile entirely reserved for Mercy. Clemency managed not to roll her eyes. At least the two of them were not dull.

She rose and moved to the side. Francis frowned. "I do not intend to evict you from your seat."

"There are many seats, and I choose to gift this one to you," Clemency said. It was only coincidence that she had moved next to Mr. Wescott. He was watching his sister play, and did not react when she stood next to him, but after a second or two, he said in a low voice, "I apologize for stirring up trouble. That struck me as an old argument."

"Lady Prudence does not need stirring up to make trouble," Clemency replied in equally low tones. "Please do not blame yourself."

"The last thing I desire is to cause you pain," Mr. Wescott said.

Clemency blushed, but said nothing. She could not imagine what she might say—that he was becoming dear to her? That his presence soothed her spirits? Everything that occurred to her felt far too intimate.

The music broke off mid-phrase. Clemency turned her gaze on Miss Wescott, who was looking at the doorway. "Is this yours?" she asked. "It does not sound like you."

Prudence stood in the doorway, her usual frown less severe than Clemency could remember seeing in years. Her hand on the door frame made her look hesitant. Then she said, "It is expected of a young lady to play such music."

"You have done what is expected for far too long," Miss Wescott said. She stood and indicated that Prudence should take her place. "Play something you love."

Prudence paused for another moment in the doorway. Then she walked forward and took her seat at the pianoforte. She adjusted the candles as if intending to shed a brighter light on the music sheets, but when she began playing, it was not the song Miss Wescott had played from the sheet music. Instead, it was something else, sweet and heartbreaking at the same time. Mama gasped, but Clemency did not know why. The melody was so familiar at first she could not remember where she had heard it last, as if the music had surrounded her all her life.

Then it came to her, all in a rush, memory washing over her with the melancholy music. She had never known the name, because music was all music to her if it had no lyrics, but she knew it was a minuet by Handel. And it had been their father's favorite.

She drew in a short, sharp breath and held it, willing Prudence to continue, willing her not to remember anything about where she was or whom she was playing for, willing her with all her heart not to come to herself and remember why this song mattered. But Prudence showed no sign that she knew anyone else was in the room. Her fingers moved deftly up and down the keyboard, playing with the sure precision that had always enthralled listeners.

Tears filled Clemency's eyes as she recalled the last time she had heard her sister play this piece. Their father had been ill by then, but he had insisted on joining them after supper, and Prudence had played and played for an hour or more, everything he asked for. Five days later, he was dead.

The last chord rang out softly through the silent room. Clemency's hand hurt, and when she looked down, she realized she held Mr. Wescott's hand in hers and was crushing it. She snatched her hand away. "I beg your pardon," she said, "I did not mean—I was caught up—"

"I understand," Mr. Wescott said. "That was beautiful."

Clemency met Prudence's eyes. For once, she felt no anger or resentment of her sister. "Thank you," she said, and found herself at a loss for more words.

Prudence looked down at her hands, still resting lightly on the keys. "I don't want to forget," she said, so quietly Clemency could barely hear her.

"You should not," Clemency said. "None of us should."

Roger laughed, a harsh sound that cut the silence like the crack of a whip. "Sentiment," he said derisively. "Father is gone. Music can't change that."

"*Roger!*" Clemency's temper snapped. "Show some respect for once in your life!"

Roger took an involuntary step backward as if the force of Clemency's words had shoved him. "You're a fool," he said. He turned on his heel and strode out of the room.

Clemency stared after him, her fists clenched. That had been a mistake, but it was not one she regretted making. She closed her eyes and calmed herself. "I apologize for my display of temper," she said. "Pray, do play more, Prudence."

Prudence stood. "I can't."

"We will play together," Miss Wescott said. She put a hand on Prudence's shoulder. "You have played the past, and now we will play the future, because I do not believe you have had a partner for duets before."

Prudence did not jerk away from Miss Wescott as Clemency expected she would. "Very well," she said after a few seconds. "There are duets in the cabinet."

"That is a hopeful thing, to buy music without knowing if you will ever play it." Miss Wescott selected some sheets of music and seated herself. "I have never heard this one; will you join me?"

"I do not know it, either," Prudence said. "But I am willing to learn."

The sprightly tune filled the drawing room as no music had in years. Clemency did not know how Miss Wescott's diffidence in playing compared to Prudence's forthright confidence, as far as musical theory went, but the one sounded like a fairy echo of the other, and the combination calmed Clemency's heart.

To Mr. Wescott, she murmured, "That is another miracle I owe you for."

"Join me at the theatre in three days' time, and I will consider myself repaid," Mr. Wescott replied.

Excitement shot through Clemency faster than she could Fly. "That seems a remarkably low price for a miracle. And in truth, it is your sister's miracle for which I am obligated. Perhaps I should join *her* at the theatre."

Mr. Wescott shrugged. "It is entirely your choice, though I should point out that Lydia does not care for plays, and she is not the one you kissed so beautifully."

"A gentleman would not remind me of my lapse in propriety."

"A gentleman would not remember those kisses with such pleasure." Mr. Wescott smiled, and the depth of emotion in his smile reminded Clemency of how much she had enjoyed his kisses as well. "Naturally we should not go in company, Lady Ashford, but if we encounter one another there, well, who would fault us for exchanging our views on the play? I find I enjoy seeing the world through your eyes."

Clemency smiled back. "Very well, Mr. Wescott. In three days' time. I look forward to it."

She closed her eyes and let the music wash over her. Mr. Wescott's closeness burned in her imagination like a brand, and she wished she dared take his hand—or that he would dare to take hers. Three days seemed suddenly an interminable length of time.

CHAPTER 22

IN WHICH ARMAND EXPLOITS
A WEAKNESS IN CLEMENCY'S
DEFENSES

C lemency passed through Emeraude House's small but elegant ballroom and covered her nose to suppress a sneeze. Mama's idea of proper decoration for a young lady's first ball involved bringing a vast quantity of green boughs indoors, holly and yew, as if anticipating the Christmas season. The greenery twined over the high, narrow window frames and across the sills; it draped across the broad doorways, dripping ripe red berries that would certainly be crushed underfoot, ruining many a lady's shoe. Clemency reminded herself to have Slater send the footmen around to sweep up the loose berries before the guests arrived. It was typical of Mama not to think beyond the beauty of the moment.

Again, her nose tickled, deep within, and she pinched its bridge and breathed shallowly through her mouth until the urge to sneeze passed. The gesture was indelicate, but no one was around to notice. She sniffed lightly once and inhaled the fresh, sharp scent of yew, stronger than mint and more appealing to her. The tapers in the wall sconces and both brilliantly-lit chandeliers gilded the greenery like a summer sunset, warming the room as if in anticipation of the guests who would fill the ballroom in just under an hour.

Clemency put away her pocket watch and circled the ballroom one last time, admiring the white walls and the dark floorboards that contrasted so beautifully with them. There had been no gatherings here since before she went away to war; though Mercy had been presented at court, she naturally had not expected to dance, and Clemency recalled the letter she had received from her sister, imploring her to influence Mama to stop pestering Mercy to attend dances where she would, in Mercy's words, "be nothing but a figure of pity."

She paused at the top of the three steps leading down to the ball-room floor. Prudence had not seemed enthusiastic about the ball that morning at breakfast, but neither had she been antagonistic, and Clemency hoped that boded well for the evening. Mama had told Clemency, in hushed tones as if imparting a great secret, that Prudence had shown an interest in the guest list, "and perhaps she will make a fine connection, too, would that not be wonderful?"

Since Mama had not followed this sally with a comment on how *Clemency* needed to make a fine connection, Clemency had not objected, though in her heart she felt Prudence was still too young to contemplate marriage. But Mama's habit of making matches for all her friends' unmarried daughters was well known, and Clemency did not take her remarks seriously.

She encountered Mercy in the hall at the top of the stairs. "Oh, I am not yet dressed," Clemency said. "If you will wait for me, I will hurry so I may convey you downstairs."

"Francis will be here shortly, and he will help," Mercy said. She wore a lovely silk gown of pale green, and her dark hair was pinned up with a golden net securing her curls. "I declare Movers are so very useful, everyone should marry one."

Clemency laughed. "If that were so, I should be besieged by suitors, so I hope no one else shares your opinion!"

"No, you have your heart set on a single suitor," Mercy teased. "Will he attend tonight?"

"I fail to understand your meaning," Clemency said, and hurried away so Mercy would not see her blush.

She chose a gown that was plain and bland so she would not outshine her sister. Prudence, of course, would wear white muslin, which meant not outshining her was difficult, especially when one was a titled Extraordinary permitted to wear any color or fabric one liked. Clemency settled on dark cream satin with a gauzy white over-gown and white shoes, accompanied by her customary pearls. She preferred their sheen and perfection of shape to faceted stones, with the exception of her father's garnet pendant.

When she left her room, Prudence was just shutting the door to her own chamber. They regarded each other silently. Clemency had not realized her sister was now as tall as she; Prudence usually hunched as if hoping not to draw attention to herself. Now Prudence stood straight-shouldered with her hand on the door handle and glared at Clemency as if daring her to judge her appearance.

Clemency stayed where she was. "That gown is lovely. It suits you."

"I feel foolish," Prudence said. "White is a terrible color."

"That is how I always felt," Clemency said. "Our family is not one suited to white. I regret custom does not permit you to wear something richer and darker."

Prudence's eyes narrowed. "Yet that is not something you ever needed worry about."

"I was always afraid to wear anything but white," Clemency said. "I feared people would believe I was putting on airs. It was not until after I entered the Flight Corps that I discovered, firstly, that no one cared whether I wore white or green or puce, and secondly, that what I wore mattered less than how I behaved."

"I never realized," Prudence said. For once, she did not sound antagonistic.

Clemency smiled. She offered Prudence the long jewelry box she held. "Father entrusted this to me," she said. "I believe he feared Mama would lose it, or forget it, and it mattered very much to him that it reach its rightful owner at the proper time."

Prudence opened the box. Her eyes widened. "For me?" She withdrew a strand of pearls identical to Clemency's except for the pendant, which was sapphire instead of garnet.

"Father was fascinated by the history of gemstones. The history of what people believed about their influences." Clemency gestured, and Prudence put the necklace into Clemency's hand. "He chose a stone for each of us that reflected our natures. Garnet for me, for constancy and enduring love—I am not sure how right he was about that, but I am mindful of it. Diamond for Mercy, for purity and light." Clemency laughed. "You should have seen Mercy's face when I told her."

"Father saw the best in us," Prudence said.

Clemency fastened the necklace around Prudence's neck and adjusted it so the sapphire settled in the hollow of her throat. "And sapphire for you, for inner peace and creativity. You know he always said you should share your music with the world."

Prudence rested her fingertips on the sapphire. "I don't see how," she said, but without the sullen heat she usually managed.

"Neither do I." Clemency stepped away, but Prudence did not turn to face her, and she did not press the issue. "Women of our social class perform for their families, usually, but there are many ladies who sing or play musical instruments for larger gatherings. Still intimate—you would not have to go on the stage—but how many would love your music if they were permitted to hear it?"

Prudence still did not turn around. She ducked her head slightly. "Perhaps," she said, and hurried away toward the stairs.

Clemency watched her go. She felt heartened by that interaction. For the first time in years, she recalled how bright and cheerful Prudence had been as a child, how eager to share her interests. Guilt struck Clemency. Mercy was right; she had neglected her sister. Well, perhaps it was not too late to make amends.

She brushed her fingers over the garnet as Prudence had done her sapphire. It was not until she was older that she had learned garnet meant passion as well as love. She did not know whether her father had known it, or had intended that second meaning for his eldest daughter. She and Armand had had passion, and the memory burned hot embarrassment through her. He had taunted her with the past, as if desire was something shameful, something no lady would experience, and now Clemency could not decide where the truth lay. Surely passion was not wrong if one shared it with one's beloved, within the bounds of matrimony? And yet her memories of what she had done with Armand shamed her, so suppose it was the passion itself that was wrong, and not the fact that she had been Coerced?

She flung her head back and let out a heartfelt groan. Damn Armand. Damn Napoleon. Damn herself for not being able to leave the past in the past.

With those harsh words ringing in her heart, she descended on foot to the ground floor.

It lacked a few minutes of the hour, but Clemency took up her station near the door where she would, as official hostess, greet Prudence's guests. She, unlike Prudence and Mama, had not looked over the list of those invited; Mama's flightiness did not extend to a careless disregard of the social niceties, and she would not invite anyone improper. Unfortunately, Lord Winder was not among the "improper" set, but Clemency had wagered with herself that he would not attend even if invited, as he knew she disapproved of him.

She wished now that she had seen the list, to see if Mr. Wescott and his sister had been included. It was unlikely, as they were not part of Clemency's usual social circle, but Mama had spoken highly of Miss Wescott after the party on Monday, and perhaps it had occurred to her to make a late addition to the guests. Clemency told herself not to build her hopes high. If Mama had made the invitation, and the Wescotts chose to attend, that would be lovely. If not, Clemency would not permit herself to be disappointed.

She heard footsteps, and turned to see Francis approaching from the ballroom. "Clemency, do say there will be a waltz?"

"I fear not," Clemency said. "Mama considers the waltz indecent. But I did not believe it mattered to you what dances we will have, unless you intend to abandon your betrothed for another?"

"I daresay I could waltz with Mercy. It is not so difficult to Move a partner in time with oneself, so long as the pace is not too rapid." Francis retrieved his snuff box and took a pinch. "But attempting any other dance would likely end in disaster. So the experiment will have to wait for another time."

"You do not mind? That Mercy is infirm?" Clemency shook her head. "I beg your pardon, that was a foolish question."

Francis struck an affronted pose. "I should think so! It is my own true love of whom you speak, and I would not wish her different."

The bell rang, and Slater sailed into view. "Then return to your own true love, and if you don't mind, ask the musicians to strike up a tune," Clemency said, and composed herself to greet the first of many guests.

Mama had done her work well. The tide of guests swelled quickly and did not ebb for more than an hour. Many of them were known to Clemency only by name, and most of those were friends of Mama's. Lord Winder did not appear. Nor, to Clemency's disappointment, did the Wescotts. She bridled her disappointment and cheerfully greeted the next guest, and the next.

She did recognize more than a few eligible bachelors and again saw her mother's hand in the guest list. Clemency did not like most of them, not because they were unappealing, but because so many of them were ten or fifteen years older than Prudence. Perhaps that would not matter in the abstract—Francis was eight years older than Mercy—but Prudence was, in Clemency's opinion, very young for seventeen. She looked each of these men in the eye and held their hands a trifle more firmly than necessary, hoping to remind them that Prudence was not without a protector.

When Jane arrived, Clemency had begun to weary of greeting strangers. She fell on her friend gratefully. "Thank you for attending," she said, and in a lower voice added, "I do not believe this is Prudence's ball, given how many of Mama's friends are present."

"Prudence is likely to be swallowed up in this mess," Jane agreed. "But your home is beautiful, and Prudence's consequence cannot help but be elevated if this ball is as popular as it appears."

Clemency turned to face the ballroom. Through its doors, she saw couples moving in a sprightly country dance, with other men and women strolling around the room. She could not see Prudence and hoped the girl was enjoying herself, wherever she was. "I must give Mama credit for knowing how to entertain."

She turned around—and found herself face to face with Armand.

Shock and fear made her gasp and take a step backward. Armand's smile broadened. "I beg your pardon, Lady Ashford, I appear to have startled you." He bowed, a shallow but polite gesture, and did not look at all abashed at her reaction. "I suppose it is rather too loud for you to hear my approach."

Clemency, keenly aware of Jane at her side, watching this interaction, forced a smile. "That is true, I did not hear you," she said. "I was unaware you had been invited."

Armand's smile was now brilliant enough to outshine the chandeliers. "The Dowager Countess is most gracious. I count myself fortunate to have made her acquaintance. Surely you do not suggest I should not have come?"

"Of course not," Clemency lied.

Jane cleared her throat. Clemency startled again. "I beg your pardon, Miss Pilgrim. May I introduce to you General de Villiers? General, this is Miss Pilgrim."

"We were introduced at the Cabinet of Curiosities," Jane said, "but I fear we had no opportunity to speak then. My father speaks highly of your military prowess, General."

"I have heard of your father, Miss Pilgrim," Armand said, accepting the hand Jane extended. "He is quite the world traveler, I understand. Do you accompany him on his journeys?"

"Very rarely, General," Jane said. She lowered her lashes demurely and gave Armand a sideways, shy smile. "I prefer England."

"As do I," Armand said with an answering smile. "Perhaps you will tell me what you love about your homeland?"

Jane accepted his arm. "If you will share with me your impressions of London. Everyone can talk of nothing but General de Villiers."

"All true, I assure you," Armand said, laughing. He led Jane in the direction of the ballroom and soon passed out of Clemency's earshot.

Clemency closed her eyes briefly and let out a deep breath. She did not know whether to curse Jane for attempting to add Armand, horrid seducer that he was, to her covey of swains or to bless her name for diverting Armand so he would leave Clemency alone. Of course Mama would have invited him; he was the guest of the hour, fêted everywhere, a man with a tragic past and an exciting future. No doubt mamas everywhere were plotting how to snatch him up for their daughters.

Clemency's heart pounded sharply, a single pulse that numbed her body for a second. Mama could not *possibly* intend Armand for Prudence! The idea was absurd. Prudence was far too young—and yet Armand was eligible, he was charming, and as far as Clemency knew his fortune, while not large, was intact despite his having been Coerced. Clemency clenched her teeth against rising bile. Well, she was the head of the family, and so long as Prudence was underage, she had the final say in Prudence's marriage plans. *Unless she elopes to Scotland*, her heart whispered, and the bile surged again.

She greeted a few more latecomers before concluding that everyone who intended to come had arrived, but instead of proceeding into the ballroom, she retreated to the small drawing room for a moment's peace. This was where all the guests' coats and wraps were held, and the smell of damp wool—it must be raining, though she had heard no sound of raindrops striking the windows—comforted her, made her feel warm and secure and able to forget Armand's presence.

Flying would be an even greater comfort, but not while she was dressed like this. As well, she recalled Roger's jab about how she took to the skies whenever anything troublesome occurred. She did *not* avoid her responsibilities. If anything, Flying calmed her spirits and made her more capable of handling her responsibilities. Roger's words stung nonetheless.

After about a minute, Clemency crossed the foyer to the ballroom door and stood at the top of the short flight of stairs. She searched the crowd for Prudence, and eventually saw her dancing with an attractive man Clemency recognized as a Mover she had seen at the trials before. She could not recall his name. He was one of Mama's eligible bachelors, perhaps. He and Prudence seemed very intent on each other, which worried Clemency; she did not like the idea of Prudence making a connection with a near-stranger. Then she chided herself for her foolishness. It was not as if the man would propose marriage in the middle of the ballroom.

The dance came to an end, and all around ladies and gentlemen began to shift as they sought out partners for the next. Clemency indulged in a brief regret that Mr. Wescott was not present. He was likely an excellent dancer, but she was smitten enough that she would not care if he was not.

"Lady Ashford."

The voice she heard over the noise of the crowd was Mr. Wescott's. Excitement filled her, and she turned swiftly to greet him.

But the man addressing her was not Mr. Wescott, but Armand.

He did not react to how quickly her smile disappeared, nor to the disappointment she was sure was palpable to everyone within ten feet of her. "My lady," he said with a bow, "may I solicit your hand for the next two dances?"

Clemency could not help herself; she glanced rapidly around to see if anyone was paying attention to this interaction. No one stared, but Clemency saw eyes shifting as the women surrounding them pretended not to have been watching Armand and hoping he would ask them to dance. Cursing inwardly, Clemency said, "Certainly, General."

Armand took her gloved hand and led her to join the line forming up at the center of the room. "I consider it my good fortune that I claimed you," he said. His smile deepened, and Clemency's cheeks heated as she took in his double meaning. "You are no doubt popular, and I would hate to lose an opportunity to speak with you."

"Speaking is not considered the primary purpose of a dance," Clemency said, keeping a light tone.

"No. There is also the intimacy of sharing one's time with another, just the two of you, promised to one another for the space of half an hour." Armand bowed as the music began. "And we are not chance-met strangers, are we?"

Clemency chose not to respond. Already she regretted not finding a socially acceptable way to turn down his request. He looked at her with those eyes that had seen her naked, his hand clasped hers lightly and caressingly as if he had the right to touch her any way he chose, and she wished she could flee the ballroom and Fly away until she reached a land where no one had ever heard of Armand de Villiers.

The steps of the dance brought them close together. In a low voice, Armand said, "You are as beautiful as I remember, Clemency. My heart, my love—how I long to hold you again."

Her name on his lips sounded like profanity. "I am not your love," she said, all she could manage before the music drew them apart. Her heart pounded, her heavy breathing hurt her chest, and her eyes ached with suppressed tears.

They danced in silence until the music brought them back

together. "You are my love," Armand said. "You are mine, now and forever. I can wait for you to see the truth."

"I was Coerced," Clemency said, trying for defiance, but her voice sounded weak and her hands shook. "I feel nothing for you, and I wish nothing more to do with you. Do not approach me again."

Armand merely smiled. When next they drew near, he said, "You will marry me, darling. It is inevitable."

"I choose whom I will marry, and it is not you," Clemency replied.

"You think any other man will have you, after you have given yourself so fully to me?" Armand's smile gleamed in the light of a hundred white tapers. "You will marry me, and make me a Comte. I have always felt the lack of a title."

"An Earl," Clemency said automatically. "And I would rather die unwed than marry a cur and a scoundrel like you."

Armand jerked as if she had slapped him. His smile faded briefly. Then it returned at full brilliance. "I see you need convincing, my love. Very well. We shall not speak of this again tonight."

Clemency clenched her teeth on a scream. He tormented her, he taunted her, and yet *she* was the one who would appear unstable if she shoved him away and ordered her servants to throw him out. She would have to have words with Mama about not giving Armand access to Emeraude House again.

They finished their dances in silence. Clemency's curtsey was perfunctory, and she made no effort to disguise the fact that she was fleeing Armand. Immediately, she was approached by another partner, whose invitation to dance she accepted gratefully. He was the Mover Prudence had danced with. She smiled brightly to conceal her forgetting of his name.

"Mr. Montague, my lady," he said immediately. "I do not know that you recall me—it has been some time since last we met."

"Of course," Clemency said. Despite his words, she felt as if she had seen him recently, perhaps in passing at the aborted trials. "Thank you for attending."

"I appreciate your invitation, Lady Ashford," he said as the dance began. "You have a lovely home."

"Thank you, Mr. Montague," Clemency replied. "I do remember you. We have never competed against each other, have we?"

"I am a Mover only, not an Extraordinary, and my skills pale beside yours," Mr. Montague said. "Though perhaps this is an oversight worth remedying, if the public trials are ever held again."

"Why would they not be?" Clemency said, puzzled.

Mr. Montague's eyebrows raised. "This threat to Extraordinaries means Mr. Jinks, whoever he is, is likely to strike again where he is least expected—but I believe something so overt as the trials would be too much temptation for him to ignore. It may not be safe to gather hundreds with talent in one place."

"I hope that is not the case. Mr. Jinks cannot be permitted to control this city."

"That is true." Mr. Montague shrugged. "But we should not discuss such dire events tonight. I have been introduced to your sister, and she is charming, but—may I be honest?—you are as beautiful, and I find myself drawn to you."

Clemency managed not to slap him. "That is kind of you to say, but I do not consider it a compliment that you admire me over my sister whose day this is."

Mr. Montague appeared taken aback. "I meant no offense. I believed you admired plain speaking. It is what everyone says of you."

"Plain speaking is not the same as a disregard for politeness," Clemency said. "Pray, let us speak no more of it."

Mr. Montague nodded and said nothing else. Clemency felt a twinge of guilt at her harshness, which she knew had been enhanced by her anger and misery over her interaction with Armand, but she found herself incapable of casual conversation. Perhaps Mr. Montague was not an awful person, but she did not care enough to discover more about him.

As one dance became another, tension gradually built in Clemency's back and shoulders, rising from her irritation with her partner and compounded by her inability to stop comparing him to the partner she wished she had. Mr. Wescott would not try her patience; he would not torment her with words calculated to hurt and humiliate her. She wished with all her heart she had influenced the guest list in this one small thing.

At the end of their dances, she bade a polite but icy farewell to Mr. Montague and wished she dared roll out her shoulders, but that would be uncouth. When she was again addressed, she turned and once more startled at her unexpected companion. "Francis!"

"I have permission to dance just this once with someone to whom I am not betrothed." Francis bowed slightly. "In truth, Mercy told me to dance as much as I like, but I find I prefer to converse with her. However, you seem out of sorts, and I intend to interrogate you as to the cause of your disquiet."

Weariness spread over Clemency like a river fog, dimming her sight and making her long for her bed. "Very well," she said.

Francis chuckled. "That is the least enthusiastic acceptance I have ever had. Tell me, Clemency, what troubles you?"

She did not wish to reveal her inner misery to her best friend. Francis was not likely to shun her, but she did not care to have him know her shame, and at worst he would challenge Armand, either privately or publicly, and that would truly be a nightmare. "I am so very tired," she said. "I believe I will turn my duties over to Mama after our dances and go upstairs."

"Then it has nothing to do with General de Villiers?"

Clemency blinked. "With General de Villiers? Why would you say that?"

"Because I watched you as you danced with him, and he looked very satisfied, and you looked as if you wished him to the devil." Francis drew near and nearly missed his step. "Did he say something to displease you?"

Clemency's heart sped up again. Not telling Francis the facts was one thing; actively lying to him was quite another. "He—he reminded me of events in France that were unpleasant," she said. "They were memories I would prefer not to dwell on."

"I had forgotten you knew one another in France," Francis said. "When was that? It must have been quite late in the war, after he broke Coercion."

"What did he say happened after that, do you know?" Clemency asked, hoping to divert Francis. "I only know that he was no longer Coerced to follow Napoleon."

"It is quite the dramatic story. General de Villiers broke free of Coercion and took command of a division of the Grande Armée, bringing it against Napoleon's troops and stopping his advance on Paris. You did not know?"

Clemency shook her head. "That is dramatic." It also could not be true, for even had Armand no longer been Coerced, all of the Grande Armée still was, so how could he have turned some of its soldiers against Napoleon's orders?

"Well, you should not have to endure unpleasantness," Francis declared. "Perhaps he is mistaken about what memories you will find pleasing, and you will have to tell him to speak on other topics." He laughed. "He does seem interested in you. Mr. Wescott may have to fight for your affections, if de Villiers intends courtship!"

Clemency smiled, and hoped it looked natural.

CHAPTER 23

IN WHICH DISASTER STRIKES

Clemency had not expected the Theatre Royal to have changed much in the four years she had been gone, but its recent remodeling left her with an odd, twinned sensation, as if past and present had collided. Though the red-curtained stage still dominated the theatre, the curtain was newer and more vibrant, cherries rather than plums. Despite the curtain's heaviness, the space felt more open, no doubt because of the dozens of chandeliers illuminating the seats and the stage and filling the theatre with the smell of fire and hot wax.

She could not tell if anyone else found the new theatre beautiful and odd at once. Four tiers of seats rose above the floor as always, but she recalled those tiers being packed with spectators, whereas now the boxes held only a handful of people each, giving them a more elite air. It meant the other patrons were far enough away Clemency could imagine them dolls, or figures in a dream. She did not know how she felt about that, either. Nevertheless, she herself had taken advantage of the trend, and she and Jane were alone in her box.

Inviting Jane to join her had been a mistake. Clemency had dimly recalled, when she delivered the invitation, that Jane was not a comfortable companion at theatrical events, but she had not remem-

bered why. Barely half an hour into the performance, the reality had
become clear: Jane thought nothing of talking over the performers in a
voice just loud enough to distract her companion, and of talking of
matters completely unrelated to the play.

Now, as *The Merchant of Venice* neared its midpoint, Clemency
leaned forward and tried to ignore her friend. She had heard of
Edmund Kean, of course, but this was the first time she had seen him
act, and she could not recall the last time she had been so enthralled
by a performance. A sympathetic Shylock was the last thing she had
expected.

"And the plans for my revel move forward nicely," Jane said. "Fancy
dress, naturally, but one must provide for the entertainment of all one's
guests, so there will be cards—you will come, won't you?"

"Of course," Clemency said, though she was not paying full attention. "Whatever you say. Now, hush. This is an important speech."

"Oh, bah, it is Shakespeare, one can barely understand two words
in five," Jane said. "I intend to acquire my costume early, you know
how quickly the good ones are taken."

Clemency nodded. She sat up straighter and applauded with the
rest of the audience as the act drew to its close, overcome by the way
the sound filled the enormous space like the roaring of a great wind at
altitude. There must be nearly three thousand people in attendance,
which to Clemency was a vital part of the theatre experience. Sharing a
performance with so many others filled her with a tingling excitement
only Flying could match.

She had not looked for Mr. Wescott, who might be anywhere in the
crowd. She herself was conspicuous in rose-pink satin, seated at the
center of the second tier of boxes above the floor. He would come
to her.

She had also not told Jane of her assignation—that seemed such a
furtive, sneaking word for what she intended, which was a respectable
public conversation complete with admiring glances and some flirtation. It was a pity Jane needed to be there at all. Immediately
Clemency regretted that ignoble thought. She would not be the sort
of person who threw her friends over for the sake of an attractive
man.

Jane stood. "I see Lauretta Hughes, and I should speak to her. Will you join me?"

"No, but please give her my regards." Clemency's heart beat a little faster at the idea of being alone in the box when Mr. Wescott appeared.

Jane regarded Clemency skeptically. "Your color is high. Are you well?"

"It is so hot," Clemency said, fanning herself with her hand. "So many people, and so many lights—naturally I am over-warm."

"I declare I feel as stifled as if I were drowning in a featherbed," Jane said. "Do not sit here all night, Clemency, that is what boring people with no conversation do." She shook out her skirts and left the box.

Clemency sat and watched the crowds. So many well-dressed men and women, and not all of them were there for the play. Seeing others and being seen were favorite pastimes of Clemency's social class, almost as popular as dancing or riding in Hyde Park, though come to think on it, both those things invited observation as well. She herself could think of only one man she was interested in seeing that evening. Why he was not yet here, she could not understand, but his absence tuned her impatience to the breaking point.

She heard footsteps over the noise of the crowd and turned eagerly to the door, saying, "You are late. I had begun to believe you would not join me."

Armand smiled. "Now that is the kind of greeting I like," he said. He was dressed as finely as any gentleman, his puce coat drawing attention to his broad shoulders and fair complexion.

Clemency's face felt numb. "What are you doing here?"

"Come now, you will make me feel unwanted," Armand said, displaying his dimple. "Do you suggest you expected another man? I will have to take steps to defend my rights."

"You have no right to me, and I insist you leave now." Clemency's hands clenched into fists. Would that she were a man, that she might strike the smile from his face!

Armand walked forward to the front of the box and put a hand on the nearest supporting pillar. "It is a delightful performance, is it not?

Though I am not certain I like Kean's interpretation of Shylock. One prefers a Jew to be a thorough villain, does one not?"

"I told you to leave, Armand. I am not interested in discussing theatre." Clemency rose. "Leave, and never return."

Armand continued to look out across the theatre. "Why red curtains, I wonder?" he mused. "Theatre curtains are always red." He turned to face Clemency. "I will not leave, my love. You belong to me, and it is past time you admitted it. Coyness is only attractive for so long."

If she screamed in fury, how many people would hear her over the din? Clemency stepped closer until she was inches from Armand's face. "You cannot believe this ploy will work," she hissed. "I am not some powerless girl you can overwhelm. I am the Countess of Ashford. Get out of my box now, or I will have you removed."

Armand's smile did not waver. "You will change your mind. I am certain of it." Swifter than Flight, he kissed her. His lips tasted of wine and sweet cream, and memories of kissing him in passion flooded Clemency's mind, sickening her. Before she could react, he had stepped away, out of her reach so slapping him was impossible. He bowed, and with a last mocking smile slipped out of the box.

Clemency's breath rasped in her lungs, and her cheeks hurt from the blood surging through them. He dared! She glanced over the crowd, but she could see no evidence that anyone had witnessed that; no one pointed in her direction or appeared to be laughing at her. Several men and women were looking her way, but it was only her imagination that it was she and not any of a hundred other women in the vicinity they stared at. There were too many other things to look at for anyone to care about staring at her, however beautiful or powerful she was.

She sank into her chair and stared sightlessly at the red curtains. She knew Armand well enough to realize he would not stop pursuing her unless she did something drastic. Unfortunately, she could not imagine what she might do that would rid her of Armand as well as protect her most shameful secret. The idea of enduring Armand's "courtship" until he grew bored of it filled her with weariness. Making a public scene was not something she was comfortable with. No other possibilities came to mind.

Perhaps it was time to tell someone, the right someone. Mr. Wescott was clever, and he might come up with a plan she had not. But when she contemplated telling him the truth, shame and humiliation still stopped her tongue. He might be the one who would support her most completely, or he might be the one to condemn her and wish never to see her again.

She had friends, though—Francis might understand, or Jane, and of course Mercy would not shun her. She pushed aside the frightened, embarrassed instinct that said she should not tell anyone ever and made herself face the truth. No one who cared about her would think less of her for having been Armand's doxy. And if she was honest with herself, she could admit she wished to tell.

She turned eagerly when she again heard footsteps. But the visitor was still not Mr. Wescott. It was Jane. Disappointment made Clemency say, "Oh, it is you. Did Mrs. Hughes not wish to converse? I believed her to be the most talkative woman of our acquaintance."

"She had much to say," Jane said. Her usual cheerful demeanor was gone, her normally expressive features still and so neutral Clemency almost did not recognize her. "About you."

"About me?" Clemency, taken aback, stared at Jane. "What about me?"

"About you and General de Villiers," Jane said.

Dread filled Clemency's heart. "Jane," she began.

"Of course it is impossible," Jane said. "You would never behave with such abandon as to take a lover."

Clemency swallowed. "I was Coerced," she said. "Napoleon Coerced me to love General de Villiers."

Jane's eyes narrowed. "Coerced? Then you *were* intimate with him."

"Yes, but it was not my choice," Clemency said. She did not like the way Jane continued to look at her as if she were a stranger. "It was Coercion."

Jane walked to the front of the box and gripped the rail, looking down at the floor beneath. "You never used to conceal things from me," she said.

"Would *you* have told anyone?" Clemency could not bear to go to her, to make Jane face her and compel Jane to hear the truth. "You do not understand what Coercion is like. I could not bear to have anyone know how I was humiliated."

"And now you say it was Coercion," Jane said. "I never believed you were a liar as well."

Clemency jerked. "What?"

Jane turned around. Her mouth was a tight, straight line, and a muscle jumped in her rigid jaw. "General de Villiers is handsome, and charming. Anyone would understand if you were carried away into intimacy with him. But for you to take a lover and then pretend you were Coerced so as to be absolved of your sin—"

"Jane!" Clemency's skin felt tight and hot. "How can you accuse me of lying? I was Coerced!"

"Can you prove it?" Jane asked. "Please, Clemency, do not pretend to impossibilities. Coercion cannot change someone's nature so thoroughly."

The pleading tone of Jane's voice cut through the numbness enveloping Clemency. She swallowed to stop her throat from closing up. "You know nothing of the matter," she said. "Nothing. And my word has always been good enough for you before."

"You have never claimed a patent falsehood to be true before," Jane said. "Please, Clemency. There is no shame in having been weak. No one will fault you."

Clemency gazed across the theatre. She no longer believed it was her imagination that everyone was staring at her, staring and whispering her shame to their neighbors. She saw Armand in a box on the highest tier, conversing with a finely-dressed couple Clemency did not know. As he turned away, his eyes met Clemency's. Even at that distance, his smile was clearly visible. He saluted her, the precise gesture of a soldier in the field, then touched his fingers to his lips and flicked them away as if tossing her a kiss.

Clemency had her hands on the rail at the front of the box, preparing to leap over it, when she came to her senses. She could not Fly in a fine gown through the Theatre Royal and seize hold of Armand, and she could not carry him away and drop him to his death on the stage. Armand's smile widened. Then he turned his back on her, so clear a mark of disdain fury and humiliation surged through Clemency again.

"No one will fault me?" she whispered, and swallowed again. Her eyes were as hot as her face now. "Is that what you believe—that I went to him willingly?"

"You know what the War Office is like," Jane said, and now her voice cajoled Clemency like a mother coaxing a stubborn child. "We had freedoms there—perhaps it is to be expected if those freedoms went to your head."

Unexpected fury surged through Clemency. Jane's pleading expression, her obvious desire for Clemency to be reasonable, were so at odds with her terrible words Clemency felt she had stepped into a play, one taking place on the wrong side of the red curtains. Surely Jane was having a joke at her expense, and any minute now she would laugh and exclaim that she had meant none of what she said.

"How can you say that?" she cried out. "You really believe I am so lost to decency that I would carry on an affair and then lie to protect myself from the consequences? Jane, do you not know me at all?"

"I believed I did," Jane said.

Clemency wound her fist into her gown to prevent herself slapping Jane. "I am not a liar," she said in a low, harsh voice. "And you are no true friend." Then she ran from the box.

She shoved her way through crowds that had on other occasions moved aside for her, even when they did not recognize her. Now it felt as if they were closing in on her deliberately. Everywhere, she heard laughter, not the sound of happy amusement but of derision and scorn. Memories plagued her, these fresh and close at hand: Armand's mocking salute and blown kiss. She had believed him at least honorable enough not to reveal the truth, but now she had no idea why she had ever assumed that. And now the world knew her shame.

She pushed harder, and people made way for her, but their abrupt silences as she passed revealed they had been talking about her. She held her head high and ignored them, but each new silence burned through her until tears spilled over her cheeks. She did not wipe them away. Acknowledging them would make her break down entirely and give London more to talk about.

She bumped into someone, shouldered past him, and came to an abrupt halt as the person took hold of her wrist. "Release me," she commanded, wrenching at his grip. She might as well have tried to break an iron manacle.

"Lady Ashford," Mr. Wescott said. "I beg your pardon, I intended only to draw your attention. I spoke your name and you did not respond. What troubles you?"

Clemency snatched her hand away, and this time he released her. He looked concerned, but not repulsed or angry, and she let out a sound that was half barking laugh and half heartrending sob. "You do not know?" she cried out. "Someone will tell you soon enough."

She turned to go, and he put a hand on her shoulder. "I would prefer you tell me," he said, quietly enough she had to strain to hear him.

It was all too much. Jane's betrayal, all those stares and whispers—she could not bear to see him shun her, too. "I cannot. Do not ask me," she exclaimed. "I wish we had never met!"

She tore herself free from his grip and ran, Moving people out of her way in her desperation. Most of them stumbled and fell into one another. She did not care if she hurt them; she only knew she needed to Fly.

She burst through the crowds onto the street and launched herself skyward. She felt the cold, but at a distance, as if her skin were already ice and the air could not touch her. Of all the horrors she had imagined, that her own friend would not believe her had not been one of them. She threw her head back and screamed out her pain, filling her lungs with frozen air so she was ice inside and out. Then she curled into a ball and floated, buffeted by the winds that said a storm was coming, and wept tears of anger and humiliation.

Eventually, she realized she was shivering, though she still did not feel the cold. She no longer felt anything. Numbly, she Flew for home. Clouds blotted out the full moon, and she smelled snow in the air. Clemency hated snow; it made Flying nearly impossible and turned the city grey and depressing. She hoped she would arrive home before it fell, so she might hide in her bed and pretend Armand had never existed.

As if taunting her, the first fat flakes fell when she was still a quarter mile from Emeraude House. She gritted her teeth and Flew faster, wiping snow from her eyes with her hands because snowflakes driven by the wind were too numerous and small to Move. Clemency knew of a few Movers whose precision with their talent was so refined they could manage snow, but she had never had the patience to learn the skill. She did not even regret her lack now; the horrid snow gave her a focus for her anger.

She slammed her window back, catching it before it could break, and landed on the hearth rug, shaking snowflakes off her gown. Some had melted and left spots. At the moment, she was too miserable to care if they ruined her lovely gown. She used her Moving to ring the bell while she removed her shoes, hovering above the hearth with her legs drawn up beneath her. The position rucked her gown up around her thighs, but there was no one present to be offended at her lack of modesty, and she would not have cared if there were.

Tatton entered. Her eyes widened as she took in Clemency's condition. "My lady," she said, "did you Fly home?"

"I did," Clemency said, managing not to add anything cutting that would have temporarily soothed her spirits at the cost of hurting Tatton's feelings. "Please help me undress."

Tatton said nothing more, but it was the sort of silence that burgeoned with unspoken words. Clemency stared into the fire as she undressed. Her decision to remain silent seemed foolish now. Armand had revealed the truth—no doubt he had done so in the most underhanded way imaginable, to make her seem whorish—and now anything Clemency claimed would seem a lie, calculated to absolve herself. Had she been open about her experience—

She cursed aloud, drawing a gasp from Tatton. "Forgive me," Clemency said. No. She should not have had to tell the world about her private shame. This was not her fault, it was Armand's, and ultimately Napoleon's. But it was too late to have regrets about past decisions.

"Tatton," she said, "you know I have not been forthright with you."

"Your business is your own, my lady," Tatton said. She brought Clemency's nightdress, warm from the fire, and helped her put it on.

"Well, that ends now," Clemency said. "You will hear the story soon enough, and I prefer you hear the truth from me first."

Tatton, her arms full of Clemency's gown, nodded. She looked perplexed.

Clemency took a deep breath. "Napoleon Coerced me while I was in France, a week or so before the battle of Waterloo. He made me believe in his cause, and he also made me love General de Villiers—to desire him so I would go to his bed."

Tatton gasped. "My lady, how horrid! But you broke free of Coercion, yes?"

"I was injured, and it dispelled the Coercion. But now Armand—General de Villiers has told the world what happened, and he has done it in a way that makes me appear licentious and abandoned. I will tell the truth, but I fear no one will believe me."

"*I* believe you, my lady. And I will tell anyone who repeats the story the truth." Tatton's narrow face bore all the marks of someone ready to die for a cause.

Clemency's heartache eased somewhat. "Thank you. I did not imagine anyone who knows me would disbelieve me, and yet Miss Pilgrim—oh, it does not matter. I must sleep now, and see what the morning brings."

Tatton nodded. "Good night, my lady."

Curled up in bed, Clemency's weariness from Flying through the storm overtook her. But her mind was too full to permit her to sleep. Jane, Tatton, and—

Her heart sank. Mr. Wescott. She could barely remember what she had said to him, only that it was something awful she now regretted. She should have told him what she had told Tatton and trusted him to react properly. Now he would hear the tainted story Armand had spread, and he would believe the worst of her, and... A sob escaped her, and then she was weeping hard enough that the tears hurt.

Once more her mind threw up alternative scenarios that would have changed the past. If she had turned down War Office service in favor of tending to family matters. If she had been attached to a different regiment. If she had turned down Jennet's request that she Fly in reconnaissance in the direction where Napoleon's forces were hidden. If she had resisted the Coercion—but no one resisted Coercion except a Discerner, so that was not something she should blame herself for.

She squeezed her eyes shut and drew in a deep, shuddering breath. Dwelling on the past would not change the present. She had not done any of those things, and as a result she had lain with Armand, and that had led to where she was now. She needed to face the truth like a woman and not hide from it like a child. Whatever came tomorrow, she would endure.

With those bold thoughts ringing through her body, she fell into sleep.

CHAPTER 24

IN WHICH CLEMENCY'S NOTORIETY RESULTS IN AN ALTERED SOCIAL STATUS

The storm worsened as the night passed, waking Clemency repeatedly with its rising howls and, an hour or so after midnight, the window slamming open like a thunderclap. The abrupt noise propelled Clemency out of bed and into the air. Her heart beat a terrified rhythm as she cast about for the monster she had been fleeing in her dream. The noise of the wind brought her to her senses, and she drifted back to sit on her bed until she felt calmer. Then she Moved the window shut and latched it more securely.

She never could Fly in Dreams, or Move anything; instead she strained to influence the world, gesturing and pointing as if that might Move objects or people. The dreams she hated most were the ones where she remembered being a Mover. They made her dreaming mind's impotence so much worse. At least tonight it had only been a monster she ran from.

The storm had dropped a pile of snow on the floor beneath the window from where it had accumulated on the sill. Clemency tried to Move it, shape it into a ball for removal, but it was already half-melted and too slushy to Move in a discrete form. She watched it melt instead, saw it turn from white to clear and then to water slicking the floor. Tatton would clean up the remaining puddle in the morning. Clemency felt slightly guilty at leaving it to her maid, as if she were responsible for the spill. But that was foolishness, and she should not entertain foolishness.

Her few hours of sleep had restored her enough that she could view her problem in a more sanguine light. Armand was a charming novelty, but she was well known and popular, and whatever lies Armand spread, they would not survive her witness to the truth. She would likely have an uncomfortable few days, perhaps a week or two, and all would be forgotten.

She lay back, but sleep eluded her. Even as she told herself nothing horrid would happen, her mind insisted on conjuring scenarios in which she was laughed to scorn, or shunned, or ignored by her friends. Finally, she made herself count the strands on the tassels of the bed curtains, and that boring exercise carried her off into sleep again. This time, she did not remember her dreams.

The storm had abated somewhat by morning, but not enough to make Flying possible, so Clemency determined on a late morning and a day spent indoors. She refused to admit that her nocturnal imaginings influenced her decision. Her situation would not be resolved in a day, and likely she would endure whispers and mocking for a while, but knowing this did not make her happy.

She eventually descended to the drawing room, where she found Mercy alone. Mercy greeted her, saying, "Did you enjoy the play, dearest?"

Mercy's cheerfulness sat like a stone in Clemency's stomach. All her earlier resolve deserted her. She had considered how she might counter Armand's lies, but she had not imagined being forced to tell the truth to people she loved. And yet she could not permit Mercy to learn of Clemency's humiliation from gossips who might have the worst of intentions.

Clemency sat near her sister. "Forgive me," she said. "I have kept secrets from you. You will understand when you hear, but please do not speak until I have told you everything."

Mercy's eyes widened. "You frighten me."

"It is not—no, just listen." Clemency breathed in and out, calming herself. "It began in France, before Napoleon's defeat…"

She told Mercy everything, every horrid detail—not the specifics of what she and Armand had done together, but everything else, all the way to the blow to the head that had broken Napoleon's Coercion. She told her of how ashamed and fearful she had been, and how she had carried that secret for months until Armand had revealed it. Mercy listened in still silence, her face growing gradually paler until she looked carved of ice. When Clemency had explained her fears of what Armand's telling of the story might do, she said, "I understand why you said nothing, but you must realize how your situation appears."

"I do," Clemency said. "Armand has told everyone I was willingly intimate with him, and my claiming Coercion sounds like an excuse for my bad behavior. But it is true, Mercy, I swear it."

"I believe you." Mercy rested her hand on Clemency's knee. "Of course I believe you. Who among your friends will not?"

"Jane Pilgrim, for one," Clemency said bitterly. "And if she does not, I cannot assume any of them will."

"Francis will stand by you, I am certain of it," Mercy declared. "And if he does not, he will suffer my wrath."

Clemency smiled. "A dire fate, indeed."

At that moment, the door opened, and Slater said, "Mr. Daubney," just as Francis said, "Clemency, I cannot believe—tell me it is not true!"

His tone was not one of censure, but Clemency's heart constricted regardless. "I do not know what you have heard."

Francis hesitated, glancing at Mercy. "It is perhaps not a story for Mercy's ears—"

"Clemency was Coerced by Napoleon into being that horrid General de Villiers' lover," Mercy said.

Francis blinked. "Ah," he said, "well, that is definitely not what I have heard. I assumed the report of your—well, those reports to have been entirely invented. But you say—" His cheeks were bright red, giving him the appearance of a cherub who had found the port decanter and gone swimming.

"I could not bring myself to tell anyone," Clemency said. "Please forgive my deception."

"There is nothing to forgive," Francis said. "I could have gone to my grave without that knowledge." He began pacing in front of the fire, four quick steps and then a sharp pivot on his heel, over and over until Clemency felt dizzy.

"Francis, sit," she said. "I already feel ill enough without your pacing."

Francis sat in the chair beside Mercy. "I will challenge him, if you like."

"Dueling is illegal, Francis. And killing Armand will do no good in any case. I must just spread my story to counter his, and wait for the furor to die down." Clemency hoped she sounded more certain than she felt.

"Waiting will not satisfy me. I cannot believe all of London celebrates him as a hero, when he—" Francis' color rose again. "The very idea infuriates me."

"That cheers me, Francis. I was worried...Jane did not believe me when I told her I was Coerced."

"Jane?" Francis absently took Mercy's hand. "I cannot credit it. Why would Jane disbelieve you?"

"I cannot understand it myself, but you have heard more stories than I. Is not Armand—General de Villiers spreading the word in a way that makes me sound like his willing bed partner?"

Francis nodded. "Yes, but surely your friends know you better than that."

Clemency shrugged. Again, she hoped her fear and insecurity did not show. "Perhaps it will pass. But I—" Again, she remembered her incoherent words to Mr. Wescott, and the memory struck her to the heart.

"What is it? You suddenly looked as if you'd been struck," Mercy said.

"It is nothing," Clemency lied, then decided she was tired of deception. "I met Mr. Wescott yesterday evening, after I discovered what story the general had spread. I was—I would not speak to him, and I fled, and now he will have heard the lies and I cannot imagine what he believes."

Francis and Mercy exchanged glances. "He thinks too highly of you to be influenced by lies," Francis said. "I am certain of it."

"You have barely exchanged two words with him, Francis, I cannot see how you can know this."

"But I know you, and you have never felt this deep an attachment to any man." Francis put his other hand over his and Mercy's joined ones. "He must be worthy to have captured your interest, and no one worthy would be fooled into taking a stranger's word over yours."

"Mr. Wescott is a good man," Mercy said. She ran her fingers over the rail on her chair wheel. "He will at least be willing to listen to an explanation."

Clemency groaned and flung herself to lie on the arm of the divan, pressing her face into her crossed forearms. "Everything about this is wrong," she said. "Why should my private affairs be the concern of anyone but myself?"

"Because you are a countess, and therefore a veritable wellspring of gossip-fodder." Francis' solemn face invested what might otherwise have been a lighthearted comment with deep significance. "In truth, Clemency, had it not been this it might have been anything else. At least in this case, the story is an outright lie."

"A lie with some tinge of truth to it. I *was* Armand's lover." Clemency sighed and sat up. "Perhaps I should have denied everything, but that never occurred to me."

"And if *that* lie came out, it would make the truth much less believable." Mercy sounded as solemn as Francis. "It is better to tell the truth."

"I hope you are right," Clemency said.

⁂

THE SKIES CLEARED AFTER TWO O'CLOCK, AND DESPITE HER EARLIER resolve, Clemency left the house to go Flying. Hours of enforced confinement had made her irritable, a feeling not tempered by listening to Mercy and Francis talk and laugh in low, intimate voices. She could not help remembering Mr. Wescott and what she had said to him, remembering too his look of concern when she had run from him. Now, in the bright post-storm light with the wind in her face, she was clear-headed enough to realize how foolish she had been to believe he would shun her. Granted, she still would not have wished to have had that conversation surrounded by thousands of theatregoers, but she might have left him more gracefully.

She had nearly reached Hanover Square when she remembered it was Friday, and Mr. Wescott would be at his place of employment. She considered stopping by regardless, visiting Miss Wescott, but ultimately decided against it. She liked Miss Wescott, but it was the lady's brother she longed to see.

She returned home to a collection of notes on the silver salver. Suppressing her relief that she had not been at home to receive visitors, she gathered them up and drifted upstairs to the drawing room. She encountered Slater in the hall outside. Slater bowed when she drew near. "Lady Mercy instructed me to inform you she and Mr. Daubney were going for a drive," he said. "I apologize for not delivering those cards to you myself, my lady."

"Never mind, it is not as if I was here to receive them," Clemency said. "Thank you, Slater." She was a little surprised that Mercy and Francis had gone out, given the icy, slushy state of the streets, but if Mercy had felt even a fraction of the restlessness that had driven Clemency into the skies, she would not have permitted something as insignificant as poor roads to keep her indoors.

She settled herself near the fire and flicked through the cards to see who had come calling. There were more than she had expected, but fewer than she had hoped. If these represented the women, and a few men, who did not think worse of her because of Armand's story, she was not yet shunned by society. What disturbed her were the names she did not see: Jane, of course—though Clemency had hoped she would enjoy a change of heart—and Elizabeth and Tobias and a handful of other Movers she considered friends. Well, Elizabeth was nearly a shut-in, and Tobias might only be following Jane's lead, but those justifications did not make her feel better.

She turned her attention to the few notes that had lain among the cards. A penknife lay on a nearby table, left behind by Mercy; Clemency Moved it to her hand and slit open the first envelope. She extracted the folded paper within and scanned its few lines:

My dear Clemency,

What a dreadful state of affairs! I never was so appalled as when I heard of your situation. The French simply have no sense of decorum, do they? You will understand, I know, that I must regretfully ask you not to attend next week's gala—it simply would not do to entangle myself in trouble of this nature. I do hope you were not too terribly eager for the event. Perhaps another time?

Florentia, Lady Wyckburn

A sick feeling started in Clemency's stomach. And so it began. Florentia was not very intelligent, but she knew how society moved, and her disinvitation spoke volumes about how others would view Clemency's "situation." She found herself crushing the note and cast it into the fire with a muttered oath. Not everyone would consider the matter as Florentia had.

She swiftly opened the other envelopes, and as she read, her sickness grew. Uninvited to this party or that, uninvited from a theatre outing—they were not important events, and none of them had been ones she was eager for, but each marked one more person who believed Armand. She could not even say "believed Armand over her" because she had not yet had a chance to tell her side of the story.

She stood with the last envelope unopened in her hand and stared blankly into the fire. Anger replaced the sick feeling. These people were her *friends*. They should not be so quick to assume the worst of her. For heaven's sake, an Extraordinary's word was meant to be her bond! And here they were assuming she had voluntarily thrown away all decency and honor to be Armand's light o' love. *They* should at least have the decency to ask her to confirm or deny Armand's story.

She considered burning the last envelope unopened, but a bitter sense of seeing an unpleasant duty through to the end stayed her hand. She slit the envelope and tugged out the paper.

My dear Lady Ashford,

I hope you have not forgotten my invitation to tea tomorrow afternoon. It will be a lovely gathering, and Mrs. Godfrey has promised to recite her latest poem. Your presence will be so welcome.

In great anticipation,

Lady Deirdre Bristow

Surprised, Clemency read the few lines again, squinting occasionally to make out Lady Deirdre's crabbed handwriting. She did not consider Lady Deirdre a close friend, as the woman was rather shallow and prone to seeing conspiracies everywhere, but she was still a friend, and her invitation heartened Clemency more than it ordinarily would have. Clemency set the invitation on the hearth as if enshrining it. She would attend, and she would take the opportunity to counter Armand's gossip. It would be the first step toward regaining her life.

SNOW AGAIN FELL THE NEXT AFTERNOON, NOT HEAVILY, BUT ENOUGH to prevent Clemency Flying to Lady Deirdre's home. She sat impatiently in the carriage, wishing it might speed along faster even as she appreciated that the weather did not permit racing. Besides, the coachman was a steady, sedate driver, accustomed to transporting Mercy, who disliked a fast ride that jostled her. Clemency usually did not care what kind of driver he was, given that she rarely used the carriage, and now she reminded herself that Mercy's comfort was more important than her impatience.

The footman handed her down outside Lady Deirdre's town house, and Clemency floated above the slushy, dirty street to the front door. It opened before she rang the bell, and the butler startled her with his sudden appearance. "Lady Ashford," he said in his dull, low-pitched voice, and bowed her in.

Lady Deirdre's town home was decorated elaborately with Greek-inspired furnishings, urns and fluted pedestal columns crammed into the small foyer, oil paintings of Greek landscapes and ruins hanging on every wall. The items were all very expensive, but the overall impression was not, as Lady Deirdre probably believed, of an elegant home; rather, it reminded one of a Mediterranean bazaar, lacking only a display of copper pots to make the illusion complete. Clemency tried to be generous of heart, but she could not help imagining how beautiful the house would be if its decorator had greater sensibilities and a modicum of taste.

She followed the butler down the hall to the drawing room. Clemency had visited many times before, but as the butler opened the door for her, she was struck by a sudden feeling of uncertainty, as if everything that had happened might have worked a transformation on Lady Deirdre's home, rendering it alien.

The feeling made her pause on the threshold, casting about for something she recognized. The furnishings bore the same Grecian influences as the foyer, low couches and the occasional pedestal-base table, and the room looked just as it always did, but the post-storm light slanted through the diaphanous drapes oddly, illuminating the walls with a strange glow that made the women present look pale and faded.

She collected herself and walked forward before her hesitation could be commented on. Lady Deirdre rose from her seat and came to meet her with hands outstretched. "Dear Lady Ashford," she said, sounding like a twittering bird. "How good of you to come. Pray, be seated. We have yet to see Mrs. Godfrey, but she is always late—personally, I believe she enjoys making a dramatic entrance, don't you agree?" Her voice dropped low as she spoke, inviting Clemency to share in this gentle indictment of the poetess.

"I have never met Mrs. Godfrey, so I cannot say," Clemency said.

"Well, we will introduce you, and then you will be able to judge!" Lady Deirdre giggled. "Ladies, you all know Lady Ashford, do you not? Mrs. Eustis, Lady Kendall, Lady Frederica..."

Clemency let the names wash over her. She did know most of the ladies present, though none of them well, and the ones she knew were clever and had good conversation. Some of her unease vanished. She was being foolish. This was just afternoon tea with friends, one like a hundred others, and her uncertain imaginings were just that.

She took a seat between Lady Kendall and Mrs. Dane and accepted a cup of tea. The tea was excellent as always, and she sipped and exchanged pleasantries with the ladies, discovering that Mrs. Dane was preparing for a trip to France and that Lady Kendall's daughter had recently been delivered of a healthy baby boy.

"He will be a Speaker, the Extraordinary Shaper told them," Lady Kendall said with a smile. "It is astonishing that we now have the ability to identify talent before it manifests. Only think what a blessing it is to parents of Scorchers and Discerners, to know to look for signs of their talent appearing! Perhaps now we will see more Scorchers survive their manifestation."

"So dreadful, the fear of immolation by a child no one knew to suspect," Mrs. Dane said. "I wish your daughter well. I am a Speaker myself, you know, and my reticulum is a great comfort to me."

"My sister Lady Mercy is also a Speaker," Clemency said, "and she says the same."

"Of course, I had forgotten," Mrs. Dane said. "She is the crippled one, yes?"

Irritation shot through Clemency. "She has lost the use of her legs, yes, but we hardly believe that defines her."

"Indeed not. I did not mean to give offense," Mrs. Dane said, sounding not at all contrite. "And she has a special wheeled chair, does she not? I imagine that helps."

The indirect reminder of Mr. Wescott made Clemency's throat close up briefly. She wished she could apologize for her behavior, beg him to understand, throw herself into his arms—but of course that was impossible. "She does," she said, and found herself incapable of elaborating.

Lady Kendall cleared her throat with a discreet cough and a sip of tea. "And you are newly returned from the War Office," she said. "That must have been quite the experience."

Clemency was spared answering by the drawing room door opening and Lady Deirdre's exclamation of, "Oh, Mrs. Godfrey! Do come in. Ladies, this is Mrs. Godfrey, my latest discovery. Pray, have a seat, Mrs. Godfrey, and may I—oh, yes, just sit anywhere."

Mrs. Godfrey took a seat near Clemency and her companions. She was a short, round woman with deeply-set black eyes like currants in a loaf, but her smile was pleasant. Her gaze immediately fixed on Clemency. It was an intense gaze that made Clemency feel as if Mrs. Godfrey could see through her skin to her bones and all the way to her heart.

"Oh, my, I am sadly remiss! Lady Ashford, may I introduce Mrs. Godfrey," Lady Deirdre twittered. "Mrs. Godfrey, the Countess of Ashford."

"Charmed," Mrs. Godfrey said. Her voice was the opposite of Lady

Deirdre's, being deep and rather gravelly. Clemency reflected that she sounded ill-suited to declaim poetry, even her own. She set that thought aside as unworthy and extended her hand in greeting. Mrs. Godfrey's grip was firm, almost masculine.

"We will be pleased to hear Mrs. Godfrey's poetry later," Deirdre said. She sat opposite Mrs. Godfrey and leaned forward so the five of them in that corner formed a little knot. "Dear Lady Ashford, I am so pleased you could attend."

"It was kind of you to invite me," Clemency said.

"Oh, the pleasure is mine, I assure you." Lady Deirdre leaned closer, and the other women echoed her movement. "I cannot credit the talk I have heard. Of course I do not believe rumor."

Since Lady Deirdre's chief consolation in life was rumor, gossip, and speculation, Clemency chose to consider this lie a polite acknowledgement that Clemency's actions had not put her beyond the pale. "Thank you, Lady Deirdre," she said. "I welcome the opportunity to tell the truth."

Lady Deirdre's eyes gleamed. "What truth is that?"

"That I was Coerced to love General de Villiers," Clemency said.

The ladies in their little group gasped. "We believed that was untrue," Mrs. Dane said. "You were...you were intimate with the general? And admit to it?"

"I was Coerced," Clemency repeated, "and I see no shame in that. Napoleon Coerced millions, and none of them are held to account for their Coerced actions."

"Of course, of course," Lady Deirdre said. She put a hand on Clemency's arm. "No one blames you."

"I fear that is untrue," Clemency said. "But it is good to know there are some who are willing to listen."

Lady Deirdre nodded. "It is only fair," she said. "Nor does anyone blame you for choosing not to bear an illegitimate child."

CHAPTER 25

IN WHICH A MORE SERIOUS
CHALLENGE ARISES

"I beg your pardon?" Clemency gasped.

"Is that not why you have kept this secret?" Lady Deirdre said. "I assure you, you should feel no shame—you would not be the first—"

Clemency shot to her feet. "You are gravely mistaken," she said. "Is that the story you have heard?"

Lady Deirdre rose as well, more slowly than Clemency. "If you were Coerced, you would have told the world. You must have felt ashamed, to keep the secret. An illegitimate child could not inherit the Ashford title, so you—"

"Stop this instant," Clemency said, putting the full force of her anger into her words. "You know nothing of the matter. I did not speak because I did not believe my intimacy with General de Villiers was the business of anyone but myself, not because I had some other secret to hide. Do not voice that foul supposition again."

Lady Deirdre's eyebrows rose. "Well, I declare," she said. "You need not take that tone with me, Lady Ashford. I have spoken in support of you despite the many voices who would call you a fallen woman."

Clemency considered what Lady Deirdre's supporting words would have been and felt ill. "I beg your pardon, but I cannot stay another moment," she said. "If you wish to share gossip about me, I hope you will tell the truth—that I was Coerced to love General de Villiers. I did not conceive a child, thank God, and I am free from Coercion now. Anything else is rank speculation." She turned and strode out of the drawing room, slamming the door behind her.

In the carriage, headed home, she cursed herself, then Lady Deirdre, and then herself again. She had no illusions about what those women would say about her now. A dramatic, titillating story was always more interesting than a pedestrian truth. They would no doubt believe her anger covered a darker reality, and they would certainly not refrain from speculating on it and sharing that speculation with the world.

She leaned against the damp canvas of the carriage side. She should have remained to try to counter the gossip, direct it in a more useful path. But even as she entertained this idea, she knew it was impossible. It would not matter what she said; all that mattered to London society was the story. Her heart ached at the thought that the story benefited Armand.

She rapped on the roof. "Hanover Square," she called out. The Cabinet of Curiosities would still be open at this hour, and she wished for nothing more than to speak to Mr. Wescott and learn whether he, too, despised her.

By the time the carriage approached Hanover Square, snow was once more falling, tiny white specks like grains of fine sand. Clemency's foul mood swelled with the rising snow. She closed her eyes and willed herself calm. Nothing would be gained by flying into a rage, and she certainly did not wish to rage at Mr. Wescott.

She opened her eyes when the carriage came to a stop and waited impatiently for the footman, then Flew rather than walked to the door and tried the latch. The door did not open. Silently cursing, she extracted her watch from within her coat. Three minutes and ten seconds after five o'clock.

She floated above the stoop and considered her options. Everything had been simple when she had believed she could encounter Mr. Wescott in public, so to speak, or at least surrounded by strangers. She might have pretended she was there to visit the collection. Now, if she knocked on the door, she would be there solely for the purpose of speaking to him, and that idea felt awkward, as if she had a right to his time. She also still feared being shunned. And suppose he had heard Lady Deirdre's story about her supposed illegitimate child? She did not feel equal to having *that* conversation.

On the other hand, she had come all this way, and leaving without achieving her goal would make her a coward. It had been the only thing her father had ever reprimanded her for, cowardice. She had needed a tooth extracted when she was fifteen, and in fear of the surgeon had pretended not to be in agony for six days until her father discovered the truth. "A coward lives her fear over and over again," he had said, "but the courageous woman endures the moment and is afterward free. You've built up a terror in your mind that does not resemble the truth, Clemency. Don't ever be a coward."

With her father's words ringing in her memory, she rapped lightly on the door and waited. No one answered. After thirty seconds had passed, she knocked again, trying not to make her knock sound impatient. She waited again. Hammond would be there even if the Wescotts were not, and he would take her message. But time passed, and still no one came to the door. Clemency shivered. The sand-speck snowflakes had become fatter and wetter, and an occasional gust of wind blew them into her face. Feeling disheartened, she returned to her carriage and directed the driver to return home.

On the way back, she told herself it was for the best that she had not seen Mr. Wescott. If rumor said she was with child, or even if it only claimed she was willingly intimate with Armand, explaining the truth meant speaking of things never discussed in polite society, Lady Deirdre's bluntness aside. That was an embarrassment Clemency was not eager for. Waiting until tomorrow would strengthen her resolve, prepare her for possible unpleasantness. She was almost sure that was not cowardice.

Upon her return, she spent an hour in her study, going over matters of business Baxter had brought to her attention previously that she had put off as being boring or complicated or both. No one intruded on her, and she was able to forget for minutes at a time that her secret was out. Occasionally, she considered whether she should not act to counter Armand's lies, but she concluded that going door to door declaring the truth would only make her appear unstable. Besides, the snow continued to fall, and no one was going anywhere.

Roger was not present at the dinner table, cheering Clemency. Mama was gone as well, reminding Clemency that she had not spoken to her mother since Armand's revelation. It surprised her that Mama had left, as the Dowager Countess hated the snow as much as any Extraordinary Mover. Even more surprising was that Prudence, rather than skulking off to her bedroom after supper, followed Clemency and Mercy to the drawing room, seating herself near them both. Clemency chose not to draw attention to her change in behavior. Instead, she asked Mercy, "You have been very quiet tonight. Is anything amiss?"

"I have been waiting for word on another bombing," Mercy said. She had not picked up her embroidery, but sat with her hands folded quietly in her lap. "The Bank of England on Threadneedle Street."

Prudence drew in a sharp breath. Clemency said, "That is the most prominent institute Mr. Jinks has yet attacked. Why have I not heard?"

"It was when you were gone to tea, and my reticulum is not large enough to receive all the news as it occurs." Mercy's lips were pale and trembled. "I only know of it because a member of my reticulum, Miles Cavanaugh, is an employee of the Bank, and we have heard nothing from him since this afternoon. We fear the worst."

Clemency gripped Mercy's hand. "You appear close to fainting," she said. "Perhaps you should lie down while you wait for word."

Mercy shook her head. "I could not bear being alone. You do not understand what it is like, being a Speaker—all their voices echo in my head unless I shut them out, and I fear shutting out the most important one, the one that will know the truth. It is occasionally unsettling."

"Then should we—" Clemency began, but at that moment Mercy tilted her head back in a Speaker's attitude, and Clemency hushed. She exchanged glances with Prudence, who looked as worried as Clemency felt. They waited in silence for a full minute. Mercy's solemn expression gave way to a deep frown, and the muscles of her jaw twitched rapidly as if in silent speech, something Clemency had never seen her sister do while Speaking.

Finally, Mercy lowered her head and opened her eyes. She was still pale, but her expression was not as worried as it had been. "Mr. Cavanaugh was injured badly, but his life was spared. He is in hospital being treated, and Emily expects him to survive. I am so relieved."

"We are relieved on your behalf," Clemency said. "I do not suppose there is more information on the bombing?"

"Just that Mr. Jinks has again claimed responsibility. It seems the bombing took the life of a prominent member of the board, Lord Deverell, who is—was—an Extraordinary Seer." Mercy twisted her gown between her fingers as she stared into the fire, seeing Clemency knew not what. "Mr. Jinks threatened to kill more Extraordinaries if his demands were not met, and his note included the reminder that ordinary people will suffer as well."

"But then why does the government not comply?" Prudence exclaimed. "Surely they will not permit more deaths, not when they can stop them."

"Because it is wrong to give in to those who would use terror to achieve their goals," Clemency said. "Doing so now will signal to others that our government is weak and vulnerable to more of the same kind of threat. But even if that were not true, eliminating all Extraordinaries from positions of power would cripple England. It is not a matter of those Extraordinaries being special; it is that so many of them hold key government positions, and replacing them all at once would devastate Parliament."

"And who is to say Mr. Jinks will content himself with gaining this one point?" Mercy ran her fingers over the rail on her chair's wheel. "He may decide eliminating Extraordinaries is not enough. Suppose he further insists that all those with any talent step down? We may be outnumbered by those without talent, but we should not be punished for being who we are."

"But Mr. Jinks," Prudence said, bit her lip, and rushed on, "whoever he is, he has only acted to right an imbalance in our society. There are Extraordinaries who abuse their privilege, and surely they should not be permitted to continue."

"Murder is not the way to address that imbalance," Clemency said. "I do not agree in any way with Mr. Jinks' aims or methods, and I feel no sympathy for his cause thanks to the manner in which he has forwarded it. Reining in Extraordinaries who break the law is a matter for the courts."

"Who never act, because they are dominated by Extraordinaries themselves," Prudence persisted. "It is not fair."

"That, I agree with." Clemency watched Mercy carefully, but her sister had regained some of her color and no longer appeared on the verge of collapse. "I believe, though, that it is a problem that will have to be resolved one case at a time, not through violence."

"May we not speak of other things now?" Mercy said. "Now that I know Mr. Cavanaugh is safe from immediate harm, I would like to put talk of bombings and death far from me."

Clemency nodded. She turned to Prudence, who looked as if she wished to continue their argument, and said, "I understand your ball was a success. I hope you enjoyed yourself."

Prudence shrugged, one shoulder raising higher than the other. "I suppose."

"Do not fret if you did not make any grand conquests," Mercy said with a straight face.

"I did not wish for—" Prudence began hotly, then subsided as she realized Mercy was teasing her. Some of the stiffness went out of her manner. "Making grand conquests is Mama's pleasure," she said.

"Yes, and she is a force of nature, not to be stopped," Clemency intoned. To her surprise, Prudence laughed, a short, quiet sound, but unmistakably merry.

"In seriousness, Prudence, you did enjoy yourself, yes?" Mercy asked.

"I suppose." Prudence shrugged again, but it was not a dismissive gesture intended to silence. "I danced with several men, and some of them were charming. But I do not intend to make a connection until I am much older. I prefer not to sacrifice my independence."

Clemency suppressed a smile. She agreed with Prudence, but her youthful visage was incongruous with the adult sentiment, and Clemency would not for the world have made Prudence believe she mocked her. "You have time to meet many men, and time to discover what you would like in a husband."

"Or perhaps you will choose not to marry," Mercy said. "You have money settled on you, and there is no reason you should wed simply for the sake of being married."

"Is that what you intended?" Prudence asked.

"I never saw anyone I could love other than Francis," Mercy said with a smile. "And if I could not marry him, I did not wish to marry anyone. Since I believed him indifferent to me, I had resigned myself to spinsterhood."

"I am so glad you will not be my poor dependent," Clemency said. "That would be tedious."

"I have my own fortune, thank you," Mercy said primly, "and you know I am delightful company."

"I do, and it is for your own sake I am glad, because you and I might have suited one another well as spinster companions." Clemency Moved the poker to her hand and stirred the fire idly. She was capable of Moving the coals, but she liked the grip of the poker and how it felt like an extension of her hand.

"You will not remain a spinster," Prudence protested. "Surely many men would like to marry the Countess of Ashford."

"Only one Clemency cares about," Mercy said, smiling archly.

Prudence sat up. "Clemency has a beau?"

"I do *not* have a beau, Prudence, and *you*, Mercy, are wicked to tease me." Clemency's cheeks felt even hotter than the fire could manage.

"She is attracted to Mr. Wescott, of Wescott's Cabinet of Curiosities," Mercy told Prudence, ignoring Clemency. "And he has an interest in her!"

Prudence gasped. "Why does no one ever tell me anything interesting? Clemency, if you are to be married—"

"Now, that is rather putting the cart before the horse!" Clemency exclaimed. "I am not even near to marriage. Mr. Wescott is no more than a friend—"

Mercy let out an indelicate sound somewhere between a cough and a snort.

"*As I said*, Mercy—should I fetch you some water for that horrid cough?"

Mercy shook her head, her eyes bright with mirth.

Clemency rolled her eyes. "Prudence, I am very fond of Mr. Wescott, but he and I have not made one another any promises, and I am certain it would embarrass him to know the speculation the two of you have engaged in with regard to the two of us." She would never tell them about the kisses.

Prudence's brow furrowed. "Then whyever not? You never blushed like that in all the times we have mentioned men who were interested in you, and that must mean *something*."

Clemency reminded herself not to underestimate Prudence's observational skills. "It means nothing, so long as he has not spoken."

"That is so unfair," Prudence said. "Why can the woman not declare herself first? Only think how much pain Mercy would have been spared if she had been able to tell Mr. Daubney of her feelings, instead of waiting for him to speak!"

"I suppose it is unfair," Clemency admitted, "but there are ways a woman can indicate her interest so she may encourage a man to turn his eyes in her direction. And imagine how difficult it must be for the man, if he does not know the woman will respond favorably? So it is not unfair in only one direction."

Prudence still wore her familiar stubborn expression. "Well, when I fall in love, I shall tell the person of my feelings and not wait for him to declare himself!"

"Then let us hope you are not approached until you are ready to be so bold," Clemency said. "Though that Mr. Montague certainly gave you enough attention."

Prudence's face paled. "Mr. Montague?"

"Yes, I intended to gently warn you away from him. He made up to me while we danced—a fine thing after he had been so attentive to you! But now that I know you have no interest in anyone, I feel I can speak freely."

"He is not interested in me," Prudence said. "I—he and I spoke of nothing in particular. He is handsome, yes, but—no."

Clemency regarded her sister more closely. "Prudence," she said, "did Mr. Montague say something to distress you? Because you look rather ill all of a sudden."

Prudence shook her head. "No, truly it is nothing."

Clemency opened her mouth to pursue the matter, and the door opened. Slater said, "I beg your pardon, my lady, but there is a person waiting at the door to speak with you. I told him the hour is late, and he became insistent." He wore the affronted look of someone whose dog has just insisted on a seat at the master's table.

Clemency rose. "He did not give his name?"

"No, my lady. I apologize if I was remiss in not insisting."

"No, Slater, it does not matter. I will speak with him." She ought to tell Slater to turn the man away if he would not give his name, but curiosity had reared up inside her.

She walked rather than Flew down the stairs, conscious of her gown, and crossed the foyer to where the man stood. She was not inclined to call him a gentleman, though he was dressed well enough; he had a hangdog air about him, as if it would take only one wrong word to make him grovel before her. Despite this servility, he faced Clemency with no sign of fear.

"I am Lady Ashford," Clemency said. "May I ask what brings you to disturb my home at this hour?"

"I bring a message," the man said. His voice had a strange, halting quality, a hiccup between "bring" and "message" that nearly swallowed the "a" bridging them. "From Lord Ashford."

For a moment, Clemency was transported to the past. "My father?" she said. "No, you are mistaken. My father passed away."

The man shook his head. "From the new earl. Roger, Lord Ashford."

"*Roger?*" Clemency exclaimed. "He is not the earl!"

"Not yet," the man said. "Lord Ashford challenges the right of his sister, Clemency Northrup, to hold the title on grounds of immorality. This is a formal notice of Lord Ashford's intent to bring suit against you."

CHAPTER 26

IN WHICH CLEMENCY RECEIVES SUPPORT FROM UNEXPECTED SOURCES, BUT IS ULTIMATELY NOT REASSURED

"It is intolerable," Clemency said for what felt like the hundredth time. "Intolerable. How *dare* Roger turn against me?"

"Dearest, you should sit," Mercy said. "You will wear a groove in the hearth rug."

"This is no time for levity," Clemency snarled, but she sat opposite Mercy. She still held clutched in her hand the official notice, crushed beyond repair. "What am I to do?"

"Fight him, naturally," Mercy said. "This is a frivolous case. You have nothing to fear."

"But...is it not true Clemency was that man's lover?" Prudence said.

"*I was Coerced,*" Clemency said through gritted teeth. "But it seems almost no one believes that."

Prudence paled. "I meant only that if it is true, all it will take for Roger to win is for enough of your peers to disbelieve your story of Coercion and for those peers to wish to make an example of you. I mean the ones who believe Extraordinaries should not have so much privilege. That means it is hardly a frivolous case."

"That is exactly right, Prudence." Clemency shot to her feet and resumed pacing. "The moral issue is simply a cover for those who seek to reduce the privileges of Extraordinaries, and they are joined by those who opposed my elevation because it threatens their precious primogeniture traditions. It will not matter that most of those men are unfaithful to their wives as a matter of course—"

Mercy gasped. "Surely that is not true!"

Clemency gave her an ironic look. "It is not something discussed in polite society, but men hold themselves to a different standard than they do women. It is part of what makes my situation so monstrously unfair—were I a man and Armand a woman, my peers might even applaud our liaison."

"I cannot believe that," Mercy said, but weakly. "Surely they must believe your word, Clemency. You are an Extraordinary; your word is legally your bond."

"Apparently that is only true when it is not a matter of one's moral purity," Clemency said. "I imagine many will believe as Jane does—that I have claimed Coercion to cover my bad behavior. And I have no idea how to counter that."

"It is so unfair," Prudence exclaimed. "General de Villiers can say whatever he likes, and everyone believes him!"

Clemency let out a deep breath. "Armand is charming, and charming men get away with so much in our society. Well, his plan has backfired. He wishes me to marry him and make him an Earl, but if Roger's suit is successful, I will no longer have a title to drape over him." Bitterness surged through her. "Though that will not be enough to force him to retract his story. Oh, how I wish—" She closed her mouth on the rest of that sentence. She could not bring herself to wish Armand dead, whatever he had done to her.

The drawing room door opened, and Mama entered. She was dressed for an evening out, in silks and jewels and with her hair arranged elaborately in curls and ringlets, but she did not look as carefree as she always did. Lines drew down the corners of her mouth and her eyes, and for once she looked her age. She stared at Clemency with her lips trembling. "Why did you not tell me?" she said. "I should have to hear of it from another?"

Clemency's jaw tightened at the unexpected attack. "It is none of your business," she snapped, "and I apologize for interfering in your heedless pleasures. I am certain my poor reputation reflects badly on you."

Mama's mouth fell open. "How dare you," she whispered. Then, in a louder voice, she said, "You think so little of me? That I care only for myself? Clemency, that man hurt you dreadfully, and you could not bring yourself to come to your mother for comfort? Did you assume I would criticize, or condemn?" She gripped the door frame as if she would fall without its support. "And I brought him into this house—oh, my dear, I regret that so terribly!"

Stunned, Clemency said, "Mama, I believed you were as captivated by General de Villiers as everyone else."

"Not so captivated that I will take his side over my own daughter's." Mama took a step forward and reached for Clemency's hand. "What a fool you must imagine me. Please forgive my ignorance and the hurt I have done you." Tears ran down her cheeks. "I truly would never have maintained the acquaintance had I known your history."

Clemency took her mother's hand and was nearly pulled off balance when Mama put her arms around her, sobbing. "Mama, please—you could not have known, and I do not blame you for anything," she said. "I am so glad you believe me."

"Of course I believe you," Mama said, sounding indignant through her tears. "You were never a liar, not since your youth, and that is why I do not understand why you kept this secret from all of us. You could not have believed we would not support you."

"I wished for it all to go away," Clemency said, and found she was weeping as well. "I wished to pretend it did not happen. I felt so ashamed."

"It is that vile general who should feel ashamed," Mama said. She held Clemency at arm's length and gave her as stern a look as her lovely face could manage. "I told everyone at the Comstocks' party this evening that you were not to blame, that you were Coerced, and that anyone who believes otherwise should consider himself unwelcome here. *Including* Lord Winder."

Clemency laughed and wiped her eyes. "Bold words, Mama!"

"It is nothing less than the truth," Mama said. "Your family will always stand by you, Clemency. Your father would have expected it."

"It is unfortunate Roger does not believe it," Mercy said.

"What do you mean?" asked Mama.

Mercy glanced at Clemency. Clemency said, "Roger is suing for the title on grounds of my immorality."

Mama's perfect lips made an O of horror. "Surely not! He must know the allegations are untrue. Roger could not be so spiteful."

"I am afraid he can," Clemency said. "Mama, I know you always believe the best of your children, but you cannot deny that Roger has always wanted the title, and he was willing to challenge Father's intentions to get it. I am only astonished that it did not occur to me that he would try something like this."

"I will speak to him," Mama said, firming up her jaw the way she did when she was determined on a thing. "He simply has not considered how his behavior reflects on the Northrups."

"Thank you, Mama." Clemency did not bother protesting that Mama's influence would have no effect on Roger. "I am grateful to you. For everything."

"It is only what a mother should do for her children," Mama said. She let out a huff of breath. "I declare I am weary from all this arguing. Doing the right thing is so exhausting sometimes."

A quiet cough from the doorway alerted Clemency to Slater's presence. "I beg your pardon, my lady, but you have a caller," he said.

Clemency examined the butler closely. Slater did not have the affronted look he got when someone displayed ignorance or willful flouting of society's mores, but neither did he look overwhelmed the way he might if the visitor were someone of higher social status than his mistress. Her first instinct, to chastise him for admitting yet another stranger to her home, faded away, replaced by curiosity. "At this hour?"

"It is Mr. Wescott, my lady," Slater replied. He still looked calm and indifferent, not at all as if he had just delivered words that struck Clemency like a knife to the chest.

She vainly tried to slow the rapid beating of her heart and ignored the way her sisters and mother all turned to stare at her. "Did you show him to the drawing room?" she asked.

"No, my lady, he instructed me to ask for a moment of your time, and to tell you he did not intend to lay claim to more hospitality than that."

Clemency wondered how much of her attraction to Mr. Wescott had communicated itself to her staff. Slater's demeanor suggested he approved of Mr. Wescott as he had approved of none of Clemency's previous would-be suitors. Her embarrassment over her transparency faded beside the surge of emotion she felt when she contemplated Mr. Wescott's presence downstairs. "Pray, show him to the small drawing room, and tell him I will join him shortly," she said.

Slater bowed and disappeared.

Clemency continued to stare at the empty doorway, trying to calm her tumultuous emotions. She had to face him, finally, and learn—but would he have come to her house, intruded upon her private space, only to tell her he despised her? And if he did not, what else might he have to say?

Mercy cleared her throat. "Clemency," she said, "Mr. Wescott?"

"I do not know," Clemency said. "We do not have a secret understanding, if that is what you ask. He has no claim on me."

"Why should he have a claim on you, dearest?" Mama said.

Clemency shook her head. "Pray, excuse me," she said, and left the room.

The walk to the small drawing room had never felt so long. Clemency's emotions had risen so high she could no longer conjure scenarios in which Mr. Wescott revealed his purpose in coming to Emeraude House so late in the evening, without an invitation and without sending advance notice. Her mind was a white blur, incapable of coherent thought.

She found herself deeply aware of her surroundings, of how her feet struck the runner of carpet filling the hall and made almost imperceptible thuds, of how the chilly air made her skin tingle now that she was away from the drawing room fire, of how the silk of her gown rustled with every step, explosively loud in the silence. The scent of the flowers in vases at intervals along the wall, her mother's passion, drifted to her nose, faint but pervasive; she might have imagined herself in a field of wildflowers if not for the cold and the rustle of her skirts and the carpeted floor. Perhaps it was not an apt comparison, after all.

She hesitated with her hand on the doorknob, reminded herself that she was no coward, and opened the door as decisively as if the moment of hesitation had not happened.

Mr. Wescott turned from where he had been examining one of the paintings on the wall, an indifferent landscape Clemency kept only because it depicted the Italian countryside as did the rest of the paintings in the drawing room. She felt a moment's guilt at having mediocre art displayed in her house, then immediately felt ridiculous at caring for anything so unimportant. Her home's décor surely did not interest Mr. Wescott.

They stared at one another in silence for a few seconds. Finally, Clemency said, "Mr. Wescott. It is rather late." She instantly felt stupid at her inanity. Or would he take her comment as a criticism? She could think of no polite way to ask the questions burning in her heart: *Why did you come?* and *Have you heard Armand's story?* and, most terrible of all, *Do you hate me now?*

"I apologize for my presumption," Mr. Wescott said. He made no move toward her. "I have no right to impose on you, but after what I have heard, I guessed you would not approach me."

"I shudder to imagine what you have heard," Clemency said, trying for a light tone and managing only to sound stupid again. She wished in that moment she had bade Slater send Mr. Wescott away. What she felt for him was immaterial; they owed one another nothing, and that made everything she wished to say impossible.

"Things I should not repeat to anyone," Mr. Wescott said. "Let alone challenge you with. You owe me no explanations, Lady Ashford, and I will not insult you by demanding you tell me what is true. I simply wish to offer you whatever help is in my power to deliver."

Clemency examined him, how he stood ready to walk away if that was what she demanded, and her heart ached for a different reason. "Why?" she asked, surprising herself. "I might be a liar, or a woman lost to all decency. I might have traded on our acquaintance to make myself appealing to you so you would believe my lies. Why would you wish to help me?"

Mr. Wescott did not move toward her, but he flexed one large hand open and shut as if he had struck someone and was working the blood back into his fingers. "You are not a liar," he said. "You kept secrets—secrets no one would reasonably wish to divulge—and you are paying the price now for your justifiable reticence. I am outraged at how readily society has turned on you, Lady Ashford, and I assure you I will support you whatever the outcome."

Tears stung Clemency's eyes, and she blinked them fiercely away. "Thank you," she said. "I do not know my future, and that frightens me."

"This storm will pass." Mr. Wescott's grim expression belied his hopeful words. "I know. Miss Wescott knows. You are not the only one —ah, but that sounds like criticism. I mean only to offer my support. Miss Wescott suffered the taint of rumor and speculation years ago, when she was considered mad. No one believed she would ever rejoin society. And then the rumors passed, and now only she and I and our mother remember those days. I do not mean to disparage your current suffering." His grim expression gave way to a lopsided smile. "I am perhaps not the ideal person to offer comfort. My instincts are always to beat a problem to death."

Clemency choked on a laugh and covered her mouth to hold it back. "Would that this were a problem that responded to beating," she said. "My brother has laid claim to my title on the grounds that I am a fallen woman."

Mr. Wescott's eyes narrowed. "And how is that not the appropriate solution? I might beat Mr. Northrup senseless, and we would see what effect that had on his intentions."

Another laugh shook Clemency, and she controlled it before it could turn into a weeping fit. "I wish I might take that offer. I fear it would only land you in trouble."

Mr. Wescott sobered. "I hope you understand," he said, "that trouble would be a small price to pay if it meant helping you."

Her heart began beating rapidly again, urging her to act, though she had no idea what action to take. "Thank you," she said again, wishing she knew the words to express what his help meant to her. "I know of nothing I can ask of you, if delivering a deserved beating to my brother is not a possibility. But the fact that you wish to help heartens me more than I can say."

"You are an Extraordinary," Mr. Wescott said. "Surely that is a protection."

"Not as much as I would like." Clemency let out a deep, frustrated breath. "I believed at first this would go away as soon as I countered General de Villiers' claims. Now it seems my word is useless. Which means I need other testimony. But few people know I was Coerced to adore Napoleon, and I told only one person of my Coerced affection for the general."

"Who is that?"

"A woman named Jennet Falconer. She—" Telling Mr. Wescott the whole story of her interactions with Jennet, whose true name she had not known until the woman sought her out months after Clemency's Coercion, was an impossibility. "She and her husband, Captain Falconer, were present when my Coercion was broken, and it was Mrs. Falconer who saved me from that nightmare. I told her the truth of my unholy attachment to Armand. But I do not know where she is. I inquired after her and the captain only to learn he had sold his commission and the two had set off on a tour of Europe. No one knows their location."

"And what of those in the War Office? Surely they know your story?"

"They know I was Coerced to follow Napoleon, and they have attested to that truth. But I never told them the rest of the story, and now even some of them believe I am using my Coercion to cover my willing affair." She let out a harsh laugh. "I suppose it is more dramatic to believe in a noblewoman's forbidden tryst. Everyone likes to see the mighty brought low."

"Do not speak that way," Mr. Wescott said harshly. He took a step toward her. "You have done nothing to deserve this treatment. Nothing. You cannot accept the calumnies of your enemies, even in jest."

"Then what am I to do?" Clemency exclaimed. "Nothing I say will make a difference to those who already know what they wish to believe. I cannot defend myself. I cannot seek redress. All I can do is refuse to bow to Roger's will, and even that may not be enough."

"I cannot solve this problem for you," Mr. Wescott said. "I can only urge you to continue to tell the truth, and stand steadfast against your accusers. I realize how impotent that advice is, and I wish—"

When he did not immediately continue, Clemency said, "You wish what?"

Mr. Wescott shook his head. "Many things, none of which are practical," he said. "But I hope you know you can call on me at any time, for anything I can do to help you."

He had taken another step toward her, and without thinking, she closed the distance between them until they were but an arm's length apart. His eyes were intent on her, and a powerful urge to put her arms around him and take comfort in his embrace struck her. But he did not regard her the way he had in his drawing room before she had kissed him; he did not move to take her in his arms, or kiss her. She hesitated, and the moment was lost.

"I will remember," she said, hoping her voice only echoed with sadness in her imagination.

Mr. Wescott bowed, and with a faint *pop*, he Bounded away.

Clemency stared at the place where he had been. His words should have reassured her, and in a way, they did, but that reassurance was as nothing beside the ache in her heart that said perhaps he did not care for her, after all. His offer of help might not have arisen from any affection he felt for her; it might simply have been a product of his hatred of injustice. If only she had reached out to him—but that, too, might have been a mistake. She realized she was crying, and realized further she lacked the fortitude to make herself stop.

It took her nearly a minute to collect herself, and then she trod wearily upstairs to rejoin her family. Mr. Wescott was right; she had to endure. She wished she did not feel so uncertain about her capacity for endurance.

CHAPTER 27

IN WHICH PRUDENCE'S ODD BEHAVIOR CAUSES CLEMENCY CONCERN

The next few days proved bright and sunny, if not warm. Clemency did not go Flying and told herself it was because the wind was strong and chilly. No more envelopes arrived, either inviting her to gatherings or rescinding earlier invitations. Jane did not appear on Emeraude House's doorstep, begging Clemency's forgiveness, but Clemency had not expected that.

She did have visitors, all of whom assured her of their belief in her veracity. Their assurances eased Clemency's heart somewhat. Most of the women told her they had spoken in her defense to others, which also cheered her. Not everyone believed she was an unrepentant liar. But Elizabeth still did not appear, and neither did Tobias, and their absence hurt.

Tuesday, the day of Jane's fancy dress party, came with no note from Jane. Clemency paced the house all morning, fretting over what it meant. Jane had not uninvited her, which was something, but neither had she renewed the invitation. It was as likely that Jane expected Clemency to intuit she was not welcome as that Jane wished for Clemency's attendance. Choosing wrongly could be disastrous.

Ultimately, Clemency chose to stay home. She knew Jane well enough to guess the worse choice would be to attend when she was not welcome. If she was wrong, and Jane had hoped to mend their quarrel, Jane would not assume Clemency had rejected her olive branch simply based on her non-attendance.

Wednesday morning, Clemency passed Prudence in the upstairs hall. She noted Prudence's heavy coat and plain grey bonnet and said, "Are you going out?"

Prudence jumped as if startled. "Oh! Yes, I am—it is so tedious being cooped up like this all winter."

Clemency examined her more closely. "Are you quite well? You look rather pale."

"It is merely that I have been indoors for too long," Prudence said. "The wind will put color into my cheeks, I am certain." She hurried away before Clemency could say anything more.

Clemency considered going after her. Prudence was never nervous, and yet she had just now behaved as if there were something furtive about a drive or a walk in the brisk December air. And yet— Clemency shook her head and continued to the drawing room. At least Prudence was speaking to her again. Clemency did not wish to destroy any chance of them regaining the sisterly affection they had once shared by prying into Prudence's affairs.

She sat alone in the drawing room for a few minutes, trying to read, when Slater entered and said, "You have a caller, my lady. It is Lady Elizabeth Cantrell."

Clemency's heart lurched once. "Show her up, please," she said, maintaining her calm. She could assume nothing about Elizabeth's feelings from the fact that she now paid Clemency a visit. Elizabeth was kind, but she was also forthright, and if she believed Clemency was lying about Coercion to conceal her immoral behavior, she would see it her duty to confront Clemency directly. This possibility did not disturb Clemency's calm; in fact, now that Elizabeth was here, she felt as if a cloud of impending awfulness had lifted. It was better to know the truth than imagine all manner of horrors.

Presently, Clemency heard footsteps approaching, and she rose from her seat as Slater opened the door and said, "Lady Elizabeth, my lady."

Elizabeth entered. She was dressed in a forest green redingote with matching bonnet she handed to Slater, and her face was paler than usual and her eyes dark-circled. "Forgive me," she said. "I should have come sooner, but Mr. Cantrell has been quite ill and I did not like to leave him alone."

"I understand," Clemency said. "I hope it is not too serious."

Elizabeth shook her head slightly. "I fear so. He is—oh, Clemency, I am so afraid for him."

Clemency felt instantly ashamed of herself. How awful, that she had forgotten others had trials beside which hers paled to nothing. She put her arms around Elizabeth and held her while her friend wept, and cried a few tears of her own that for once were not self-indulgent.

When Elizabeth's weeping subsided, Clemency guided her to a seat near the fire and rang for tea. "You should not have worried for me, not when your own worries are so great," she said. "I regret so much that I did not consider whether you might need my support."

Elizabeth wiped her eyes. "Oh, my dear, if only half of what I have heard is true, you have had troubles enough without adding mine to your burden. Forgive me, I know it is inappropriate, but I must know —you were Coerced into an affair with that general?"

"Then you believe me," Clemency said.

"I know you would not lie to make yourself seem an innocent victim if you were not." Elizabeth let out a deep breath that shook only a little. "It is too dreadful to imagine. One believes Napoleon Coerced others only into worshipping him, but naturally Coercion can take many forms, if the stories are to be believed."

"I wish they were not true." Clemency paused as a servant brought in the tea tray, then took a moment to pour tea for herself and Elizabeth. When she was again seated, she continued, "I cannot imagine Napoleon did not do the same to many women, making them complicit in their own degradation. I was—" She lowered her cup to her saucer to still her hand's trembling, sloshing the cup's contents. "I wish not to speak of it, except it seems not speaking of it has got me into this nightmare."

"Half of those I spoke to insisted your affair was voluntary, on the grounds that you kept the secret." Elizabeth's pale face contorted with anger. "I daresay most of those vultures would bemoan their fate pitiably if *their* secrets were aired so publicly. It is so monstrously unfair, Clemency."

"Unfairness is irrelevant when it comes to gossip." Clemency shook her head. "And now Roger demands that he be given the title. Speaking of unfairnesses."

"I had not heard," Elizabeth said. "Surely his suit will not succeed —except I know of many who would like to see an Extraordinary brought low. Oh, my dear."

"I have heard nothing more from Roger since I received notice of his suit. It would be nice to believe that meant it has gone away, but I know Roger, and more likely he is gathering his resources." Clemency drained her cup and set it down again with a *tink*. "I will have to do the same, but that is difficult when I do not know what form his attack will take. But I have spoken with my solicitors, and with members of the House of Lords, and I believe I have at least some support."

"Would not the Prince Regent control such a challenge?"

"Fortunately for me, no. The Articles of Regency prohibit him from interfering in the inheritance of peerages, presumably so he cannot use his influence to uplift his cronies. Someone was foresighted in that respect." Clemency sighed. "Were he the one to decide my fate, I might as well pack my bags and vacate Emeraude House at once. The Prince Regent favors his fellow Scorchers in every instance, and he would support Roger unquestioningly."

"That is something, at any rate," Elizabeth said. "Then if not he, who?"

"It will be my peers in the House of Lords, just as it was when Roger and I had our original wrangle over the title," Clemency said. She set her cup aside and rose to pace in front of the fire. Its heat felt at a distance, as if it burned beyond a pane of thick glass, and yet it crackled as loudly as ever. "My peers, and those who study the law— they will present arguments demonstrating precedence in support of each of us, and Roger and I will speak, and the lords will make a decision based on what they hear."

"And based on their feelings about the legal influence of Extraordinaries," Elizabeth said.

Clemency stopped and gripped the edge of the mantel as if she might break off some of it. "That is the other thing I fear. I cannot help but be the focus of this unrest. Mr. Jinks, whoever he is, represents a threat to our country, and suppose some of those responsible for determining my fate decide to vote against me for the sake of appeasing him?"

"You have no control over that," Elizabeth said. "Pray, do not let it trouble you. You can only present your case in the most convincing way; you cannot force anyone to believe as you wish."

"I know." Clemency sighed again. "I hope it will be enough."

The door opened, and Slater entered. He extended his silver salver to Clemency in silence. A single small envelope lay atop it. Clemency took the envelope and turned it over; her name was written on it in a bold hand she did not recognize. Quickly, she slit the envelope and extracted its contents.

"Oh, my," she said. "This is from the Marchioness of Lychfield, inviting me and my sisters and mother to a gala tomorrow night. She apologizes for the short notice, but gives no explanation for it. I don't understand."

Elizabeth smiled for the first time since entering the room. "I may have suggested to Catherine that you could use some cheering up. She is Mr. Cantrell's sister, you know, and a dear, though rather oblivious to other people's trials. That is, she knows of the rumors surrounding you, and does not believe them, but it did not occur to her that her support might be of some benefit to you."

"I cannot," Clemency said. "All those people, staring—oh, Elizabeth, I don't believe I can bear it."

"Of course you can," Elizabeth said. She stood and put a gentle hand on Clemency's wrist. "Hiding in Emeraude House will do you no good. You must show the world that you are not ashamed of having been the victim of Coercion. That will lead others to accept your story."

"Or it will make them believe I am a hardened wanton with no sense of decency," Clemency said bitterly.

"Anyone who believes that will do so regardless of your actions. Come, Clemency, have faith. You are in the right. Let that be your support."

"I cannot help but remember all the martyrs who died despite being in the right," Clemency said.

⊛

SHE DITHERED OVER HER WARDROBE THE FOLLOWING NIGHT SO LONG that Tatton finally said, "My lady, if you do not choose *something*, you will be forced either to stay home or attend the gala as you were the day you were born."

Tatton's forthrightness surprised a laugh out of Clemency. "You are right, of course," she said, and sank onto the chair of her dressing table and rested her arms across the table's marble top. "I lack decisiveness because I fear others judging me for my appearance. Should I pretend nothing is amiss, and dress boldly? Or should I wear something modest so I may appear humble? Oh, it is all too difficult for words!"

"If I may suggest, my lady," Tatton said, not sounding at all reticent, "you should dress as you normally would. You are not prone to extremes of fashion nor extravagances of hair and clothing, and if you were to appear in something other than what is typical for you, that will be noticed."

"I shall be guided by your wisdom, Tatton. Thank you."

She chose a gown of jade green satin gathered at the rear, with a cream satin band around the high waist. Her father's necklace did not precisely match, but wearing the garnet gave her courage, as if her father were there guiding her. Clemency regretted his loss more than ever. It was hard not to remember with bitterness the illness that had taken him, how no Extraordinary Shaper nor doctor had been able to cure him. Everything would be so different if he were alive. She looked her reflection in the eye and firmed up her jaw. There was no point revisiting the past, and her father himself had always told her one could never know if changing the past would have improved the present. "Might-have-been is a fool's game," he had told her, "and you are no fool."

She slipped her feet into shoes that matched her gown and waited patiently for Tatton to finish arranging her hair. "You do such lovely work," she told her maid.

"Thank you, my lady." Tatton's hands paused in pinning another lock of hair with pearl-tipped hairpins. "May I ask...we have all heard of Mr. Northrup's suit. What will you do?"

"Rebut his challenge, naturally." Clemency wished she felt as certain as she sounded. "I will not permit him to take my title without a fight."

"We are all—the staff, that is—we hope you will succeed. I should not speak ill of Mr. Northrup, and he is not a bad man, but we all know how much the earl wished for you to succeed him, and we remember him fondly." Tatton resumed her pinning. "I hope that is not too bold."

"No, I am so glad you cared for my father," Clemency said. It was tempting to criticize Roger knowing Tatton would join in willingly, but that was the sort of sneaking, shabby behavior Clemency despised in others and therefore tried not to indulge in herself.

When Tatton pronounced herself satisfied with Clemency's appearance, Clemency thanked her again and left her room. A slight chill in the air raised gooseflesh on her arms and made her face tingle. She heard the distant sound of the front door closing, probably the source of the cold air, and hurried to the stairs to see who had opened it.

She was in time to see Prudence hurrying across the foyer, clad in a hooded cloak that shrouded her face. Clemency leaned over the rail and called out, "Prudence, we are leaving soon! You did not change your mind, did you?"

Prudence looked up as she ran up the stairs. Her cheeks were red with cold. "No, forgive me, I had an errand that took longer than I expected," she said. "I will dress quickly—I do not wish to miss the gala."

In some bemusement, Clemency watched her sister rush past and enter her room, shutting the door behind her with a bang. This was the first time Prudence had ever been excited for a party; she had not acted so eager even for her own ball. Clemency could not understand her mercurial behavior, nor her frequent absences. She would suspect her sister of concealing a beau were she not convinced Prudence meant what she said about not wishing to form an attachment at her young age. And yet she could imagine no other reason for Prudence's secrecy.

With a shrug, Clemency continued down the stairs to wait in the drawing room for the others. Prudence would eventually tell her, or not, and either way Clemency still did not wish to interfere in her sister's business.

Mercy arrived shortly after, carried to her chair by Albert, with Mama trailing in a few minutes later. Clemency settled herself to wait on Prudence, suppressing her annoyance, but only five minutes after Mama's arrival, Prudence hurried into the drawing room, garbed and coiffed as neatly as if she had not been in a rush. "I beg your pardon for making you wait," she said, somewhat breathlessly.

"It was not such a long wait," Mercy said. She gathered up a woven blanket that lay on the nearby divan and folded it over her lap. "But let us go quickly, as I am certain the carriage ride will be cold."

Once they were all settled in the carriage, Clemency sat so she could see Mercy's chair where her Moving held it behind them and drew it along with them as the carriage set out for the Marchioness of Lychfield's house. "This is so comfortable, the four of us," she said.

"It is what I always dreamed of, watching my daughters enter society," Mama trilled. "Clemency, you really must make a match soon. It will not do to have your younger sister married before you."

"No one minds that anymore, Mama," Mercy said. "Not with all these Extraordinaries serving in the War Office until they are twenty-five, and unable to marry before that time. It is hardly fair to make their sisters wait on their return."

"Nonsense. Many women in the War Office are married," Mama said. "Clemency, you—oh, I did not remember your trouble. I beg your pardon. Of course you cannot become engaged until Roger's ridiculous suit is resolved, and your good name restored."

Sometimes Mama was too direct in her innocence for Clemency's comfort. She reminded herself Mama meant well and said, "I am not interested in marriage at the moment, and I will not demand Mercy postpone her marriage until I am."

Mercy looked as if she wanted to say something, but she remained silent when Clemency looked her way. Clemency could not imagine why Mercy would refrain from teasing her about Mr. Wescott, but she was grateful for her reticence.

"Perhaps it is Prudence who will make an attachment next," she said with a smile to let Prudence know she was not serious. But Prudence was looking out the window at the darkened streets and did not respond.

Mama put a hand on Prudence's knee. "My dear, you must tell us who interests you!"

Prudence startled. "Who interests me? Well, no one. No one at all!" Her hands gripped one another tightly.

"That sounds like too much of a protest," Mercy said in a teasing voice. "Now you must share your secrets."

Prudence shook her head. "I have no secrets. How could I?" She drew away from Mercy, shrinking in on herself as if Mercy's joke had been a physical assault.

Clemency regarded her carefully. "Does something trouble you?" she asked.

Shaking her head again, more vehemently, Prudence said, "It is just that I have not been out in society much yet, and I do not know what to expect. The gala is sure to be a mad crush, and well attended, and I am unaccustomed to much noise."

"You need not fear," Mercy said. "When it was I who was first out, I took shelter in the card-rooms, as I could not dance. They are much quieter, and you will be safe, I assure you."

Clemency said nothing. Prudence's reply had come too quickly, as if she had prepared that response. She was worried about something, Clemency was certain. "Are you sure—" she began.

Prudence fixed her with an unexpected glare. "Mercy is right, I am certain," she said. "I am being foolish, I know. Pray, let us speak no more of it."

Clemency subsided. Prudence was a woman grown, and she was capable of managing her own affairs. Whatever her worries, they were none of Clemency's business. And yet she wished she might press Prudence for the details, if only to ease her burden. Perhaps their relationship had not yet regained the closeness that would require.

The Marquess and Marchioness of Lychfield lived in one of the largest mansions in London, twice the size of Emeraude House. Crenellated walls gave it the look of a castle rather than a mansion, as did the round towers flanking the entrance. Set back from the street somewhat, with hedges defining its territory, it crouched on its plot of land like a tiger confident in its power, blazing with light as if it was on fire.

Prudence had been right about the size of the gala; their carriage waited in line for nearly fifteen minutes before depositing them at the door. Clemency set Mercy's chair on the pavement and Moved Mercy to sit in it, then Moved the chair and its occupant to rise above the three steps leading to the front door. She was grateful for Mr. Wescott's chair and its narrowness, for the mansion's front door was unexpectedly small. Then she had to suppress a pang at the memory of the chair's creator. She had no expectations of seeing him there that night, but she could not help hoping she was wrong.

The tall, brightly lit foyer had been transformed into a fairy palace for the evening. Green boughs honoring the season decorated the walls and twined around the banister of the spiral staircase leading to the first floor, while gauzy fabric in pale blue and lavender hung like drifting curtains from every bough. Clemency breathed in the piney scent and covered her mouth to keep from coughing; the smell was lovely, but too strong even for this large space.

She looked up to where two chandeliers illuminated the room, their crystals trembling in the draft produced every time the door opened and sending fractured rainbows across the walls to catch in the draperies like drops of sunlight. It was an effect she liked, and she considered how she might replicate it in her own ballroom. Standing in the doorway Moving the small crystals was impractical, but surely there must be a way.

The Marchioness, Lady Lychfield, a plump, attractive woman in her early forties, swept across the foyer to greet them. "Lady Ashford, thank you for accepting my invitation," she said. Her smile was genuine and welcoming and made her look even more attractive despite the prominent front teeth it revealed. "And Lady Ashford, Lady Mercy, Lady Prudence—it is so good to see all of you."

"Your invitation was so kind," Clemency said, clasping the Marchioness's hand lightly in her own.

"It truly was no trouble, no trouble at all." Lady Lychfield's smile disappeared. "I am grateful to Elizabeth for suggesting it. I wish to offer you my condolences on your situation. A dreadful thing, truly dreadful. I cannot believe anyone would be so impolite as to disbelieve an Extraordinary's word."

"It has shown me who my true friends are, and I choose to take heart in that fact," Clemency said.

"I have given the matter much consideration—do you not find it so, that others' misfortunes often give us the opportunity to consider how we would react in their position?" Lady Lychfield said. "I am an Extraordinary Speaker, and I daresay I should be furious, quite furious, if anyone doubted my word—are you very angry, Lady Ashford?"

"I am not angry," Clemency said, "at least, not at the moment. It is disappointment I chiefly feel."

"Well, anger would be justified, in my opinion," Lady Lychfield said in a confiding manner. "Please enjoy yourselves, and do not fear, Lady Ashford, everything will work out for the best. At least, that is what my husband is fond of saying, and he is quite the most intelligent man I know!"

As Clemency did not know the Marquess, she could not argue with this statement, but she clung to it as she left the foyer for the ballroom. The dancing had not yet begun, and the room was barely half full, but it was already much warmer even than the foyer with all its hundreds of lights.

She turned to speak to Mama. "I believe—but where is Prudence?"

"She left while you were speaking to Lady Lychfield," Mercy said. "I tried to stop her, as she was not going to the ballroom, but she was too fleet of foot. I expect she needed to refresh herself."

Unease filled Clemency's heart. "I expect you are correct," she said. "Will you both mind if I excuse myself as well?"

"I see Mrs. Bakly, and I wish to speak with her, she is such a dear," Mama said, and hurried off in the direction of the fattest woman Clemency had ever seen.

"Do not worry about me, Clemency," Mercy said in some amusement. "I will find a quiet corner and Speak with Emily until the dancing begins."

Clemency squeezed Mercy's hand and set off to find Prudence.

The resemblance to an ancient castle ended at the mansion's front door. Lady Lychfield's house was as opulent and ornate as a palace, with gilding striping every molding and every door. Once away from the foyer and the ballroom, the lights were fewer, and Clemency soon had to slow to avoid running into the many pedestals bearing vases of flowers blooming out of season. Their scent filled the air like a tangle of ribbons, rose and lilac fighting for dominance. Clemency was not fond of strong floral scents, which reminded her of Armand, but she was enough intent on locating Prudence that the smells were only a small annoyance.

The woven carpet beneath her feet was so thick she felt as if she were leaving footprints in wet soil. It silenced her footsteps, but that meant it would also make the sound of Prudence's tread imperceptible. Clemency surveyed the floor, but either the light was too low or her fancy about footprints was untrue, because she saw no trace of anyone else.

She had been walking less than a minute, but that was enough to take her well away from the public parts of the house. Her awareness that she was being an impolite guest was swallowed up in her increasing worry for Prudence, who might be brash and outspoken but knew what her behavior should be in public. That included not wandering uninvited through someone else's home. And Clemency was certain Prudence had not gone in search of the water closet.

The wide halls gave way to narrower ones, these lacking the gilding and the vases, though they were not servants' quarters. Paintings indistinct in the low light covered the walls, their gilded frames glimmering like windows on the same fairy realm the foyer was part of. Clemency paused to listen at a place where two halls crossed. One of the new passages was dark, too dark for anyone to find her way. Of the others, one ended a few paces away at a plain, unadorned door. Clemency tried it; locked. That left only one direction.

This one led straight as an arrow to another door, much sturdier than the other. It was also ajar, and a freezing draft blew through the crack. Without hesitating, Clemency opened it.

As she suspected, the door opened to the outdoors. Beyond was a small garden, bare and winter-dead, with a path that wound at random through the empty beds. The mansion enclosed it on two sides, with stone walls protecting its other two sides. With the moon not yet risen, the garden lay in near-darkness; Clemency stood in a wedge of pale grey from the dim light of the hallway.

Ahead, near the wall, someone crouched, her white-gowned figure the brightest thing in the garden. Clemency took a few steps forward, then paused, feeling uncertain. She shivered, not certain if it was the cold or the eeriness of the setting that chilled her. "Prudence?" she said.

Prudence shot upright and turned, revealing a face as pale as her gown. "Go back!" she exclaimed. "You must not—please, Clemency, go back to the others!"

The desperation in Prudence's voice compelled Clemency forward. "Prudence, what is wrong?" She lifted a few feet off the ground and Flew toward her sister, ignoring the path and passing over the dark earth of the beds.

Prudence glanced over her shoulder at something on the ground, then back at Clemency. "No, you mustn't!" She stepped toward Clemency, hesitated, then took another few steps, waving Clemency off.

Clemency alit next to Prudence. "What is that?"

Prudence took Clemency by the shoulders and tried to steer her away. Clemency removed Prudence's hands from their hold on her and gently Moved her out of the way. Surprisingly, she met no resistance to her Moving; Prudence, rather than fighting Clemency's talent, gripped her arm and tried to draw her away again, to no avail.

Clemency walked forward until she could see the thing on the ground more clearly, or at least as clearly as she could see anything in the garden. It was a wooden box, oblong, about as long as her arm and half as wide and deep. For a few seconds, Clemency was puzzled. She ignored Prudence's hands on her arm, tugging at her. "Is that—"

"No!" Prudence cried out. "We must go! Leave it, just come with me!"

Clemency turned to look at Prudence, and in that silent moment, the sound of ticking came to her ears. She sucked in a horrified breath. "A bomb," she said.

She did not stop for anything, not even to wonder why Prudence was here or why she clearly knew what the object was. As the ticking grew louder, she snatched the bomb up with her Moving and shot away into the sky. She Flew as fast as she dared, gradually widening the distance between herself and the box while keeping it as still as she could manage, and cast about for a solution. She was nowhere near the Thames, there were no convenient empty fields, and she was definitely not far enough from the bomb to escape its blast.

She stretched herself to her limit and extended the bomb as far from herself as she could manage, feeling like Mercy straining to reach a workbasket just barely within her reach. As she frantically evolved plans and discarded them, she continued Flying, heading north. Perhaps she could pass the city limits and drop the bomb to detonate in uninhabited land—

She felt the bomb shift, snatched at it, and missed her grasp. It fell, and instinctively Clemency Flew after it, reaching for it. She could not hear the ticking now over the sound of the wind. With a tremendous effort, she wrapped her Moving around the box and halted its fall.

White light exploded, banishing the darkness. A tremendous blow like the biggest fist in the world smashed into Clemency, knocking her backward in an uncontrolled tumble. Unable to stop herself, she fell out of the sky and into a bottomless well of darkness.

CHAPTER 28

IN WHICH MANY SECRETS
COME TO LIGHT

S he came to herself slowly, rising out of blissful numbness into sharp, all-encompassing pain. Her head ached, her supine body felt like it was being prodded by sharp-pointed knives, and something was clamped around her left leg that seemed to be trying to remove it. Blinking, she looked up at the sky. Her vision was blurry, and nothing about what she saw made sense; the sky appeared to be crisscrossed with iron bars arranged at random. She blinked again and tried to rub her eyes, but moving her arm made the knives dig deeper. Finally, she focused on the nearest iron bar and realized it was actually a tree branch. Awareness struck: she sprawled within the embrace of a bare-branched tree.

More information flooded in as she regained her senses. She lay at an angle, her head lower than her feet, which accounted for the ache in her skull. She hoped that was the reason for the ache; she had suffered a severe head injury once and had no desire to repeat the incident. But her vision was clear, not doubled as she remembered from that earlier injury, and she felt no urge to vomit. When she shifted her weight, the branches cradling her shifted as well, stabbing at her body. She craned her neck to see her left leg. It was wedged into a cleft in the tree trunk and held fast, but it did not seem broken. All in all, she reflected, she had been remarkably fortunate to survive yet another bombing at such close range.

She floated upward, gingerly freeing herself from the branches until all that held her was her foot caught in the cleft. Hovering in a seated position, she gripped her leg just above the ankle and pulled. It shifted, sending pain from the abrading bark through her leg. Clemency stopped pulling and regarded the problem. She would free herself at the cost of a torn and shredded leg.

Instead of pulling on her leg, she shifted her grip to the tree itself. The cleft was formed where two branches separated from the trunk, and she took hold of the smaller of the branches and pulled with both her natural strength and her Moving. The branch snapped off, and Clemency, unprepared, fell a foot or two, crying out when she hit more branches on the way down before she caught herself. Then she disentangled herself from the tree and drifted to the ground.

Her injured foot hurt when she put her weight on it, so instead she floated a few inches off the ground and assessed her condition again. Her gown was torn in a dozen places, and the skirt had come free from its gathering at one side and hung low enough to drag the ground. Scratches covered her arms, her hair was disordered, and—

With a gasp, she touched her throat. Her father's necklace was gone.

She fell to her knees, heedless of the pain, and frantically felt around the base of the tree. The ground was frozen hard in a series of lumpy hillocks, pitted where rain had battered the earth before it froze once more. Her hand fell on wizened, gnawed apples she flung aside, not caring how disgusting they felt. The necklace had to have been torn from her in her collision, which meant it was somewhere near. She refused to listen to the tiny gibbering voice that told her it was lost forever.

She circled the tree twice, searching with eyes and fingers, then backed away to widen her search. The freezing air numbed her arms and face, but she ignored that as well. Losing the necklace was unthinkable. She wished for a bright full moon, or even the half-moon that would not rise for hours, anything to guide her search.

Then her eye fell on a line of white some distance from where she had already searched. She scrambled toward it. The string of pearls had snapped, and the frayed ends of the thread waved in the breeze when she picked it up with trembling fingers. A few pearls were missing, but the rest were securely knotted in place. She clutched the garnet pendant in her left hand and sagged in relief. That was two miracles God had blessed her with that night.

She lifted into the air and finally took in her surroundings. She had passed beyond the bounds of London's official limits, past its northern border into the countryside. She had not realized how far she had Flown in her urgent need to dispose of the bomb somewhere it could hurt no one.

The tree that had caught her, probably saving her life, was one of many that grew at such regular intervals Clemency guessed she had found an apple orchard. Through the trees, she saw a grey stone cottage, low to the ground with a thatched roof that was light even in the dimness. No light came from its windows, and its chimney, which tilted slightly to the right, emitted no smoke. Even without that evidence, Clemency was certain it could not be inhabited, or the residents would have responded to the explosion.

Clemency began to drift in the cottage's direction, but in only a few seconds, reason asserted itself. There was no one there, and even if there had been, that person could not help her. She needed to return to—but where? Going back to the Marchioness's house would rouse questions she did not know how to answer. Going to her own home meant disappearing from the gala with no explanation, which would cause trouble of a different kind, not to mention abandoning Mercy. She ought to inform Mr. Rutledge about the bomb, but she did not know how to reach him, and she did not feel comfortable going to Hanover Square at this hour to entreat Mr. Wescott to contact him.

And then there was Prudence.

Clemency did not know what to believe. Prudence had clearly been aware of the bomb's presence, and she had known what it was. But she had not brought it to the gala; Clemency would have noticed if Prudence had carried anything so large and visible. It was barely possible Prudence had gone for an innocent walk in the garden and come across the bomb, but her hurried exit from the gala argued against that possibility, that and the fact that no one could wish to walk in the garden at that season. Which all meant she was somehow complicit.

Wearily, Clemency took to the skies. Speaking to Prudence was more important than any uproar she might cause by returning to the gala in this condition.

Now that the immediate crisis and her terror over her necklace had faded, she was aware of her aching, bruised condition. She was not so badly injured that she could not use her talent, for which she was grateful, but it was a close thing. Her ankle throbbed; she did not believe it was broken, but it might be sprained. Her back, her thighs, and her posterior hurt as well, likely from her collision with the tree. She would be black and blue come the morning.

In contrast with her earlier wild flight, the return to the Marchioness's house seemed to take forever. So as not to become lost in the darkness, she flew low over the streets, which were unusually crowded with people. She gathered from their movement they were intent on the northern boundaries of London. Well, it was not as if that explosion could have gone completely unnoticed. Even so, no one abroad looked up to notice her.

Not for the first time, she considered whether it might not make sense for her to wear drawers or short trousers beneath her gowns. She had certainly made enough flights in inappropriate attire to wish to protect her modesty, if not keep herself warm.

After an eternity, the blazing brilliance of the Marchioness's mansion drew Clemency's eye, bright as a torch in the distance. She altered her course and made for the garden. She would enter by the back way, and seek out a servant to ask the Marchioness to join her. Lady Lychfield was an Extraordinary Speaker, and possibly a member of her reticulum was aware of Mr. Rutledge and could help Clemency contact the man. Then she would challenge Prudence.

She landed, careful of her injured foot, in the center of the garden, and once more put her weight on that foot. It still hurt, but not as sharply as before. Clemency lifted off the ground nevertheless.

In the next moment, a white figure rushed at her, flinging its arms around her neck before Clemency could react by Flying away. "You are not dead," Prudence sobbed. "You took the bomb—Clemency, that was so dangerous! You should have left me to it."

"Don't be ridiculous," Clemency said, but she returned Prudence's embrace. Her sister's heart was beating hard and fast enough Clemency could feel it against her chest. "I could not leave it where it might hurt others."

"But you—" Prudence released her and took a step back. "Your gown, and your hair—Clemency, what happened?"

"The bomb detonated, and I was close enough that it blew me out of the sky. But I am not seriously injured, and nor is anyone else." Clemency gripped Prudence's shoulders. "We must leave without alerting anyone to what has happened."

"We?" Prudence swiftly looked away. "Why 'we'?"

She looked so guilty Clemency felt ill. "Do not imagine me ignorant," she said. "You and I are going to have a talk. But it must wait. Unless you would like me to tell the world what happened here? Because that is what I must do if I walk back into that gala in this condition."

Prudence ducked her head, an even more furtive gesture. "I do not know how we can escape telling."

"You will have to lie." Clemency refrained from saying *You are clearly experienced at that*. "Go find Mama and tell her you feel ill and that I will take you home. If she expresses concern, explain that it is a sour stomach and nothing dire. Then return here, and we will leave."

"But if we take the carriage, how will Mama and Mercy return home?"

Clemency smiled. It could not have been a pleasant expression, because Prudence took half a step back and her eyes widened in fear. "Not the carriage. You and I, dear sister, will Fly home."

Prudence's mouth fell open. "I cannot," she said.

"You don't have to. I can manage your slight weight."

"No," Prudence said, shaking her head. "I am afraid of heights."

"Then close your eyes," Clemency said, feeling not at all repentant. If Prudence was involved with the bombings, she deserved a little fear.

Clemency waited, growing increasingly cold, while Prudence was gone. She rubbed her bare, scratched arms, which prickled with gooseflesh briefly, and wished for the warm coat she could not retrieve without causing an incident. To distract herself, she examined the garden. Yew hedges that showed signs of recent pruning lined the walls, rising to within three feet of the tops of the walls. There were no other hedges defining the path, and no trees, just the dark soil of empty beds. Clemency had never seen a garden so completely denuded for the winter. It was as if someone intended to start completely anew come the spring. She had to admit she liked the effect. So much less depressing than a tangle of wilted leaves and dead plants.

Prudence returned far more rapidly than Clemency expected. She had imagined Prudence would dawdle, either out of guilt or out of fear of Flying. But she appeared only a few minutes after leaving and shut the garden door behind her. "Please," she said, "can we not take the carriage?"

"I will have to return to transport Mercy's chair," Clemency said, "but if Mama or Mercy needs to leave before that, I would not wish to deprive them of transportation." She extended a hand to Prudence. "There is nothing to fear. I will not drop you. Besides, you know what Father always said about cowardice."

Prudence nodded. She took Clemency's hand and gripped it painfully tight. "What do I do?"

"Relax, and do not fight," Clemency said. She Moved Prudence off the ground so they were side by side, then Flew away, bringing Prudence with her. Prudence squeaked and closed her eyes. Her grip on Clemency's hand became intolerable. Clemency pried her hand free, making Prudence scream and flail about for something to cling to and forcing Clemency to exert herself to maintain her hold. Despite her anger and frustration with her sister, Clemency felt a twinge of sympathy for her fear.

She hooked an arm around Prudence's waist. "Hang on to me, if you must," she shouted above the wind of their flight. Prudence immediately wrapped both arms around Clemency's shoulders and clung to her. She was not the first to fear Flying, Clemency reflected, as she remembered other flights, other passengers. Most had been afraid; a few had relished the experience.

She recalled the night flight in which she had taken Jennet

Falconer, who at the time was posing as a young man, from Valenciennes to Brussels. Jennet had loved the flight, and Clemency had Flown high and fast in response to her enjoyment. She had not believed she would ever see Jennet again after they parted outside the city, and then a few months later Jennet had found her in Paris, bringing with her news of her new identity and marriage. Clemency had been surprised and pleased at how Jennet had taken the trouble to seek her out. They might become true friends with time and propinquity. But that would mean finding Jennet again.

Clemency adjusted Prudence's grip on her neck so her sister did not choke her and Flew faster. She had reached out to every contact she had in the War Office and the Army, and none of them knew where the Falconers had disappeared to. Her friend Miranda Sherburne, an Extraordinary Speaker, had promised to continue the search, but even Miranda's reticulum could not cover all of Europe. That was all Clemency knew: the Falconers were somewhere in Europe. Unless they had returned to England, and Clemency's contacts were searching in the wrong place...oh, it was impossible, and Clemency needed not to put her hope in impossibilities.

She swooped down, eliciting another terrified cry from Prudence, and unlatched her window when she was still several feet away, swinging the window open and alighting within. She let go of Prudence, who staggered and fell, landing on her posterior with another cry, this one of pain. Clemency latched the window and crossed the room to stoke the fire. When it blazed brightly, she snatched the coverlet from her bed and wrapped it around Prudence, whose lips were blue-tinged with cold.

"Now," she said, searching her dressing room for the warmest wrap she owned, "talk."

Prudence burrowed into the blanket. "I have nothing to say."

"The devil take you," Clemency shouted. "Do not imagine you can get away with a lie. You knew that bomb was there and you knew what it was. What is your involvement? Did you place that bomb? What of the others—have you been complicit—"

"*No!*" Prudence shouted back. "I mean, yes, I knew—"

Clemency swore again, more viciously. "You fool. You utter fool.

Why on earth would you involve yourself in such foul business? *How* did you even encounter Mr. Jinks or his organization?"

Prudence's mouth fell open. "How did you know it is not one man?"

"You are in no position to ask questions," Clemency said. "Tell me everything. And pray there is something in your story that will spare you the noose."

"The noose?" Prudence's eyes widened more. "But surely—"

"These bombings are murder, and murder is a capital offense," Clemency said. "Did you believe your youth would spare you a hanging?"

"But I—" Prudence swallowed. "I have never placed a bomb, never—"

"I am not interested in your excuses." Clemency took two steps to stand looming over Prudence where she sat on the hearth rug. She no longer felt the pains in her ankle or the rest of her body. "Tell me what happened. Start at the beginning."

Prudence nodded. "It was because I hated the power Extraordinaries have in our society," she said. "It is wrong and unfair that some people should receive privileges simply because they are born with an unusual talent. And I am not the only one who feels this way," she added defiantly.

Clemency glared at her until she looked away, abashed. "Spare me your rhetoric," Clemency said. "How does this relate to the bombings?"

Still looking away, Prudence said, "I met someone who agrees with me. Someone who said we should do something about this injustice. But I did not know he meant killing them! When I heard about the first bomb, I did not realize it was this group. Then they told me they —we—were responsible, but they said they only intended to gain attention for the cause. To frighten people."

Clemency ground her teeth together to keep from calling Prudence a fool again. She was only seventeen, after all. It was easy to be fooled by people you believed in when you were seventeen. "But you must have realized the truth eventually. Why did you not break ties with them immediately you did?"

Prudence did not immediately answer. Clemency was about to repeat herself when the girl said, "I was afraid. They told me I would be in trouble if they were caught, because I knew their plan and was therefore complicit. Then they told me if I helped them more, they would be successful, and no one would ever find out the truth. I believed I had no choice."

"You always have a choice, Prudence!" Clemency exclaimed. "Beginning with telling me. Did you not believe I might be able to help?"

Prudence's head snapped around, and she glared at Clemency with such ferocity Clemency was taken aback. "You abandoned us," she snarled. "You left, and when you returned you were a stranger. And you treated me like a child when you noticed me at all. What makes you believe I could have come to you for help, when you so clearly wanted nothing to do with us?"

"That is not true, Prudence," Clemency shot back. "I was preoccupied, true, but I have always stood ready to help any of you." But she remembered the last two months, how she had never made an effort to reach out to Prudence, had assumed she was a sulky child, and had never suspected beneath the sulky façade lay genuine pain and confusion.

"So you say," Prudence said. "If Father were alive—"

"Don't," Clemency said, but without anger. "It does neither of us any good to dwell on 'if' or 'maybe.' You are right, none of this would have happened if Father were alive." She sighed deeply and knelt before her sister. "And you are right that I have not been a true sister to you. I forgot you are a woman grown, and I forgot you might still be grieving. I regret so much my part in making you feel unwanted."

Prudence blinked. "I never expected to hear that from you."

"I never expected to need to say it." Clemency took Prudence's hand, still chilled from their flight, and gripped it gently. "Tell me, though—have you ever taken part in the bombings? What were you meant to do tonight?"

Prudence shook her head violently. "I found out what they intended after they attacked the Flying trials. I never wished for anyone to die, and they told me the other deaths were accidents, but then you were nearly killed, and I told them I wished nothing more to do with them. Which is when they threatened me. They said I needed to prove my commitment to their cause." She swallowed. "They left the bomb in the garden, and I was to put it beneath the Marchioness's bed."

"Prudence!"

She waved her hands as if urging Clemency to stop. "It was at the last minute, when I told them of the invitation. I was the only one who could do it. But I never intended to! I was trying to discover how to disable the bomb when you found me."

"That could have killed you," Clemency said.

Prudence's eyes were haunted, and her mouth trembled. "I know. But I was responsible—no, not responsible, but involved in the other attacks, which means those deaths are on my conscience. I did not care if the bomb killed me."

Without a second thought, Clemency gathered Prudence into her arms and held her tightly. "Never say that," she said as Prudence began weeping. "We would all be devastated to lose you."

"Not Roger," Prudence said in a muffled voice.

"Even Roger, may he be damned to live a thousand eternities without a title," Clemency said. Prudence choked out a laugh. "Prudence, you have made mistakes, but you are in a position to repair them, something you could not do if you were dead. I know a man who is investigating the bombings, and we can tell him what you know. That will help him stop these murderers. But you have to tell me— who is Mr. Jinks? Or am I right that that is a name your group uses, and there is no such person?"

Prudence sat back so she could look at Clemency. "It is true Mr. Jinks is an invented name," she said. "But there is a real person behind the name. It is Mr. Montague."

CHAPTER 29

IN WHICH CLEMENCY RECEIVES ADVICE FROM AN UNEXPECTED SOURCE

The revelation did not surprise Clemency. She had a feeling, as Prudence spoke, that she already knew the answer to "Mr. Jinks'" identity. Mr. Montague's behavior to Prudence at Prudence's ball had not, in hindsight, been that of a lover, and his rather abrupt declaration of interest in Clemency now struck her as forced. Why Mr. Montague had believed it necessary to feign interest in her, she did not know, unless he meant her to take him in dislike, also something that made no sense.

She dismissed this line of reasoning and focused her attention once more on Prudence. "Mr. Montague," she said. "How was he introduced to you? I believed you had not gone out in public until that ball."

"It was at a concert," Prudence said, wiping her eyes. "He spoke to Roger—they belong to the same club—and Roger introduced him in that way Roger has, dismissing his sisters as nothing because they are not men. He made me sound like a child, but Mr. Montague was so polite, and he seemed interested in speaking with me." Now she sounded pleading. "I believed him, not romantically interested, but friendly, and I liked being treated as an adult."

"I understand. He preyed on your youth and your loneliness,"

Clemency said. "I regret so much leaving you vulnerable to such an approach."

Prudence shrugged. "We spoke of many things, and I may have mentioned my dislike of Extraordinaries, for Mr. Montague sympathized and told me of others who intended to promote the interests of the non-talented. There were many women in his group, it was not all men, so I believed it was not improper."

Clemency's eyebrows rose. "Did you?"

"I—" Prudence blushed. "No. But I enjoyed feeling as if I made a difference. I enjoyed being important finally. So I told myself I was justified."

Clemency caught herself before she could challenge Prudence's assumptions. It did not matter whether she had been wrong or right. "And you met with these people frequently? Where?"

Prudence blushed harder. "It was in many different places, none of them fashionable. That made the meetings more exciting, knowing I went to places you and Mama would disapprove of. It was all talk, at first. And Mr. Montague did not seem to be in charge. But I realized after a time that his was always the voice that directed us in making decisions. After the first bomb, when I discovered these people were responsible, he was the one who assured me I had done no wrong."

"I see. So Mr. Montague gradually assumed a more explicit leadership position."

"Yes," Prudence said, with some vehemence, as if she intended to convince Clemency of the truth of her words. "And it felt as if we all wished him to do so. Miss Honeycutt in particular, though I believe she has a more personal interest in Mr. Montague."

"Who is Miss Honeycutt?" Clemency asked.

Prudence shrugged again. "I suppose one could call her Mr. Montague's most devoted follower. She is a Scorcher, and I have never seen her when she is not angry about something. She would do anything for Mr. Montague."

Clemency recalled dodging fire above St. Paul's Cathedral. "Including set a bomb?"

"Yes, certainly." Prudence wrapped Clemency's blanket more

closely around herself. "Miss Honeycutt frightens me. A Scorcher in a temper might not control her fire."

"At least Roger has never misused his talent," Clemency said. "So, on the night of your ball, Mr. Montague threatened you?"

"That is when he told me I needed to prove myself. My commitment to him and to the cause." Prudence drew in a shuddering breath. Her gaze roved the room, never settling on anything, but Clemency did not believe she was lying. "He told me they would inform me of when I was to act, and that I was to make contact with him frequently for instructions. I told him I would not, and he said...he said I was not the only one in danger. That he could kill you, or Mama, or Mercy, whenever he chose."

"Surely you did not take that threat seriously?" Clemency exclaimed. "I am far from helpless, and I can protect any of you."

"You do not understand," Prudence cried out. "Mr. Montague is clever, and devious, and he—I did not know for so long, but he cares nothing for others, and he enjoys causing death. He will find a way to hurt you, I know he will. And now that I have failed—" She burst out weeping again.

"Prudence, it will be well," Clemency said, laying a hand on Prudence's knee. "I will stop him."

"How?" Prudence demanded in a thick, tearful voice. "You are not a man, to challenge him."

"I am a War Office veteran, and I wager I am far more skilled with Moving than Mr. Montague," Clemency said, "given that he has only ever used his Moving talent in the public trials. If it comes to a fight, he will not find me easily overwhelmed." She stood and looked down at Prudence, feeling all her aches return with a vengeance. "But it will not come to a fight. I will turn him over to someone who has authority to pursue these villains, and Mr. Montague will go to the Catterwell, and you need not fear his reprisal."

"But you said I was complicit," Prudence said, weeping harder. "You said I would be hanged."

"I will see to it that Mr.—that my contact understands that you were manipulated into taking part. You never set any bombs, and you revealed Mr. Jinks' identity; that should be enough to protect you." She swore a silent oath that it would be enough. Prudence's youthful foolishness would not condemn her, not if Clemency could stop it.

Prudence nodded and wiped her eyes again. "I have been so afraid," she whispered. "I regret so much not trusting you."

"I should have made myself more trustworthy," Clemency said. She helped Prudence to her feet and hugged her. "Go to your room and try to sleep. I must return for Mama and—" She caught sight of her reflection, saw her disheveled, bruised appearance, and swore, making Prudence gasp. "I cannot go looking like this," she added. "No, do not worry, Tatton will help." Tatton had been understanding of Clemency keeping her other secret; it was past time she was aware of Clemency's other doings.

Tatton proved as reliable as Clemency had ever hoped; she did no more than exclaim once over Clemency's condition, and then helped her don a new gown with no comment. Clemency briefly explained about the bomb, omitting Prudence's role in the evening's events, and ended by saying, "You understand why it is imperative you not discuss this with anyone. Capturing Mr. Jinks and his organization requires secrecy, and I will not be able to inform my contact of his identity until morning."

"I would never speak of your affairs to anyone," Tatton said, somewhat indignantly. She finished arranging Clemency's hair and added, "Your face is bruised and scratched, my lady. It is obvious you have been in a fight."

"That cannot be helped, unless you have access to theatrical cosmetics," Clemency said with a smile that made her bruised cheek throb. "I will not enter the gala—oh, how I regret not being able to attend! I might have said much in my defense. It is a terrible lost opportunity."

"And a lost opportunity to enjoy yourself, my lady," Tatton said, pretending to scold her.

Clemency prodded her poor broken necklace where it lay on the dressing table. "I shall have to see about getting this mended," she said, and stood. "Thank you again, Tatton. I will return shortly."

Tatton left the room, and Clemency opened her window. She hesitated as the first chill blast of wind struck her. Then she lifted her mattress and whisked her Army trousers toward herself. She held them with her Moving and examined them. They would be bulky under her gown, but they would protect her as she Flew. And, she realized, she did not care what others thought of her. She donned the trousers, smoothed her skirt over them, and leapt out of her window.

HER VARIOUS ACHES AND SCRAPES HURT WORSE THE FOLLOWING DAY, and when she woke—late, due to a night made sleepless by excitement —she lay still in bed and considered whether she might not stay there for a few hours, as all her pains lessened when she did not move. Sighing, she reminded herself that Mr. Montague might strike again at any moment, and made herself rise.

The mirror revealed several long scratches across her forehead and temple and one large bruise across her cheek, none of which she could conceal. Her arms were similarly battered. She determined on telling anyone who asked that she had been Flying by night and collided with a tree. It was embarrassing, but believable, and had the advantage of being mostly true. With luck, she would not encounter anyone who would ask.

It did not occur to her to wonder what Mr. Montague's reaction to the failed bombing of the previous night might be until she had finished her breakfast and donned a comfortable gown with long sleeves that concealed the worst of the bruises. He would obviously know his attempt at murdering the Marchioness of Lychfield had failed, and if he or some of his men had been on watch, they might have seen the detonation far from the Marchioness' home, but he could not know more than that. Which meant he would likely try to contact Prudence. The thought chilled Clemency. Mr. Montague had no idea his identity had been revealed, but imagining his presence in Emeraude House worried Clemency.

She went in search of Prudence and learned that her sister had gone out with Mercy and Francis for a walk in the nearby park. Clemency's worry subsided somewhat. Mr. Montague would not approach Prudence if Francis was present, and Francis was as strong an Extraordinary Mover as she was. There was no imminent danger. Still, Clemency felt the urgency of her need to speak to Mr. Rutledge. She could not believe she had ever resented his interference. She did not fear Mr. Montague for himself, but when she contemplated the things his organization had done, and how Prudence had been caught up in them, she wished devoutly to turn the mess over to someone else.

She moved restlessly through the house for an hour or more, aware that it was Friday and Mr. Wescott would be at his place of employment, even more aware that she had no idea at what time he would return home. Finally, impatient with herself and her uncertainty, she changed into her Flying gear and Flew to Hanover Square.

The sky was clear, the sun was bright, and she could easily see why Prudence and Mercy wished to spend some of the day outdoors. If not for her sense of urgency, Clemency would have dawdled through the sky, enjoying the weather. Instead, she Flew at nearly her top speed, ignoring the airborne specks that were Bounders going about their business. Perhaps one of them was Mr. Wescott.

She felt no frisson of excitement when she thought of him. She did not know if she had been wrong in believing he cared for her, and that left her feeling despondent. He was not the sort of man to offer his help if he despised her as a fallen woman, she was sure, but not despising her was a long way from feeling a warmer attachment. Yet when she considered addressing him directly, her courage failed her. Kissing him in a moment of spontaneous excitement had not prepared her for declaring she wanted more from him than kisses.

She alit on the Wescotts' doorstep and knocked politely, banishing her tumultuous feelings to somewhere she hoped Miss Wescott could not perceive them. This was no personal matter, and she had no reason to believe she and Mr. Wescott would converse on anything but Mr. Rutledge's whereabouts. She should not be nervous.

The door opened. "Lady Ashford," Hammond said, bowing.

"I would like to speak to Mr. Wescott. On a matter of business," Clemency said, and immediately felt like a fool. It was none of

Hammond's business why she was there, and she owed the butler no explanations.

Hammond's expression did not change. "You are not expected, my lady," he said. "Pray, permit me to show you to the drawing room, and I will inquire."

Furiously willing her embarrassment not to show on her face, Clemency followed Hammond up the stairs to the drawing room. There, she sat by the fire—not too near, not too far—and settled her divided skirts more than they actually required. She had never been one to fidget before returning from the war, and she did not know if it was Armand, Roger, or Mr. Wescott who had inspired the habit in her. Likely all three.

Shortly, she heard light footsteps in the hall, lighter than Hammond's, and before she could stand, Miss Wescott entered. She did not look at all taken aback by Clemency's presence, nor by her bruised appearance. "Lady Ashford," she said in her high, musical voice. "I beg your pardon, but my brother is not here."

"Oh," Clemency said, "I know he is employed on Fridays, and I— perhaps I should have sent word before simply appearing on your doorstep." She stood. "I can return later."

"He will not be here later," Miss Wescott said. "I cannot say when he will return."

Confusion, and then a dawning realization, struck Clemency in rapid succession. So he would not see her at all. Hot embarrassment flooded her cheeks, and she looked away from Miss Wescott at the fireplace. The crackling of the fire devouring the wood seemed suddenly to surge in her ears like a high wind. She watched a slim log, eaten away at the center by the flames, sag and snap in half, making the fire roar in triumph over its victim. "Oh," she repeated. "I understand."

Miss Wescott took a step toward her. "No, do not feel so," she said. "He truly is gone from London, and I cannot say where he has gone or when he will return. It is not—" She stopped abruptly and put a hand to her lips as if trapping words inside. "I cannot say that, either," she concluded.

Confused, Clemency looked at Miss Wescott. The young woman showed no signs of embarrassment or concern; she looked placid, as if she felt none of Clemency's turmoil, though Clemency was certain that was untrue. Clemency did not know what to make of her words. "This is not a personal visit," she heard herself say. "I need to speak with Mr. Rutledge, and Mr. Wescott is the only person I know who can reach him. I don't suppose Mr. Wescott left you any word? Instructions for— but no, that is unlikely."

"No, I know nothing of Mr. Rutledge's whereabouts." Miss Wescott shifted her weight, and then her eyes widened. "I beg your pardon, I forgot myself again. Will you sit? Or perhaps you do not like to, if this is not a visit for pleasure."

"I suppose I should not take up your time," Clemency said, feeling downhearted again. "Mr. Wescott left you no way to contact *him?*"

Miss Wescott walked past Clemency without answering and took a seat near the fire. Feeling awkward, Clemency resumed her seat and clasped her hands in her lap to still their trembling. Miss Wescott took the poker and stirred the fire, one neat half-circle clockwise, then another counterclockwise. "I cannot say," she said without looking at Clemency. "He made me promise. Tell no one, he said, not for any reason."

"But that is not the same as not knowing!" Clemency exclaimed. "Miss Wescott, this is quite urgent. I have information about the bombings Mr. Rutledge must know. If you cannot tell me his location, surely you can convey a message to Mr. Wescott!"

"No, that I truly cannot do," Miss Wescott said. "I know where he went. I do not know where he is. I realize that sounds confused."

"You mean you know his destination, but not his current location," Clemency said.

Miss Wescott brightened. "Ah, then I am not as confused as I believed. Such a relief. And you—your anger has not yet got the better of you."

"I am not angry, Miss Wescott, certainly not with you," Clemency protested. "I do not understand why you persist in claiming otherwise."

Miss Wescott's jaw hardened briefly, and then she regained her calm. "It is unimportant," she said, "but I hope—no, it is not my place to comment on others' emotional states. You are actually quite calm for one in your position, vilified by society and challenged by your brother."

Clemency did not know what to say to that. She settled on, "I will survive. I must survive, because the alternative is too terrible to imagine."

"It will pass," Miss Wescott said.

Rather than being angered, Clemency found those three words comforting. Miss Wescott had spoken not as someone offering useless reassurances, but as one who knew the future and had total certainty as to what it held. "I look forward to that time," she said.

Finally, Miss Wescott turned to face her. "I hope it is a happy time," she said with a brilliant smile. "Your emotions are always so strong and easily distinguishable from my own, and that is a rare enough thing I cherish it when I encounter it. Have you not spoken to Mrs. Rutledge?"

Her change of topic was abrupt enough Clemency did not at first remember who Mrs. Rutledge was. Then she said, "*Mrs*. Rutledge? Of course! I was so intent on finding her husband that seeking her out did not occur to me. I do not know her well, nor do I know her direction here in London. But of course she will be able to put me in contact with her husband."

"I do not know her, either," Miss Wescott said, her brow furrowing in a little V above her nose. "I fear I do not have many acquaintances in the city yet. It is so unfortunate. I believe Colin is afraid I will break if I go out in society, but I am not so easily overwhelmed as that, not after what I have experienced."

"I am certain Mr. Wescott cares for your well-being very much," Clemency said, but she recalled what Mr. Wescott had said the day she had met Mr. Rutledge in Miss Wescott's company, how he had admitted to perhaps too much caution over his sister, and it prompted her to add, "Perhaps you will call on me sometime? It is not the same as a large gathering, but I enjoy your company, and I believe Lady Prudence would like to pursue your acquaintance."

"I would like that very much," Miss Wescott said. "I do not enjoy being alone in the house with Colin gone."

"I understand," Clemency said. She rose and added, "I should seek out Mrs. Rutledge. Thank you for your hospitality. I hope Mr. Wescott's errand will not take too long."

Miss Wescott smiled again, the beatific expression that said she felt something wonderful. "Yes, you do," she said.

Clemency blushed and let herself out.

CHAPTER 30

IN WHICH CLEMENCY
ENLISTS HELP IN HER QUEST

The sun had set while Clemency was speaking to Miss Wescott, and the western sky was a hazy deep blue fading to gold along the horizon. Gas lamps illuminated the streets of Hanover Square, giving her paths to follow as she returned home in the darkness. The chill in the air made her face tingle, and she was grateful for the layers of Flying gear and coat and gloves to warm her as she Flew ever higher.

The path home was so familiar she paid only enough attention to it to ensure she did not Fly too far off course. The rest of her attention was caught up in making plans. Even had she known where the Rutledges lived, she could not burst in on them at this hour. She would have to spend the evening in searching, and approach Mrs. Rutledge in the morning, assuming her search was successful. She would enlist Mercy and her reticulum. Mrs. Rutledge was a well-known Extraordinary Seer, and someone would know her direction.

She entered Emeraude House by way of the front door rather than her window and divested herself of her outerwear. Slater, who accepted her coat and gloves, said, "There was another messenger for you, my lady. He informed me it was to do with Mr. Northrup's suit."

Rather than filling her with apprehension, the news irritated Clemency. Roger's selfish demands mattered little beside her other concerns, and yet his demands had to be addressed. "Is the man here?"

"No, my lady. He left papers for you. I took the liberty of delivering them to your offices."

At least Clemency would not have to deal with yet another unsatisfactory encounter before supper. "Thank you, Slater, I will look at them shortly."

"Yes, my lady." Slater did not bow or turn to leave.

"Was there something else?" Clemency asked.

Slater cleared his throat. "My lady," he said, "I fear Mr. Northrup approached each of the footmen privately earlier today. He offered them money to speak against you, in his favor."

Now sick dread filled Clemency. "I take it they refused, or you would be telling me a different story."

"They came to me immediately. Most of them turned him down unceremoniously. One, the lad William, was rather more clever, and gave Mr. Northrup the false impression that he might choose to be swayed. From the conversation he provoked, he learned that Mr. Northrup wished specifically for the footmen to claim that General de Villiers was a frequent visitor to this house and that you—excuse my bluntness, my lady—that you permitted him unrestricted access to your bedchamber."

Clemency realized her nails were cutting into the flesh of her palms and made her hands relax. "I am so grateful they were not suborned."

"I do not permit disloyalty among the servants," Slater said. "They know their duty, and they know to whom they owe respect. You were my lord's choice, and none of us would care to see you displaced."

"Thank you," Clemency said. "All of you. I will ensure your loyalty is rewarded."

Slater bowed and carried her coat and gloves away.

Clemency Flew to her room and removed the white knit cap, causing little tendrils of hair to stick up in all directions from the braid coiled around her head. She smoothed them down in vain. So Roger had stooped to conniving. That was good, in a sense, because it meant he felt insecure in his chances of winning the title. But it also meant that he might try other tricks she was unaware of, and that was dreadful to contemplate. She dared not dwell on who else he might find to lie on his behalf, for that would demoralize her completely.

Prudence was not at supper. "She has a head-ache," Mama announced to the table at large. "She has been ill so frequently of late —a head-ache tonight, a sour stomach last night—the poor child. And she had looked forward so to the gala."

From these words, Clemency concluded Mama had no idea of the trouble Prudence was tangled in. That was a blessing. Mama was kind and would be understanding, but she was not always careful in keeping secrets.

She regarded Mercy covertly. Mercy ate as neatly and placidly as always, showing no sign that she knew anything was amiss. Then Mercy said, "Prudence and I had a lovely walk this afternoon. She told me of some new friends she had made recently."

"New friends?" Clemency said.

"Oh, how delightful," Mama exclaimed. "Prudence is sadly isolated. I am so glad she has friends. Who are they? Anyone we know?"

"A society of like-minded individuals," Mercy said. She shot Clemency a meaningful glance. "Ones with an interest in societal change. Their ideals are unusual. Quite *explosive*."

"Did she meet any of them in the park today?" Clemency asked, tensing.

Mercy shook her head. "We were quite alone, Francis and Prudence and I. I imagine they are not the sort to pay visits unless they believe Prudence is not otherwise engaged."

Clemency relaxed. She did not know what had prompted Prudence to confide in Mercy and Francis, but having others know the secret, others who could help protect Prudence from being approached by Mr. Montague or others of his group, relieved her mind.

Mama left for an engagement with friends— "*Not* Lord Winder, my dear, he is quite, quite unsuitable, and I wonder that you ever permitted him to attend on me!"—and Clemency and Mercy settled, not in the drawing room, but in Clemency's bedroom, where they could be assured of greater privacy.

"I was so shocked when Prudence told me what had happened last night, and what she has been doing," Mercy said. "She was quite brave to confide in us, really. Especially as Francis was present for two of the bombings and lost friends. He assured her he did not blame her for being foolish. Tell me, Clemency, how much danger is she in?"

"That depends on whether Mr. Montague discovers she was partly responsible for his plot's failure," Clemency said. "Which means I must act quickly. I need your help."

"My help? What can *I* do?" Mercy sounded puzzled but not dismayed.

"It is actually your reticulum I need," Clemency said. "I must locate a man, Mr. Rutledge, who is involved in investigating these bombings. His wife is a famous Extraordinary Seer, but I only know her from her work in the War Office, and I do not know her direction here in London. I hoped perhaps your reticulum might have that information."

"I can try," Mercy said, somewhat dubiously. "My reticulum is not large, but some of its members have many more contacts than I have, and if I find the right connections, that web might be very far flung."

"Please try. If I cannot locate Mrs. Rutledge this way, I will have to inquire among my acquaintances, and so many of them have shunned me..." Clemency stared into the fire, which crackled and popped as merrily as if it did not care about her troubles.

Mercy shifted her position on Clemency's bed. She had arranged her legs beneath her for added balance as she leaned on one hand for support. "Something else disturbs you," she said. "Was it another disinvitation?"

"No, it is only that I suspect Mr. Wescott is not as interested in me as I believed." Clemency closed her eyes so the sound of the fire and the feel of its heat on her face filled her immediate world. "He does not hate me, at least, but—oh, I am a fool. My emotional entanglements hardly matter when I have so many other, more pressing cares."

"The state of one's heart is never unimportant." Mercy's voice came to her as if from a great distance. "Have you spoken with him?"

"He has left London, and his sister cannot say where he went or when he will return." Clemency sighed. She felt at that moment it would be a great comfort to be an Extraordinary Scorcher; the fire's heat soothed her, and she wished she might take it in her hands and mold it to her desires. "There will be time for that later. Now we must see about saving Prudence. If I cannot convince Mr. Rutledge she is innocent of any real wrongdoing—" She closed her mouth, unwilling to speak the worst for fear speaking might make it come true.

"Then permit me to search," Mercy said, and fell silent.

Clemency opened her eyes to see her sister tilt her head back in the attitude of a Speaker. She knew Mercy never perceived anything around her when she was engaged in Speaking, but she rose quietly anyway so as not to disturb her and Moved her chair closer to the bed. Then she sat and contemplated her hands, resting loosely in her lap. She often had to remind herself to use her hands rather than her Moving in social settings; Moving one's teacup or fork was considered impolite. A hundred years ago, Movers did such things as a way of displaying their talent and were honored for it. How strange, the ways in which society changed.

She considered what might change in the future. Suppose female Extraordinary Movers began wearing trousers beneath their gowns so they might Fly whenever they chose. Suppose garb for all Movers became trousers or pantaloons instead of gowns. That was something Clemency could barely imagine. To sacrifice one's modesty—and yet, was it truly immodest for a woman to display her legs in such a fashion? It was not as if people did not know women had legs. She laughed, and then covered her mouth to silence herself. Such a fancy!

"I hope your amusement means you are not so despondent anymore," Mercy said without looking her way. "You need not be silent on my account. I know watching someone Speak is tedious. Perhaps you should find a book."

"My nerves are too agitated for anything so passive. Do not worry about me," Clemency said.

She fell into a waiting fugue in which time did not pass. Memories presented themselves for review, memories of her father, memories of the War Office, memories of her childhood. For once, her memories of Armand did not trouble her, and she remembered Mr. Wescott once before banishing those memories as well. So she did not know how long it took before Mercy said, "Emily has met Mrs. Rutledge, but she does not know her direction, so instead she is Speaking to one of Mrs. Rutledge's close friends who can tell her what we wish to know."

A little of the tightness in Clemency's chest disappeared. "Such a relief."

"We still cannot communicate with Mrs. Rutledge tonight," Mercy pointed out.

"Yes, but I can send a message in the morning, and—oh, I must not feel as if the problem is solved." Clemency rose and paced the room. "There are still so many obstacles in the way."

Mercy did not respond. Clemency saw she had resumed her Speaker's pose and fell silent, watching her. Shortly, Mercy opened her eyes and said, "Pen and paper, if you please."

Clemency provided her with the requested articles, and Mercy swiftly wrote a few lines. She handed the paper to Clemency. "I know you will not be content until you have written your message, even though you may not deliver it tonight. Why do you not simply approach Mrs. Rutledge directly?"

"Because an Extraordinary Seer is a popular person, and one does not simply appear on her doorstep, even if one is not interested in a Dream or a Vision," Clemency said. "And as I wish to speak to Mr. Rutledge, not his wife, I should first ensure that he will be present. Though my instincts are to Fly there tonight and rap on the door until I am admitted." She was already engaged in writing a note, which she blew on and then folded. "I will send this in the morning, and hope Mrs. Rutledge is not a late riser. She never was when I encountered her in the War Office, but perhaps her peacetime activities are different."

"Do not fret," Mercy said. "I have faith that all will be well."

Despite her sister's injunction, Clemency did not sleep well. She dreamed of bombs exploding, of herself tumbling endlessly through the air, and woke in a sweat to discover her surroundings unchanged. She slept again, and dreamed of speaking to Mr. Rutledge, but in the dreams he could not understand her because they did not speak the same language, and he walked away from her, but when she tried to follow, her feet felt mired in thick honey that dragged her down. Then

Mr. Wescott took her hand to pull her free, and in her dream she imagined she could feel the touch of his skin against hers, but when she reached for him to kiss him, he dissolved into vapor, leaving her to weep with longing.

When she finally woke to find the sky paling toward dawn, she decided against suffering any more dreams and rang the bell for chocolate and toasted bread. How long, she wondered, should she reasonably wait before sending William the footman on his way?

Two hours turned out to be the answer to that question. William, bright-eyed despite the earliness of the hour, took the message cheerfully. Clemency recalled that he had been the clever footman who had drawn Roger's purpose out of him. Some kind of bonus was definitely in order.

William returned as speedily as Clemency had hoped, bearing a folded note. Clemency broke the seal and read the note there in the foyer, where she had been pacing awaiting his return:

Lady Ashford,

Your unexpected message leaves me filled with questions. It is unusual for a woman to write to me requesting an interview with my husband rather than myself. Mr. Rutledge will be home after eleven o'clock this morning, and you are welcome to call on me then.

Sophia Rutledge

In her haste, it had not occurred to her how odd her message must have seemed—asking a woman to provide another woman access to the first woman's husband, and with no explanation, given that Clemency did not know how much in Mr. Rutledge's confidences Mrs. Rutledge was. The Extraordinary Seer was unusual indeed.

Clemency hurried to her room and changed into her Extraordinary Mover's Flying garb. While she was donning her soft boots, her glance fell on her pocket watch. Four minutes and ten seconds after ten o'clock. She would arrive far too early. Imposing on Mrs. Rutledge's good nature after she had already challenged propriety was unthinkable. And yet Clemency could not bear waiting one second longer.

She cast her gaze about her room, searching for inspiration, and saw her broken necklace lying where she had left it on her dressing table. She had enough time to Fly to the jeweler's to leave it for repair.

That would put her properly in time for meeting Mr. Rutledge. Gathering up her necklace, she put it into its box and dropped the box into her reticule. Having a purpose eased her agitation considerably.

She Flew low that morning, feeling a need to connect with other people, even if that connection was merely the symbolic one of observing others walking or riding through the streets. A few people looked up and stared as she swept past. She wished she might wave at them, but waving at strangers was considered the equivalent of pointing and was therefore impolite. The knowledge unexpectedly saddened her. That a friendly gesture might be taken as rudeness made her wonder what other traditions of society made no sense.

Harrell's in Bond Street had been her family's jeweler for more than fifty years. They were not so popular as others, but Mr. Harrell's skill was exceptional, and he always attended on Clemency himself rather than putting her commissions to one of his subordinates.

"Everyone wants the Prince Regent's custom," he had once confided in her, "but no one realizes what that custom does to hamper one's business. One must carry stock with his Highness's tastes in mind, and be prepared to drop other work for his sake—and too great a demand by customers who wish to patronize the same shop as royalty leads to poor quality as one rushes to meet that demand." Clemency had never considered the matter at all, and in a lesser craftsman she might have suspected a ploy to cover his disappointment, but when she considered the jewels he produced, she could not believe him less than honest.

That morning, she delivered the necklace to Mr. Harrell, who commiserated over her accident but was polite enough not to mention the marks on her face. "I will endeavor to match the pearls," he said in his usual prim way, "but as there are only four missing, it will not be much of an endeavor." He smiled, dispelling the illusion of primness. "I recall your father buying these. He was insistent that the pearls be of the highest quality, and the stones be matched in size and clarity."

"His daughters thank you for your care," Clemency said.

Having established that the necklace would be ready in a week's time, Clemency stepped outside and examined her watch. Thirty-seven minutes and forty seconds after ten o'clock. A leisurely flight would put her at Mrs. Rutledge's house just after eleven o'clock.

Still intent on her watch, she stepped aside from the door to avoid another patron and immediately ran into someone she had not noticed. "I beg your pardon," she said, looking up. Then she gasped in surprise.

It was Mr. Montague.

CHAPTER 31

IN WHICH CLEMENCY ENDURES A LITERAL AND A FIGURATIVE ASSAULT

S he knew instantly that her reaction had been too dramatic. Her surprise at encountering the man who had preoccupied her thoughts since Prudence's revelation had made her recoil as if from a dangerous animal, and her gasp had been almost theatrical. Mr. Montague's eyes narrowed. "Lady Ashford," he said, "I beg your pardon."

Clemency collected herself with a powerful exertion of will. "No, sir, it is my fault, I was not looking where I was going," she said, striving for a light tone, apologetic and yet unconcerned, as if their collision was no more than a trifle. Someone passed between her and the building to enter the shop, and she was aware she and Mr. Montague stood in the middle of the throng, but she felt incapable of stepping out of anyone's way, irrationally afraid Mr. Montague might attack if she moved aside.

Mr. Montague's gaze took in the bruise and the scratches. "You appear to have had more than one collision," he said with a smile that frightened Clemency with its lack of warmth and humor. "I hope it was not serious."

"I struck a tree while night Flying," Clemency said with a laugh she instantly regretted for how false it sounded. All her self-possession had deserted her; she could think only of how this man had orchestrated seven bombings in the name of his terrible cause. Looking at him, at his implacable expression, she remembered what Prudence had said of him, that he delighted in causing death, and felt ill.

"A tree," Mr. Montague said. "Was this last night? Your injuries appear new."

"Two nights ago," Clemency said without thinking.

Mr. Montague's expression grew harder. "I wonder that so skilled a flier as Lady Ashford should have such an...accident."

Warning bells rang in Clemency's head. "Oh, it is embarrassing," she said, again pretending to an offhanded indifference. He suspected something, she was certain of it, and she had just linked her supposed accident to the same night as the thwarted bombing. "I do not wish to speak of it further."

"Very well," Mr. Montague said. "May I ask how Lady Prudence fares?"

"Lady—? Oh! She is well," Clemency said, taken aback at the sudden change of topic.

"I enjoy speaking with her. She is quite mature for her age." Mr. Montague's eyes never left Clemency's. "And possessed of some radical opinions. Most intriguing."

"Prudence is young, and does not always know what she believes," Clemency said.

"Ah, but the young are so passionate in their beliefs. They are not afraid to act on what they believe, too. And they achieve great change." Mr. Montague smiled. It was a predator's smile, toothy and malicious.

"They are also easily led, don't you agree?" Clemency's awareness of how half their conversation was happening below the surface loosened her tongue. "And if they listen to the wrong influences, their passion can be warped to serve the wrong master."

The smile widened. "How unfortunate for them," Mr. Montague said, "that they will be held responsible for their action regardless of who led them to it. One does not, after all, blame the knifemaker if a woman stabs her husband in a fit of passion. It is the woman who will go to the gallows."

His veiled threat frightened and angered Clemency all at once.

Without considering, she said hotly, "But a woman manipulated into acting on behalf of another is not ultimately guilty, and it is unjust to permit that man to walk free."

Mr. Montague tilted his head in an expression of bewilderment. "My, my, Lady Ashford, such vehemence on behalf of a nonexistent woman! It is not as if anyone could prove that a particular someone was behind that woman's actions. Particularly if the woman was, mmm, *persuaded* not to speak against him."

"Can I not?" Fear for Prudence made her heedless of her surroundings, of the men and women passing and entering and leaving the jeweler's. "That man would do well to fear, because there are those interested in stopping him, and I intend to see justice done. And do not approach Prudence again."

Mr. Montague's eyes widened in feigned dismay. "You speak as if you believe I am a threat," he said. "Why should I wish to harm Lady Prudence? She is such an enthusiastic, clever young woman. In fact, I intend to dance with her at Almack's Wednesday next, and have an enlightening conversation."

Clemency took a step nearer. Mr. Montague was somewhat taller than she, but she bore down on him as if she towered over him. "You will not be in a position to dance with anyone Wednesday next. The Catterwell does not, to my knowledge, permit for much of a social life."

To her surprise, Mr. Montague smiled as if she had just given him a great gift. Then he staggered backward, crying out loudly, "Lady Ashford, why do you attack me?"

Clemency took an involuntary step back, startled at his reaction. Two men passing stopped and turned at his exclamation. Then they shouted as a large, dark shape that screamed in terror hurtled at them and Clemency. Reflexively, Clemency caught the thing and Moved it up and away from the men before realizing it was a carriage, and the screams came from inside as well as from the horse still harnessed to it that now hung head-down, jerking against Clemency's hold.

"Lady Ashford has gone mad!" Mr. Montague shouted. "She attacked me!"

"I, mad?" Clemency exclaimed. "You attacked me!"

The screams were growing louder, and the lady inside the carriage, unimpeded by either Clemency or Mr. Montague's Moving, clung to the seat and kicked at the door. Mr. Montague shouted, "I won't stay to be killed!" and ran.

Clemency made a grab for him with her Moving. Mr. Montague stumbled, caught himself on hands and knees, and wrenched away from her. Clemency tried to hold him again, feeling as if she were trying to contain wet sand that slid and slipped through her fingers. The carriage swayed wildly, and the lady inside shrieked and fainted. In Clemency's moment of distraction, Mr. Montague twisted out of her grip once more. He caught her eye, laughing, and then turned and fled.

The fainting woman, whom Clemency had not been able to restrain, slid toward the front of the carriage. Clemency caught her now inert body and felt the carriage shift as her Moving balance altered. Cursing inwardly, she gently lowered the carriage to the ground, laid the woman to rest on its floor, and then righted the horse, holding it still so it would not injure itself in its panic. She now saw, beyond the carriage, a man in coachman's garb lying very still where he had fallen and two other men crouching over him.

"Help!" she shouted. "I need help containing this horse!"

There was quite a crowd now, drawn by the commotion. One of the men rose from where he knelt and hurried to the horse's head. The animal's eyes were wild and white-ringed, and its head jerked in panic. The man put out a hand to touch the horse. "What should I do?" he asked.

"Be ready to calm him—in fact, there should be three of you," Clemency said. "I have done this in the field—the horse is panicked, but if you soothe it, I will be able to release it and it will not run mad. But someone should release it from the carriage so the horse will not drag anything away if this goes wrong. Please, we need more men here!"

A few other men emerged tentatively from the crowd and joined the first, surrounding the frightened horse. Clemency eased her grip on it so she only held its legs with her Moving. Moving animals was only difficult in how panicked they became; they had no will to oppose hers, and she might Move the horse anywhere she chose, but if she was incautious in releasing it, it would hurt itself.

Gradually, under the calming influence of the men, the horse's frightened movements subsided until it was only trembling. One of her helpers had worked the harness free, and Clemency gently Moved the carriage a few feet from the horse. She was peripherally aware of men and women gathering near the carriage door, but the horse was now her primary concern. She steadied its legs, holding them with the lightest touch of Moving, and watched the animal closely, observing its rapid breathing and the occasional toss of its head.

"Hold it steady now," she said, and released her hold.

The horse took a few awkward steps as it regained its balance, but otherwise did not move. Clemency let out the breath she had been holding and shook out her hands, which were as tense as if she had held the horse in place with them instead of with Moving.

A surge of motion drew her attention back to the carriage. The gathered crowd had drawn the fainting woman out and laid her on the street, and as Clemency approached, the woman's eyelids fluttered, and she tried to sit. Clemency considered restraining her with Moving, decided that was a bad idea, and instead knelt beside her. "Are you hurt? I see no obvious injuries."

The woman's eyes widened, and she shied away. "Why did you attack me?" she said in a hoarse whisper, as if she wished to shout but could not manage it. "I might have died!"

"It could not have been this lady," one of the bystanders said. "She would hardly have flung your carriage through the air with Moving and then stayed to repair the damage and save the horse."

Clemency had, in her haste, temporarily forgotten Mr. Montague's odd behavior. "That was—" she began, then thought better of announcing Mr. Montague's secret identity in public. That would cause more of a panic than the flying carriage had. And she did not believe she could tell even part of the truth without entangling herself in explanations that would prevent her making her rendezvous. Capturing Mr. Montague now was likely out of the question, after so many delays.

"I do not know why that man pretended I was the one attacking," she declared, "but it is certainly true that he was the one who Moved the carriage. I caught it when he flung it at me and those gentlemen."

"But he claimed you attacked him," a weedy little man said. "I heard his words myself."

"Perhaps he believed I was someone else," Clemency said. "Or he is mad. Really, I must go."

"A madman? Unlikely," said the weedy little man. "I say you attacked *him*."

"Don't be a fool," said the first bystander. "That makes no sense. An Extraordinary, attacking another Mover on a public street? It's absurd."

"Thank you," Clemency said. She stood and brushed off her divided skirts. "Madam, are you well? I fear I cannot stay to see you to a hospital, or to your home."

"I won't be touched by you," the woman said as several people helped her to her feet. Most of them got in the way of the others, and ultimately the woman had to fight her way free of the crowd to stand unsupported. "I am not certain you did not have something to do with this attack. Perhaps you did not Move my carriage, but if not, that other Mover must have had a reason to attack you."

Clemency's gratitude faded, replaced by irritation. "I have said I do not know what motivated him," she said, as politely as she could manage. "Perhaps you might consider what would have happened to your horse and carriage, as well as to yourself, had I not been present when he Moved you."

The woman shrugged. "He would not have Moved us had he not wished to hurt you. So it is ultimately on your head."

Clemency felt the seconds slipping away from her and made a decision. "Madam," she said, walking slowly toward the woman, "I am Lady Ashford, and while I sympathize with your justifiable anger, I refuse to permit you to place the blame on me. You have suffered a tremendous shock and I believe you should return home to rest." She gestured at the carriage and to the driver, standing next to it now. He had been the fallen man, she realized, and was relieved that he, too, seemed not seriously injured.

"Your carriage is undamaged," she continued, "your horse unhurt, and in all I daresay this is the best conclusion to a terrible ordeal that anyone might expect. Now, if you don't mind, I believe I should find the man who *is* responsible and see that he is brought to justice."

She glared at the woman and was pleased to see her duck her head away from Clemency's gaze. Then she leapt into the air and Flew straight up, wishing to put as much distance between herself and the crowd as possible.

It was unlikely Mr. Montague had remained on the streets to be captured, but Clemency Flew along the path he had taken, surveying the ground. Almost immediately, the street outside Harrell's jeweler's shop crossed another, broader street, one crowded with pedestrians, carriages, and horses. Clemency swept a wide circle over the intersection, but it was no use. Frustrated, she Flew toward the Rutledges' house.

With nothing to do but remember the confrontation, Clemency became increasingly angry—with Mr. Montague, of course, but also with herself. Had she not given herself away, had she not given her anger free rein and revealed that she knew Mr. Montague's secret identity, she might have manipulated him into giving away information she could use—no, that she could give to Mr. Rutledge. Now, not only did Mr. Montague know that his secret was revealed, he had escaped and might be anywhere in London. Clemency silently berated herself for her foolishness.

She alit in front of the Rutledges' door at three minutes and seventeen seconds to eleven o'clock and stood for a moment, pretending to herself she needed to regain her breath. She was alone on the street, and everything was so still she might have imagined herself in a distant land, far from the bustle of London.

The rows of houses lining the street looked perfectly ordinary until one noticed how broad their faces were, with the doors set so widely apart one might have fit two average houses in the space between. Ornamental lintels of grey stone decorated the windows, preventing the street from seeming a canyon of blank stone, featureless and dull.

Each door had its own Grecian-style porch, complete with ornate carvings of men and women draped in Greek robes. Clemency glanced at a handful of them, curious: indeed, every porch was unique. She was wealthy enough, and Emeraude House was beautiful, but this was the sort of understated beauty that declared its owners were accustomed to true wealth.

She approached the door and rang the bell, then composed herself to wait. One could tell so much about a person by how she answered her door. Sending the butler immediately put oneself in a subservient, eager position; making the guest wait suggested indifference, or a desire to maintain the upper hand. Clemency had sometimes considered whether there was a limit to how long one might make a guest wait, and what it did to the balance of power, so to speak, if one overshot the mark. She did not take out her pocket watch; the door would open when Mrs. Rutledge chose, and Clemency had no power over her.

The door opened—not so soon as to be eager, not too delayed as to be arrogant—and an elderly man, somewhat stoop-shouldered and with thick white hair, peered out at Clemency. "Lady Ashford," he said, his voice stronger than she would have guessed from his appearance. "Pray, enter."

Clemency entered and immediately had to restrain an impulse to gasp. She had never seen a house so elegant and finely constructed as this that was not a royal holding. Only two windows illuminated the foyer, and that not well due to the wan sunlight fighting the overcast, but that light was enough to show rich mahogany paneling and a pillared first story balcony. A broad, curved freestanding staircase, a marvel of engineering, swept up to that balcony, suggesting grand entrances and women in archaic full skirts descending. The stillness of the street had penetrated to this room, and Clemency breathed lightly, not wishing to disturb the quiet.

"Mrs. Rutledge will see you in the Eastern drawing room," the butler said. Clemency followed his halting steps across the black and white tiled floor and tried not to become impatient at his slow pace. Unlit halls led away from the foyer, but the butler ascended the beautiful staircase instead.

Clemency had plenty of time to look about her. She knew very little of architecture, but she could compare this to Emeraude House and conclude that the Rutledges' home was very new, surely no more than ten years old; it lacked the small details that said the architect had restored an older house but left earlier elements in place. Again, Clemency was impressed at the probable size of the Rutledges' fortune. An Extraordinary Seer was likely very wealthy in any case, but to have a home such as this required a great deal more than "very wealthy."

The first floor hall was more brightly lit than the foyer, lined with lamps in sconces that shed their light over paintings lining the hall. Again, the butler's pace was such that Clemency had plenty of leisure to examine the paintings. Some were portraits done by masters; others were oils depicting, not pastoral landscapes, but classical subjects, mostly famous battles. Clemency did not know what to make of those decorating choices. Certainly these were valuable paintings, but from what little she knew of Mr. Rutledge, she did not believe he would choose art at random simply because it was expensive. And she had no reason to believe Mrs. Rutledge less canny than her husband.

Her soft Flying boots made little sound on the carpet, and the butler's tread was only a little louder, so when he opened a door on the right, the *snick* of the latch sounded like rifle fire in the stillness. "Mrs. Rutledge," he said, "Lady Ashford."

Clemency entered the room and paused just past the threshold. Technically, Mrs. Rutledge should be introduced to her, however wealthy and talented she was, but Clemency had never been one to stand on ceremony when it did not benefit her. And she remembered Mrs. Rutledge, in any case: the woman just rising from the settee was familiar, her ruddy hair seeming darker in the pale light from the windows, her gaze as intent as Clemency recalled. She had put on weight since the last time Clemency had seen her, and her movements were more contained, less gawky.

"Lady Ashford," Mrs. Rutledge said. "Pray, have a seat. Mr. Rutledge will join us shortly."

Clemency sat on a nearby chair and made herself as comfortable as her nerves would permit. She immediately saw why the butler had referred to the room as the "Eastern drawing room;" the furniture, wall hangings, and rugs showed the influence of the Orient in their design and arrangement. It reminded Clemency of Jane Pilgrim's father's house, and she suppressed a pang of sadness at the memory.

"I appreciate your generosity," she said. "I realize my request is odd."

"Indeed," Mrs. Rutledge said with a smile. "But I assumed you would not have approached me so openly if you were interested in an illicit liaison with my husband."

Her directness startled and embarrassed Clemency. She nearly protested when she registered the gleam in the woman's eyes and realized Mrs. Rutledge had made that indelicate remark as a test. "I seek only for information," she said. "But were I so lost to decency, I hope I would not be so foolish."

Mrs. Rutledge's smile broadened. "No, you would not," she said. "How long have you been home from your War Office service?"

"These two months."

"And they have been tumultuous months, I expect." Mrs. Rutledge leaned back against the settee, her gaze never leaving Clemency's face. "I have heard of your troubles. An illicit, Coerced affair. A challenge to your title. But that is not why you requested this audience."

"I should speak only to Mr. Rutledge," Clemency said. "I beg your pardon, but it is a private matter—"

"And you do not know how much I know of my husband's affairs," Mrs. Rutledge said. "I understand perfectly. And I do not expect you to change your mind, even if I tell you I am deep in Mr. Rutledge's confidences. I might be lying to gain your confidence."

"I would not call you a liar."

"And I would not be offended if you did." Mrs. Rutledge's smile faded. "I imagine," she went on in a slow, contemplative manner, "you never expected to be forced to defend your rights a second time."

"Nor the first time," Clemency said. "My father believed he had arranged things to everyone's satisfaction. We did not imagine my brother would not be satisfied."

"I followed your suit with great interest. After my first husband's death, I inherited his property, but there was a distant relation who wished to lay claim to it. My case was not as dramatic as yours—an Extraordinary Seer has more clout than an Extraordinary Mover, you know—but I felt sympathy for you nonetheless."

"Thank you," Clemency said, feeling awkward. She would prefer not to speak of her past or even her present woes when her worry over Prudence and Mr. Montague was so much more immediate. But it occurred to her that enlisting Mrs. Rutledge on her side might benefit her with Mr. Rutledge, if the Extraordinary Seer was actually in his confidences as she claimed.

"I don't suppose—that is, are you familiar with a Captain Falconer?" she asked, feeling inspired. "He was with the 95th Rifles before selling his commission."

Mrs. Rutledge's eyes narrowed. "I am not," she said. "Is he someone of importance?"

"Only to myself," Clemency replied. "He and his wife know the facts of my case and would be invaluable witnesses on my behalf."

"I see," Mrs. Rutledge said. "It sickens me that you should be forced to defend yourself against vile calumny. You were Coerced; that should be the end of it." One hand closed into a fist as if Clemency's accusers were present for her to beat. "But to men, such doings are either unthinkable and therefore a lie, or unconnected to them and therefore unimportant. I imagine they would not be so quick to believe the worst of a woman if they were vulnerable to the same attack."

Clemency did not know what to say to that. She ducked her head and hoped she was not too red with embarrassment.

"I apologize," Mrs. Rutledge said. "I am often too direct for other people's comfort. Forgive my bluntness—I mean only to express my support."

"I understand." Clemency still could not bring herself to meet Mrs. Rutledge's eyes.

The door opened again, and as Clemency turned to see Mr. Rutledge standing in the doorway, Mrs. Rutledge said, "Ah, there you are. I never expect you to be so punctual, sir. Have you that much interest in Lady Ashford's information?"

Mr. Rutledge took a step forward so he loomed over Clemency. "Not as much," he said, "as I have in discovering why she persists in interfering in my investigation."

CHAPTER 32

IN WHICH AN UNFAIR
ACCUSATION LEADS TO A
TENTATIVE ACCORD

Clemency gasped. "I, interfere?" she exclaimed. "I have done no such thing!" She chose not to dwell on the many times she had considered defying Mr. Rutledge's instructions.

"Then you did not go to the Marchioness of Lychfield's home intent on stopping another bomb?" Mr. Rutledge's voice was low and cutting, the voice of someone containing his anger. "I warned you, Lady Ashford, that there would be consequences if you chose to ignore me. Tell me why I should not take action against you!"

Clemency shot to her feet. "My attendance at the Marchioness's home was by invitation," she said, matching him tone for tone, "and my discovery of the bomb accidental. I acted the only way I could, by removing it at great personal risk. Or do you suggest I should have left it and gone crying into the night for help—help I had no reason to believe was forthcoming?"

Mr. Rutledge continued to glare at her. "So I am to believe your involvement was a grand coincidence? That is asking much, considering your past actions."

"Every time my *actions* have run up against your investigation, it has been by coincidence. And I have been extremely forthcoming with you." Clemency kept her temper in check, though she wished dearly to fling one of the Oriental vases at his head. "I came here today intending to tell you what I have learned about Mr. Jinks and the bombings, but it is clear you are uninterested in anything that does not increase your personal power!"

"Lady Ashford," Mr. Rutledge said, his voice rising to a shout, "I can have you locked up as complicit in these crimes, and I no longer see any reason not to do so!"

"That is quite enough," Mrs. Rutledge said. Her voice, quieter than her husband's, nevertheless cut across the noise, silencing him and Clemency both. "Mr. Rutledge, surely you see that bullying Lady Ashford will get you nowhere. Lady Ashford, you must realize how your involvement appears. Need I remind you both that you are on the same side?"

Clemency did not take her gaze from Mr. Rutledge's furious face. He, in turn, continued to stare her down. After a long, silent moment, he said, "Have a seat, Lady Ashford. I agree, fighting will get us nowhere."

Clemency waited until Mr. Rutledge lowered his considerable bulk into a chair that creaked under his weight, then resumed her seat near the settee. Mrs. Rutledge, who had not risen during the shouting match, said, "I believe the two of you have much to say to one another. We did not at first know, Lady Ashford, that you were the one who removed the bomb from the Marchioness's home."

"I will do the speaking, my dear," Mr. Rutledge said, but he smiled as he said it, a rueful smile that surprised Clemency with its tenderness. Again she reminded herself not to underestimate this man simply because he was large and stern and had a commanding presence. "Lady Ashford, my men discovered Mr. Jinks' intent to murder the Marchioness of Lychfield only hours before her gala. When no bomb exploded at her mansion, we assumed it was a false rumor that had led us there, possibly to distract us from the real target. What became of the bomb?"

"I found it in the garden, and carried it out of the city so it detonated harmlessly—or at least without killing anyone." Clemency gestured at her bruised face.

"And how did you happen upon it, if you did not know of its presence to go there intentionally?" Mr. Rutledge's demeanor had calmed, but his eyes, dark brown and fathomless, remained fixed on hers.

Clemency drew in a deep breath. "Mr. Rutledge," she said, "what I am about to tell you will very likely anger you. I wish you to listen to my whole story before reacting."

Mr. Rutledge pursed his lips. "You seem fond of setting conditions on my behavior. First I am not to tell of your nocturnal activities, and now I am, what, to refrain from shouting at you for your foolishness? You have no right to tell me what to do."

"It is not my foolishness, sir, and this is a request, not a command." Clemency drew in another breath. "I have learned the identity of Mr. Jinks from one of his...well, from someone who knows his business. But this person is not guilty of anything but being young and idealistic, and I do not wish to see the person condemned for Mr. Jinks' crimes."

Both Mr. Rutledge's eyebrows drew down over his nose in an epic scowl. "Anyone complicit in these bombings will suffer the full force of the law. No exceptions."

"Even if the person is responsible for revealing Mr. Jinks' identity, and providing valuable information that leads to capturing him?" Clemency exclaimed. "There must be some provision for mercy in the law, Mr. Rutledge."

"Perhaps we should hear the full story, sir," Mrs. Rutledge said.

Mr. Rutledge shot his wife a warning look she ignored. She went on to say, "Lady Ashford, stopping Mr. Jinks is imperative. He grows bolder by the day, and we can depend on luck for only so long. Please, tell us what you know. And have no fear. The law *is* merciful as well as just." She glanced at her husband. "We know this to be true from experience."

Clemency hesitated. Mr. Rutledge still looked as if he was prepared to disembowel her. Her heart ached for Prudence even as she railed silently at her sister for her foolishness. But Mrs. Rutledge was correct; stopping Mr. Montague was what mattered.

"Mr. Jinks is the pseudonym of an Alistair Montague," she said. "My sister, Lady Prudence, fell under his sway and was temporarily involved in his organization. She told me everything she knew of their plans, and I intend to share those details with you. But I must—no. I beg of you, do not condemn her. She never took part in the bombings, and she intended to disable the one intended for the Marchioness, which would almost certainly have cost her her life. She does not deserve to hang for mere foolishness, not when her knowledge may save hundreds or even thousands of lives."

Mr. Rutledge's expression had changed as she spoke, becoming still and impassive as she spoke of Prudence. When Clemency ran out of words, he said, "Tell me what you know."

Clemency repeated for him everything Prudence had said, emphasizing Prudence's regret at having been taken in. Mr. Rutledge listened as intently as a hawk stooping to prey. Across from him, Mrs. Rutledge was equally silent, but her expression was thoughtful, as if she were mulling over possibilities.

At the end of her speech, Mr. Rutledge said, "I do not know this Mr. Montague. Sophia?"

"Nor I," Mrs. Rutledge said.

"I do," Clemency said, feeling apprehensive. "And I fear I have given the game away. I met him on the street, quite by accident, before coming here, and in my surprise I revealed that I knew his secret identity."

To her surprise, Mr. Rutledge did not shout or rail at her. His lips thinned in a straight, hard line. "I suppose I should not expect anything less—no, that is not a criticism of you, Lady Ashford, I simply mean that this entire investigation has been plagued by misfortune."

"It is not as if there is any precedence for an inquiry of this nature," Mrs. Rutledge said. "You are inventing something beyond what local magistrates or even the Bow Street Runners do. Difficulties will arise."

"Such excuses do nothing to end Mr. Jinks'—Mr. Montague's reign of terror," Mr. Rutledge said. "What do you know of the man, Lady Ashford?"

"Very little, I fear," Clemency said. "He is one of likely thousands of well-to-do gentlemen in London, not titled, not possessed of great fortunes, but socially acceptable. Oh! I know his club—it is Hepburn's in Clarke Street. Perhaps you might catch him there!"

"We will search for him, but it is likely he will not go there if he believes you know of it and are likely to tell the authorities." Mr. Rutledge rubbed a large hand over his chin. "Though our advantage is, as always, that the bombers do not know what forces are arrayed against them or what they are capable of. Therefore, I will send men to Hepburn's. Even if Mr. Montague has fled, his fellows at the club will know more of his habits and residence."

"I could go," Clemency said. "I know him by sight, which your men do not—"

"You," Mr. Rutledge said, "will return to your home immediately. I do not wish for you to be further entangled in this nightmare."

"I am, as you say, already entangled," Clemency said, "and I have already proved myself competent. I have disposed of two bombs, I brought you the identity of the villain—"

"You know nothing of my investigation or methods, and your inter-ference has twice cost us vital information," Mr. Rutledge said. "It is sheer luck that you provided knowledge to compensate, and even greater luck that you survived three separate bombings. I will not be responsible for the death of a peer, particularly a female one."

"If you were to tell me of your methods, I could help," Clemency insisted. "I am a powerful Extraordinary Mover, and Mr. Montague is a Mover of no small talent; suppose your men were to come upon him, and he attacked them with his Moving? I would be capable of thwarting his attacks better than your people, I am certain."

"We are competent enough, thank you, Lady Ashford," Mr. Rutledge replied drily. "No. I insist you stay out of this. Do not mistake me; I am grateful for the assistance you have provided. But your ongoing help will only confuse matters. Pray, go home. Protect your sister."

"Protect—but you said you would not prosecute her!"

"I said nothing of the kind. But as it happens, I meant protect her from reprisal from Mr. Montague and his organization." Mr. Rutledge looked grave. "He knows you know his identity, and he must guess you learned it from Lady Prudence. I have no doubt he will attempt to punish her for betraying him. And I do not have the resources to protect her myself."

Clemency was about to shout at him again when she caught Mrs.

Rutledge's eye. The Extraordinary Seer gave a tiny shake of the head as if to warn Clemency to be still. Clemency stilled, unsure as to why, but certain that Mrs. Rutledge had something in mind.

"Then you will go to apprehend this vile monster now?" Mrs. Rutledge said.

"Eager to see me out the door, Sophia?" Mr. Rutledge said with a smile. He stood, his gaze still fixed on Clemency. "Do not mistake me," he said. "I will not hold your sister's fate over your head to make you obey me. But the success of my investigation is key to whether or not she hangs. Your continued interference may hinder me, and in that case, Lady Prudence may suffer." He inclined his head politely and let himself out.

After the door shut, Mrs. Rutledge let out a tremendous sigh and slumped against the settee's arm. "That is better. Alexander is under a tremendous strain, and I fear that means he sees anything that does not fit neatly into his plans as an obstruction. Would you care for tea?"

"I—no, thank you, Mrs. Rutledge, I should go," Clemency said, standing. Mr. Rutledge's words about Prudence's safety had struck her to the heart.

"I would like you to wait a moment. Give me time to Dream on your behalf." Mrs. Rutledge shifted her position until she was lying on the settee. It was such a careless, informal gesture Clemency felt uncomfortable, as if she had intruded on a private moment.

"But," she began, and decided against protesting further. If an Extraordinary Seer of such skill as Mrs. Rutledge possessed offered her talent as a gift, Clemency did not like to refuse it.

Mrs. Rutledge closed her eyes, and in the space of a few seconds, her face relaxed into sleep. It was clearly not a normal sleep, however; Mrs. Rutledge's body held perfectly still, and her eyes did not twitch beneath their eyelids as Clemency had observed in other people as they slept. One hand rested below her breasts, while the other lay loosely curled above her navel. Slowly, Clemency settled back into her chair, though she did not believe any movement of hers would wake Mrs. Rutledge.

She spent the next few minutes examining the furnishings, the many vases and rugs, the wall hangings and the couches. Whoever had furnished the room had made an effort to blend European influences with Eastern design, and the result was charming to the eye as well as, once again, revealing that the Rutledges were extremely wealthy. Perhaps it was Mr. Rutledge's wealth that permitted him to employ men to search for Mr. Montague.

Mrs. Rutledge stirred and sat up, and Clemency pretended she had not been gawking at the room. Mrs. Rutledge put a hand to her head, patting a stray lock back into place. "You must send your sister into the country at once," she said. "I hope it is not already too late."

"I beg your pardon?" Clemency exclaimed.

"Mr. Montague intends to harm her in retaliation. His people approach her now. You can best protect her by putting her out of his reach, meaning that you should take her out of the city." Mrs. Rutledge stretched, an indelicate maneuver she seemed not at all embarrassed about. "This is the extent of my Dream. I hope it is enough."

Clemency sprang to her feet. "Thank you, Mrs. Rutledge. For everything. I must—" But of course Mrs. Rutledge did not need Clemency's explanations. With no further politenesses, Clemency ran from the room and Flew to the front door, bypassing the beautiful stairs.

Once on the street, she leapt into the sky and headed for Emeraude House. Her divided skirts dragged at her, filling her with unexpected fury. If she was too late to protect Prudence because of some stupid societal expectation— She pushed herself faster and refused to dwell on possibilities. She would be in time, or she would not, and if she were not, to the devil with Mr. Rutledge. Clemency would destroy Mr. Montague herself.

She alit on the street in front of her house, stumbling in her haste, and thrust the door open, shouting Prudence's name. Her voice echoed through the foyer into the upper stories, but no one appeared, not even Slater. Fear surged through her, and she Flew over the balcony and sped toward the drawing room. That room was empty as well.

Frustrated, she turned around and nearly bowled Slater over. "Oh, I beg your pardon," she exclaimed automatically. "Slater, where is Lady Prudence?"

Slater did not react to her abruptness. "She has gone out for a walk with Lady Mercy, my lady."

"Lady Mercy? Slater, was Fra—Mr. Daubney with them? Tell me quickly!"

"I fear I do not know, my lady. I met Lady Prudence in passing below, and she was so good as to inform me of her plans and ask me to notify you, but she did not mention Mr. Daubney."

Clemency cursed under her breath. "Where did they go?"

"That, I also do not know. She did not order the carriage, so I presume it was not far."

"Thank you, Slater," Clemency said, and Flew back downstairs.

Once outside again, she Flew skyward and searched the nearby streets. She realized now she should have asked Slater how long ago Mercy and Prudence had left, but returning to question the butler, delaying her search, was intolerable. Instead, she flew a spiral pattern, gradually widening the spiral to include the streets leading away from Emeraude House. Impatience insisted she should Fly straight to the park, but without knowing how long her sisters had been gone, she did not wish to miss them on the street and leave them unprotected.

Beneath her, the city went about its business, quietly humming along in a way that drove Clemency's fear and impatience to new heights. No one looked up as she sailed overhead; the sky was still grey and cloudy, and she cast no shadow that might draw attention. Her gratitude for Mercy's chair expanded to include gratitude that it was obvious even in a crowd. She swept lower, ignoring the carriages, searching clusters of pedestrians for the chair.

She realized the hum of the city had grown louder and more fright-ened just as she recognized screams coming from behind her, in the direction of the park. She swung around and saw bright, hot light flick-ering through the trees. Fire. Without pausing to puzzle out that mystery, she Flew as fast as she could toward the fire.

Men and women stampeded past like horses fleeing in terror from a conflagration, shoving one another in their fear. Some fell and did not rise. Clemency could not stay to help. She sped to where fire burned the leafless trees, spreading gleefully from branch to denuded branch. The trees grew close together, following a path through the park, and from a distance, the line of burning oaks looked like a string of molten gold.

She had almost passed the burning line when she heard her name being shouted. As she hovered, searching for the voice, it shouted again: "*Clemency! Move!*"

A ball of fire some ten feet across hurtled from the fiery woods, engulfing her.

CHAPTER 33

IN WHICH CLEMENCY FIGHTS FIRE WITH FIRE

Clemency dropped immediately, plummeting like a stone to the ground and rolling as she landed. The warning had been enough to take her quickly out of the fire's path, and she was not even singed. Dead leaves crackled beneath her as she rolled and came to her feet. The burning trees were some ten feet away, and the flames darted and waved in the rising wind. Clemency cast about for the Scorcher who had tossed fire at her. He had to be stopped before the fire spread throughout the park and the wind carried it to the nearby houses.

A brighter flame, low to the ground, caught her eye, and she flattened herself so the ball of fire passed over her to impact on a nearby tree. Clemency sprang to her feet and Flew in the direction the fire had come from, but came up short against the wall of burning trees. This could not be an Extraordinary Scorcher, immune to fire and capable of hiding within the blaze, but if it was, Clemency might be outclassed. She dodged another fireball and rose higher, searching for a way past the wall.

Someone again screamed her name, and she turned, searching for the voice. And there was Mercy's chair, tipped on its side like a barricade, and the next time the person shouted at her, she recognized

Francis' voice. She was too afraid to feel relieved. She darted toward the chair, dodging another fireball that scorched her back, and dropped behind the nearest tree.

"Thank God," Francis said. He knelt behind the massive trunk, occasionally glancing past it at the burning trees. "Every time I try to take us out of here, that damned Scorcher sets the air on fire, and I cannot protect myself and Mercy *and* Lady Prudence." He nodded at Prudence and Mercy, who crouched behind him, clutching one another tightly but making no sound. Prudence's face was streaked with tears; Mercy looked white but resolute.

"I have told him to flee and seek help—" Mercy began.

"That is impossible, and I do not wish to hear any more nonsense," Francis said. "Clemency, you should take the ladies and go, and I will distract the Scorcher."

"Francis, no!" Mercy cried out.

"Clemency, this is my fault," Prudence said, weeping harder. "That is Miss Honeycutt, I am certain of it, and she is here to kill me."

Clemency squeezed in closer to Francis so the oak's broad trunk protected them against the next fireball. "You must take them," she said. "I may need to make a firebreak, and you know I have the greater Moving capacity."

Francis' lips pinched tight with anger. "You expect me to flee and leave you in danger?"

"I expect you to save my sisters," Clemency said. "Please, Francis. Get Mercy and Prudence to safety."

Francis turned his head away briefly, and a muscle leaped in his clenched jaw. Then he said, "Very well. Mercy, Lady Prudence, continue to hold one another. It will be easier to protect you if we are not all spread out against the sky." He shifted to where he could put his arms around both of them, his back to the Scorcher. "Where should I take them?"

"It will have to be Emeraude House, for now," Clemency said. "That will not be safe forever, but for now—go inside, and lock the doors, and have Slater and the other men secure the entrances and all the windows except mine. I will return soon."

"Brave words," Francis said with a tight smile.

Clemency gripped his hand. "Wait until I draw this Miss Honeycutt's fire, and then Fly!"

The last thing she saw before turning away was Prudence's tearstained face. For once, Clemency did not feel annoyed with her sister's foolishness. Prudence did not deserve this, no matter how foolish she had been, and Clemency intended to see her safe.

Clemency waited for another fireball to splash against the oak before speeding low and fast across the ground away from the tree. It had not yet caught fire, she saw as she glanced back once, but its bark was blackened and the smell of char filled the air. Then she turned her attention to the line of burning trees, coming up fast before her.

Most of the fire was in the branches, not the trunks, but the wind tore the flames so they danced like mad sylphs, and they leaped from tree to tree faster than they devoured the trunks. Clemency drew her arms and legs close in, cursing her skirts, and made herself as narrow as possible just before shooting between the first ranks of trees.

The heat beneath the burning branches was intense, but not unbearable, and there was no smoke thanks to that same wind carrying it away. What else it was carrying away, Clemency chose not to dwell on. She tried not to breathe too deeply for fear of scorching her lungs. Flying low and fast near the ground, she searched for the Scorcher, Miss Honeycutt.

She had begun to fear she had gone in the wrong direction when a ball of flame, diffuse and hot as all the others had been, erupted almost in her face. She jerked, did a backflip in the air, and landed prone on the dry, fire-seared earth. Another fireball passed over her head almost immediately. Clemency observed the direction it had come from and leapt to her feet, propelling herself off the ground and Flying toward the Scorcher.

This time, she saw the woman. She was dressed in trousers and a man's greatcoat, and had Prudence not identified her as Miss Honeycutt, Clemency would have assumed her male. She grabbed the Scorcher with her Moving and tried to lift her. Miss Honeycutt's feet left the ground, but Clemency only managed to raise her a foot or two before the woman's struggles freed her from Clemency's grip. Clemency snarled at her, though she was almost as angry at herself as at the Scorcher. She was supposed to be one of England's finest, and yet she could not Move any of these villains more than a few inches!

Miss Honeycutt scrambled backward and flung another ball of fire that Clemency dodged. "Give up now, Miss Honeycutt," Clemency shouted over the roar of the wind and the flames. "You see we know your identity—give up, and you may yet receive mercy."

Miss Honeycutt laughed, a horrible, vicious sound that sickened Clemency. She raised both hands in a dramatic gesture, and suddenly Clemency was on fire—not surrounded by one of the fireballs, but burning as if the Scorcher had put a match to her clothes. She dropped and rolled, but the fire would not extinguish. Panting with terror, she sped away out of Miss Honeycutt's sight and rolled on the ground again. This time, the fire went out. Clemency lay on her back, staring up at trees that had not yet begun to burn, and gasped for air. She did not hurt as if she had been badly burned, but her clothes stank of burnt wool, and she was certain they were ruined.

After a few indulgent seconds, she propped herself on her elbows and regarded the fire. She could no longer see Miss Honeycutt, but no more balls of fire erupted from the tree line, and she hoped that meant Francis had got clean away. In the distance, a sharp crack and a rushing sound told her a tree had fallen. With luck, enough of them would burn through before the fire spread past the park that the houses would not catch on fire. Clemency decided she did not wish to count on luck.

She rolled to her feet and, crouching, crept rather than Flew toward the burning trees. As she approached, she surveyed the fire, making note of which trees burned hottest and which were nearest being eaten away by flame. The fire was gradually spreading westward, in the direction the wind blew, which meant the trees most completely destroyed were on the east. The last she had observed, Miss Honeycutt lurked nearer the western side. Perfect.

Clemency lifted off the ground and, using the unburned trees as cover, made her way eastward. The sound of the devouring fire filled her ears, drowning out even the noise of the wind that shook the branches. She hoped that meant Miss Honeycutt would not perceive what Clemency had in mind until it was too late.

She chose a tree that was fully on fire, red-gold flames flowing across its trunk and branches like molten gold, sparks snapping and leaping from the fire to burn out like tiny fallen stars. With very little effort, she wrenched it free from the ground and wrestled it away from the entangling branches of its fellows. Then, pushing it along in front of her, she set off in search of her prey.

And it seemed luck was with her, because she saw Miss Honeycutt before the Scorcher saw her. Miss Honeycutt was engaged in setting more trees on fire, laughing her terrible laugh. Clemency did not hesitate. With one swift movement, she swung her tree at Miss Honeycutt's back.

The tree slammed into the Scorcher, lifting her off the ground and propelling her a few feet into the air. Miss Honeycutt fell and lay motionless for the few seconds it took Clemency to Fly at top speed toward her. She had barely begun to stir when Clemency landed nearby and Moved the tree again, this time bringing it close to the Scorcher's face. Miss Honeycutt froze.

"That is right," Clemency said, crouching to avoid the greater heat that burned above her. "You are not immune to fire, are you? Do not attack me again unless you wish to discover how close I can bring my weapon."

"You will die, too," Miss Honeycutt croaked.

"I do not intend either of us to die. Now, I offer you a choice: relax and permit yourself to be Moved out of this conflagration, or fight me and die pinned under a burning tree." Clemency ignored the tiny part of her that said she was no killer. This woman had intended Prudence's death, she might have killed dozens of people with her talent, and Clemency felt a fierce, hot joy in stopping her that rivaled the fire itself.

Miss Honeycutt again lay still. Then she said, "You would not kill me."

"I would," Clemency said, and in that moment, she meant it.

In the pause that followed, another distant tree cracked and fell with a crash. Miss Honeycutt said, "I will not fight you."

Clemency tossed the burning tree aside and gathered up the Scorcher, keeping her arms pinned to her side, though that would not stop a Scorcher from using her talent—but had Clemency not seen the woman gesture, now and before at St. Paul's, when summoning fire? That was irrelevant at the moment. As quickly as she could, she Flew with Miss Honeycutt out of the burning trees and into a clear, cold patch of grass well past the part of the park that was on fire.

She dropped Miss Honeycutt with no consideration for the woman's comfort and stood where she could see both her captive and the burning park. The wind, she realized, was both blessing and curse: it drove the fire wild and made it spread, but it also blew the flames so they spread in only one direction, and that direction was away from the nearest houses. That gave the city some time to contain the fire.

Clemency cast about to see who else the fire had drawn. There were crowds on either side of the park, none of them coming too close, and they did not appear to be doing anything, though Clemency could not hear them over the noise of flame and wind. Then it came to her. This was a park on fire, not a building, and there was not a fire brigade in the city contracted to stop a fire that was not on someone's insured property. The firefighters might be drawn to where the fire would spread to a house or store, but they would not act before that.

Clemency put a warning foot on Miss Honeycutt's shoulder when the woman tried to rise. "Do not make me change my mind," she said. "I might yet throw you back into the inferno."

"There is nothing you can do to me that is worse than the disappointment I have given my master," Miss Honeycutt said, her voice slightly muffled from where her face was pressed into the grass.

Clemency doubted this, but she did not care about Miss Honeycutt's delusions. "I know your master is Alistair Montague. He sent you, did he not?"

"That snip of a girl will pay for her betrayal. If not from me, then from another. You cannot protect her all the time," Miss Honeycutt sneered.

"We shall see." Clemency pressed harder, and Miss Honeycutt fell silent.

Clemency examined the trees. There were not enough of them to be a true woods, though they completely bracketed the path where it led through the trees. The fire had not yet spread to the far side of the path, which gave Clemency an idea. She had mentioned a firebreak to Francis, and if she could identify the correct trees to uproot, she might stop the fire spreading farther.

But there was Miss Honeycutt to deal with. Clemency eyed the woman. She was peaceful enough for now, but Clemency had no doubt the Scorcher would try to set her on fire and run if Clemency's attention wavered. And she did not believe she could contain Miss Honeycutt *and* uproot a line of trees.

She wished she had not had to send Francis away. Two of them would solve the problem neatly. Frustrated, Clemency cast her gaze about, searching for a solution she knew would not appear. What mattered more, stopping fire from ravaging the city, or keeping Mr. Montague's right-hand woman a captive? The fire brigades would assemble quickly...but the fire would damage property and possibly kill people before that...on the other hand, Mr. Rutledge might make good use of whatever Miss Honeycutt knew...

Feeling as if she might scream and count it a release, Clemency turned her attention on the trees. She would do as much as she could to make a firebreak, and hope Miss Honeycutt did not realize she was distracted.

At the eastern end of the woods, two trees stopped burning.

Clemency blinked. Surely her vision was not clouded with smoke, not when there was almost no smoke in the area. Another tree was extinguished. Then another. Then the fires were going out so rapidly it looked as if a wave of shadow had rolled over them, leaving behind cold, ashy branches that quivered in the wind. Some of them snapped off and fell, rattling, to the ground, where they made soft thumps as they landed.

A jerk brought Clemency back to herself. Miss Honeycutt had pushed to her feet and turned to face Clemency, bringing up her hands as if preparing to conduct an orchestra. Surprise, and then fury, filled Clemency until she felt surrounded by fire again. She took two quick steps and punched Miss Honeycutt in the face, snapping the woman's head back. Before Miss Honeycutt could recover from being stunned, Clemency gripped her with all the force her Moving could manage and lifted her to hang upside down thirty feet in the air.

"I suggest you do not struggle," she hissed, "because you have a strong will and would certainly break free of my Moving, and it would be the last thing you ever do."

Miss Honeycutt did not fight.

"Hello?" a woman's voice called out. "Is that the Scorcher responsible?"

Clemency turned to see a woman about her own age, dressed plainly in a wool gown the same color as Clemency's Flying garb—at least, the color it had been before Miss Honeycutt happened to it—approaching from the direction of the burned woods. She seemed not at all concerned by the sight of a woman dangling in midair, nor by Clemency's ragged state.

"I was a few streets away when I heard someone shouting that there was a Scorcher destroying the park," the woman said. She had heavy eyebrows and very direct grey eyes that gave her the appearance of a fierce bird of prey, though her voice was pleasant enough. "Is that she? How fortunate that you were near as well, though of course not for her."

Clemency blinked as everything fell into place. "You are Lady Enderleigh," she said. "The Extraordinary Scorcher."

"I am—and I believe I recognize you. Lady Ashford, is it?" Lady Enderleigh smiled. "Such *very* bad luck for this one." She tilted her head back to regard Miss Honeycutt. "I regret that I was not close enough to prevent most of the damage, but better the trees than people's homes, I say. And what are we to do with her?"

Clemency remembered her earlier bloodthirsty thoughts and felt ill. How could she have ever considered killing someone—worse than that, torturing someone to death? "She must go to—" In time, she realized she could not reveal Miss Honeycutt's involvement in the bombings, nor Mr. Rutledge's role in the investigation. And she did not believe she should haul Miss Honeycutt through the skies to leave her on the Rutledges' doorstep.

"To the Catterwell, of course," Lady Enderleigh said. "I can transport her, if you wish. I am better qualified than you to contain her talent—I hope that is not rude of me to say."

"No, you are correct," Clemency said. She would have to tell Mr.

Rutledge where Miss Honeycutt was, and permit him to deal with her in whatever way he saw best.

No. First, she must see to Prudence.

"May I leave her with you?" she said. "There is something I must do, and it is terribly urgent—though perhaps you require my Moving assistance, but it really is—"

"Pray, think nothing of it," Lady Enderleigh said. "My husband will be along shortly; he is an Extraordinary Mover as well, you know, and we are both of us experienced in dealing with talented miscreants." She smiled, a rather impish expression, and added, "Though I daresay you are as experienced as we, if you were able to capture this one!"

Rather than encourage Lady Enderleigh to speculate further on this topic, Clemency nodded politely and Flew away.

She had never Flown so fast, not even in the races, but her fear for her loved ones sped her along, and in almost no time she unlatched her window and slipped inside. She threw the latch and raced from her rooms, crying out, "Oh, where is everyone?"

Immediately she heard Mercy saying, "We are here—oh, Clemency, are you injured? Please say you are well!"

Clemency Flew to the drawing room, nearly bowling over Prudence, who opened the door just as Clemency reached it. Prudence burst into tears. "Clemency, you stink of fire—Miss Honeycutt burned you—this is all my fault!"

"Hush, Prudence, it is the fault of Mr. Montague," Clemency said, drawing her sister into her arms. "Hush, now. Miss Honeycutt has been captured, and she cannot hurt you now."

"That is small comfort, given how many other men Mr. Montague must have at his command," Francis said grimly. "Do not look daggers at me, Clemency; we must be sensible. Prudence cannot stay here, no matter how well guarded the place is."

"I know," Clemency said. "Prudence, hush. Mrs. Rutledge, the Extraordinary Seer, Dreamed for me, and she said Prudence must leave the city if she is to be safe. Francis—"

"We will leave immediately," Francis said, "and you are coming with us, Clemency. No argument."

"Yes, I will feel safer if you are both there," Prudence said.

Clemency scowled. "I cannot—"

A knock on the door preceded Slater's entrance. "I beg your pardon, my lady, for my inappropriate behavior," he said, "but this is something that should not wait." He held out a rolled piece of parchment, tied with ribbon and sealed with a wax coin that dangled from one of the ribbon ends. Clemency's heart, which had nearly calmed, thumped once painfully hard before settling into a sharp, fast rhythm.

She accepted the parchment and slid the ribbon off. The parchment did not like being unrolled, and she had to hold it open with both hands. She scanned the fine script, though her racing heart told her what it contained. "It will have to be just you, Francis," she said. "I am to present myself before the House of Lords Monday at noon."

CHAPTER 34

IN WHICH A CHANCE ENCOUNTER BRINGS CLEMENCY TO A HORRIFYING REALIZATION

"You will be alone and unaided," Francis said for the third time. He and Clemency stood by the fire in the drawing room, which made noises so like those of the fire in the park Clemency felt ill.

"That cannot be helped," she replied. "And you would not be permitted in the hearing chamber in any case. Besides, it matters more that you protect Prudence and Mercy. We do not know the extent of Mr. Montague's resources, and suppose he has enough followers to send some of them to Ravenwood Hall?"

"Norfolk is too far for him to reach," Francis said, but he sounded less forceful than he had before. "I agree that we should be careful, but there is no reason I should not install Mercy and Lady Prudence in your country estate and return to assist you."

"I will be unable to give my full attention to this hearing if I am worried for my sisters' safety, Francis." Clemency turned away and poked the fire restlessly, making the flames surge up. "Please. This is the most important thing you can do to help me."

"I cannot feel but that I am abandoning you instead." Francis took the poker from her and made her face him. "If you are certain—"

"I am certain."

Francis blew out his breath. "How long do you intend us to remain in the country?"

"I cannot say. Surely it will not take Mr. Rutledge's men long to run Mr. Montague to ground." She did not feel at all superstitious about saying this. Without knowing the details of Mr. Rutledge's organization, she should not make such an assertion, but she remembered the hard look in his eyes every time he spoke of the investigation and felt he was a man who would not rest until he had captured his prey.

"I will send word when Mr. Montague is captured," she continued. "A few days, no more."

"You will not come yourself?"

Clemency flicked the dangling seal of the parchment roll with her fingernail. The click it made was almost inaudible, but it felt to her like the stroke of midnight, promising doom. "If I can," she said. "I have no idea how long this will take. It would be nice to believe I will make my statement and be immediately believed by my peers, but that is so unlikely I dare not even imagine it."

"It does not matter that you are in the right. How I wish I could beat sense into your brother!" Francis strode away from the fireplace, his head bowed as if he faced a terrible wind. "And none of this addresses the issue of General de Villiers. Though I do not know what you intend to do about him, if anything. It might be best to let the rumors die."

"If that is even possible, with Armand still roaming London, spreading the news wherever he goes." Clemency sighed. "He will not be satisfied unless I marry him."

Francis' head snapped up. "Surely not!"

"I will never marry him," Clemency said. "Never. But he will go on making my life miserable unless something changes."

"Suppose he disappears," Francis said. "Or...was made to disappear."

Clemency gasped. "Francis, what are you suggesting?"

"We are experienced veterans of the War Office," Francis said. "It is not as if we lack the skill."

"But we are not murderers," Clemency protested. "We do not kill to benefit ourselves. It is—not unthinkable, obviously, but nothing we should consider. I could not live with myself if I solved my problem that way."

Francis scowled, but he nodded. "It is a satisfying fantasy, but nothing more," he said. "I should return to my home to pack a few things, but I will return shortly. And—you might have someone stand guard over the carriage. If Mr. Montague's men think to place a bomb in its frame—"

Clemency shuddered. "That had not occurred to me. Go, Francis, and do not delay."

She walked with him to the front door and then returned through the house to the small stable yard behind. None of the Northrups except possibly Roger were riders, and Clemency kept only the one horse that drew the carriages and a quiet mare Mama occasionally took out to be seen in Hyde Park. She did not imagine anyone could enter the stable yard without drawing the attention of Ross, who did double duty as driver and ostler, but she was disinclined to be careless after the day's events.

Ross was as stolid as a boulder and equally taciturn. He made no comment on her charred and torn clothing, merely assured her that only he had been in the stable yard all day and that he would assign two of "the lads" to watch the carriage. Clemency checked it anyway. She found no sign of anything amiss, no strange boxes affixed to the undercarriage, no odd bundles piled on top. She thanked Ross and returned to her room.

She had only had the one Flying costume, and she could hardly be seen in the trousers and coat of her secret night flights. So she rang for Tatton and with her maid's help removed the ruined gown and bathed quickly. Then she changed into a comfortable morning gown and returned to the drawing room. Prudence and Mercy both waited there. Prudence still looked pale, but she had stopped weeping. Mercy looked unexpectedly calm. "I regret that you cannot come with us," she said. "Why is Roger so abominably selfish?"

"He believes in the superiority of men over women," Prudence said, "which is foolishness. And yet everywhere one looks, one sees evidence that others believe as Roger does. Why do you not have a seat in the House of Lords, Clemency?"

"Because women do not govern," Clemency said. "Which proves your point, to an extent. With the war over, and talented women returning, that point will be challenged. Businesses will not wish to be hampered by hiring only men if there are women with greater Bounding or Moving skill available. Whether that philosophy will penetrate to our government, I have no idea. But the time may not be far off when women's voices are heard in Parliament."

"Roger has also always been prone to looking to others to get his way," Mercy said. "Do you recall when he was a child, how he used to run to Mama for favors when Father told him no? He does not like standing on his own merits, likely because he knows those merits are not exceptional." She frowned. "The more I consider the matter, the more evidence I see that Roger's behavior has always been that of someone dissatisfied with the great bounty he has, for whom no reward is ever good enough so long as someone, somewhere has something better."

"I should reprimand all of us for speaking ill of our brother, but it is nothing more than the truth," Clemency said. "Let us move to the foyer. Francis should return shortly."

By the time Clemency had Moved Mercy's chair and her sisters' small trunks downstairs, Francis was there, another, slightly larger trunk hovering in front of him. "The chair will have to be strapped to the carriage roof," he said. "If we are attacked, I will defend us more efficiently if I am only Moving one object, so to speak."

Clemency helped him arrange all the baggage securely and settled Mercy in her special seat within the carriage. Prudence sat opposite her. "Clemency, you will be well, will you not?" she said.

"Do not worry for me," Clemency said with a smile. "I will feel reassured to know you are all safe. And you are not to fret over Mr. Montague," she added, seeing Prudence about to speak again and guessing her intent. "That is all well in hand. You are to—" Inspiration struck. "You will write down everything you know about Mr. Montague's organization. Names, places you met, the plans they made. That will help Mr. Rutledge's investigation tremendously."

Prudence's face lit. "Truly? Because that is something I can do easily."

"Truly. Write it all, and I will see that it gets to him." It could not hurt, and the task would keep Prudence from falling into despair.

Francis joined Clemency at the carriage door. "We are ready," he said. "Good luck, Clemency. Send word whenever...whatever happens." He closed the door and lifted into the air, bringing the carriage with him.

Clemency tilted her head back to watch him Fly away north. When the carriage was nothing more than a speck in the sky, she went indoors. That was Prudence settled. Now she must take care of her own concerns. She wished she could be more certain what the future held.

THE FUTURE, IT TURNED OUT, HELD A HACKNEY CAB.

In all the last-minute meetings with her solicitors, her advisors, and even Tatton, whose sensible advice—"Dress as if you deserve to be a countess, my lady"—reassured Clemency more than any of the legal advice she received, she had not connected the fact that she needed to drive to the hearing with the fact that she had sent Francis off with the carriage. She dared not drive herself, and be thought fast, not when her defense hinged partly on proving that she was not a fallen woman. She dared not Fly, and arrive looking windblown and disrespectful of the gravitas of Parliament. So on Monday she had Slater summon her a hackney, and in her most formal and sober attire set off for the Palace of Westminster.

A fog had rolled in off the river overnight, and while most of it had cleared, the streets were still misty, as if someone had shrouded the city in grey gauze. With the fog had come a dank, smelly, clinging dampness in the air that made Clemency wish even more she could have left London with the others. She eyed the clouds and the fog, assessing how long it would take for them to dissipate. The sun's yellow-white disc was fuzzy around the edges, but still remained bright enough that Clemency could not look at it directly.

She sat back and watched the city pass her by. Men and women strolled past, not huddling into cloak or coat—the fog might be smelly and uncomfortably damp, but the air was also warmer than if the sharp wind blew it away. The fog softened the edges of every building she passed, and Clemency marveled at how the effect made even stern institutions like banks seem inviting. It was probably fortunate that the effect was not permanent. How dreadful if people assumed everyone they encountered meant them well!

The hackney rounded a corner, and the Palace of Westminster loomed up out of the fog. Unlike the rest of London, the fog made the palace look sinister, like a castle out of a gothic novel. If not for the continued pedestrian and carriage traffic, Clemency would have felt overawed, as if she were about to meet a brooding German Graf with sinister designs upon her.

The carriage passed the long row of low, arched entrances to the colonnade, and then it drew up before the great door beneath the arched window that filled most of that side of the palace. Clemency waited for the coachman to open the door and help her out, feeling grateful for his assistance because her legs had become unexpectedly wobbly.

She stood for a moment before the entrance, looking up at the window. Its shape echoed the door, but it was far bigger, and the glass panes looked dull in the foggy light. This, she felt, was how St. Paul's ought to have looked, grand and dramatic to match its beautiful dome. And she was stalling. Straightening her spine, she walked to the doors and was bowed inside by a man who held the door open for her.

Within, the air was moderately drier and very cool, enough that she was grateful for her wool Flying coat. The hall was full of men—all men—dressed in varying degrees of finery. Some were plainly clad and appeared to be clerks or message runners, while others wore fashionable frock coats and knee breeches like gentlemen of fashion. None of them looked directly at her. Clemency was certain by how still they all became as she passed that they were, in fact, very aware of her presence. She held her head high and ignored them. None of them wore the white-trimmed red robes of the House of Lords, and therefore none of them were a danger to her.

She walked with a measured pace through the halls, not slowing to examine the portraits on the walls or the halls that branched off to other rooms. She remembered this walk clearly, though it had been nearly four years since the last time she had stood before her peers, arguing her right to the earldom. Mingled with her satisfaction at having won her point and her father's will were sorrow and anger over Roger's frustrating, selfish behavior. He had apologized and made amends, and she had accepted his apology even though she knew it was rooted in fear of being without the benefits accruing to the Northrup family.

Now she wondered if she should have seen this coming. Not *this* precisely, for who could have predicted Napoleon's Coercion? But she might have guessed Roger would be alert to anything that would give him grounds to challenge her again. On the other hand, did it matter if she should have predicted this if there was no way for her to prevent it? Clemency realized she had clenched her left fist and relaxed it. Dwelling on what might have been was pointless now. She could only move forward, and hope for the best.

There were fewer men in the halls this deep into the palace, and the ones wearing clerk's garb now greatly outnumbered the fashionable gentlemen. *Now* everyone stared at her overtly. Clemency gave up on pretending they were not there and smiled pleasantly at everyone she encountered.

Ahead, two guards flanked the entrance to the chamber where the House of Lords met. They looked stern and completely without humor, and Clemency eyed their halberds and considered what it would take to disarm them. Not that she had any intention of doing so, but her awareness that Mr. Montague was still at large had her on edge and devising plans to disable anyone she met, even the ones not obviously a threat.

Two men ahead of her entered the chamber, brushing past another man who was emerging. The third man had a large belly and a crooked mustache, and Clemency slowed to observe him. She was certain she had seen him before, though she could not recall where. He was one of the clerks, and held a thin but large book under one arm. His mustache was odd; it was bushy, hiding most of his mouth, but it also grew crookedly, as if it had been glued on in a hurry.

Clemency stared at him as they drew near one another. Memory flashed before her mind's eye, of passing this man in the Cabinet of Curiosities, how he had bumped against Mercy. It was so unexpected Clemency's steps slowed.

The man caught her eye. He smiled politely—and then he winked. And in that wink, Clemency finally recognized him as Mr. Montague.

"Stop!" she shouted, lunging for him. Mr. Montague danced out of her reach and took off running for the front doors. Clemency collected herself and made a grab at him with her Moving. He tripped, caught himself, and kept running. Clemency looked about her frantically for a weapon. Her eye lit on the guards with their sturdy halberds. "Excuse me," she said, and wrenched both of them out of their owners' hands and sent them hurtling down the hall after Mr. Montague.

A group of men, two of them robed in red and white, emerged from a room ahead of Mr. Montague. He glanced back, saw the flying weapons, and darted into the middle of the group. The men exclaimed as one of them was knocked over, and then the exclamations turned to shouts of fear at the sight of the halberds flying their way. Clemency flung the weapons aside to impact harmlessly against the opposite wall. Mr. Montague did not look back. Clemency made one final snatch at him. This time, she grabbed his ankles and pulled. Mr. Montague fell face-first on the floor.

Hands grabbed Clemency, forcing her to lie on the floor just as Mr. Montague had and making her lose her grip as she lost sight of her quarry. "Do not resist," a man said. "You have used weapons against a peer of the realm, and the penalties for doing so are severe. You will—"

"Let me up," Clemency shouted. "I am Lady Ashford, and that man is Mr. Jinks—you are permitting him to escape!"

"Do not think to deceive us," a different man said, hauling on her wrist and bringing her to her feet. "You will not escape punishment by lying."

"I am *not* lying," Clemency insisted, breaking the guard's grip with an experienced twist of her wrist. "The man I attempted to stop—that man there—" She pointed down the hall. Mr. Montague was gone.

Clemency bit back a curse. "He has escaped," she shouted at the two guards. Their expressions were still stolid and uncomprehending, which infuriated her further. "He has escaped, and he is free to bomb—"

Free to bomb.

Clemency looked past the guards at the door they had left unattended. Many men in red robes gathered around it, peering out and murmuring to one another. All the blood drained from Clemency's face. "God help us," she whispered. Then she Moved the guards aside, flinging them into opposite walls, and ran for the chamber.

"Get out!" she shouted. "There is a bomb in the House of Lords chamber!"

CHAPTER 35

IN WHICH CLEMENCY'S ANGER FUELS HER RETRIBUTION

T he Lords blocked the doorway almost completely and showed no inclination to move. One or two of them even stepped forward as if to bar her way. Frustrated, Clemency leaped and Flew over their heads, flattening herself so as to fit in the gap between them and the door frame. She rolled midair and alit neatly in the row between the many benches. To her relief, not many of the benches were occupied yet. An even greater relief was the empty throne at the far end of the chamber. Clemency had not expected the Prince Regent to attend, but all this debacle needed was his presence, so she was grateful anyway.

"Everyone, listen to me!" she shouted. "Listen! There is a bomb hidden somewhere in this chamber. You must all leave immediately!"

A few men stood. The rest remained where they were, sitting or gathered around the table some five feet from where Clemency stood. One of the Lords at the table turned his gaze on her. "Lady Ashford," he said. "I expected you to attempt to distract us from our purpose. I did not believe you would stoop to lying."

She recognized him—Lord Sacheverell, a War Office liaison who was chief among those who not-so-secretly wished Extraordinaries to have fewer rights and protections than the law currently afforded.

Where Mr. Rutledge was heavily built, Lord Sacheverell was fat, but the two otherwise resembled one another closely in their stern demeanors and powerful presences. At the moment, Lord Sacheverell's glare might have melted iron.

Clemency calmed herself, though her mind was shrieking at her to get these men to safety. "My lord," she said, "this is not a ruse. I saw Mr. Jinks leaving this chamber, and I am certain he has left a bomb. You are all in terrible danger. Please, move outside, and I will find the bomb and dispose of it."

The murmuring that had begun when she burst into the chamber rose in volume as the red-robed Lords and the few black-clad clerks began arguing. A few men stood and headed for the door. "Stop," Lord Sacheverell commanded. "This woman intends to frighten us so we will not pass judgment on her case. If there is a bomb, which I doubt, she is clearly complicit in its presence here."

"I beg your pardon?" Clemency exclaimed. "I have just told you what you need to do to save yourself. How does that make me complicit?"

"You could not have known of the bomb unless you were in league with the bombers," Lord Sacheverell said. He walked toward Clemency, his slow pace sending her heart racing. "You and your accomplices placed something here you intend to claim is a bomb, and you will pretend to save us from it, thereby earning our gratitude so we will find in your favor."

The sheer horrid unfairness of Lord Sacheverell's theory combined with the spine-chilling awareness of the bomb's presence sent a spike of rage through Clemency. Everything she had experienced in the past weeks, Armand's torments, Roger's stupid and selfish challenge, even Mr. Wescott's desertion, broke some dam within her.

In her memory, Miss Wescott said, *It is what the anger fuels, the desire to stop others being hurt.* The anger. Miss Wescott had said it, over and over again, that Clemency was angry, and Clemency had denied it every time. Now the anger flooded through her, fury at having been abused by Armand and slighted by Jane and insulted by this petty, infuriating man, anger she had suppressed and denied and told herself she did not deserve to feel. Before she could stop herself, she lifted seven feet into the air and shouted, "*Ignore me at your peril!*"

Lord Sacheverell was red in the face. "You dare——" he began.

Clemency lifted him off his feet with her Moving and slammed him against the wall. He let out an *oof* of breath and slid in a boneless heap to the floor. Part of her, the part that hung on to sanity with both hands, whispered that she would never be able to repeat that maneuver, not against someone as strong of will as Lord Sacheverell, but the rest of her saw the chamber in a bloody haze of fury and did not care about her victim's fate.

She Flew forward to light on the steps of the dais and dropped to her knees, searching. Behind her, the commotion indicated that people were tending to Lord Sacheverell, and that others were cautiously approaching her. She ignored them for the moment. There was no bomb under the throne.

She moved on to the nearer benches, none of which were occupied, and began Moving them, lifting them high so she could see beneath. As she Moved each one, she set it in a stack to one side, not very carefully except as was needed to keep the stack from tumbling down and interfering with her search. Bench after bench joined the pile with no bomb in sight.

"You will stop immediately," a querulous voice behind her said.

Clemency turned on her heel and glared at the speaker, who was an elderly man in red robes. He looked nervous but resolute. Sanity admired his courage. The rest of her said, in a quiet but forceful voice, "I am going to save your life, you fool. Stay out of my way."

The man swallowed. "By the authority——" he began.

"Out," Clemency said. "Or your authority will be scattered in a hundred pieces, along with your corpse." Fury still surged through her. This stupid, arrogant little man believed he could tell *her* what to do.

She shifted another bench, and froze. Beneath it lay a wooden box the size of a clock case, bigger than the other bombs she had seen. It was tucked back where it could not be seen except by someone crouching to look beneath the bench—or by a person Moving that bench away. The noise in the chamber was too great for her to hear ticking, and the box looked so harmless Clemency wondered for a moment if she had imagined the whole danger.

Clemency heard the elderly Lord gasp. Then he clutched her arm. "Is that—" he said.

"It is," Clemency said. "Get everyone out of this chamber immediately. Find someone to carry Lord Sacheverell, if he is not yet conscious." She hoped he was not yet conscious. That would make things so much easier.

The elderly Lord turned and shouted, "It is true! There is a bomb, and we must leave now! Leave!"

The muttering murmur became even louder and terrified. Clemency's gaze did not leave the bomb, but she heard the scrambling sounds of two dozen men all trying to fit through a door at the same time. She considered flinging the box through a window, but she recalled what Mr. Rutledge had said about all the bombs having detonated prematurely, and she decided she did not like the idea of shaking the thing accidentally and blowing herself up.

She looked around for inspiration. The room was empty, though she heard shouts and cries of fear in the distance. There were no windows at ground level, and the walls were covered with enormous paintings of fleets of ships, possibly the most appropriate imagery to associate with ruling the nation of Great Britain. Above the paintings, arched windows with dozens of square glass panes let in the grey, foggy light. The effect was of being becalmed at sea, peering out of one's cabin at the ocean waves where a low mist rolled.

She glanced around once more and then seized the topmost bench on her teetering pile, Moving it into position beside the window directly above the bomb. She Flew backward, as far as she could get from the window, and swung the bench at it. Glass shattered, sending shards everywhere. Sanity hoped no one was beneath to be hurt, but it was growing difficult to hear its silly notions of what Clemency ought to do.

She used the bench to clear away the remaining shards that clung to the window frame and then dropped the bench well away from the bomb. Breathing deeply and steadily, she Moved the bomb, holding it as still as she could manage, and carried it with her as she Flew through the empty window.

Beneath her, the streets were in chaos. Figures in red ran away from the palace and came up against a sea of others pressing forward to discover what the commotion was about. Their cries were distant, like the calls of seabirds over the ocean when one stands on the shore. Now Clemency could hear the ticking of the clockwork mechanism. She could not tell if it was faster than it had been, only that it was loud and very slightly irregular, not a steady *tick-tock* like her pocket watch, but a *tick-tick-tock* and then the faintest pause before another *tick*.

She surveyed the scene. The Thames was right there, but at nearly noon, the river teemed with ships and boats, and dropping the bomb in the river would be certain catastrophe. She was far from the outskirts of the city, too far to take the bomb where there were no people. All that was left to her was—up.

She Flew, carrying the bomb as gently as cradling a child, up and away from the Palace of Westminster, all the while looking down rather than up to gauge the distance at which the palace would be safe if the bomb detonated. She dared not speed, though her heart demanded she get herself as far from the deadly object as possible. All the time, she listened to the *tick-tick-tock...tick* until she imagined she had gone mad. *Tick-tick-tock...tick.*

Then the ticking sped up.

Clemency Moved the box up fast, past herself and farther still until it was at the limit of her Moving range. Then she flung it as hard as she could and Flew downward, speeding away from the bomb, praying a devout, incoherent prayer that her efforts had been enough.

White light banished the fog, and an explosion rocked Clemency in her mad flight, but she felt no pain, no buffeting as when she had been blasted into the Thames. She steadied herself and turned, hovering, in time to see the light fade and shards of wood come hailing down upon her. She raised an arm to deflect the splinters from her face and made herself breathe normally. Then she Flew slowly groundward, searching for a place to land that would not leave her surrounded by people who would want to know what had happened.

Everyone she saw in her flight was looking upward. Some of them stared at her; others pointed and exclaimed at the remnants of the bomb. Everyone except one man, who was making his way steadily through the crowds toward the river. He was dressed in the somber black clothing of a clerk, and from above he looked like an ink spot against all those pale faces.

Clemency hissed. The rage began building again. He had escaped her once. He would not do so again.

She Flew after Mr. Montague, keeping her distance though she dearly wished to drop upon him and snatch him screaming into the sky. But he had resisted her Moving before, and she dared not attack him while he was surrounded by innocents. So instead she followed him, feeling grateful that the overcast sky meant no shadows to give her pursuit away.

Mr. Montague eventually fought free of the crowds, emerging near the riverbank, but he did not run. He kept a measured pace as he walked toward the wall preventing anyone walking accidentally into the Thames on a cloudy night. There was a door in the wall, and stairs leading down to the river's edge, and a shallow rowboat drawn up at the stairs. As Mr. Montague walked, he removed his clerk's coat and reversed it, revealing an ordinary gentleman's greatcoat. Clemency watched him peel the false mustache from his lip and remove a stiff, oddly-shaped pillow from beneath his shirt. He had nearly reached the wall. Clemency dove.

Instead of using her Moving, she swooped low and with her arms caught Mr. Montague below the knees, lifting him off his feet and carrying him aloft. The man shouted, but with surprise, not fear, and immediately kicked Clemency in the chest, sending the breath whooshing out of her. She dropped Mr. Montague, who managed to land on his feet. Mr. Montague stood upright as Clemency Flew down to hover in front of him.

"You again," he said. "How is your sister?"

"Safe, and out of your reach," Clemency said, refusing to be drawn. "And you are going to prison."

"I find that idea disagreeable," Mr. Montague said with a mocking smile. "I believe I will kill you instead."

Something struck Clemency, knocking her sideways and sending pain shooting up her ribs. Instinctively, she Flew higher, and the next blow missed. It was a boat, Clemency realized, an actual boat some fifteen feet long, still dripping river water and sludge. She seized it before Mr. Montague could hit her again. For a moment, the two of them battled for possession of the weapon, until another boat came flying out of the river and Clemency had to dodge again to avoid being crushed between them.

She heard screams from the river and was distracted long enough that Mr. Montague hit her again, this time a glancing blow that numbed her ankle. Someone thrashed and flailed in the water, and Clemency snatched the person up and dropped him on the riverbank. Then she Flew higher, wheeling and dodging to confuse Mr. Montague. She needed her own weapon, something more efficient than an awkward rowboat.

Her eye fell on a cluster of trees with thick boles growing at the river's edge. She picked one with roots showing above the water line and *pulled* with all her Moving talent. Slowly, with a ponderousness that felt as if she were dredging the tree from a black morass, the roots came free, and Clemency swung the tree around in time to catch one of Mr. Montague's rowboats amidships. With a mighty crack, the boat splintered and fell apart, the various pieces hanging in midair, still controlled by her enemy's Moving.

Clemency did not stop to admire her handiwork. With the tree in tow, she Flew in search of Mr. Montague. He had not run for the boat at the foot of the stairs, which was unfortunate for Clemency as sitting in the boat would have made him an easy target. Instead, he stood near the road, surrounded by a moving, shifting cloud of fist-sized objects. In the next moment, Clemency identified them as river stones, damp from where they had lain on the bank. Then Mr. Montague hurled the first of them at her.

She Moved the tree to deflect the stone. It bounced off and was followed by two more, also deflected. At first, Clemency could not see the point of the attack. Eventually Mr. Montague would run out of missiles, and she would have him. Then she realized he was catching the rocks as they rebounded toward him. He could maintain his supply indefinitely, and unless Clemency did something to change the situation, they were at an impasse. And Clemency had never liked fighting a defensive battle.

The next time Mr. Montague hurled a stone at her, she caught it rather than permitting it to bounce off the tree. She collected six stones before Mr. Montague realized her change in tactics. He ducked, ran, and hid behind a tree so large Clemency did not believe she could fit her arms around it. She flung a stone, which bounced harmlessly off the bole of his hiding place. He need not even fight her. Now they were at a worse impasse than before.

Or—perhaps not.

Clemency set her tree down and stood where Mr. Montague could see her. "Attack me, if you dare!" she shouted. "The law will not be kind to someone who tries to kill an Extraordinary."

As she had expected, Mr. Montague did not show his face. He flung another river stone that Clemency caught. "You believe you are above the law," he shouted, "you and all your useless kind. I am a more powerful Mover than you, and yet you are the one celebrated and praised. I will do the world a favor in killing you." Another two stones flew and were again caught.

Clemency began Moving her collection of stones in a flat circle, parallel to the ground. "Will you?" she said. "A paltry little criminal like you? You could not even set a bomb properly."

Three more stones sailed out of the space beneath the tree. Clemency added them to her circle without losing hold of any of them. Mr. Montague laughed. "I will see you all dead," he exclaimed, in a voice edged with mania. "All of you!"

Clemency let out a breath. Without a word, she extended her grip on the circle of stones and flung them fast as a series of lightning strikes behind Mr. Montague's tree, out of her sight. There was a series of thuds, and a groan, and then many more thuds as the stones Mr. Montague had been holding fell to the ground.

Clemency Flew low and fast across the intervening space and behind the enormous tree. Mr. Montague lay sprawled beneath the branches, blinking dazedly. Blood streamed from beneath his hair on his right temple and from a cut at the center of a spreading bruise on his chin. Clemency held him with her Moving. "I will see you imprisoned first," she said.

To her surprise, Mr. Montague laughed weakly. "You?" he whispered. "You are nothing, you degenerate specimen of a degenerate race. I should have seduced your sister when I had the chance so I could fling it in your face that there is nothing you have that I cannot take from you."

The fury rose again. Clemency found she had swept two dozen stones into the air and held them straining against the urge to crush the man's head. Sanity told her this was wrong. But he had threatened her, he had abused her sister's trust, he had killed and destroyed and would go on killing and destroying if no one stopped him. If *she* did not stop him.

She heard footsteps coming up behind her. "Lady Ashford," Mr. Rutledge said. "Step away, please."

"He deserves to die," she said, and was distantly surprised at how calm she sounded when every nerve screamed at her to batter Mr. Montague into a crushed mass of blood and bone.

"Indeed," Mr. Rutledge said. "But not by your hand. You have won, Lady Ashford. Leave him to his fate."

"Forgive me if I do not trust your assurances," Clemency said. "You believed me complicit, you threatened me—"

"We have misunderstood one another, you and I." Mr. Rutledge was not visible except as the edge of a shape just out of full sight to her left. "But we have always desired the same outcome—to see this man brought to justice. Please, Lady Ashford. Let this be enough."

Clemency drew a deep breath that shuddered through her. Then she released the stones and let them fall harmlessly to the ground.

Mr. Rutledge stepped past her and rolled the unresisting Mr. Montague onto his stomach. He removed his long, narrow neckcloth and bound it over Mr. Montague's eyes. "He will not recover from your attack quickly, but I do not wish him free to Move anything in the meantime," Mr. Rutledge said.

Clemency stood still and watched Mr. Rutledge bind Mr. Montague's hands behind him and then haul the man to his feet. "If you wouldn't mind?" Mr. Rutledge said. "I do not believe he is capable of walking far."

He was addressing her. Clemency came to herself with a start and Moved Mr. Montague out of Mr. Rutledge's grip. "Where?"

Mr. Rutledge led the way through the strip of lawn near the river and to the road, where a number of carriages and men in nondescript clothing waited. Clemency imagined she recognized one of them from the attempt to arrest Mr. Wescott at the lecture; he bore the same hard, indifferent look she remembered. This time, she glared at him and was pleased to see him look away quickly.

Surrounding the nondescript men was a growing crowd, all of whom stayed well back. Mr. Rutledge opened a carriage door, and Clemency guided Mr. Montague's unresisting body inside. Two of Mr. Rutledge's men immediately followed. Mr. Rutledge closed the carriage door, but did not walk away.

"I wish you had not been involved," he said, "but I am grateful for your assistance."

Clemency chose not to quibble over "assistance." "Because I am a woman?" she snapped.

Mr. Rutledge regarded her with those fathomless brown eyes. "Because you have enough troubles without a deranged bomber inflicting more of them on you," he said.

It was said so gently Clemency did not know how to respond. All at once, her fury collapsed, leaving her cold and aching and horrified that she had nearly caused the deaths of two men that day. "I," she began, groping for a response. "I could not permit him to escape."

"I know," Mr. Rutledge said, again so gently he seemed a completely different man. "I wish I could order you to return home and forget your troubles, but—" He looked past her. "I believe your troubles are coming for you now."

Clemency turned. A mob of men in white-trimmed red robes hurried in their direction, implacable as the oncoming tide. At the head of the mob was Lord Sacheverell. Aside from favoring his left leg, he did not seem injured.

"Lady Ashford," he said, "you will come with us."

CHAPTER 36

IN WHICH CLEMENCY'S BATTLE ENDS IN DIVINE INTERVENTION

C lemency could not help herself; she glanced at Mr. Rutledge, instinctively seeking his support. Mr. Rutledge did not look at her. He said, "Lady Ashford was injured in apprehending Mr. Jinks. Her case should be deferred."

"This is not about her case, Rutledge," Lord Sacheverell snarled. "She attacked me, she destroyed the House of Lords' chamber, she manufactured a threat to manipulate us—"

"Mr. Jinks left a bomb in that chamber, Sacheverell," Mr. Rutledge said, calm in the face of the lord's sputtering anger. "Lady Ashford saved your life, whatever you may make of her methods. You ought to give her your thanks."

"You have no authority here, Rutledge." Lord Sacheverell's face was red, and his lips quivered, spraying droplets of spittle in his agitation. "I decide—"

"You do not decide, Sacheverell," said a man who had been pushing his way through the crowd and now faced Lord Sacheverell. "Or have you forgotten that you are one of many? Lady Ashford saved us all." Clemency remembered him; he was the elderly man who had faced her so bravely.

"She knew the bomb was there," Lord Sacheverell said. "She must be complicit with the bomber. What else are we to make of her ludicrous claim that she recognized Mr. Jinks leaving the chamber?"

"I see you are still demonstrating the keen wisdom for which you have always been famous," Mr. Rutledge said. "Lady Ashford has been instrumental in discovering the identity of Mr. Jinks. She knows his face, a fact for which you should be extremely grateful. If you choose to continue to lay false accusations against her, I will be forced to take notice."

Clemency held her breath. The magnitude of what she had done in her fury bore down on her, terrifying her. She had turned her talent on a peer of the realm, and that bore consequences her title and status could not protect her from. She wondered in passing how Mr. Rutledge, with no title nor talent, could possibly hold power over a viscount such as Lord Sacheverell, but the wondering was merely a distraction from her fear.

"She used Moving on me," Lord Sacheverell said as if he could hear what echoed through her mind, "and for that crime, she must be tried."

"She did so to save your life," the unknown elderly lord said. "Staying in that chamber and ignoring Lady Ashford's instructions would have killed us all. I am certain Lady Ashford acted as she did out of the exigency of the moment. Had you been less of a fool, you would not have suffered."

"I, a fool?" Lord Sacheverell exclaimed. "Winfield, you dare—"

"I grow tired of your posturing, Sacheverell," Lord Winfield said coldly. "Your animosity toward Extraordinaries is well-known. Would you have preferred me to turn a mental attack on you, rendering you helpless? For I am certain your stubbornness would not have responded to anything less than an assault. I say Lady Ashford acted appropriately."

"You Extraordinaries are all alike," Lord Sacheverell spat. "Defending one another against any possibility that you might be charged with a crime—"

"That is untrue," said another lord, this one tall and thin to the point of gauntness, with black hair parted in the middle and slicked down on both sides. "I am no Extraordinary, but I recognize the part they play in our society, and I say your antagonism is both unwarranted and unfair." He bowed to Clemency. "Lady Ashford, if you are in need of medical care or Healing, I will propose your case be postponed a day."

"I thank you, my lord, but I am not badly injured," Clemency said, which was a lie; her ribs stabbed her sharply if she moved incautiously, and she could not put weight on her left foot without wincing. "I would prefer to see this challenge ended as soon as possible."

"Very well," the black-haired lord said. "As Lady Ashford's actions have prevented the destruction of the palace, I suggest we adjourn to the meeting chamber and proceed. Unless you have other irrelevant charges to lay at her ladyship's door, Sacheverell?"

Lord Sacheverell's countenance had become less florid, but Clemency did not have to be an Extraordinary Discerner to know he had not given over his anger. He glared at Clemency. "This changes nothing," he said. "You will still have to defend your right to hold that title. And I warn you, the House of Lords does not appreciate the peers of England displaying low moral character."

There was an uneasy shifting in the crowd of red-robed men behind Lord Sacheverell. Clemency's fear receded slightly. If enough of those lords felt guilty of the same charge Clemency was accused of, perhaps they would not be quick to condemn her, out of fear that the same fate might befall them.

She caught Mr. Rutledge's eye. His expression did not change, but he nodded once before turning away. That he might become an ally was something she had never imagined, and yet he had spoken in her defense, had threatened Lord Sacheverell—perhaps she had misjudged him as much as he had misjudged her.

Lord Sacheverell led the way back to the palace doors. Either he had regained his confidence, or he intended to reclaim his authority over his peers by taking the lead. Clemency, having no power to stop either of those things, drifted at the rear of the crowd of red robes, careful of her ankle. Her momentary hope had vanished, leaving her feeling unmoored and helpless. It was sheer luck she had not been handed over to Mr. Rutledge to be confined in the Catterwell, luck and the assertion of Lord Winfield. Her guilt at having lost control of her temper battered at her. It did not matter that she had been sorely provoked; she should never have lashed out. Suppose she had killed Lord Sacheverell? The idea shook her to her core.

The chamber where the House of Lords met was still in disarray, benches flung everywhere, glittering glass shards on the floor. There were not many of those, but some of the lords began picking them up with Moving, while other Movers righted and arranged the benches. Clemency did not offer to help. She did not wish to remind anyone of her role in making the mess.

When the room was cleared and settled, the red-robed lords filed in and took their seats. Clemency waited near the door. She recalled standing at the center of the room the last time, but she decided it would not look good for her to presume. So she waited, and wondered where Roger was. It was well past noon by now, and she had not seen him. Hope again spiked in her heart, but she suppressed it. This hearing was not actually about herself, or her moral character, or Roger's claim; the fate of Extraordinaries in government and perhaps the entire empire lay at the heart of the challenge.

Finally, the lords were all seated, and Lord Winfield stood. "Lady Ashford, please stand here," he said, gesturing at a spot near the long table where sat Lord Sacheverell, Lord Fotheringham, and two other lords whose names she did not know. She should have informed herself about the men who would be hearing her case. Not knowing some of them struck her as a potentially dangerous oversight now.

Lord Winfield took a seat at the long table. Lord Sacheverell rose. "Where is Mr. Northrup?"

Everyone turned and looked at the door. No one entered. Lord Winfield stood as well. His shoulders were rounded and his stance a trifle bent, but his voice no longer trembled as it had done when he faced Clemency near the bomb. "The Honorable Mr. Roger Northrup has made the claim that his sister, Clemency Northrup, Countess of Ashford, is unfit to hold the Ashford title and estates due to her illicit affair with General Armand de Villiers. As Mr. Northrup has not bothered to present himself, I move to dismiss this case as frivolous."

"Expecting a peer of the realm to comport herself with modesty is not frivolous," Lord Sacheverell said. "What is worse, Lady Ashford has made mock of our oldest institutions by claiming she was Coerced into her lewd behavior. The very idea is preposterous."

"Lady Ashford's word, as an Extraordinary, is her bond," Lord Winfield said.

"And there we come to the heart of the matter." Lord Sacheverell no longer looked suffused with rage; his demeanor was calm, his voice smooth and reasonable, and Clemency's heart sank. "It is her Extraordinary status that permits her to flout law and tradition. Anyone with a lesser talent, or no talent at all, would not dare to pretend to innocence in such a matter. I say Lady Ashford should be held to the same standard as anyone else."

A commotion at the door caused everyone to turn once more. This time, Roger stood there, breathing heavily. His hair and clothes were disordered from running. "I beg your pardon, my lords," he said. "I was detained." He thrust a shaking hand at Clemency, pointing. "My sister arranged for men to set upon me as I journeyed here so I would not arrive in time to see justice done."

"I have done no such thing!" Clemency protested. "My lords, Roger Northrup attempted to suborn my servants to lie on his behalf. This is another one of his schemes to put me at a disadvantage because he knows his suit is groundless."

"Of course you would say that," Roger said. He was the very picture of wounded innocence. "You have already shown that you have no morals to speak of."

This time, Clemency tamped her anger down hard. Attacking Roger would do no good, however much she longed to fling him about the room or tear one of the golden chandeliers free to batter him. "My lords," she said, ignoring her brother, "I have said repeatedly that I was Coerced. I was forced into those actions Mr. Northrup claims prove my lack of morals. But even had I acted voluntarily, I am not certain this august body wishes to apply a virtues test to its members, nor to the peerage of England as a whole."

"Do you accuse us of immorality?" Lord Sacheverell sounded angry, but there was triumph in the way he threw his shoulders back and held his head high.

"I accuse no one," Clemency retorted. "I do suggest that we have a biblical example of what happens when one is invited to throw stones. We are none of us perfect, Lord Sacheverell, and I believe expecting perfection of its members would decimate the House of Lords."

She had made a telling point; that much was obvious from the murmurings and occasional nodding of heads that rose up. But Lord Sacheverell's next words dampened the relief she felt. "First you say you are not guilty," he said, "and in the next breath you say you are. You should choose your story more carefully, Lady Ashford."

"I did say 'if,' Lord Sacheverell," Clemency replied, hoping her despair did not show on her face. "I have never deviated from the facts. I was Coerced into that relationship."

One of the unknown lords rose from the table. "You should have evidence of that," he said. "We cannot know that you did not simply invent that story when your misdeeds became known."

"I apologize for not being willing to spread the news of my degradation," Clemency said, with such force that the lord blanched and resumed his seat quickly.

"This hearing has spun out of control," Lord Sacheverell said. "We will ask the questions, if you please." He turned to Roger. "On what grounds do you seek to be awarded the Ashford title?"

"It is as I have said," Roger replied. He walked forward to where he could face the table, which put him within arm's reach of Clemency, just as if they were not now mortal enemies. "My sister has demonstrated her unfitness for her status repeatedly. She abuses her wealth by controlling the finances of her household and making her dependents beg for her approval, she permits men access to her bedchamber, she uses her Extraordinary status to protect her from reprisals—"

"*None of that is true,*" Clemency ground out. "Mr. Northrup—"

"You will be permitted a chance to speak," Lord Sacheverell said. "My lords, are we to give free rein to such excesses? To permit the nobles of England to do whatever they desire with no consequences?"

"You are out of order, Lord Sacheverell," Lord Winfield said. "We have not proved Mr. Northrup's statements, and we should not speak as if we have. Lady Ashford, do you dispute his claims?"

"Entirely," Clemency said. She drew in a calming breath and wished her voice did not shake so. "Mr. Northrup has always resented the fact that our father wished his eldest child to inherit and took steps to ensure that that child, despite being female, would take the title after him. You all remember that we have stood before you once already, and at that time you ruled my father's will legitimate. I have done nothing to bring shame upon my family or my father's memory, and I ask you to believe that Mr. Northrup's current claim rises out of spite and jealousy."

"Which is not the same as refuting his claims," Lord Sacheverell said.

"I will be happy to provide character witnesses," Clemency retorted, "but I would hope my word would be enough for all of you."

"And again we come to the crux of the matter." Lord Sacheverell's eyes gleamed. "An Extraordinary's word should not bear so much weight it overbalances the body of testimony in opposition."

"Lord Sacheverell," Lord Winfield began.

"My lord, may I speak?" Clemency interrupted. Lord Winfield hesitated, then nodded. "My lords, I will not deny that Extraordinaries wield great power and are afforded great respect. But when I ask you to believe my word, it is not that of an Extraordinary I request you hear. It is Clemency Northrup, Countess of Ashford. I have served my country for four years, I have lived a blameless life, and I have used my title and fortune to benefit others. I believe I have set an example that makes my word my impeccable witness. I ask you to consider that carefully and make the right decision."

Again, the muttering rose, and it continued until Lord Sacheverell banged his fist on the table and shouted, "Pray, be silent!" When the room was still, he said, "That is a moving plea, Lady Ashford, but we deal in facts, not emotions. You have both had your say and are invited to withdraw while we deliberate."

"Lord Sacheverell, this is most irregular," Lord Winfield said. "And most hasty. We have not heard enough to draw conclusions."

"I have," said one of the unknown lords. "I agree with Lord Sacheverell."

"I would like to ask more questions," said Lord Fotheringham.

Clemency's eye was drawn to the door, which had opened slightly, as if it had not been properly latched and someone had bumped it ajar. Beyond it, she heard voices, male and female, raised in argument, though not loud enough that she could make out words.

"I said, Lady Ashford—are you listening?" Lord Sacheverell said.

"I beg your pardon, my lord," Clemency said. "I fear I was momentarily distracted. Would you mind repeating yourself?"

Lord Sacheverell's lips thinned. "I said, can you—"

The door swung open, silencing Lord Sacheverell as he turned with the rest of the lords to observe the interruption. Clemency, who was already facing the door, at first did not recognize the woman who stood there, followed by a tall, exceptionally handsome man. She took in the woman's curly black hair, the odd blue-grey eyes she had never seen on another person, and her mouth fell open in astonishment.

Jennet Falconer.

"What is the meaning of this intrusion?" Lord Sacheverell demanded in what to Clemency seemed a rather theatrical denunciation. "No one is permitted access to this chamber."

"I beg your pardon, my lord," Jennet said in her lilting Scottish accent. She showed no sign that Lord Sacheverell intimidated her. "I believed my husband and I were summoned here to speak on Lady Ashford's behalf. If we were mistaken, I apologize."

This calm statement made Lord Sacheverell hesitate. In that moment, Lord Winfield said, "Speak for Lady Ashford? Who are you, pray?"

"I am Mr. Thomas Falconer," the tall man said, "and this is my wife, Mrs. Falconer. You are familiar with my father, Mr. William Falconer, I believe, Lord Winfield."

"Indeed I am, sir," Lord Winfield said with a smile. "As I imagine most of us are. Your father is held in high esteem by his fellows. I understood you to be an officer in the Army; is that not so?"

"I rose to the rank of captain before selling my commission," Mr. Falconer said. He held his head as proudly as any prince, and Clemency recalled the many times she had admired his beauty. The memories felt distant now, as if their encounters belonged to some other time.

"This is an irrelevant intrusion," Lord Sacheverell said. "You are invited to withdraw, Mr. Falconer, Mrs. Falconer."

"We have important testimony to share on Lady Ashford's behalf," Jennet said. "Unless you prefer to condemn my lady out of hand."

A peculiar expression came over Lord Sacheverell's face. Clemency, puzzled, saw his jaw relax and his complexion, which had once again reddened, gradually pale back to its normal shade. "Very well," he said in a much calmer voice. "You may speak."

Clemency caught sight of Lord Winfield, who looked as puzzled as she felt over Lord Sacheverell's apparent change of heart. Lord Winfield opened his mouth to speak, and his eyes met Clemency's. He closed his mouth and shook his head slightly.

"Thank you, my lord," Jennet said. "I understand there has been some question as to the truth of Lady Ashford's story. My husband and I were present when she received the injury that freed her from Napoleon's Coercion. We were traveling in company with a Discerner who verified that Lady Ashford had been doubly Coerced, though she did not know to what end. And Lady Ashford confided in me afterward the truth of her relationship with Armand de Villiers, that she was Coerced to love him."

"And how are we to know you are not saying this to protect your friend?" Lord Sacheverell still sounded unnaturally calm, though his words were at odds with his demeanor.

"I would not have crossed Europe to stand before you and lie, my lord," Jennet said, her cool voice sharp as a blade of ice. "I hope you will not insist on every word in Lady Ashford's defense being false, for there is no proving anything to someone who has made up his mind."

Clemency drew in a sharp breath. Jennet was correct, of course, but that kind of condemnatory statement could not help but hurt Clemency's case. She held that breath and waited for the explosion.

It never came. Instead, a hush fell over the chamber. Everywhere Clemency looked, she saw nodding heads. At the table, the two unknown lords bore identical expressions of dawning awareness, as if they had just made a wonderful realization. Lord Winfield's brow furrowed slightly, deepening the wrinkles across his forehead and at the corners of his eyes. "Then you attest to Lady Ashford having been Coerced, Mrs. Falconer?" he said, somewhat skeptically.

"I do," Jennet said in that same cold voice. "And, my lords," she added, "I had hoped for better from those who rule this country. It might have been your own daughters in Lady Ashford's position had Napoleon succeeded in conquering Europe. How fortunate for all of us that he did not." There was an odd note of amusement in Jennet's voice now, one Clemency could not explain.

"We cannot, of course, direct your decision," Mr. Falconer said. "But we hope our witness added to that of Lady Ashford is enough to persuade you that she does not deserve the calumny she has no doubt endured these past weeks." He bowed. "Thank you for permitting us to speak."

The unknown lord at the table who appeared to side with Lord Sacheverell stood. "I still say," he began. Jennet turned to regard him, her expression one of polite interest. A peculiar, inward-turned look crossed the man's face. "That is," he continued, "I believe we have heard enough."

Clemency, stunned, could not stop herself saying, "Have you, my lord?"

The man gestured at the Falconers. Mr. Falconer was smiling slightly, his gaze directed at Jennet. Jennet continued to watch the man, still appearing unconcerned about his words. "Mr. Falconer is well respected, and of course Mrs. Falconer would have no reason to lie. If this case hinges on your virtue, my lady, I believe we have established that you have acted with propriety at all times." He cleared his throat. "Has anyone anything they wish to add?"

Clemency was certain that was not what he had intended to say. She waited for Lord Sacheverell to rail at him, to shout at her, to insist that she was a liar and that Mr. and Mrs. Falconer were her tools. Instead, Lord Sacheverell said, "An Extraordinary should not be permitted to flout the law," in such a dull tone of voice it sounded like rote learning.

"But this testimony has nothing to do with Lady Ashford's talent," Lord Winfield said. He was still watching Lord Sacheverell narrowly.

"The charge at hand is a lack of moral character, and that charge has been refuted. There is nothing more to say."

Lord Sacheverell blinked. "You are correct," he said.

"But you cannot simply ignore my assertions!" Roger declared. "I will have justice!"

"This is justice," Lord Winfield said. "I decree that Clemency Northrup, Countess of Ashford, shall retain her title. If any man insists we visit this claim further, speak now."

This, too, seemed not at all the proper procedure, or at least it felt so informal Clemency could not believe it was how such things were handled. She scanned the room, searching each face for some hint as to whether Lord Winfield had acted inappropriately. And as she searched, she noticed something odd. About two-thirds of the lords looked puzzled, as if they had expected something different, but none of them spoke or stood to be recognized. The rest all wore that same expression of pleased realization she had seen on the other two lords. She could not explain it, but it worried her.

"Thank you, my lords. Lady Ashford, you are free to go," Lord Winfield said with a smile that wavered slightly when he again looked at Lord Sacheverell. Lord Sacheverell looked confused now, as if he had been addressed in a foreign language that sounded almost but not quite like English. Clemency took an incautious step in her hurry to get out of his sight and hissed in pain as she put weight on her injured ankle. She lifted two inches off the ground and came face to face with Roger.

"You think you've won," Roger said in a low voice that did not carry past the two of them. "You don't deserve the title. I won't stop until I've gained my point. There is nothing you can do about it."

Clemency rose a few more inches until her eyes were level with his. "I can, in fact," she said, managing calm though she once more longed to beat him senseless. "Great-Aunt Edith's bequest has not been finally settled on you. If you persist in attacking me, I will challenge that will and see to it that you receive nothing. And I can do it, Roger. I am the one with the resources, not you."

Roger blanched. "You wouldn't dare."

"You care for no one but yourself," Clemency said. "Father was right not to wish you to inherit, because you are a spoiled, selfish, arrogant monster who was willing to see his own sister vilified in public to gain her estate. From this moment, I cut you off from our family. Expect no more support from me. And if I hear so much as a breath of rumor that you have spoken against me, I will break Great-Aunt Edith's bequest. Now—get out of my sight."

Roger took an involuntary step back. Then he turned and strode from the chamber. By the time he reached the door, he was running.

All around Clemency, the red-robed lords were gathered in groups of three or four, conversing in low voices. She could not make out individual voices, but she found she did not care about eavesdropping. Instead, she approached the Falconers. She came close enough to hear Mr. Falconer say quietly, "...too big a risk with Lord Sacheverell, as antagonistic as he was," and Jennet's reply, "Not when no one knows to look for it." Then Jennet saw Clemency, and smiled. "We made a dramatic entrance," she said. "I promise it was unintentional."

"After all I have been through, I believe I am due a dramatic divine intervention," Clemency replied with a smile that made her face ache. She had not smiled in so long; she had had nothing to smile about. "You certainly made an impression on Lord Sacheverell."

Jennet's smile wavered momentarily. "Oh, I suppose he simply needed the right push," she said.

Realization struck Clemency as a dozen different impressions, a dozen different facts, slotted into place. The strange expressions on those lords' faces. Lord Sacheverell's sudden change of heart. Jennet's odd smile when she spoke of Napoleon. And earlier memories of Jennet bending over her and her Coercion disappearing as if it had been unraveled. The right push.

"You are an Extraordinary Co—" she began, and snapped her mouth shut on the rest of that sentence. She had always assumed Jennet had no talent, but suppose the woman instead had a talent she dared not reveal to the world? An Extraordinary Coercer's talent?

Jennet eyed her closely. She seemed calm enough, but there were lines of tension at the corners of her mouth, as if she expected Clemency to hurl an accusation at her. Clemency shook her head. "I am grateful to both of you," she said, "and I believe I would be most *un*grateful if I were to quibble about the details."

Jennet relaxed. "You are quite welcome, though I believe you should be more grateful to your messenger. It was he who got us here in time."

Puzzled, Clemency said, "My messenger?"

"The Bounder you sent after us," Mr. Falconer said. "Mr. Colin Wescott."

CHAPTER 37

IN WHICH THERE IS A HORRID MISUNDERSTANDING

The sounds filling the chamber seemed suddenly to be coming from very far away. Nearer at hand, she heard Jennet say, "Clemency?" in a voice that echoed through Clemency's skull. She blinked, and the world came back into focus.

"I am well," she said automatically. She was not well, but even her injuries felt at a distance. "No, truly, I was just surprised," she added as Jennet put a steadying hand on her elbow. "I did not send Mr. Wescott."

"He told us you had need of our testimony," Mr. Falconer said. Clemency focused on him. He was every bit as beautiful as she remembered, but she found herself regarding him the way she might an exquisite statue, with no desire to flirt with him as she once had. True, he was married, and she had principles, but that was not the cause of her lack of desire.

"I mentioned you to him," Clemency said. "I told him—but I did not ask him to go. That was all his decision. And I cannot understand why he would not tell me."

Jennet exchanged glances with her husband. "He was quite determined to find us," she said. "I understand he crossed most of Europe in his search. I did not realize anyone might wish to locate us, or we might have left a better trail."

"It truly is a miracle, then," Clemency breathed. She blinked again and shook her head to dispel the lingering fog. "Where is he? I must thank him as well."

"He took us first to your home," Mr. Falconer said, "and when your servant informed us where you had gone, he carried us here and bade us farewell. I assume he returned to his house, because he appeared to be at the end of his reserves."

"I must go," Clemency said. She clasped Jennet's hands. "You must both come for supper—you will stay in London for a time, yes?—I would like you to meet my mother and sisters. In a few days, perhaps. But I truly must go now."

"We understand," Jennet said with a smile that suggested she understood more than Clemency did. "I will call on you soon."

Clemency nodded and hurried away.

She Flew through the halls as fast as she dared, carefully avoiding the men who watched her curiously. Her ribs now hurt abominably— she hoped they were merely bruised and not cracked, but she had a suspicion that her luck had not held out that far—and her ankle throbbed, but her heart drew her on so inexorably she felt the pains as annoyances rather than infirmities. When she reached the outer door, she shot into the sky, not caring about her modesty.

She Flew across London, cursing the lack of her goggles that would have permitted her to Fly faster, because every second felt as if it lasted an hour. Mr. Wescott had found the Falconers. He had done that for her. The oddity of his having kept it a secret niggled at her, but only slightly. He had spent more than a week quartering Europe in a search she would have called futile, and he had found the Falconers and brought them to England in time to rescue her. No other man had ever done anything so wonderful for her sake.

Despite the feeling of urgency that propelled her and the pain in her side, she rolled in midair, laughing. He would not have done such a thing if he felt nothing more than friendship for her. All her sorrow over his presumed abandonment vanished. He cared for her deeply. And she loved him more than she could express.

The clouds pressed in, darkening, as she crossed the city, and a few heavy, wet snowflakes had fallen by the time she reached Hanover Square. Clemency alit on the Wescotts' stoop, rubbing her arms for warmth. She was too happy to care about snow, though she retained enough sensibility to be grateful she did not have to Fly in it. She knocked, and waited.

Presently, the door opened, and Hammond appeared. "Lady Ashford," he said. "Pray, enter."

"I wish to speak with Mr. Wescott," Clemency said. She brushed dampness from her coat's shoulders. "Is he at home?"

Hammond bowed. "I shall inquire, my lady," he said, and retreated to the stairs. Clemency, surprised at his abruptness, watched him until he vanished down the first floor hall. That he had left her hovering in the foyer rather than inviting her to the drawing room struck her as odd. Still, she did not care about standing on ceremony, not when she longed to see Mr. Wescott.

The foyer was as chilly as ever, and Clemency incautiously hugged herself and hissed when she compressed her ribs. Yes, they were likely fractured, and she needed to find an Extraordinary Shaper soon, but it could wait. Her ankle still throbbed as well, but the pain had lessened somewhat during her flight. She realized she was smiling like a fool and made herself stop.

She had almost retrieved her pocket watch to check the time when she heard footsteps above. To her surprise, the man who appeared at the top of the stairs was not Hammond. It was Mr. Wescott.

Clemency's heart gave a little leap of excitement. Its excitement diminished when she caught sight of Mr. Wescott's face. It was not at all welcoming. In fact, he looked terrible, his eyes dark-circled as if he had not slept well in days, his hair not perfectly kempt, his mouth drawn down at the corners. He was in his shirtsleeves as he had been the first time Clemency had ever seen him. He looked down at Clemency, unsmiling, and her first eager greeting died unspoken.

"I apologize for bursting in on you," she said instead, and immediately regretted how timid she had sounded, for Mr. Wescott's lips curved in a frown.

"I fear I cannot invite you in," he said. "My sister is sleeping—she had a bad night—and it is better that you and I not meet without her company."

Confused, Clemency said, "Oh. But surely—oh. I suppose you are correct." This was not at all what she had expected. Dreams of throwing herself into his arms and kissing him dissolved around her. Outside, the wind picked up, sounding a high, shrill threnody that cut Clemency to the heart.

"Did Mr. and Mrs. Falconer reach you in time?" Mr. Wescott said. He did not descend the stairs, and Clemency, unwilling to Fly to meet him, had to tilt her head far back to meet his gaze.

"They did," she said. "Mr. Wescott, I cannot thank you enough for finding them. I owe you a great debt."

"I did not do it to put you in my debt." Mr. Wescott's voice sharpened, and again Clemency felt stabbed, though this time it was he and not the wind that wielded the knife.

"Then why did you do it?" she shot back, her confusion and hurt filling her with a terrible desire to strike him the way he had struck her.

Mr. Wescott looked away. "I told you I wished to help you in whatever way you needed. This was something only I could do. I am glad to have been of service."

His words were cold, and indifferent, and Clemency cried out, "But I believed—I did not realize you saw me as an obligation." Her eyes ached hotly with unshed tears she blinked away. If she gave herself leave to cry, she might break down entirely.

"Not an obligation." Mr. Wescott turned his gaze on her again. "Lady Ashford, I know how my behavior must seem. But surely you can see how unsuitable our relationship is."

That felt like a blow to the stomach. "Unsuitable?" she managed.

"Who you are, who you have been," Mr. Wescott said. "It would be wrong for me to pursue the connection."

Who you are. Who you have been. Memories of Armand battered at her as they had not in weeks. Coerced or not, she had been his lover. "I did not believe that mattered to you," she said, her voice echoing with despair.

"I could hardly call myself a man if it did not," Mr. Wescott said.

The ache in her eyes had become a terrible numbness in her throat that spread throughout her body. She had been so wrong about him, so very wrong.

"I see," she said, and now her voice sounded so colorless, so lacking in spirits, she barely recognized it as her own. "I regret that you did not come to this conclusion sooner."

"As do I." Mr. Wescott actually sounded apologetic now. "It is simply impossible, for both of us. I am glad you understand. If you were not—"

"Pray, say no more," Clemency said. "I am grateful for what you have done for me. Let us leave it at that." She turned and fumbled at the latch for a moment, unable to see clearly for the tears filling her eyes. Mr. Wescott did not speak. Finally, she flung the door open and Flew away, not closing it behind her.

Immediately she knew Flying was impossible. The snow was falling in earnest, and she could barely see a foot from her face. Flakes burned her cheeks, as frigid as her tears were hot. For a few seconds, perhaps a minute, she hovered above London and wept. Of all the reactions she had imagined, that he might actually hold her violation against her was farthest from her expectations. She had been so terribly wrong. And yet her heart still yearned for him—not the man who had just devastated her, but the one she remembered, the one who had built Mercy's chair and admired her beside the silver swan. The one she had kissed. That man was a figment, and the sooner she forgot him, the better.

Snowflakes collected on her eyelashes and her hair—she had lost her bonnet during the fight with Mr. Montague, a fight that now seemed ages in the past—and she realized she was becoming dangerously cold. She descended to the street and hailed a hackney.

Having promised the driver a large sum of money upon arrival at Emeraude House, she curled up in a corner of the cab and stared at nothing. She should send word to Ravenwood Hall that Francis and her sisters could return home. Based on Prudence's assessment, it was unlikely "Mr. Jinks" could continue to function without its leader, and Clemency was certain Mr. Rutledge intended Mr. Montague not see the light of day ever again. She ought to be the happiest woman in

London. The idea made her laugh, a bitter sound she never had dreamed she might make.

The drive, like her journey to Hanover Square, seemed to take forever. She would have suspected the driver of taking the long route in hopes of more money had she not already settled on the amount. More likely, he was taking the quickest route, and it was only Clemency's despair that made it feel so horridly long. Nevertheless, the carriage's sudden stop startled her out of her numb reverie. She climbed down with the coachman's assistance and floated over the already slushy streets to the front door. "Thank you," she called over her shoulder. "Please wait, and someone will bring you your money."

The warmth of Emeraude House enveloped her the instant she crossed the threshold, and for a moment, the pain in her heart lessened. As she closed the door, Slater came down the hall that led from the servants' quarters. "My lady," he said. He jerked in surprise as he took in her battered condition. "My lady, are you well?"

"Slater, will you see to the coachman? I fear I took nothing with me with which to pay his fare," Clemency said. She drifted in the direction of the stairs.

"Yes, my lady," Slater said, "but—"

"Oh, and Roger is not to be admitted to this house ever again," Clemency went on, remembering her final words to her brother. "If he wishes to collect his things, you may tell him I will have them sent to him."

"Of course, my lady, but—"

"And I will need someone to send to Norfolk to tell my sisters they may return." Oh, there was such a welter of things to take care of, and Clemency wished only to lie on her bed for a moment's rest before sending for an Extraordinary Shaper.

"Yes, my lady, I will do so immediately, but you have a caller." Slater had followed her across the foyer to the foot of the stairs, and while he still looked aghast at her condition, his voice was as perfectly correct as ever.

"A caller? Slater, why have you permitted someone to wait for me when I have not said I wish to be at home to callers?" Her dream of a quiet bed seemed now completely out of her reach.

"I beg your pardon if I overstepped, my lady. The caller is Mr. Wescott."

Clemency jerked to a stop. Slater's words made no sense. "Mr. Wescott is in Hanover Square," she said, stupidly. "I have just left him."

"That may be so, my lady, but I assure you he is waiting in the drawing room. Forgive me for admitting him." Slater did not sound at all apologetic. "He was greatly distressed when he arrived, and I believed it was the right thing to do."

Greatly distressed did not square with how Clemency had left the somber, cold Mr. Wescott. Curiosity supplanted the aching sorrow that filled her. "The coachman, Slater," she said, and when Slater had gone to the door, she Flew upstairs and floated along the hall.

She hesitated at the drawing room door. The idea of giving Mr. Wescott another opportunity to wound her made her feel ill, and she briefly considered retreating to her room and sending Tatton to tell Mr. Wescott to go home. But Slater's behavior puzzled her. He was usually very protective of her time, and she had never known him to admit a guest without ensuring that guest was welcome. However much he approved of Mr. Wescott as a romantic possibility for Clemency, he would not have acted to promote Mr. Wescott's interests over Clemency's unless he believed he was doing the right thing. And Clemency trusted Slater's instincts. She turned the latch and pushed open the door.

Mr. Wescott had been standing in front of the fire, staring at the flames, but at Clemency's entrance he turned so rapidly it almost appeared that he had Skipped in place. He looked even worse than he had at Hanover Square, his hair wildly disordered, his breathing heavy, and his large hands clenched into fists.

"Mr. Wescott," Clemency said, alarmed, "what is the matter?"

"Lady Ashford," Mr. Wescott said. "I cannot—please, hear me out. I believe I have given you the most terrible misapprehension."

This extraordinary statement confused Clemency further. "I cannot imagine how that could be. You were very clear—and how did you manage to arrive here before me?"

"I Skipped," Mr. Wescott said, "faster than I have ever Skipped before, though I could barely see through that storm. I had to, because

I could not bear for you to believe I love you less simply for what was done to you. That is not at all what I meant."

"Love—" Shock at his words made Clemency drop onto the nearest sofa. "But you said—"

"It did not occur to me that you might assume I spoke of Coercion, and of your unwilling liaison with General de Villiers. I swear to you, Lady Ashford, that was nowhere in my thoughts. I am a fool, but I am not such a fool as to believe your violation makes you in any way unworthy. I beg you to forgive my misspoken words." Mr. Wescott's entire body was rigid with the intensity of his speech.

For the second time that day, Clemency felt as if everything were happening at a remove, as if the drawing room and the fire and Mr. Wescott were all part of some dream realm, and she was the only real thing in the world. She swallowed. "You may not have meant what I believed," she said, "but you must have meant *something*, for I have never heard anything so decided a rejection as what came from your lips."

Mr. Wescott closed his eyes briefly as if she had struck him. "I told you I was a fool," he said quietly. "Will you permit me an explanation before I go?"

Clemency hesitated. The part of her that still longed for him despite everything that had passed between them urged her not to send him out of the house immediately. "Very well."

Mr. Wescott took a few steps toward her, but he did not sit. For once he towered over her. "I have never known another woman like you," he said in that same quiet voice. "You have such spirit, and such confidence, I was drawn to you from the beginning. But you are also wealthy, and titled, and possessed of a social rank far above my own. At first, I told myself it did not matter, for surely I was the only one who felt an attraction. But then you kissed me, and from that moment I gradually realized I could not continue as if you were an ordinary woman."

The sense of the dream realm receded, leaving Clemency with the beginnings of anger. "*You* could not continue?" she said, in a voice that to her sounded dangerously calm.

Mr. Wescott apparently did not hear the warning. "It was wrong of me to court you, however indirectly, when you are of noble birth and I am not. And yet I could not bear to stop. When your liaison was revealed, and your brother challenged you, I told myself I would do this one final thing for you, find the Falconers, and then say goodbye to you forever. But I inadvertently led you to believe—well, you know. I regret so much causing you pain."

"And you believe the pain would have been lessened if I had understood you were rejecting me on grounds of differences of birth?" Clemency said. Anger was growing inside her, but this time it was a good, clean, hot anger that scoured away her sorrow and filled her with a sense of rightness. "In our misunderstanding, I gave you the impression that I agreed with your...your wrongheaded, ridiculous notions, is that it?"

Mr. Wescott blinked. "I beg your pardon?"

"As well you should!" Clemency exclaimed, springing to her feet and ignoring the twinge of pain that shot through her ankle. "You— you addle-brained fool! As if I were a child dependent on others to make my decisions for me! Did it not occur to you, Colin Wescott, that if I permitted you to court me, however indirectly, I must believe our connection not only desirable, but appropriate? How dare you treat me like a witless girl!"

Mr. Wescott's eyes were wide, and his mouth hung open. "Lady Ashford," he began.

"I am *not finished*," Clemency raged. "I believed for so long that you did not care for me, that you had run away so you might never see me again. Then I learned what you had done for me, in searching all of Europe for the Falconers, and I have never been so happy. So for you to say such horrid, cruel things to me in the name of doing what is best for both of us, and then to tell me that you love me—I am not sure I believe you." She turned her head away from him and resumed her seat. Her anger had drained away with her speech. "No one who loved me could possibly believe I would be happy without him, whatever the difference in our circumstances."

For a moment, the room was still save for the crackling of the fire and the howl of the wind battering the windows. Then Mr. Wescott knelt in front of Clemency. From her position, she could see nothing of him save his thighs and his hands clasped in front of him. "I am a greater fool than I realized," he said. "Clemency. Look at me. Please."

She lifted her head to meet his gaze and was struck all over again by the strangeness and beauty of his sea-blue eyes. Mr. Wescott let out a deep breath. "Perhaps it is too late, and I will never convince you," he said. "I imagine in my heart I could not believe someone like you could care for someone like me, virtually penniless, somewhat obsessed with an odd profession, possessed of no remarkable beauty. But I should have been honest with you about my worries instead of deciding for both of us how the future should go."

He hesitated, and then took her hand in his. "Tell me," he said. "If I had come to you and said, 'You are my love, my dearest desire, the one woman in all the world I long for.' If I had said, 'You have captured my heart, and I wish nothing more than to stay by your side for the rest of our lives.' What would you have said?"

The dreamlike state retreated entirely, and Clemency's whole world narrowed down to her hand in his, how rough and warm his skin was against hers, how his hand trembled in her grasp as if her answer meant everything to him. She let out a breath. "I suppose," she said, "I would not have said anything," and she leaned forward and kissed him.

His lips on hers were warm as he kissed her fiercely in return, melting away the last of her misery. Kissing him before had been beautiful, and exciting, but it was as nothing compared to how her heart soared to know he loved her, and she could feel that love in his kiss. His hand closed over hers firmly but gently, and he once more slipped his arm around her waist, drawing her closer.

Her ribs twinged, and she let out a hiss of pain. Startled, Mr. Wescott pulled away and said, "I have hurt you."

"No, it is only that someone hit me with a boat," Clemency said, gingerly prodding her ribs.

Mr. Wescott's eyebrows raised nearly to his hairline. "I never know what you will say next," he said. "Hit you with a boat? Should I prepare to defend you from an irate captain?"

Clemency laughed, and a little more of the ache in her chest vanished. "It is a rather long story," she said, "and I would like you to sit here with me while I tell it, because there is nothing I wish for more in the world than to feel your arms around me."

"Now that," Mr. Wescott said, "is something we can agree on."

CHAPTER 38

IN WHICH MR. RUTLEDGE MAKES AN UNEXPECTED OFFER

E mbracing had to wait. Mr. Wescott—Colin, she loved his name and the intimacy of using it—Colin immediately Bounded to St. Margaret's Hospital in search of an Extraordinary Shaper. Dr. Imbrie, a dark-haired man with narrow blue eyes who was unusually short for a Shaper, did not ask questions about Clemency's injuries and how she had got them. He said only, as Colin prepared to return him to the hospital, "You should take care in Flying, Lady Ashford. Colliding with trees is a dangerous activity." He smiled and winked as he said it, and Clemency guessed he had deduced that she had engaged in much more dangerous activities than that.

Once she was Healed, she and Colin sat close together talking for the rest of the afternoon. After Clemency shared everything that had happened since he had left, and the events of the day, Colin told her of his journey across Europe. "Not to make myself sound heroic, but it was extremely difficult," he said. "I knew no Bounding signatures in Europe, and I had to enlist other Bounders to carry me from place to place until I learned enough signatures to transport myself. I would have fallen into despair early on had I not had your memory to encourage me."

"I do not understand why your quest required such secrecy,"

Clemency said. "I believed the worst when your sister said you had instructed her not to tell where you had gone."

"It does seem rather sinister now I consider it from your perspective." Colin chuckled. "I simply wished not to give you false hope. I knew how impossible the thing was, and that even if I found the Falconers, I was likely to find them too late."

"I cannot tell you how stunned and relieved I was to see Jennet— Mr. and Mrs. Falconer enter the lords' chamber. It was a near thing."

"Perhaps you were due a miracle."

"That is what I said." She did not tell him what she had guessed about Jennet's secret talent. Even if Jennet was the Extraordinary Coercer who had stopped Napoleon as Clemency believed, Jennet had not chosen to reveal that fact, and Clemency respected her privacy.

She said, "You did not say what drove you here, desperate for me to forgive you. How did you realize that we had misunderstood one another?"

"It was Lydia," Colin said. "She woke when she heard our voices and was coming downstairs just as you left, and Discerned your emotional pain. I wish I could kick myself for causing that, darling. Lydia was very clear that you were in extreme distress."

"I forgive you. Go on."

"She asked me what I had said to you, and I repeated what I could remember and told her my motivations as well. Then she called me some names I did not realize she knew and informed me that you believed I considered you unworthy of me, and then told me if I did not wish to be called more vile names, I should come here immediately."

Clemency laughed. "Such a dire threat. Miss Wescott is not the fragile flower I at first believed her to be."

"I am continually forced to reevaluate my assessment of her. My instincts to protect her seem less appropriate every day." Colin clasped Clemency's hand in his. "And she brought us together. I owe her everything."

"I came so close to sending you away unheard," Clemency said. "But I prefer to look to the future, and not dwell on past misunderstandings."

"I will say in my defense," Colin went on, "that I have never insisted you stop Flying headlong into danger as I am sure many men would."

"I would likely just ignore you if you did." Clemency smiled. "That is not entirely true. I trust you to share your concerns with me, and I will listen to them because I love you and I would rather not give you cause for alarm."

"Has Mr. Rutledge repeated his demand that you stop your night flights?"

"He has not." Clemency sighed. "But it is implicit in what he does not say. Perhaps he is right. I have not considered how my actions affect those I love. Suppose I were seriously injured or even killed in the act of apprehending criminals?"

"As I said, I will not tell you what to do. But I also cannot deny fearing for you. Being hit by a boat is not the worst that could happen." Colin's expression was somber, and he idly ran his thumb over her knuckles as if unaware of the gesture. "What do *you* wish for, my love?"

Clemency stared in the direction of the fire, which burned lower than before. The flames danced across the coals in their endless tangle of runes she wished she could read. "Miss Wescott was correct. I was angry about having been Coerced, and more than that, I was angry that my father was gone, and that anger fueled my desire to see justice done. I feel ashamed, now, that I took such delight in frightening criminals."

"But you did much good, regardless of your motives," Colin said. "Those you protected did not care why you acted in their defense. And I do not believe your desire for justice only existed so long as you were angry and vengeful."

"I think you may be right. I simply do not know where that leaves me. I understand Mr. Rutledge better now, and I believe he understands me; at the very least, we are no longer enemies, though it is possible we are still at odds." Clemency sighed again. "I intend to forgo night Flying for a time, perhaps a week, and make a decision at the end of that time. There is still so much to be done, and Prudence's fate is not as settled as I would like."

"I will Skip to Norfolk in the morning if you like," Colin offered. "I don't suppose you have a Bounding chamber at Ravenwood Hall?"

"No, but I will rectify that lack immediately." Clemency smiled impishly. "After all, my husband will wish to Bound there at will—and of course we will need one here in Emeraude House as well."

Colin blinked. "Husband?"

"Come, dear heart, you did not imagine I would permit you to escape me?" Clemency said. "Remember that despite what society believes, I am not actually a fallen woman, and I insist on legitimizing our kisses as soon as possible."

"Of course, but traditionally it is the man who proposes to the woman. Suppose you have ruined my plans for an elaborate, surprise proposal?"

"You had no such plans. And I am of higher rank, so of course it is my responsibility." Clemency turned to face him more directly. "My love, please say you'll marry me. I could not bear it if you left this house without being my affianced husband."

Colin put his arms around her waist, bringing her close to him. "I will," he whispered, brushing his lips across her cheek, "and I would like to point out that I am the only man you will ever meet who is unafraid to accept that proposal."

"Am I so terrifying, then?" Clemency murmured.

"So powerful," Colin said, kissing her lips, "so confident, so remarkable. A lesser man might fear he has nothing to offer you that you do not already have twice over."

"And you are not a lesser man?"

"You tell me," Colin said, and they were finished speaking for a time.

When they finally parted, Clemency, rather breathlessly, said, "We are perfectly suited to one another, my lord."

"I beg your pardon?" Colin's brow furrowed in puzzlement.

"Lord Ashford," Clemency said. "You will have to become accustomed to your title, you know."

"Lord Ashford?" His puzzlement deepened. "Surely not."

Understanding struck Clemency. "You did not know—it was part of my inheritance, that as countess in my own right and an Extraordinary

I would elevate my husband to my rank, and not the other way around. No wonder you were so certain I was above your touch!"

"I did not know." Colin's puzzlement became stunned amazement. Then he laughed, a rueful, self-mocking laugh. "Likely I would still have been too proud to aspire to your hand, but—that would have made a difference."

"Well, that is all in the past." Clemency rested her head on his shoulder. "I choose to look to the future."

※

THREE DAYS PASSED. FRANCIS, MERCY, AND PRUDENCE RETURNED. Clemency dispatched Prudence's account of Mr. Jinks' operation to Mr. Rutledge and received no reply. She chose to believe that meant Mr. Rutledge was too busy rounding up actual criminals to worry about Prudence.

She arranged for Roger's things to be packed and sent to his club. After some consideration, she paid his fees up until his twenty-fifth birthday. She had no desire to help him, but this ensured he would not come crawling back, begging to be permitted to live at Emeraude House until his majority, and she did not wish to see him ever again.

She did not go Flying by night, though the weather after that single short storm was clear and warm. She told herself Flying under a dark moon was a bad idea regardless of any other promises she had made to herself.

Though the House of Lords' decision had been made public, she continued to receive letters of disinvitation from those she had considered friends. She burned each one, making them sacrifices that carried her ill feelings away. As hurtful as it was to discover she was still a pariah to some, it was good to know who her true friends were. Jane did not write or call.

On the third day, she sat in the drawing room with Colin and Lydia, for so Miss Wescott had asked Clemency to call her now that they were nearly related, and Mercy and Francis and Prudence, listening to Prudence play the pianoforte. Gone were the days when Prudence played love songs and airy tunes; now it was Bach and Beethoven,

381

Mozart and Haydn. The music thrummed through Clemency's bones. She resolved to find a way to promote Prudence's musical talent.

The sound of a throat clearing alerted her to Slater's presence, as well as to the fact that he had likely addressed her once or twice already. "Yes, Slater?"

Slater offered her the silver salver, upon which rested a card. Clemency read the name *Mr. Alexander Rutledge*. Apprehension took the place of pleasure. She considered for a moment. "Bring him here, please, Slater."

Slater bowed. "You do not wish to meet him privately?"

The rest of the conversation had stopped, though Prudence, lost in her own world, continued to play. Clemency watched Prudence for a moment. "No," she finally said, "no, I believe privacy is not my friend in this case."

Slater bowed again and left.

"Prudence," Clemency said.

Prudence left off playing. "Yes? Is there something you would prefer to hear?"

"Prudence, Mr. Rutledge is here."

Prudence blanched. Lydia, who had been standing behind her, put a steadying hand on her shoulder. "You should not fear," she said. Her eyes unfocused, and she tilted her head as if listening. "He is not angry, and he feels no guilt or regret. I do not believe he is here to take you into custody."

"But that is why I wish to meet him here, with all of you present," Clemency said. "What he has to say—" In that moment, she recalled what else he might intend to discuss, and her heart gave a quick, hot pulse of fear. Then she told herself to take Lydia's advice. Her friends and family would not judge her for her nocturnal activities, and as those activities affected them, perhaps the time for secrecy was past.

Slater opened the door and bowed Mr. Rutledge in. Mr. Rutledge showed no surprise or disquiet at the crowd. "Lady Ashford," he said politely. "May I sit?"

Clemency gestured at the largest chair in the room. Mr. Rutledge's lips quirked in acknowledgement of a telling blow. He took his seat and leaned back, the picture of a gentleman at ease. "I did not intend to interrupt a private family gathering," he said. His gaze fell briefly on Colin, whose expression remained carefully neutral.

"I would not have permitted you entry had I felt you were an interruption," Clemency replied. "Tell me, what of Mr. Jinks?"

Now Mr. Rutledge's gaze focused on Prudence, who still looked near fainting. "Mr. Montague is safely imprisoned in the Catterwell, and his organization, thanks to some very thorough intelligence, has dissolved. Lady Prudence, we thank you for your contribution."

Prudence remained silent. Clemency said, "How thankful are you, sir?"

Mr. Rutledge said nothing for a moment. "I choose not to look closely at the source of Lady Prudence's information," he finally said. "I do not believe justice would be served by such scrutiny. And I have never been one to show ingratitude to those who assist me."

Prudence sagged. Lydia caught her elbow and helped her remain upright. Prudence drew in a deep breath. "Thank you, sir," she said.

Clemency waited for Mr. Rutledge to say something warning Prudence to watch her behavior in future, or reminding her to be careful in her choice of friends. Instead, he addressed Lydia. "Miss Wescott. I am pleased to see you out in company."

"Should I not be?" Lydia said. Again, she tilted her head like an inquisitive blonde wren.

"Extraordinary Discerners are not always capable of enduring public gatherings. The ones I know are not mad, but they are rather fragile." Mr. Rutledge's gaze on Lydia was narrow-eyed and calculating. "You are quite remarkable."

"Miss Wescott is sometimes overwhelmed by large groups of people," Colin said. There was an edge to his voice that Clemency heard as a clear warning.

Mr. Rutledge seemed unaware of Colin's cautionary words. "Miss Wescott," he said, "my name is Alexander Rutledge, I am possessed of a large, inherited fortune, and the Prince Regent fears me. What do you say to that?"

Lydia smiled. "You are good at concealing a lie beneath another, more obvious one, that is what I say."

"And which lies are those?"

"You hoped to distract me by mention of your fortune." Lydia released Prudence's elbow and walked around the pianoforte until she stood before Mr. Rutledge. "You are a self-made man, are you not? But the Prince Regent does not fear you—I cannot say how he actually feels unless I speak to him, but your feelings of scorn suggest *you* believe he is unaware of half the threats to his regency you have stopped. What do you say to that, sir?"

A smile slowly spread across Mr. Rutledge's face. "Extraordinary indeed," he said. "I may have a use for you."

Colin rose. "My sister is a person, not a tool," he said. "She is not something you can use at your pleasure."

"Miss Wescott should be the judge of that," Mr. Rutledge said. He stood as well. Next to his full height, Lydia looked like a wisp, a fairy out of a stage play whom Mr. Rutledge might crush under one of his massive feet, but she held herself tall and regarded him fearlessly.

Mr. Rutledge pursed his lips in thought. "I have need of someone who can tell lies from truth," he said. "Someone who can pass through a crowd unnoticed, Discerning those who might be a threat. You are not only skilled at Discerning, you are the very picture of innocence. No one would ever suspect you of being other than you appear."

"Mr. Rutledge," Colin said angrily.

"Colin, do not worry," Lydia said, holding out a hand in warning. "Mr. Rutledge only believes he has the upper hand. He truly does need my help, and he would like me to believe he is doing me a favor."

Mr. Rutledge's expression of shock and dismay only lasted a few seconds before his face smoothed back into a thoughtful placidity. "I see I should reexamine my assumptions," he said. "Very well, Miss Wescott. You are correct. I am not accustomed to laying all my cards on the table, so to speak, but deceiving you appears impossible. I am offering you a position in my organization, doing what I mentioned before. You would prove a valuable asset."

"Your organization apprehends criminals. That does not sound safe," Colin said. He put his arm around Lydia's shoulders. "Lydia is not even of age. You cannot propose to put her in danger like that."

"I will be twenty-one in February, Colin. That is close enough. And —" Lydia tilted her head again. Clemency, who could see her face clearly, was chilled at the unexpectedly calculating expression she wore. "And I have had enough of hiding and being afraid. I am stronger than you realize, you know. If Clemency can Fly about at night capturing criminals, I do not see why I cannot attend balls and parties and the like and Discern people's lies."

"Capturing criminals?" Francis said.

Mr. Rutledge rode over his interjection. "That is almost exactly what I have in mind. I cannot promise there will be *no* danger, but I do not intend to throw Miss Wescott to the wolves. She is far too valuable as she is." He smiled. Clemency guessed it was meant to be reassuring, but she felt another chill nonetheless.

"Lydia," Colin said, "I cannot permit this."

"In two months, your permission will be irrelevant," Lydia said. "Oh, do not look that way! You know I respect you so very much. It is only that you cannot protect me from myself, you know. And I know also that you are afraid for me and for Clemency and that makes you angry because neither of us will thank you for swaddling us like babes." She put a hand on his arm. "You see how your anger does not disrupt me. I am strong now, Colin, and it is all due to you. Give me this chance to prove my strength."

Slowly, Colin reached up and covered her hand with his own. "I cannot help remembering how you looked when I brought you home from that asylum, that terrible lost expression in your haunted eyes. We are neither of us the same as we were that day." He sighed, but he was smiling. "Very well. I withdraw my objection. But I reserve the right to warn you if you become overwhelmed."

"I agree," Lydia said. She offered him her hand to shake, just as if they had concluded a bargain. Colin laughed and shook it.

"Then I will contact you, Miss Wescott, sometime very soon," Mr. Rutledge said. "Lady Ashford. Do I take it you have ignored my express instructions?"

Clemency squared her shoulders and met his gaze unflinchingly. "I do not believe my business is any of yours," she said, "but I have not recently engaged in those activities you find so objectionable."

"Very good," Mr. Rutledge said as if patting a child on the head. Clemency drew in a breath for an outraged protest, but he said, "You are correct; I am not your superior, and you owe me no obedience. I wish only to commend you on the good you have done in protecting others from assault and theft."

"Protecting others?" Francis said.

"I—well, thank you, I suppose," Clemency said, startled.

"You will do as you wish, I am sure," Mr. Rutledge went on, "but in future, if you are willing, I will call on you again. Miss Wescott is not the only one whose talent I have need of."

Clemency's mouth fell open. "You...you are offering me employment? The Countess of Ashford?"

"I said no such thing," Mr. Rutledge. "Good day, my lady, and good fortune on your marriage." He bowed and left the room.

"Clemency," Francis said, rather plaintively, "what was that about? Criminals?"

Clemency stared at the closed door. "I believed him harmless at first because he has no talent," she mused. "Now I wonder if he does not have dozens of them."

"He likes you," Lydia said. "He felt pride, and satisfaction. I am not sure he realizes what he is letting himself in for in employing me. I may be good at keeping secrets, but I believe he assumes that means I will keep his even from himself, which is never easy."

"Clemency, you must tell us *something*," Mercy said. "Francis is nigh to bursting with questions."

Clemency nodded. "It is past time some secrets were revealed," she said.

CHAPTER 39

IN WHICH A CONFRONTATION ENDS IN A SURPRISING BUT SATISFACTORY WAY

Snow fell all morning the following Wednesday, but by afternoon, the sun had emerged from behind the overcast, and that evening the streets were slushy with snow-melt the carriage wheels kicked up as gaily as maidens dancing through fallen leaves. Clemency watched, not the darkening streets, but Lydia, who sat with her wrap loosely clasped about her shoulders and appeared engrossed in the gaslit lamps they passed.

"How strange," Lydia said abruptly. "Light without fire. Or I suppose it is a different kind of fire. But the modern age is certainly a marvel." She settled herself more comfortably on her seat. "You should not fear. Oh, I apologize, that is dismissive of your emotions. Of course you may fear if that helps."

Clemency, caught off guard, laughed and hoped it did not sound nervous. "I have not been to Almack's since all this began. Lady Cowper's assurances that I am still welcome are not precisely reassuring. I had expected, when she appeared on my doorstep last week, that she intended to demand the return of my voucher."

"She was determined to support you. She herself—but I should not be indelicate." Lydia turned her attention once more to the lamps. Since Lady Cowper's liaison with a man not her husband was one of those facts everyone pretended not to know, Clemency did not believe Lydia's delicacy was warranted. But she had been too grateful to Lady Cowper to cavil at the lady's veiled hints that she respected Clemency despite believing Clemency's relationship with Armand had not been Coerced. Mercy had said only, "Emily is clever, and I enjoy having her as a member of my reticulum, but she occasionally lacks imagination."

Lady Cowper had been equally obliging in the matter of providing a voucher for Lydia, and had exclaimed repeatedly how pretty and interesting Lydia was, "not at all what one expects of an Extraordinary Discerner, yes?" She had also congratulated Clemency on her upcoming marriage and made no comment on Colin's social status. Clemency had never before so fully appreciated the grace and kindness Lady Cowper was known for.

Now, as the carriage rounded the corner and the lights of Almack's became visible in the distance, Clemency straightened her spine and adjusted the fall of her cloak. She would be welcome by those in attendance, or she would not, but she had nothing of which to be ashamed and no reason to be chased away by whispers and sidelong glances.

She lifted herself and Lydia over the slush and through the door, where they divested themselves of their outerwear and then passed into the ballroom. The enormous chandeliers lit the room as brilliantly as the sun might, their candles flickering on occasion as a draft swept past. Tall, broad mirrors reflected the room and the dancers, making the space appear to be twice its size and even more densely populated. From where Clemency stood, the assembly room was a riot of color, with men and women dressed splendidly in silks and muslins and fine wools, all of them in motion so Clemency felt a moment's dizziness.

She looked up and away to steady herself and watched the musicians in their high perch for several seconds. Their somber, dark clothing made such a contrast to the dancers she could not help feeling they belonged to another world, one in which music was everything and no one cared about appearances.

Lydia hooked her hand around Clemency's arm, bringing her back to the here and now. "I did not expect the noise," she said.

Clemency felt guilty. "I did not think to ask how you fare. Are you overwhelmed?"

"Not at all. This is exhilarating." Lydia's face was alight with pleasure. "It is—I cannot explain, and if I try, you will believe me mad. So many of them feel only pleasure that it is like being swept by the tide, except I am rooted in the sand and it cannot carry me away."

"That does not sound mad."

Lydia made a dismissive gesture with her free hand. "Then I will not tell you that I can hear the colors sing. Blue for serenity, green for passion, yellow for excitement—they are a sonata of color. Marvelous."

"Then let us walk, and I will introduce men to you. Though I imagine Colin will protest you are too young to make an attachment." Clemency smiled impishly. "I say you are never too young to flirt."

"Flirtation is less interesting when you know if the man is interested, and how interested he is." Lydia sounded much older than twenty as she said this. "There is never any mystery."

"Then you will have to discover how courtship is appealing without the mystery," Clemency said.

They strolled around the room, watching the dancers. Clemency had not realized the quadrille was danced at Almack's now, and she stopped to admire the sprightly movements. She felt unexpectedly lonely without Colin, but he had been engaged to speak to a scientific organization that evening, and now she almost wished she had gone with him instead. But Lydia had been so eager to see Almack's, and to test her fortitude against a large crowd, and Clemency had agreed that was more important.

"Lady Ashford! Such a pleasure to see you."

Clemency startled. "Oh, Mr. Davis! I apologize, I did not see you. The quadrille surprised me."

"Yes, it is a new thing, and not everyone is convinced it is a good idea." Mr. Davis, tall and sandy-haired with a long face and equally long limbs, had his eyes fixed on Lydia with an expression of appreciation. "You have been gone so long I am sure many things are new to you."

Clemency kept her smile pleasant, though she wished more than anything to laugh at Mr. Davis' obvious interest in her companion. Before Clemency had left for the War Office, he had been very interested in her. He was a flirt, but a harmless one. "Miss Wescott, this is Mr. Davis, an old acquaintance of mine. Mr. Davis, Miss Wescott."

Mr. Davis bowed. "I have not seen you at Almack's before, Miss Wescott."

Lydia curtseyed. "This is my first time, sir. It is most interesting."

Clemency decided to cut through the conversation she could see looming on the horizon; Mr. Davis would circle around asking Lydia to dance in the most roundabout way so as not to offend Clemency by not asking her instead. "Then perhaps, Mr. Davis, you would care to dance with Miss Wescott? I am certain you will show her how pleasant Almack's can be with the right partner."

Mr. Davis, well-bred as he was, did not show surprise at Clemency's abruptness. He offered Lydia his arm. "Shall we, Miss Wescott?"

When Lydia and her partner were gone, Clemency proceeded to stroll around the room, nodding at acquaintances. More than half of them pretended not to see her. Their rejections did not sting as they once would have, though the hypocrisy of it all annoyed her. Had Armand not made their relationship public knowledge, she might have endured her peers knowing of it privately the way Lady Cowper's affair was known. If she hated anyone for their treatment of her, it was Armand.

As if by some demonic spell, the crowd parted in front of her at that moment, and she saw Armand standing not five feet away, conversing with a woman whose back was to Clemency. Armand's gaze fell on Clemency. He smiled, a slow, intimate smile that revealed his dimple, and pursed his lips as if offering her a kiss.

Instead of shame and humiliation, anger filled Clemency, with, to her surprise, amusement following close behind. Armand thought to discomfit her, remind her of things she would prefer to forget. He wished to torment her so she would see no other choice but to return to him. And yet, when she looked at him, her memories were faded, not sharp and painful. It was true, she had once loved him; that that love had been Coerced did not change what she remembered. But he could not define who she was or who she would become.

She walked toward Armand, whose intimate smile wavered slightly at her approach. "General," she said politely, then, "Lady Jersey. Good evening."

"Lady Ashford," Lady Jersey said. Her lips were pinched as if she tasted something bitter. "I did not realize you had a voucher." The unspoken *still* hung in the air between them.

"Yes, Lady Cowper was gracious enough to suggest I come tonight."

The bitter expression deepened. "Did she."

Well, Lady Jersey's rudeness was legendary, and Clemency had not expected to win her over. "I am here with my young friend Miss Wescott; she is so pleased to attend."

Lady Jersey's gaze was already roving the room, examining the dancers, possibly for flaws in their morals and decorum. "Of course she is," she said.

"Lady Ashford, I am so pleased to see you again," Armand said with a bow. "Dare I ask you to dance with me?"

Clemency regarded him thoughtfully. She did not need to be Lydia to know what lay behind his invitation. If she rejected him, she would appear haughty and arrogant; if she accepted, she would have to endure half an hour's worth of his taunts and insinuations, not to mention giving her repeated denials of their intimacy the lie. None of her options were good ones.

"You may not," she said.

She had spoken loudly enough that Lady Jersey's attention returned to her. The supercilious patroness said, "You will not dance?"

"I will not dance with *him*," Clemency declared.

The men and women in the figures of the dance passed near enough Clemency could feel the breeze they raised, but they did not stop, though Clemency was sure her words had carried over the music. Armand's eyes widened in triumph for barely a second before he put on a sad, dismayed face. "Why, Lady Ashford," he said. "Surely you do not mean to reject me after all we have been to each other?"

"And what was that?" Clemency said. "I was your Coerced prize, General de Villiers. Anything that passed between us was a lie, as despicable as the lies you have spread about me. You wish to make me miserable so I will return to you, do you not? Well, general, rest assured that will never happen. I know the truth, and I will continue to declare it regardless of whether anyone believes me."

Armand's expression never wavered. "If you choose to pretend—"

"Stop," Clemency said. "Let us end this farce. I refuse to counter your lies any longer, and I refuse to be the one forced to defend myself against you. Say what you like. I am free now." She leaned in close and whispered into Armand's ear, "And I suggest you watch your back, Armand, because the man I intend to marry will not stand for your continued vilification of me. And he is an *excellent* pugilist."

Armand's eyes narrowed at Clemency's mention of marriage. "You dare," he whispered. "You belong to *me* and to no one else." In a louder voice, he said, "I cannot believe you are so lost to common decency, my lady. You should—"

"Excuse me," Lydia said, startling Clemency with her sudden appearance at Clemency's left shoulder. She had brought the entire dance to a halt and now regarded Armand with a curious, thoughtful expression. "Who is this man?"

"That is General de Villiers, the war hero," Lady Jersey said.

"I see. That explains it," Lydia said. "The general is one of Napoleon's men. He is Coerced."

A gasp rose up from those near enough to hear Lydia's words, followed by mutterings as those who had not heard demanded information from their neighbors. Armand's already pale face turned white. He stepped away and came up against a wall of men and women pressing forward to hear better. "That is a lie," he said. "I broke Coercion at Waterloo—I took command of a regiment and turned Napoleon's forces back from Paris—"

"You did not," Lydia said, her clear, high voice cutting across the murmuring like a shard of glass. "You...hmm...that is interesting. You fled the battle at Waterloo and pretended...yes, your guilt tells me you pretended to be free of Coercion so you would not be captured. I imagine you feared you would be executed when your continued attachment to Napoleon was discovered."

"What nonsense is this?" Lady Jersey demanded.

"I am an Extraordinary Discerner," Lydia said, smiling as pleasantly as if she had not just aimed a dagger at Armand's heart. "I know when someone is lying, and I am certain you are aware that a skilled Discerner can tell what truth hides beneath the lies."

Armand shrank away from Lydia. "Stop," he demanded. "You

cannot know anything. You are nothing but a chit of a girl—surely none of you believe this nonsense?"

Lydia advanced on him with all the steady implacability of a battleship sailing to war. "And then you fled France when you feared your lies would come to light," she said. "You persecuted Lady Ashford with the memory of her Coerced relationship in hopes of convincing her to marry you and afford you the protection of her title. I do not believe that is how it works, in truth, but it is certainly what *you* believed."

Armand snarled and swung his fist at Lydia. Clemency Moved Lydia out of the way of the blow and stepped into her place, bracing herself against the impact. Too late, Armand tried to stop his attack. A low cry of astonishment rose from the watching crowd as he struck Clemency in the face, rocking her back.

Armand lowered his hand. "I beg your pardon," he said, sounding desperate. "Pray, forgive me—I did not intend to hit you."

"Instead you intended to hit Miss Wescott?" Clemency gestured at Lydia, who despite her proud stance looked small and waifish in comparison with the well-built Armand.

Armand twitched. His gaze shifted in all directions, looking for an exit the way a fox might seek shelter from the hounds.

In the sudden silence, Lydia said, "You know it is your own emotions that condemn you. You cannot hide from me. And I daresay everyone here who believed your lies is considering what else they might be wrong about."

Lady Jersey cleared her throat, a delicate sound that in the silence seemed as loud as thunder tearing the sky. "I believe you should go, general," she said.

No one moved. Armand turned in a circle. "You should not believe her," he said, his voice echoing with despair. "She lies to protect Lady Ashford."

"She is an Extraordinary," a man in the crowd said. "Her word is her bond."

With a cry, Armand shoved his way past the onlookers and fled.

At his exit, loud exclamations broke the silence. Twenty people battered at Clemency, half of them concerned over her tender and bruised cheek, the others insisting they had always believed her word.

Clemency ignored them, instead moving to Lydia's side. She was even more thronged about than Clemency, but she did not appear overwhelmed. "I did not expect that," she said, her eyes sparkling with excitement. "There was more, but he did not stay for me to interrogate him."

"I am sure he prefers it that way," Clemency said. "Thank you. You spared me his continuing persecution."

"You were already free of him," Lydia said. "I Discerned that first. You freed yourself."

"I did," Clemency said. The rightness she had felt facing Armand was fading to a glowing sense of peace. In her memory, her father cheered her on.

EPILOGUE

IN WHICH CLEMENCY FINDS HER HAPPY ENDING IS NOT WHAT SHE EXPECTED

The last Monday in December was Christmas Day, and the public Moving trials were held on Tuesday instead. A clear, bright Christmas had not been enough to dry the ground, and between that and the dispirited, bare-branched trees and the mulch that was all that remained of their leaves, Clemency had to work hard at keeping her spirits up despite the sunny weather.

"This is a mistake," she said as the carriage trundled toward Hyde Park.

"It is not a mistake," Colin said. "It is the reparation of a decades-long mistake."

Clemency plucked at her trousers, whose cuffs were tucked neatly inside her Flying boots. She had considered wearing pantaloons, but ultimately had decided she wished to distinguish herself not only from the female Extraordinary Movers racing that day, but also from her male counterparts. "Suppose I am disqualified before I race?"

"Then we will return to Emeraude House and go on preparing for our wedding." Colin put his hand on Clemency's arm. "But it is past time female Extraordinary Movers stopped hampering themselves in the name of propriety. Suppose those divided skirts slowed a Mover so she did not arrive in time to rescue children from a burning building?"

"That is an unnecessarily dramatic example, my dear." But Clemency smiled. "I agree. This is not just about winning a race. It is about removing unnecessary limitations."

"So many women will applaud what you do today, regardless of what happens," Colin said. "Take heart in that."

He walked beside her as she drifted along the muddy path, past the other trials. She intended to compete in only one today. Almost everyone was intent on the competitors, but a few noticed her and stared. Torn between displaying casual unconcern and friendly smiling, she settled on nodding politely at anyone who stared, pretending their attention did not tie her insides in knots. She wished she dared take Colin's hand, but there were some social niceties she did not wish to flout.

The pillars and platforms at first looked just the same as before the bomb, tall and white like flattened mushrooms. A second glance showed that they were taller than before, the platforms wider as if in defiance of bombs and destruction. Small figures Flew between the ground and the platforms, and a dozen men and women milled about at the beginning of the Tower course high above.

Now Clemency gripped Colin's hand, so briefly no one would notice that moment's intimacy. "If I return immediately—"

"You will not," Colin said with a smile. "Go. Win this race. I wish to see Francis' expression when you outfly him."

"That would be so satisfying," Clemency agreed. The tension in her chest lightened.

She Flew to the platform and floated to where Mrs. Bonner stood. Better to know immediately if she was to be outcast. Mrs. Bonner noticed her immediately. Her mouth turned down in a scowl of epic proportions. She drifted to meet Clemency. "Lady Ashford, what on earth are you wearing?"

Clemency plucked at the fabric of her fitted thigh-length coat and smoothed her trousers. "It is Flying garb, Mrs. Bonner."

"It most certainly is not," Mrs. Bonner said. "You will leave the platform immediately, and you will not return until you are properly clothed."

Clemency drew a deep breath. "I think not. In fact, Mrs. Bonner, there are no rules governing how an Extraordinary Mover is permitted to dress for the public trials. It is tradition only that requires females to wear divided skirts."

"Do you suggest tradition is irrelevant?" Mrs. Bonner sounded as if Clemency had just declared her intent to Fly naked.

"I suggest that tradition has hampered us for too long." Clemency tilted her head to look more directly at Mrs. Bonner. "Those skirts are an impediment, and I say—" She drew in another breath. "I say by racing in these clothes, I will win by no less than a yard."

The other racers burst out in exclamations, indignant and surprised and even amused. Clemency ignored them. "And if I do not win," she continued, raising her voice above the din, "I will concede your point, Mrs. Bonner, and you will never see me Fly in trousers again."

Mrs. Bonner made a "be silent" gesture, and the crowd stilled. "Very well, Lady Ashford," she said. "Humiliate yourself if you must. The race starts in three minutes!" she exclaimed, and turned away in as decided a gesture of rejection Clemency had ever seen.

She floated to the edge of the platform, away from the other racers, and regarded the ground. She did not see Colin, though she searched the spectators' area, but knowing he was there gave her courage.

She became aware that someone had drawn near her just as Jane said, "You look ridiculous."

"I know."

"I wish I had thought of it first."

Clemency glanced sidelong at her former friend. "I am surprised you did not. You always were more daring than I."

"Not daring enough." Jane was staring into the sky, apparently searching for birds or clouds or some other aerial object that might occupy her attention. "I was so sure..."

"Sure of what?"

Jane shook her head. "I could not believe Coercion was as powerful as that. It made more sense that you wished to pretend your affair with the general had not happened."

The words did not sting as they once would have. "You did not trust me. Trust my word."

"I did not." Jane cracked her neck, making a loud, sharp popping noise Clemency had never liked. "I was afraid. Coercion scares me. I wished your story to be untrue so I could go on believing Coercion cannot take someone's will so completely."

"I understand."

Jane whipped around to stare at Clemency. "You do?"

"I believed the same before it happened to me. I simply wish you had not let that fear override what you should have known was right." Clemency felt as if the conversation was happening at a distance. She did not even know if she wished to forgive Jane.

Jane nodded. "I apologize," she said. "I should have trusted you. I will understand if you can't forgive me."

"I don't know yet," Clemency said. "But I accept your apology."

Jane looked up. "Here is Francis," she said with the air of someone happy to see the end of a painful conversation. "Does he know what you intend?"

"I do," Francis said, alighting near them. "And if Clemency believes a change of wardrobe will be enough to defeat me, she is more unhinged even than her garb suggests." He stretched. "I am feeling particularly fleet today."

"I would have beaten you last time," Clemency said.

Francis waved a dismissive hand. "I had bad luck, and that can happen to anyone. But it will not happen to me today."

A whistle shrilled out. "Form up for the Tower run!"

Francis held out a hand. Clemency covered it with hers. After a pause, Jane rested hers lightly atop Clemency's. The three of them held that pose for a second or two, and then separated, Flying for the starting gate. Clemency took a position near the top, with Francis on her right. She intended him not to lose sight of her, not because she wished to rub his nose in her victory, but because proving herself to her friend meant almost as much as proving herself to all of England.

She settled her goggles over her eyes and tugged her white cap more securely over her skull. Rising slowly into position, she drew her arms and legs in to make her body an arrow and waited for the signal.

In the next second, the whistle blew two shrill blasts, and Clemency shot away from the gate.

Despite the many times she had Flown in trousers, hunting criminals by night, she had never raced in them. Now she sped through the air faster than ever before, feeling as light and maneuverable as a bird. For a few seconds, Francis kept pace with her, but she gradually left him behind until she Flew alone through the blue sky, her whole body vibrating with the speed of her flight. She wanted to shout, to cheer, to give voice to her exhilaration, but that would slow her, and she had not yet won the race.

The wind of her flight roared in her ears, making it impossible to hear anything like the approach of another racer. She had no idea how far ahead of Francis she was, and with the goggles partly obscuring her vision, she could not tell if anyone else had gained on her. Those were more worries for a different time. It was not as if she could do anything about the others. She remembered what her father had said, years before when she had competed for the first time and lost: *In the end, we're all only racing ourselves. Defeating another is a moment in time, but outracing yourself is forever.*

She had remembered that, though she had not understood its truth until the second race, when she had surpassed her earlier time, and she had not appreciated it fully until the first time she won and felt discouraged that it was with a slower time than her best. And now she was racing for a prize bigger than any before. Winning today meant a victory for more than just herself.

She saw the Tower of London growing gradually larger until it filled the sky. This was the moment. She had not practiced this turn without the billowing skirts to anchor her as she flipped in midair, and if she was wrong in what she guessed she had to do, she would lose and she would humiliate herself in so doing. The Tower and the marker flag loomed closer, and Clemency counted down, *four, three, two—*

On *one*, Clemency curled in on herself, letting her momentum spin her around, and almost immediately straightened again. She did not pause to make sure she was oriented correctly, for fear the pause would lose her precious time; she Flew on, gaining speed as she realized the Tower was behind her and the Thames lay in a silver ribbon below. Again, she kept from screaming in joy. Ahead of her lay dozens of Flying figures, and she rose above the pack to avoid collisions. This slowed her, but that was unavoidable. A collision would slow her far worse.

Once free of the others, she Flew as she had never Flown before, speeding straight and sure toward the finish. More racers passed beneath her, headed for the Tower, and she resisted the urge to identify them. She would outrace them, and that was all that mattered.

Ahead, she saw the platforms, with the waiting Speakers and monitors. She identified Mrs. Bonner by her skirts. The woman held something that winked like a star, but Clemency was moving too fast to be curious.

Then a flash of light shone into Clemency's eyes, blinding her. For a moment, she slowed, and then sense caught up to her and she pushed herself harder. She no longer knew where she was or where the platforms lay. Despair struck her. She could not finish the race if she could not see...or could she?

She closed her eyes and kept Flying. She had been pointed directly at the platforms, and all she needed to do was keep a straight course. A tiny part of her considered what might happen if she overshot the platforms, but all there was in that direction was Kensington Palace, and... well, smashing face first into its walls would not be good, but she was certain she would stop in time.

She risked opening her eyes. The light was gone, but her eyes watered badly. She could not wipe away tears with the goggles in place, and removing the goggles would slow her. Blinking, she aimed again at the blurry spot that was the platforms, huge now before her. She was Flying so fast she felt she might shatter, sending bits of her flying in every direction. With a final titanic effort, she flashed past the finish gate and kept going a few dozen yards, just to be sure, before slowing.

She removed her goggles and wiped her eyes before looking back at the platforms. More figures were coming up fast, the first of which passed the gate as Clemency turned. Francis sped past her, slowed, and returned to her side. His eyes behind his goggles were wide and astonished.

"I feel I have spent the last ten years racing someone unfairly hobbled," he said. "You were five yards ahead of me the whole way back."

The sky was filling up with Flying figures, all of them hovering nearby in silence. Clemency's excitement at winning faded. She had not considered whether her experiment would make them feel like fools. "I am so glad I was right," she said, feeling timid.

Another figure approached. "You were right," Jane said, removing her goggles and her cap so her hair tumbled around her shoulders. "But don't believe you will get away with that kind of victory again. Next time, you will not be the only woman in trousers."

"Unfair," one of the Flying men shouted. "You already outfly me, Jane."

Laughter rose up, dispelling the horrid silence. Clemency's chest relaxed. She Flew back to the platform with Francis and Jane, listening happily to their banter. But when she saw Mrs. Bonner waiting, her good cheer dissolved.

She Flew straight to the woman's side. Mrs. Bonner said, "I refuse to accept—"

Clemency grabbed Mrs. Bonner's hand and forced it open, revealing a palm-sized mirror. "I imagine you felt fortunate to have this on you, didn't you?" she said. "You knew what would happen, and you could not bear to lose your control over us."

"I have no idea what you mean," Mrs. Bonner said.

"Do not think to brazen this out, Mrs. Bonner. You might have killed me and possibly someone else—what do you imagine a collision at those speeds would do?" Clemency made the little mirror flash light into Mrs. Bonner's face so the woman flinched. Then she Moved the mirror so it hung between them, reflecting Mrs. Bonner's face, which was distorted with anger.

"You have no regard for your modesty," Mrs. Bonner spat, "and no regard for the influence you wield. You will teach young women to be hoydenish, corrupt, immoral—"

"I will teach them to respect their talent," Clemency said. "I will teach them that their honor lies in a virtuous life and not in the kind of skirts they wear. We will no longer be constrained by your notion of our purity, Mrs. Bonner." She turned away, then looked back over her shoulder at the Extraordinary Mover. "And, Mrs. Bonner? I don't need to know how fast I Flew today. That is not the race I Flew."

She descended from the platform to be instantly mobbed by the spectators, all of them shouting. Clemency decided not to draw close enough to discover whether the shouting was in her favor or against. Instead, she Flew in the direction her carriage waited, fast enough to leave them behind.

When she was halfway there, Colin appeared in front of her with a *whoosh* of displaced air. "Congratulations," he said with a smile.

She wished she could wrap her arms around him and kiss him in full view of the competitors at the other trials, but despite what Mrs. Bonner believed, she was possessed of a sense of decorum. So she drifted close and accepted his arm instead. "It is a start."

"A good start. And from what I overheard, about half of the spectators considered your attire sensible. You may be able to guess which half."

"I doubt my appearing in trousers at the Flying trials will convince a nation of women to sacrifice their gowns," Clemency said. "But some of us require sensible clothing for the things we do."

"Women employed with public Bounding companies already wear trousers," Colin pointed out. "You are only extending that common sense elsewhere."

"Trousers are so much warmer when one is Flying high." Clemency adjusted the hang of one trouser leg. "In fact...do you mind if I Fly home, dearest? I feel the need for a few minutes alone."

"I anticipate seeing you again soon," Colin said. He took her hand and lightly kissed her knuckles. "And soon enough, seeing you every day of my life."

She rose into the sky and looked back to see him watching her with his eyes shielded before vanishing. He would likely reach Emeraude House before she did.

This time, she Flew slowly, enjoying the sight of London in the winter sun. At this altitude, which was always cold regardless of the season, she could pretend it was summer in the streets below. The skies were filled with Bounders leaping about like fleas, some of whom *whooshed* into existence mere yards from where she Flew. They looked startled, though none of them appeared frightened at the possibility of a collision. Bounders knew even earlier in their careers than Extraordinary Movers how impossible those odds were.

She rolled onto her back and drifted with the breeze. How fortunate there were no strong winds that morning, or her victory would have been less dramatic, though she had no doubt she would have won regardless. Again, she remembered her father, and wished that he could have seen her Fly that day. He would have been so proud—though he was proud of his children no matter what accolades they received. And if he were here, he would know about Roger, and Clemency could imagine how he would have felt about that.

Far below, someone screamed.

Clemency rolled again and scanned the streets, dropping lower. She was flying over Wapping, and the black scar of the fire that had ravaged it weeks ago, caused by the first of Mr. Montague's bombs, drew her eye as readily as a beacon. Again, she heard a scream, and this time she realized it was coming from somewhere just south of the scar. In a narrow alley, two people fought, and one shoved the other to the ground. Even in the alley's dimness, light flashed on the blade he held.

For a moment, Clemency hesitated. It was broad daylight, not nighttime, and surely someone else would follow the sound of screams, though in truth there did not seem to be anyone else around. No one but Clemency. And she *was* wearing trousers.

She Flew low, turned, and dove.

THE TALENTS

The Corporeal Talents: Mover, Shaper, Scorcher, Bounder

MOVER (Greek τελεκινεσις): Capable of moving things without physically touching them. While originally this talent was believed to be connected to one's bodily strength, female Movers able to lift far more than their male counterparts have disproven this theory in recent years. Depending on skill, training, and practice, Movers may be able to lift and manipulate multiple objects at once, pick locks, and manipulate anything the human hand can manage. Movers can Move other people so long as they don't resist, and some are capable of Moving an unwilling target if the Mover is strong enough.

An EXTRAORDINARY MOVER, in addition to all these things, is capable of flight. Aside from this, an Extraordinary Mover is not guaranteed to be better skilled or stronger than an ordinary Mover; Helen Garrity, England's highest-rated Mover (at upwards of 12,000 pounds lifting capacity), was an ordinary Mover.

SHAPER (Greek μπιοκινεσις): Capable of manipulating their own bodies. Shapers can alter their own flesh, including healing wounds. Most Shapers use their ability only to make themselves more attractive, though that sort of beauty is always obvious as Shaped. More subtle uses include disguising oneself, and many Shapers have also been spies. It usually takes time for a Shaper to alter herself because Shaping is painful, and the faster one does it, the more painful it is. Under extreme duress, Shapers can alter their bodies rapidly, but this results in great pain and longer-term muscle and joint pain.

Shapers can mend bone, heal cuts or abrasions, repair physical damage to organs as from a knife wound, etc., make hair and nails grow, improve their physical condition (for example, enhance lung efficiency), and change their skin color. They cannot restore lost limbs or organs, cure diseases (though they can repair the physical damage done by disease), change hair or eye color, or regenerate nerves.

An EXTRAORDINARY SHAPER is capable of turning a Shaper's talent on another person with skin-to-skin contact. Extraordinary Shapers are sometimes called Healers as a result. While most Extraordinary Shapers use their talent to help others, there is nothing to stop them from causing injury or even death.

SCORCHER (Greek πιροκινεσις): Capable of igniting fire by the power of thought. The fire is natural and will cause ordinary flammable objects to catch on fire. If there aren't any such objects handy, the fire will burn briefly and then go out. A Scorcher must be able to see the place he or she is starting the fire.

Scorcher talent has four dimensions: power, range, distance, and stamina. Power refers to how large and hot a fire the Scorcher can create; range is how far the Scorcher can fling a fire before it goes out; distance is how far away from him- or herself a Scorcher can ignite a fire; and stamina refers to how often the Scorcher can use his or her power before becoming exhausted.

The hottest ordinary fire any Scorcher has ever created could melt brass (approximately 1700 degrees F). When she gave herself over to the fire, Elinor Pembroke was able to melt iron (over 2200 degrees F).

Scorchers are rare because they manifest by igniting fire unconsciously, in their sleep. About 10-20% of Scorchers survive manifestation.

EXTRAORDINARY SCORCHERS are capable of controlling and mentally extinguishing fires. As their talent develops,

Extraordinary Scorchers become immune to fire, and their control over it increases.

BOUNDER (Greek τελεταχύς): Capable of moving from one point to another without passing through the intervening space. Bounders can move themselves anywhere they can see clearly within a certain range that varies according to the Bounder; this is called Skipping. They can also Bound to any location marked with a Bounder symbol, known as a signature. The room must be closed to the outdoors and empty of people and objects. Bounders refer to the "simplicity" of a space, meaning how free of "clutter" (objects, people, etc.) it is. Spaces that are too cluttered are impossible to Bound to, as are outdoor locations, which are full of constant movement. It is possible to keep a Bounder out of somewhere if you alter the place by defacing the Bounding chamber or putting some object or person into it.

An EXTRAORDINARY BOUNDER lacks most of the limitations an ordinary Bounder operates under. An Extraordinary Bounder's range is line of sight, which can allow them to Skip many miles' distance. Extraordinary Bounders do not require Bounding signatures, instead using what they refer to as "essence" to identify a space they Bound to. Essence comprises the essential nature of a space and is impossible to explain to non-Bounders; human beings have an essence which differs from that of a place and allows an Extraordinary Bounder to identify people without seeing them. While Extraordinary Bounders are still incapable of Bounding to an outdoor location, they can Bound to places too cluttered for an ordinary Bounder, as well as ones that contain people.

The Ethereal Talents: Seer, Speaker, Discerner, Coercer

SEER (Greek προφητεία): Capable of seeing a short distance into the future through Dreams. Seers experience lucid Dreams in which they see future events as if they were present as an invisible observer. They may or may not be able to recognize the people or places involved, so Seers tend to be very well informed about people and events and are socially active. Their Dreams are not inevitable and there is no problem with altering the timeline; they see things that are the natural consequence of the current situation/circumstances, and altering those things alters the foreseen event. Just their knowledge of the event is not sufficient to alter it.

No one knows how a Seer's brain produces Dream, only that Dreams come in response to what the Seer meditates on. Seers therefore study current events in depth and read up on things they might be asked to Dream about. Seers have high social status and are very popular, with many of them making a living from Dream commissions.

An EXTRAORDINARY SEER, in addition to Dreaming, is capable of touching an object and perceiving events and people associated with it. These Visions allow them not only to see the past of the person most closely connected to the object, but occasionally to have glimpses of the future. They can also find a Vision linked to what the object's owner is seeing at the moment and "see" through their eyes. Most recently, the Extraordinary Seer Sophia Westlake discovered how to use Visions attached to one object to perceive related objects, leading to the defeat of the Caribbean pirates led by Rhys Evans.

SPEAKER (Greek τελεπάθεια): Capable of communicating by thought with any other Speaker. Speakers can mentally communicate with any Speaker within range of sight. They can also communicate with any Speaker they know well. The definition of "know well" has meaning only to a Speaker, but in general it means someone they have spoken verbally or mentally with on several occasions. A Speaker's circle of Speaker friends is called a reticulum, and a reticulum might contain several hundred members depending on the Speaker. Speakers easily distinguish between the different "voices" of their Speaker friends, though Speaking is not auditory. A Speaker can send images as well as words if she is proficient enough. Speakers cannot Speak to non-Speakers, and they are incapable of reading minds.

An EXTRAORDINARY SPEAKER has all the abilities of an ordinary Speaker, but is also capable of sending thoughts and images into the minds of anyone, Speaker or not. Additionally, an Extraordinary Speaker can Speak to multiple people at a time, though all will receive the same message. Extraordinary Speakers can send a "burst" of noise that startles or wakes the recipient. Rumors that

Extraordinary Speakers can read minds are universally denied by Speakers, but the rumors persist.

DISCERNER (Greek ενσυναίσθηση): Able to experience other people's feelings as if they were their own. Discerners require touch to be able to do this (though not skin-to-skin contact), and much of learning to control the skill involves learning to distinguish one's own emotions from those of the other person. Discerners can detect lies, sense motives, read other people's emotional states, and identify Coercers. Discerners are immune to the talent of a Coercer, though they can be overwhelmed by anyone capable of projecting strong emotions.

An EXTRAORDINARY DISCERNER can do all these things without the need for touch. Extraordinary Discerners are always aware of the emotions of those near them, though the range at which they are aware varies according to the Extraordinary Discerner. Nearly three-quarters of all Extraordinary Discerners go mad because of their talent.

COERCER (Greek τελενσυναίσθηση): Capable of influencing the emotions of others with a touch. Coercers are viewed with great suspicion, since their ability is a kind of mind control. Those altered are not aware that their mood has been artificially changed and are extremely suggestible while the Coercer is in direct contact with them. By altering someone's emotions, a Coercer can influence their behavior or change his or her attitude toward the Coercer.

Coercers do not feel others' emotions the way Discerners do, but can tell what they are and how they're changing. Many Coercers have sociopathic tendencies as a result. Unlike Discerners, Coercers have to work hard at being able to use their talent, which in its untrained state is erratic. However, Coercers always know when they've altered someone's mood. Coercers do not "broadcast" their emotions, appearing as a blank to Discerners. Because Coercion is viewed with suspicion (for good reason), Coercers keep their ability secret even if they don't use it maliciously.

An EXTRAORDINARY COERCER does not need a physical

connection to influence someone's emotions. Extraordinary Coercers are capable of turning their talent on several people at a time, and the most powerful Extraordinary Coercers can control mobs. The most powerful Extraordinary Coercer known to date is Napoleon Bonaparte.

HISTORICAL NOTE

I first heard of the inventor John Joseph Merlin—yes, his real name—on the podcast *Ken and Robin Talk About Stuff*, and the longer they talked about stuff, the more fascinated I became. By the end of the fifteen-minute segment, I knew I had something I could build part of a plot around. Many of the inventions cited in this book, including inline skates and the invalid chair, are in fact credited to Merlin, though he seems in many cases to have refined on others' inventions rather than being the originator. For the purposes of this story, it suited me to use the mystique built up around him. (The story about the mirror is entirely true.)

As I've written, I originally intended the Extraordinaries series to both be eight books long (eight talents, eight books) and to end with the battle of Waterloo. Since *Beguiling Birthright* and Waterloo were book six, that meant reevaluating what more I could say about the larger story arc and the alternate history in which these books are set. *Soaring Flight* touches on some of the issues facing a country coming home from war; as happened in America post-World War II, society was disrupted by soldiers returning to face a glut of working men on the market, as well as women who had taken on traditionally male roles who didn't like giving up the unexpected independence of making their own money.

In this history, the existence of Extraordinaries complicates matters as non-talented men and women question whether those Extraordinaries deserve the special treatment they receive. Additionally, the world begins to move into what we would recognize as the modern era, with all the changes of thought and scientific advancement that entails. Clemency's night flights fighting crime belong to a new era, one in which Mr. Rutledge's organization has a growing part to play—but that is a matter for a future story...

ACKNOWLEDGMENTS

As always, my thanks go to first readers Jacob Proffitt and Sherwood Smith, who both provided much-needed feedback that improved this novel tremendously.

ABOUT THE AUTHOR

In addition to the Extraordinaries series, Melissa McShane is the author of many other fantasy novels, including the novels of Tremontane, the first of which is *Servant of the Crown; Spark the Fire,* first in The Dragons of Mother Stone; and *The Book of Secrets,* first book in The Last Oracle series.

She lives in the shelter of the mountains out West with her husband, two children and a niece, and two very needy cats. She wrote reviews and critical essays for many years before turning to fiction, which is much more fun than anyone ought to be allowed to have. You can visit her at her website **www.melissamcshanewrites.com** for more information on other books and upcoming releases.

For news on upcoming releases, bonus material, and other fun stuff, sign up for Melissa's newsletter **here**.

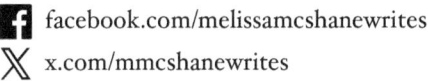 facebook.com/melissamcshanewrites
X x.com/mmcshanewrites

Stranger to the Crown

Scholar of the Crown

Servant of the Crown

Exile of the Crown

Rider of the Crown

Agent of the Crown

Voyager of the Crown

Tales of the Crown

COMPANY OF STRANGERS

Company of Strangers

Stone of Inheritance

Mortal Rites

Shifting Loyalties

Sands of Memory

Call of Wizardry

THE DRAGONS OF MOTHER STONE

Spark the Fire

Faith in Flames

Ember in Shadow

Skies Will Burn

THE CONVERGENCE TRILOGY

The Summoned Mage

The Wandering Mage

The Unconquered Mage

THE BOOKS OF DALANINE

The Smoke-Scented Girl

The God-Touched Man

Emissary

Warts and All: A Fairy Tale Collection

The View from Castle Always

www.ingramcontent.com/pod-product-compliance
Lightning Source LLC
Chambersburg PA
CBHW071640260626
47170CB00001B/172